ACCIDENTAL BONDS

MARIE REYNARD

ACCIDENTAL BONDS

ELEMENTAL BONDS
BOOK ONE

MARIE REYNARD

PEACE GARDEN
PUBLISHING

Cover by Moor Books Design

Illustrations by GetCovers

Beta read by Amy Pittel (LesCourt Author Services) and Megan Dischinger (Blue Beta Reading)

Proofread by Sandra (One Love Editing)

Standard Cover ISBN: 978-1-958002-01-8

Alternative Cover ISBN: 978-1-958002-02-5

First Edition

Published by Peace Garden Publishing, LLC

 Formatted with Vellum

CONTENT WARNINGS

This book contains scenes with elements of dubious consent and mentions of rape in a historical context.

ACCIDENTAL BONDS

It was meant to be temporary. Fate had other ideas.

Victor Mills would do anything to protect his pack, even work with magic he detests. When the wards safeguarding his territory start to deteriorate, he's forced to hire a local mage to fix them. He could tolerate the abrasive stench of sorcery, if only the mage didn't also smell like everything his wolf has ever wanted.

Elijah Lauring has no intention of tying himself to a shifter pack; his neutrality pays the bills. Repairing the Mills pack wards should be a one-off job, but the spell he casts to tap into Victor's energy stubbornly refuses to fade. The intoxicating connection that lingers between them plunges his magic into chaos right when he needs it the most.

As they grapple with their conflicting desires, they soon discover the wards aren't the only thing decaying. An evil is infecting the pack land, and they must learn to trust each other and their growing bond to defeat it. If they fail, Victor's pack will pay the ultimate price.

Accidental Bonds is a steamy 115k M/M paranormal romance featuring a broody wolf shifter, a headstrong mage, meddling friends, a perpetually unimpressed cat, and knotting. It's perfect for readers who love simmering slow burns, characters who rub each other in all the wrong ways before they realize the right ones are much more enjoyable, and shifter stories with a healthy dose of found family, thrilling action, and snarky banter. While it guarantees a happy ending for its main couple, the overarching plot does contain cliffhangers. (This series does not contain mpreg.)

ONE

Victor Mills stared out the windshield of his SUV at a dingy brick storefront, faded gold letters on the window proclaiming it *The Mystik Corner, For All Your Magik Needs*. Only shadows lurked behind the glass. It had the dilapidated look of disrepair, just another abandoned building on a neglected street in a dying town, not worth a second glance. But he could smell the disguising magic used to make human eyes slide right past, ensuring anyone unaware of the supernatural would never suspect what lay within.

He'd never been inside. His father had been a frequent visitor though, making the forty-minute drive as often as he could to see the shop's former owner, and Victor didn't like to think about what had happened because of that.

Streetlights cast a sickly glow on the crumbling building, its appeal equal to Victor's desire to be there. Hiring a mage of all people. From this shop of all places. But with the way his life had been going, he shouldn't have been surprised. Par for the course, really, and he only had himself to blame.

His jaw ached, and he forced himself to unclench it.

This had to be done. Every day he put it off, he was endangering his pack. His territory wards were failing, the protection they provided weakening and slipping out of his control. It'd been the better part of a month, and nothing had stopped them from deteriorating further. So here he was, bracing himself to ask for help from the shop's new owner, one of the few mages in the Northwestern United States who could do what Victor needed.

A voice in his mind whispered that this solution would be worse than his current problem; being there felt like a risk, like mere proximity to magic would send him spiraling out of control. But the need to know, to find out what was happening to his wards, to keep his pack safe, clawed at him.

He got out of his SUV and walked down the cracked sidewalk. Magic permeated the block, reeking of ozone and leashed power, enough to make his nose wrinkle. The idea of working closely with that scent, the knowledge that it'd cling to his skin for days after this was over, made him want to turn tail and run. Determination drove him forward. If he needed to deal with magic to fix this, he would.

This mage had been in Lost Creek for less than a year, still an outsider by most small-town standards, but he already came highly recommended. Rumor had it prominent shifters throughout the Pacific Northwest had the mage he'd apprenticed under on speed dial, and his training had been top-of-the-line. The alphas of both neighboring packs had used his services shortly after he'd arrived. He'd removed a hex on an heirloom owned by the MacFarlan pack's alpha and had run off fae that had invaded the Lucas pack's territory. Alpha Lucas had said he seemed decent—cold and aloof, as most unaffiliated mages were around shifters, but he hadn't tried to screw him over on the price. He hadn't taken more than he needed.

The way Grant Lucas had said that last part had put Victor on edge. It hadn't been meant unkindly, but even the slightest allusion to the mage who'd previously owned this shop made Victor's fingertips ache with the urge to sprout claws.

Victor stopped in front of the dirty glass door, preparing himself for the assault on his senses that would greet him on the other side.

Unbidden, an excited shiver coursed through him, raw and primal. He pushed it down. As much as Victor didn't want to be there, his wolf wanted nothing more. But it'd lost that right the last time they'd been near a mage. He'd never been at odds with his wolf before; magic was the only point of dissonance between them. Being unable to trust his instincts on something so fundamental had tilted his world in a way he hadn't adjusted to yet.

He reached out and pulled the old-fashioned handle, half-surprised it didn't fall off in his hand. The door hinges creaked in protest, almost drowning out the jingle of bells.

As he stepped inside, the omnipresent odor of magic saturated the air, impossible to ignore. It curled in his nostrils and clogged his throat. Acerbic iron sparks layered over a myriad of herbs, incense, and oils, too many to pick out and identify. But under that, another scent lingered. He inhaled deeper, trying to get more of it before he could stop himself. He caught hints of soil and snow, then his vision swam, and he had to breathe shallowly through his mouth to regain his balance. Every inhale tasted sharp on his tongue.

The shop loomed around him, long and narrow. His skin prickled, like if he touched the walls, he'd feel the buzz of electricity running through them. And somehow, even though it'd been a year, he swore a leftover trace of miasma festered. The stench was one he'd become too familiar with, one he'd hoped to never smell again.

There was no one else in the darkened shop. With the streetlights barely penetrating the hazy gloom through the window, he needed his heightened senses to see. The only sounds were the whir of an overhead fan and the ticking of four clocks on the walls, each showing a different time.

He glanced at the door, confirming he hadn't imagined the Open sign. It hung there alright, even if it was the only thing welcoming about the shop.

Bookshelves and display cases made from a dozen kinds of wood littered the space, their positions without rhyme or reason. They were cluttered with bottles and books, some battered and worn, worm-eaten and time-smudged to the point a breeze might blow them away in a swirl of dust. Candles of all shapes, sizes, and colors lent a waxy note to the air. Loose gems, polished stones, and assorted trinkets were scattered over every surface, as were bits of bone and teeth, both human and not. Mahogany-paneled walls were obscured by towering rows of shelves, stretching up to the ceiling and crowded with vials of oils, various implements of magic, and jars filled with dried herbs, flowers, and things he couldn't name. Seven small wood-carved figurines watched him as he passed, stirring the hair on the back of his neck.

Great, now you're letting knickknacks freak you out, he thought, but when he looked back at the shelf, it was empty. He quickened his pace.

A glass counter dominated the far wall. Behind it, a door stood cracked open, a warm glow spilling out, the only source of light inside the shop. More books, candles, and a half dozen boxes were stacked on the countertop. A deck of old tarot cards fanned out among the disarray, gilded edges catching the light from the door.

He took a breath, still shallow but deliberate, firming his resolve. Even though he found this unpleasant, it'd be a temporary arrangement. Once his territory was secure, he'd never have to use this mage's services again. He'd never come back. The further he stayed from magic, the better.

His wolf prowled in his mind, no more thrilled with that idea than Victor was with his current situation.

"Anyone there?" he called out.

After a moment, a man pushed the door open. Light flooded from the doorway, silhouetting him, before lamps scattered around the shop twinkled to life, casting it in a contrast of muted yellow incandescence and velvet-black shadows. Delicate wind chimes made from burnished metal and fine crystal captured the glow, then sent it back, fractured and kaleidoscopic, as they tinkled and clinked in a breeze—more magical than physical—that slipped from the door. The sound, a soft chorus that built and subsided; its final notes, otherworldly and echoing.

The air around Victor quivered. His awareness pulled taut, magic shimmering over his skin like constantly flickering lights. He took a step forward, some kind of gravity demanding he get closer, its lure a bone-deep calling.

It took more effort than it should have to halt his momentum, to keep himself from taking the last few steps to the counter. But he couldn't stop his eyes from sliding down the man's body. The refined look of his gray slacks and black dress shirt added a stylish flair that offset the esoteric nature of his surroundings and made him an oddity amongst the vials and candles and who knew what else. He was slim, with broad shoulders and pale skin that would glow under a full moon. Victor's gaze caught on his long fingers, his frost-blue eyes, and the black-brown tumble of his hair.

The man leaned forward, hands on the counter and the start of a smile on his lips. His bright eyes glittered in the dim light, dragging Victor in. "Can I help you?"

It took Victor a beat to remember why he was there, that he had business to take care of. He met the man's electric gaze. "I'm looking for Elijah Lauring."

"You found him."

A sudden, icy aversion washed over Victor.

Well, that explained the instinctual pull toward the man, the way Victor's wolf was sitting up with interest.

He'd heard the mage was young, but that hadn't prepared him for someone his age or younger, who looked like he could be a TA at the nearest university, not the owner of this shop and a respected mage. Had he even finished his apprenticeship?

His surprise must have shown. The mage quirked an eyebrow at him, his lips pressing together before he asked, "And you are?"

"Victor Mills, Mills pack alpha."

Elijah's eyes widened a fraction before his expression shuttered to detached politeness. "So you're the reason I had the chance to buy this shop."

Victor bristled, not needing the reminder.

"Alpha Lucas and Alpha MacFarlan both came to see me the first week I was here," Elijah said.

That was what custom and common courtesy dictated. Victor hadn't been able to make himself do it. "If you're expecting a welcome gift, the shop is going to have to be enough."

The air around Elijah seemed to chill. Without looking,

he flipped over a tarot card and tapped against its face. Victor caught a glimpse of an old man and frowned when it seemed like, for a fraction of a second, his lantern held a light that flared, flickered, then guttered out.

The mage walked around the counter, his fingers trailing along the edge of a shelf as he passed, his eyes not leaving Victor. For all that he looked out of place, he moved through the clutter with a confidence that thrummed off him, someone in control of his own domain.

Elijah came to an easy stop in front of him, a customer service smile plastered on his face. He brought with him a gust of candle wax, old books, and magic used so often it'd seeped into his bones. But under that was the dizzying scent of forest earth beneath a thick blanket of snow and the pinpricks of stars in an endless night sky, dark and light and eternal.

Victor resisted the urge to take a step forward, to inhale deeper.

"What brings you here?" Elijah asked.

"You operate under standard privacy and protection agreements, I assume?"

He raised an eyebrow. "Of course."

"What if I want more than that?"

"Blood oaths start at five hundred for an oath of silence and increase from there, depending on what you want sworn. I reserve the right to refuse any oaths that will compromise my current or future clients, my ability to use magic, my neutrality in any pack conflicts, or that will require me to do anything I find morally unacceptable, that will tie me to your pack permanently, or for any other reason I deem valid." He rattled off the spiel like he'd said it a dozen times before, his arms crossed loosely over his chest.

"I want you to swear you will not cause harm to or take advantage of my pack in any way while fixing the issue."

Elijah stood straighter. "Mages are honor-bound to not cause harm."

"Not all mages. It's hard to be bound to something you don't have. I want a guarantee."

"Most mages would kick you out for such a request." From the flinty steel in his tone, he was considering joining their ranks, but Victor wouldn't yield. Not on this.

"It's nonnegotiable." His wolf wanted to argue with that, but he ignored it, shoving it down as far as he could. This required a clear head, not his wolf's clouded judgment.

"I'm not agreeing to anything until I know what you want me to do."

"If what I want is acceptable, will you swear the oath?"

Elijah considered him, something calculating in his gaze. "Were the events that brought me here your only experience with magic?"

Victor raised one shoulder a fraction. The mage could interpret it however he liked.

"An oath is the only way you'll trust me?"

Trust was a strong word, but Victor nodded. "When it comes to my pack, yes."

He felt weighed and measured under Elijah's scrutiny.

"Fine," Elijah finally said. "As long as you're not asking for anything objectionable, I'll swear not to harm your pack while we work together."

Victor suppressed a sigh of relief. At least one thing was going right.

"So. What brings you here?" Elijah asked again, this time with bite.

There was no point hiding it. This was why he'd come. "The border wards on my territory. They're failing."

Elijah's cool eyes sparked with interest. "How old are they?"

"Well over a hundred years."

"No problems before now?"

"None that I'm aware of."

"And you've been alpha for what? A year?"

Victor nodded, tight and sharp, and waited for the accusation he'd been dreading. Border wards were tied to pack alphas, passed from one leader to the next. If the wards on his territory were crumbling a scant year after he'd taken over, it had to mean there was something wrong with *him*, something in him that was lacking, a deficiency in his ability to protect his pack and their land.

But the accusation didn't come. Instead, Elijah asked, "You haven't told the regional shifter council, have you?"

"No."

"Why not?"

Because he didn't want them to know he was failing already. Not yet. He didn't want to admit that weakness, that they'd been right when they'd implied he was too young to take over. As if he'd had the option to wait another five or ten years for his father to give him the reins.

He forced his hands to relax from the fists he'd balled them into. "I'll tell them if they need to know."

Elijah's expression flickered. If he didn't have magic, if they were somewhere else, maybe Victor would have been able to catch the scent of his emotions and use them to figure out what he was thinking, but there was too much magic in the room for that. It overwhelmed everything and left Victor at a disadvantage, guessing what the almost imperceptible tilt of Elijah's head and minute upward tick of the right corner of his mouth might mean.

Whatever Elijah had been thinking, he didn't comment

on it. "Ward magic is one of my specialties, but it isn't cheap. If your wards require a full reset, considering the size of your territory, you'll be looking at the mid-five-figure range."

Victor carefully didn't grind his teeth. "As long as it's a onetime payment, money isn't an issue."

"You're aware of what else this will involve?"

A growl that was entirely human threatened to rumble out of him. "I assume you'll have to use my energy somehow."

Elijah looked him over, reading his discomfort. "Don't worry. I won't take more than I need."

Victor ignored how that comment made his wolf squirm. He wouldn't let himself falter in the face of magic. "You'll swear the oath?"

"I will." Elijah held out his hand. The gesture reeked of magic and deliberate provocation. He had to have dealt with enough shifters to know they'd balk at skin contact, at a touch that would brand them with a scent they found less than pleasant.

Victor shook his hand anyway, enjoying the flicker of surprise the move caused. He refused to give a mage the satisfaction of seeing him back down.

Elijah's grip was strong and warm. It took effort not to yank away from the tingle of magic pressed against his palm. It took more not to hold on tighter.

"Do you want the oath now?" Elijah asked before dropping his hand.

"Preferably."

"Considering what you're asking for, it'll be an additional fifteen hundred. I'll send the bill to your pack."

Victor stifled another growl. "Fine."

Elijah nodded and walked behind the counter. He

pulled out a sheet of heavy vellum, a dip pen, and an empty inkwell.

Cleaning off a space, he placed the paper down, and then his fingers danced over it. White lines of light criss-crossed the surface, an intricate and precise scrollwork from a master calligrapher, except they didn't stop where he touched. They crept over the page, lighting their way across it, momentarily chasing away shadows with their glow.

Victor stared as the magic dimmed, leaving behind nothing but fleeting afterimages that faded to a blank page. He hadn't seen anything like that since he was a kid, and for a moment, he was five again, staring in fascination at the wondrous things magic could do, wanting to see and know everything. But he shook himself. He wasn't that naive kid anymore.

Elijah produced a small dagger and used it to prick his thumb, letting the blood pool before dripping it into the inkwell. Then he held the dagger out to Victor. "Cut your thumb with this and add your blood to the well."

Oaths needed blood to be binding; Victor knew that much. But he hesitated. It wasn't the pain that worried him. With his shifter abilities, such a shallow cut would heal almost instantly. Giving a mage some part of himself, even just a few drops, on the other hand...

He slid his thumb across the blade, watching the blood well up and trying to ignore his racing heart.

Elijah tilted his head slightly, studying him, that same look from before on his face, like he couldn't quite figure Victor out.

Victor exhaled and pressed against his thumb. His blood joined Elijah's. He half expected something to happen, an explosion or a glimmer of magic, but nothing did.

The pen nib drew up the blood as Elijah dipped it in the well, leaving behind spotless glass.

Metal scraping on parchment might have been reassuring, as mundane as pen to paper, if it weren't for how calmly Elijah used blood as ink. Faint lines glowed purple under the fabric of his dress shirt, the magical tattoos peeking out from his buttoned cuffs. Victor knew all mages had a few—invisible except when they channeled their magic, the color and pattern unique to the mage, spreading up their arms as their strength increased—but that didn't stop him from wondering how much of Elijah's skin they covered.

He kept waiting for Elijah to run out of blood ink, kept thinking he'd have to prick his finger again, but he never did. The letters flowed from the pen, meticulous and ornate in their style. He read as Elijah wrote.

I, Elijah Lauring, swear to Victor Mills, Mills pack alpha, that...

The pen's slide across the paper was hypnotic. Smooth strokes and crisp red lines filled the parchment.

"There." Elijah finished scribing the oath and pressed his palm against the vellum, causing it to glow once more, sealing in the magic he'd locked into the ink and paper. Or so Victor hoped.

Elijah held it out to him, and Victor felt the buzz of residual power as he took it.

"It will last until the issue with your wards is resolved or you've released me from the oath."

That assuaged a few of Victor's fears about working with a mage, but no oath would give him peace of mind when it came to his wolf's response to magic.

"When can you begin?" Even if they finished this tonight, it wouldn't be soon enough.

"I'll come to your pack house tomorrow at noon to see what I'm dealing with."

Victor grunted. It was clear Elijah knew where the pack house was; any mage worth his salt would find out everything he could about the local packs. Still, he didn't like Elijah knowing things about them. But he couldn't change that, so he nodded, turned, and left.

The hinges of the door creaked as it closed behind him.

He took a deep breath to steady himself, savoring the fresh air and catching another hint of wintry soil, unseasonable in the late-summer evening. His wolf crawled to the surface again at the scent.

A shiver of anticipation ran through him, but he pushed it aside. He clenched his hands and dug his nails into his palms. Whatever it took, for his pack, he'd do. He wouldn't accept any less from himself; being alpha meant he couldn't afford to be weak. And he'd make damn sure he didn't follow the same path his father had.

As he'd known it would, the scent of magic clung to him. He scrunched his nose. He needed to go home and shower, not that it'd help much.

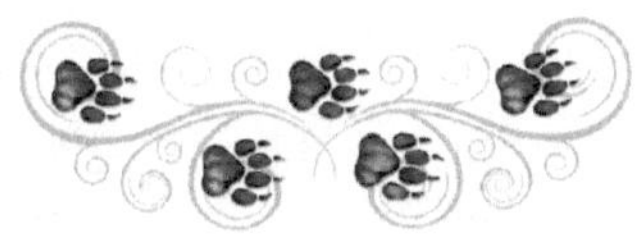

TWO

Elijah leaned against the shop window and watched Victor walk toward the lone vehicle parked halfway down the block. Streetlights caught on his dark hair and cast dramatic shadows over his muscular frame. With night fallen and the power of the waxing moon behind him, his predatory grace and strength were on full display.

His features, his bearing, his body, right down to the sound of his footsteps, all exuded a raw, primal energy that called to Elijah, the pull of it stronger than the swelling of the upcoming blue moon or Victor's alpha status could account.

Elijah shook out his hand, a tingle of that energy mixing with the magic under his skin. The fact that a trace had seeped into him from their brief contact boded well for any spell or ritual he'd need to do. Victor might be reluctant to work with magic; his energy was anything but.

Running his fingertips over the cut on his thumb, Elijah found it already closed. He didn't have the healing abilities of a shifter, but his magic helped things along. Especially when it got an unintended boost.

It'd been a petty move, making a shifter touch him, but he hadn't been able to resist, not after the insinuation he was untrustworthy. There'd been no denying his urge to needle Victor in return, to see how he'd react. The lightning-quick play of emotions across his face had been worth it. Momentary hesitation, stubborn resolve, confident challenge, with something darker and wilder underneath.

Victor was young for an alpha, but he projected authority the way a born leader should. He'd only grown more resolute when confronted with magic he clearly detested.

Elijah had wanted to push more, wanted another flash of uncertainty or suggestion of vulnerability. But he'd resisted the temptation.

Victor's dogged determination was something he could appreciate. Elijah had needed his own to convince the mage council he was competent enough to take over this shop straight out of his apprenticeship. He wondered who'd gotten more shit from their respective councils, him for going from apprentice to shop owner in a handful of months or Victor for assuming leadership of his pack a decade too soon.

The other alphas in the area had referred to Victor as young, but Elijah hadn't been expecting an alpha around his age. Most he dealt with were in their forties. He'd figured "young" meant early thirties to them, not mid-twenties.

His subverted expectations made him curious to know the circumstances under which Victor had become pack leader. The mage council had intimated the vaguest of details when they'd passed ownership of the shop to him, but the snippets—charges brought by the new Mills pack alpha of impropriety so serious the previous mage had been removed and compensation had been given to the pack—were far from the whole story.

As Victor got into his SUV, their gazes met through the grimy window, and Victor's eyes flashed gold, his wolf showing itself before either of them could look away.

Elijah watched him drive off, then flipped the sign to Closed and locked the door. The comforting hum of his wards sprang up around the building as he slid the deadbolt into place.

He wound his way through his shop, taking his time as he moved through the clutter, making mental notes of things to restock and how he needed to dust again. He did it regularly, but it was a losing battle. Whenever he turned his back, the dust slowly and surely reclaimed its territory.

One by one, the lights dimmed to darkness as he passed. When he reached the counter, the tarot card he'd drawn waited for him. The Hermit. An intriguing card for an intriguing man. It wasn't a card Elijah would readily associate with an alpha; they were too connected to their packs to qualify for the surface-level reading of solitude and isolation. But there were other meanings that might fit— healing, recovery, introspection. And beyond those, the more sinister associations. Betrayal, treason, corruption. If that was the case, Elijah doubted the territory wards were failing because of Victor.

He went into the cramped office behind the counter. The room was lit only by a desk lamp, the yellow light bright enough that the shadows beyond the door didn't trouble him. Still, he snapped his fingers at a brown candle on his workbench. The wick crackled and smoked before it caught, bathing the space in the scent of lavender and cloves with the barest hint of cedar.

Opposite the workbench, his desk was up against the right-hand wall, a scanner perched precariously on its corner while the piles of books he'd been archiving for a friend formed a barricade along one side. The chair under it wasn't the type that encouraged extended periods of sitting, but that didn't matter; it was already occupied.

His cat, Lady, was curled in a fluffy ball on the chair's cushion. The winter-morning white and gray of her fur was downy in the low light. Irritation radiated off her as she refused to acknowledge him. She wasn't a familiar; she wasn't even magical, but there was no telling her that. When he'd first moved to town to take over the shop late last summer, she'd adopted him, loitering around the shop's back door until he'd let her in, and then she'd never left.

He scooped her up and settled her onto his lap as he sat. She opened one uncannily intelligent amber eye to glare at him.

"Do I smell like dog?"

Her disgruntled trill was answer enough.

"I know, but he had that unfairly attractive alpha shifter energy going on. It's mage catnip."

One eye no longer able to convey the full force of her unimpressed disapproval, Lady opened the other.

"Don't look at me that way. It's not like I'm going to rub myself all over him."

Even if he'd been ludicrously hot and had checked Elijah out before he'd realized who he was. Even if his energy mingled with Elijah's magic with more ease than it had any right to. Getting involved with shifters was not on Elijah's to-do list.

Lady stared at him for a beat longer. Whatever her glare might say, he had self-control. He hadn't jumped any of the other shifters he'd worked with, regardless of how much their energy called to him, and he wasn't planning to start now.

Though he found something reassuring in how Victor wanted nothing to do with him. A mage could only deal with shifters who were a little too invested in getting him to join their pack so many times before he got jaded. He didn't want to contemplate what it said about his love life that someone's lack of interest was rapidly developing into a turn-on.

He scratched behind Lady's ears, half apology, half distraction, and opened his ledger to make sure his ordering system hadn't let anything slip through the cracks. When he finished, he stood and returned Lady to her throne, then tackled the books, runes, and bits of crystal that needed a final quality check and sorting before he sold them in the shop.

But his mind wasn't on his work.

A near-intangible trace of Victor's energy lingered inside him hours later, luring, tempting. It prickled its way down his spine when he attempted to capture and mold it into something, anything, just to be rid of it. But each time he tried, it remained elusive.

It shouldn't have been there at all. Normally, it was harder to siphon shifter energy. The transfer was usually more deliberate. If he'd gotten this from a touch, what would it be like to connect to Victor more completely, to channel his energy? A shiver threatened to run through Elijah.

Or if they took it one step further. If he tethered himself to Victor, that permanent connection giving him access to

Victor's energy. Whenever, wherever, as much as he wanted. To have all that power at his disposal. The things he could do with an alpha's energy.

He groaned. This wouldn't do. He knew what tethering himself to a shifter entailed. And while the energy he'd get out of the deal might be enticing, letting a shifter bond him in return most definitely was not.

It had taken him years of apprenticeship to achieve the level of respect he had and a full two months of lobbying before he'd convinced the higher-ups to grant someone his age ownership of a council-sanctioned shop, even one as run-down and rural as this. Sure, the money he'd withdrawn from his savings to use as a cash down payment, to his parents' horror, and the seventeen-page business plan he'd submitted had been the main reasons they'd permitted him to buy the shop—the money far more influential than the plan—but that made his drive to prove himself stronger.

Besides, his friends would never let him hear the end of it. Not after all the times he'd scoffed at mages that wanted nothing more than a shifter's energy to feed their magic, and an alpha's at that. His friends had agreed the life of a pack mage wasn't for them, but he'd been the most vocal about it.

Successful shops were run by unaffiliated mages. And if he wanted the council to take him seriously and let him own a shop that wasn't in the middle of nowhere, successful was what this shop had to become. The last thing he needed was to get tangled up with an alpha, to get tied to a pack. A firm handshake and surprisingly compatible magical signatures weren't changing that anytime soon.

No matter how that energy sang in his veins.

He flicked his wrist, extinguishing the candle before heading up the stairs to the loft two floors above his shop. Lady had forgiven his cheating ways enough to follow, or at least, she was willing to overlook them for food.

Once inside the narrow efficiency, he tossed his keys onto the kitchen counter. The place was as bland as they came, but it had everything he needed. A small kitchenette with a table for two was tucked into the corner near the door, bookcases with his personal library lined one wall, and a single bed was pushed as far out of the way as possible. The closet-sized bathroom had scarce room to stand, but it served its purpose. He'd been tempted to squeeze a sofa and TV in the remaining free space that constituted his living room, but he knew a lost cause when he saw one.

Council-sanctioned contract mage work was lucrative; he'd eventually be able to afford a bigger place once the shop turned a profit. But he preferred being close. Just because his wards were strong didn't mean they could keep everything out.

Besides, there was no point. If the next two years went according to plan, he'd be selling this shop, trading up to something a little more urban. It was the first of many stepping stones until he owned a sanctioned shop in a major metropolitan area. Why bother moving within the town when his intent was to move out of it altogether?

Cool night air from a partially open window eased the burn of overactive magic in his chest as he toed off his shoes.

He fed Lady and heated up leftovers for himself. The entire time he ate, he ran through a mental list of supplies he might need for his appointment tomorrow, but there were too many variables at play. He could bring half his shop and still not have what he needed.

He composed a reasonable list as he washed his dishes and got ready for bed. Lady zoomed ahead of him, claiming the pillow as her own.

As he slid between the sheets, a truck backfired out in the street and rumbled down the block, momentarily distracting him. When the night had fallen silent again, he was left with his thoughts.

What was causing the wards to fail? Was it something wrong with the land itself? Something the Mills pack was doing? Or was it an outside influence?

He shook his head. He'd figure out what he was dealing with tomorrow. Until then, there was no use dwelling on it, even if it was impossible to ignore the whisper of shifter energy still inside him, teasing his magic with the promise of more.

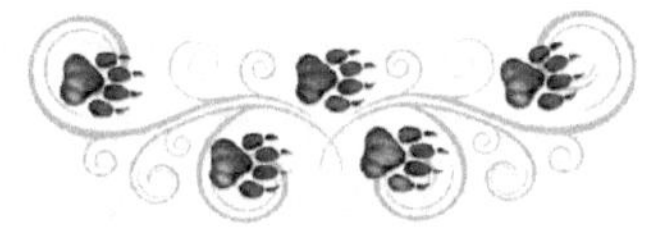

At five to noon, Elijah pulled up outside the Mills pack house. The two-story building stood at the end of a long gravel driveway. It was old but immaculately maintained, built of wood and stone, with a wraparound porch and a sprawling addition on the back. The lush greenery surrounding it was a few weeks away from erupting into the vibrant colors of autumn.

The forty-minute drive from the outskirts of town to the pack's land followed the highway before winding into the foot of the mountains. It'd afforded him time to consider his options, but everything came down to what he'd already decided. After he saw the wards, he'd determine his next step.

Elijah got out of his car, slung his messenger bag over his shoulder, and walked toward the house. The air was warm and redolent with the last breath of summer.

Victor's pack wasn't big by any means, especially compared to the more powerful ones, the largest reaching over one hundred members. But his few dozen was respectable.

Not that there was any sign of them now. The house seemed remarkably quiet.

Elijah's research had indicated a few members lived closer to town, in territory that none of the three local packs claimed, but the rest lived on pack land. He hadn't expected a welcoming committee, but it was highly unlikely every member of the pack just so happened to be elsewhere.

The lengths some shifters took to avoid magic would never stop amusing him. Though, given Victor's suspicion of mages, Elijah had to wonder if those lengths had been taken by choice or because of Victor's insistence.

Victor had to know he was there. A few miles back, Elijah had crossed into pack territory, and the wards had swept over him, not unwelcoming but letting him know his presence hadn't gone undetected. They weren't currently set to keep people out; with as large as the pack land was, it'd take a massive amount of energy to do that, but they'd give the alpha warning whenever anyone potentially dangerous entered the area. Elijah's magic alone marked him as that.

He climbed the porch steps and paused in front of the door, then strolled around to the back of the house. Knocking would be a waste of time.

Victor was sitting on a wall near a small pond. Like the house, it was well tended, man-made, but not out of place in the surrounding wilderness. Light filtered through the trees and glinted on the clear water skirted by stones. A soft breeze rippled over the surface, scattering the reflection of the sky.

Even seated, Victor was a force to be reckoned with. The direct sunlight did nothing to hide his power. He was tall, as most shifters were, with solid muscle well-defined under a simple navy T-shirt and pair of jeans, though he wasn't bulky or massive like some alphas thought they needed to be. His skin was golden, his hair short and dark, and when he turned his head to look at Elijah, his brown eyes were too bright to be entirely human.

The remnant of his energy that had persisted under Elijah's skin all night flared before fading, leaving an emptiness where it had settled beneath his sternum, but that, too, was gone with Elijah's next breath.

Victor rose as Elijah approached, his gaze steady and assessing. They took a moment to size each other up. Victor's expression gave nothing away, but tension lay in his shoulders.

"Elijah." Victor's voice was overly smooth, almost soft, a forced sort of welcoming.

"Victor." Elijah walked up to him and leaned against the stone wall.

Victor didn't answer but clenched his jaw, likely annoyed at being addressed so informally on his territory. But if he didn't want to use Elijah's title, Elijah wasn't going to use his. He wouldn't be putting up with any alpha bullshit.

There was a catch in Victor's breath before he switched from breathing through his nose to his mouth. Elijah did him the favor of not snorting. He was used to it by now, the way the scent of magic repulsed most shifters. The ones that pretended to enjoy it were worse.

"House seems quiet today," Elijah said.

"They all had things come up suddenly."

He did snort at that. "Do they know why I'm here?"

Indecision flitted across Victor's face, but he answered. "My betas do. I'll tell the rest if necessary."

"They haven't noticed the wards?"

"Only my betas and I patrol that area. The rest of the wards haven't been affected yet."

Elijah nodded, watching the ripples on the pond. He resisted the urge to toss a few rocks in to make more. Instead, he asked, "And how are the wards?"

Victor's brow furrowed, and his eyes grew distant, no doubt sensing the wards in his mind. The hesitation made Elijah pause as well.

"They're getting worse. There's an entire section of land along the western border I can't feel anymore. And whatever it is, it's accelerating."

Elijah raised an eyebrow. "How fast?"

Victor faced him again, his gaze sharp. "When it started, it was barely noticeable. Tiny slivers of land. I thought I was imagining it. But then it kept growing."

"And now?"

"A few acres a day. Last night, it was closer to a dozen."

Elijah grimaced. "Any theories as to what's happening?"

"That area is where our land meets the territories of the other local packs. From what we can tell, neither of their wards are failing. We're allies, but..." Victor's hands curled into fists.

Elijah hoped that wasn't where this was heading. Pack wars were never pretty, and the other alphas had seemed decent when he'd worked with them. He also didn't want to think about what it would do to his shop. People didn't venture near war zones to buy magical supplies. "When did you notice it?"

"Three weeks ago, a few days after the full moon. I was doing a routine perimeter check. As I got closer, something felt off, but I couldn't place it until I was right there."

"You checked the land for any signs of tampering?"

"Obviously." Victor's jaw tightened again. "There was nothing."

"Any tracks?"

"Deer, raccoons, and the like."

"No humans or shifters?"

"None."

Elijah frowned. There had to be a trace of something, a clue as to what was happening. "I need to see it for myself."

"I figured as much." Victor's eyes flickered down Elijah's body, taking in his tailored dress shirt and pressed pants. "It's a hike."

"I figured as much," Elijah said, copying his words. He wasn't dressed for the outdoors; very little of his wardrobe was suitable, but he'd worn hiking boots for a reason. He adjusted his bag and looked at Victor. "Let's go."

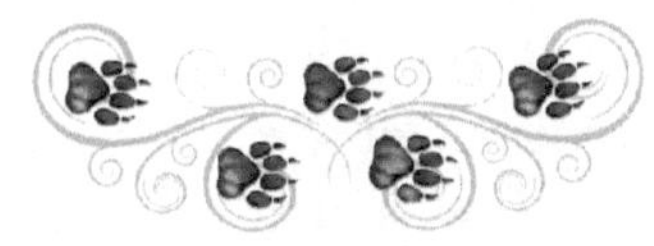

The trail wound through the forest, at places only a rough sketch of a path more suited to paws than feet. Dappled light scattered through the canopy as Elijah and Victor climbed over fallen trees and ducked under branches.

Bushes alongside the trail crowded into it, trying to claim the open space as their own.

At one point, the land to the left dipped into a valley, heavily forested and thick with growth, its depths untouched and silent, as if sunlight couldn't reach them. At another, Elijah glimpsed the frothy white of a waterfall between the trees, a sparkling gem on a canvas of deep green.

Victor led the way; the line of his broad shoulders and the curve of his ass held Elijah's attention more than was strictly professional. Or advisable, given the likelihood of him running into a tree if he got too distracted. But more than that, Victor's energy beckoned, as brilliant and enchanting as the forest, drawing Elijah in. The pull of his energy was strong enough Elijah could close his eyes and still know exactly where Victor was.

In his left hand, Elijah held a small ball of light. Its soft glow flickered. With the midday sun high in the sky, he didn't need it to make his way through the undergrowth. Instead, the spell was for detection. It was impossible for him to constantly monitor for traces of dark magic while hiking through a forest—that required too much concentration—but the pure white light would discolor on contact with the slightest foul taint.

More than once, he caught Victor staring at the light out of the corner of his eye, glancing at it over his shoulder. Maybe he was suspicious of it or checking if it'd detected anything, but there was something about his gaze that Elijah couldn't place. Something more like fascination than the revulsion he'd expected. But when he tried to identify it, Victor noticed his scrutiny, and his expression shuttered, closing off whatever emotions he might be feeling.

The silence between them was filled with the sounds of

the forest. The quiet murmur and rustle of leaves were punctuated by the groaning call of a crow and a chorus of birds chirping. Water rushed in a nearby stream, and small twigs cracked underfoot.

The smell of wet earth and moss floated on the air, the forest rich with the scents of life.

They hiked along the wards for most of the hour-long trek, following a trail carved by decades of daily perimeter checks. The barrier hummed to the right of the path, invisible, though it rippled into a translucent fog when touched by magic.

The wards around a pack's territory were a measure of their alpha's strength; they told everyone with the ability to sense them who was in charge and how capable they were of protecting their own. Sure, a mage had to make the wards, but the alpha's energy fed them, kept them alive and thriving. A powerful alpha could transform poorly made wards into something formidable, while Elijah's best work would disintegrate if left in the care of an incompetent one.

Victor's wards were strong, as strong as any Elijah had seen, not something he'd expect to be failing. They weren't the type to be easily destroyed.

But the magic encircling Victor's territory was so much more than that. It whispered against Elijah's senses. This barrier hadn't been created with brute force alone; it had been crafted, almost lovingly. The way it was so tightly interwoven with life spoke of an absolute masterclass in skill, threads of magic as fine as spider silk woven into something Kevlar-strong.

As they walked, Elijah puzzled over the wards, trying to figure out how they'd been made. No amount of money could buy wards like these. They couldn't have been constructed in a single ritual either; they must have been meticulously woven over years, dozens of rituals layering protection on protection, refining them into a masterpiece of strength and beauty.

He stumbled and came to a halt as an idea formed. A reason they might feel so different from wards he'd seen before.

Victor looked at him, an eyebrow raised in question, but Elijah ignored him. He stepped off the path into the brush and held up his hand to the wards, watching as they shimmered and swirled, reacting to his magic, recognizing he wasn't a threat. An icy electricity buzzed against his palm, not dissimilar to the way Victor's energy had.

This close, the nuances of the weave sprang into focus. These threads weren't a mage simply channeling a shifter's energy. The magic and energy that had built them were intertwined to the point there was no discerning where one ended and the other began. Inseparable, transcendent, perfectly balanced.

Of course he hadn't seen comparable wards; he couldn't imagine more than a dozen existed in the entire world.

"Were these made by your great-grandparents?" he asked, unable to keep the awe out of his voice.

"Third great-grandmother," Victor corrected. He paused before adding, "And her mate. Who was a mage."

Elijah tore his eyes from the wards to look at Victor. "They were bonded? I mean, not a transactional relationship. An actual, genuine bond."

Victor's surprise was evident. "You can sense that?"

Elijah nodded. He'd seen pack wards constructed for hire. Hell, he'd even done a few of his own. The wards created by transactionally bonded couples—mages and shifters who considered their bond a mutually beneficial business transaction and nothing more—were only marginally better. This eclipsed them all. The difference was written into the wards. "They're beautifully made. I've never seen anything like them."

Victor stepped beside him and raised his own hand, shivers of light coursing along the length of the wards as he touched them. A tendril of fog curled around his forearm before flowing back into the invisible wall. And for that one moment, he was transformed. The alpha suspicious of magic was gone. His eyes softened, and a smile played at the corner of his mouth. His fingers skated over the wards. In their wake, trails of energy gleamed before being absorbed.

A ribbon of that energy flowed to where Elijah's hand was still pressed to the wards and gathered under his fingertips, tingling against his skin. He inhaled sharply as it seemed, for one heartbeat, like another tendril of fog was forming, like the wards wanted to greet him the same way they had Victor.

But before they could, Victor jerked his hand away and turned back to the path. The nascent tendril sank into the wards.

"It's a little farther," he said, voice gruff.

Elijah exhaled shakily, then followed, not sure what had just happened and too stunned to process it.

True bonds between mages and shifters were exceedingly rare. There was too much suspicion between their kinds to allow for anything beyond the more commonplace transactional relationships. But now that he had seen what they could produce, something so striking and exquisite, still resonating with their connection over a hundred years later, he couldn't help but regret the lack. The world needed more magic like this.

As they neared their destination, the dazzling life faded

from the wards, Elijah's wonder dimming with them. Victor hadn't been exaggerating. Something did feel off.

A creeping wrongness hissed against the back of Elijah's neck, a sense of dread heavy in the air. He kept checking his detection spell, but the ball of light never discolored.

Seeing the weakened section did nothing to placate Elijah's unease.

He stopped to test the wards again, not surprised to see they barely reacted to his touch. His stomach twisted with concern as he brushed them with his magic, trying to sense the extent of the damage, tracing their wavering line. The barrier was still there, but it was muted, washed-out, the energy leached from it.

They were stretched thin—alive but shrinking in on themselves, pulling back to maintain as much coverage as they could with the little they had left. The strings of magic, tightly woven in other places, were threadbare here. At their worst, they were all but gone, wisps of energy so strained that he doubted they could detect anything that moved through them.

Whatever had caused this hadn't been focused on one point to punch a hole in the wards; it had been eating away at the entire section, spreading out, dissolving them. Another thing he'd never seen before.

"Well, fuck," Elijah muttered. His magic bristled at how wrong the wards felt. "That's not good."

"No shit," Victor agreed.

When they passed through the barrier to get to the land that was now outside the deteriorated wards, Elijah didn't feel the icy brush he should have. Even Victor's touch only caused a faint pulse of light that faded quickly instead of sweeping along their length. But still, the glowing ball in

Elijah's hand remained a steady, pure white. He let it extinguish.

"You checked for signs of a spell?"

Victor nodded. "And every detectable intrusion we could think of. Nothing."

Elijah knelt on the forest floor. "Is there anything nearby?"

"Besides trees?"

"Anything on the neighboring lands?"

"No. None of us come out here regularly. Just during patrols and maybe full-moon runs. It's mostly a buffer between our lands."

Elijah sank his fingers into the soil beneath the carpet of needles and fallen leaves. He shut his eyes, took a breath, and let his senses flow into the ground.

This forest was old and alive, sure and strong, a thick verdant tapestry both above and below. The moist earth beneath his fingers was dark and rich, the air heavy with the scent of moss and pine.

Larger animals roamed in the distance, moving through the trees, while birds darted from branch to branch. Victor waited beside him, his presence reverberating in the echoes of wolf shifters that had passed through, but that was all Elijah could sense. There were no traces of an intruder, no one with hostile intent, no sign of magic.

The forest was ablaze with life, glorious and untainted. If someone had dared to come into this territory, they might have tried to poison the land to destroy the wards that were linked to it, but he would have felt the aftermath of that, and it wasn't there. Only the wards were broken.

What would cause that kind of damage without affecting anything else? It wasn't harming the plants or creatures; there was no dark magic creeping through the land. It had just attacked the wards.

Elijah pulled his hand from the dirt, opened his eyes, and sat back on his heels.

"Find anything?" Victor asked, voice quiet.

Elijah looked up at him. "I can't pick up anything. No magic, nothing irregular or unusual. The only things remotely magical that I can sense are the wards themselves, and the only energy is your pack's."

"Do you have any idea what it is?"

Elijah stood, dusted off his knees, and took in the land around the damaged wards. It grew gorgeous and untamed. He'd never been much for the outdoors, but the wild beauty of it was undeniable. "I don't think a mage did it. It also doesn't feel like fae. There'd be residue from their magic, and I can't sense any. But beyond that, I don't know."

Victor studied him, gaze intense. "Can you fix it?"

Elijah shook his head. "Not today." A concerned expression clouded Victor's face, so he rushed on. "Not completely, at least. I'll need the full moon to do that. But I can create a stopgap, something temporary, to shield this area until next week."

He expected Victor to have doubts, but he didn't hesitate. He nodded, his dislike of magic outweighed by the instinct to protect his pack. "What do I need to do?"

Elijah took the bag from his shoulder and opened it, pulling out a jar.

"I need you to mark your territory."

Victor cocked an eyebrow at him. For the first time, there was a trace of amusement on his face. It was a good look on him. It made him seem more carefree, more like he might have been before he'd become pack alpha.

"Yeah, okay. I walked into that one. With this." Elijah

held out the jar, and Victor took it, twisting the lid open. His nose twitched, rather bunny-like, not that Elijah would say that to a wolf. "It's ground cedar, oak, fennel, and anise, used for protection. It needs a drop of your blood. I have a knife if you need it."

"I've got it covered. That's it?"

"For now. Sprinkle it where the border should be so I know where to make it. I'll set up while you do that."

Victor nodded, then slipped into the shadows.

Elijah knelt again and cleared a small patch of loose stones and leaves. He pulled out the knife he used to carve runes into wood and inscribed a circle in the dirt. Fresh soil wasn't the easiest to write on, but he'd always had a way with earth, and the forest seemed willing to accommodate him, molding itself into what he needed it to be. He leaned back to examine his work.

This spell wouldn't support itself for long, but it only had to last a week. He could do something more permanent on the full moon. Hopefully without having to tear down the current wards. If he had to start from scratch, he wasn't sure he could destroy such a work of art.

He opened his bag again and sorted out a few smaller pouches, laying them on the ground. From one, he took out a vial of dried licorice root and ginger mixed into a fragrant oil and put a drop on each of the compass points of the circle. From another, he let four black pebbles engraved with runes fall as they willed. Another still held a sachet that contained cinnamon, cloves, and marigold that he buried in the earth.

The circle was nearly ready by the time he realized Victor was back, watching him. Victor stayed silent, his gaze a heavy weight as Elijah finished his preparations.

"Any of that mixture left?" Elijah asked, setting the

brown candle from his office in the center of the circle. He opened the smallest pouch and placed three tiny bundles of cedar twigs wrapped in muslin around it.

Victor nodded. "Some."

"Bring it here and kneel beside me."

Tension rolled off Victor as he crouched, but he had no choice if they were doing this. His expression was conflicted, closed off and cautious, yet vivid curiosity glimmered in his eyes. Elijah had the strangest impression that he was holding himself back from asking questions about the purpose of everything Elijah had laid out. Not from suspicion but from a genuine desire to know.

Elijah took the jar from Victor and sprinkled the remaining mixture over the candle. He lit the wick with a short, precise snap of magic and watched the flame flare as it burned the herbs until there was nothing left but the ghost of smoky wood.

"Now, the part you aren't going to like," he said. "I can make temporary wards to close the gap, but I can't do it with my magic alone." To extend it that much, he needed more power than he could channel from the land, and he doubted the existing wards would welcome foreign magic. He wouldn't need much, but it'd be a good test to see if Victor's energy was as cooperative as he thought it might be.

Victor's gaze raked over him in assessment. His eyes held Elijah in place as they drank him in, and Elijah forced himself to weather the silent intensity of his stare.

After a long moment, Victor nodded. "Take what you need."

Elijah reached out and placed his left palm on Victor's chest, the fabric of his T-shirt soft, the heat of him spilling through.

"Should I take off my—"

"Not this time," Elijah said, but he did need skin contact, and it was interesting Victor knew that. "Wrap a hand around my wrist."

Victor obeyed, and Elijah's awareness zeroed in on that point of contact, the warmth crawling up his arm. He let out a silent breath when Victor's thumb brushed against the inside of his wrist, leaving behind a trail of heat. That simple touch was enough to feel how energy thrummed in Victor, how it seeped into Elijah's magic and combined effortlessly, far easier than any shifter's had before.

Elijah dropped his right hand to the earth, his fingers digging into the soil again as his eyes slid shut. He pulled on Victor's energy, feeling the breath under his palm hitch.

The rush of power was immediate and intoxicating, like he was casting his first spell all over again. But that had taken effort, and this was easy, so smooth and simple. Victor's energy was open to him, waiting for him, there for the taking. Where he'd expected a trickle, he received a flood.

He pushed his fingers deeper into the earth, using it to ground himself, and the forest reached back. It sent root-like coils toward him, drinking in their magic and energy.

It led him to the edge of Victor's territory. The line he'd marked lit up in Elijah's mind.

Elijah channeled more energy, threading it with the forest's essence and his magic.

Basic wards weren't difficult to make; all they required was a connection to the thing being protected and a source of power. Good wards, on the other hand, powerful ones that could rarely be broken, were another matter altogether. Those took precision and effort. Even with Victor and the forest helping, he had to set them carefully.

He reached out with his senses and tugged on the earth, pulling his magic up and out of the ground to follow the boundary line. He laid magic around the territory border, inching it toward the healthy sections.

Victor's pulse beat quick but strong under his palm, and the wide swath of forest around them breathed in time with him.

As his magic approached the wards, the anticipation grew as tangible as the crackle of energy under his fingertips. It was heady and thrilling, and Elijah inhaled deeply, Victor's energy filling him, fueling him.

His hands, his magic, his tattoos heated as he poured more power into the spell, creating a shield for the weaker section. He took another deep breath, steadying himself.

The two wards met, one pale fog, the other black earth, and he wove them together at the edges, letting them intertwine and form a pattern that faded as it reached the healthy wards. The tattered, stretched section dissolved like a relieved sigh into the reinforcements.

Elijah held Victor's energy in contrast with his own magic for a moment longer, one wild and one leashed, but more alike than he ever would have imagined. It washed over him, bringing with it the rustle of leaves, the taste of the forest on his lips, sharp power on his tongue. It was easy to see why mages often wanted more, why they might let someone convince them to join a pack so they had constant access to it.

But that wasn't why he was there. On Victor's land or in this town. He'd done what was needed; he'd extended the wards. For now, at least.

The energy he hadn't used ebbed away, returning to Victor. The lack made him dizzy, oddly empty without it filling him.

Victor's grip tightened on his wrist, his body so warm through his shirt.

Elijah opened his eyes and met Victor's dark gaze, saw it flash amber in the shadows of the forest. This close, he could only see the sharp angles of his face, the rough stubble along his jaw. Victor studied him right back.

"What?" Elijah asked, voice a breath above a whisper.

"Your eyes," Victor said. "They're glowing."

Elijah huffed out a laugh. "Yours were too." He pressed his eyelids shut and gathered his magic inside himself. It was harder than he'd expected with Victor touching him, with that energy pushing against his skin. He blinked his eyes open, knowing they'd no longer glow purple. "Better?"

Victor's expression was unreadable.

Elijah straightened and pulled back. Victor did the same, dropping his hand to his side.

It didn't take long to pack up his things, some he left behind as a thank-you for the forest lending its strength.

Doing magic usually took more out of Elijah, but this time, his body was flush with energy, almost drugged with it, his senses overstimulated as they made their way back. The forest air was cool, sweet with sap dripping from trees. Leaves tickled his skin as he passed, bark rough as he ran his fingertips over it.

It was late afternoon when they reached the pack house, still as quiet as when he'd arrived. Elijah figured the pack wouldn't reappear until they knew he was good and gone or Victor declared it was safe for them to return.

Victor walked him to his car. "How much?" he asked when they got there.

Elijah blinked at him. It took longer than it should have to realize what he was asking. Right. This was his job; he charged for this. But if he had to dismantle the pack wards, he couldn't charge for that. Not his usual rate. It'd be a crime, like offering some cheap forgery in their place.

"The damage is extensive, but I'll do everything I can to use as much of the current wards as possible. If I can make that work, it'll be in the upper four figures." Though, if he were being completely honest, part of him wanted to do it in exchange for a few hours of testing and examining Victor's wards, learning their secrets. He hadn't lied when he'd said wards were one of his specialties, but in comparison, he was no better than a novice.

"I should have come to you sooner," Victor said, not meeting Elijah's gaze. The admission seemed to cost him more than what Elijah was charging. "It would have been easier to fix then."

"It might have made patching up the damage easier, but we don't know if they'll continue to erode or what caused it. And either way, we need to strengthen the whole barrier, which can only happen on the full moon if we want to do it right."

"Still," he said, finally looking Elijah in the eye. "Thank you."

Elijah wondered how much that had pained Victor to say. He doubted he'd suddenly come to trust magic, but it was a start. "Don't thank me yet."

Victor nodded his acknowledgment. "What will you need?"

"If there's a clearing near the center of your territory, somewhere guarded, where we won't be disturbed, that'd be best. And your entire pack should be here, if possible."

"I can arrange that. Anything else?"

"I'll handle the rest."

Silence fell between them for a beat.

"If the wards start to fail," Elijah said.

"I'll contact you immediately."

Elijah nodded. "Right. I should get going."

He got into his car, tossed his bag onto the passenger seat, and gave Victor an awkward wave before turning the key and heading down the long drive to the main road.

The first few miles blurred by him. He couldn't concentrate through his live-wire thoughts, so he let them drift over him like a breeze. When he drove through the wards, they reached out after him, one final shimmering caress.

It was only once he'd put more distance between himself and the pack territory that he could focus. The rolling of his tires calmed him.

He parked outside his shop, turned off the engine, and sat there for several minutes, staring at the building but not quite seeing the boxy storefront. He touched his wrist and could swear a mark pulsed there, an invisible brand left by Victor's energy.

If that was what a basic warding spell had been like, how would the full ritual feel? The promise of all the energy he'd be handling shivered through him.

God, he was turning into a cliché. A mage drooling over alpha energy. Could he get any more pathetic?

Grabbing his bag, he got out and climbed the stairs to his apartment. Once inside, he dumped the bag on his small kitchen table and pulled his phone out of his pocket to check the time. It was ten past five.

He glanced up to find Lady surveying him with a frigid glare. The disdainful swoosh of her tail accused him of things he hadn't done.

Okay, fine, he'd looked. With an ass like Victor's, he didn't think anyone could blame him for looking. Anyone who wasn't Lady, at least.

As if reading his mind, she flattened her ears and turned her head away when he knelt beside her.

"I know, I know," he said, coaxing a reluctant purr out of her as he scratched under her chin. "If you think I'm bad now, wait until the full moon." She'd shun him for a week. But there was no helping it. If she didn't like wolf shifters, she should have adopted someone else. There was no avoiding them in his line of work.

Ignoring the buzz of the excess energy in his system, he pulled himself together. He needed dinner, and then he had research to do. If he could find the reason wards like Victor's were failing, he might be able to stop it from happening again.

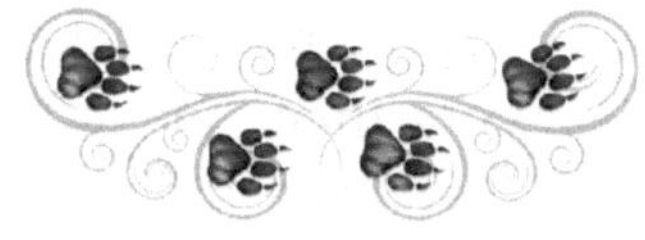

THREE

Someday, Victor would figure out how to go grocery shopping with multiple carts. One was not nearly enough, and pushing two through the store was unwieldy.

What if he lashed them together with rope and formed a train? He doubted that'd attract more stares than he was getting now with his overflowing cart, even the lower tray packed with boxes and cans, each turn more precarious than the last.

It wasn't like he could explain shifter appetites to the little old man who'd stopped dead in his tracks to watch Victor roll by, though a few middle-aged women gave him sympathetic looks.

"Teenage boys at home?" one asked as she passed him in the snack aisle.

Victor forced out a laugh. "An entire pack of them."

What he had in his cart wouldn't survive long, and that was before taking into account the fast-approaching full moon.

He rarely did the shopping; that normally fell to those lower in the pack hierarchy. Frequently, it was a team effort, with a couple of members loading up on as many groceries as possible.

But Victor was restless. He'd needed to get out of the house, needed to do something. Sitting around, waiting for the full moon, had been driving him insane, driving *his wolf* insane, and they still had three days to go.

Kade, his second-in-command, had told him in no uncertain terms that if he didn't find a way to work off his excess energy, Kade and his other two betas would consider mutiny as a serious possibility.

His actual words had been, "With all due respect, Victor. *Alpha.* If you bounce your leg another goddamn time, I will not be responsible for my actions. Actions that I will carry out with love and respect."

He'd then implied, with the graceful subtlety only Kade was capable of mustering, that Victor needed to get laid. Which was ridiculous. How could Victor think about sex when he had his pack to protect, and all he'd been able to smell for the last four days had been the lingering scent of magic? It had faded since Elijah's temporary patch of the wards, but with the moon waxing and the ritual looming, Victor only became more aware of the cobwebs of wintry earth that clung to his skin.

Even now, in this store filled with too-bright light and far too many scents, with the aisle of coffee four over and the racks of spices past that, with the two-day-old fish in the meat department and the man that'd walked by him, fresh from the gym but not the shower. None of that stopped the filaments of soil and snow from coiling around him, curling inside him with every breath.

He turned down aisle five, the rows of cereal stretching out before him, and a can of vegetables tipped over the edge of his cart. Only his quick reflexes enabled him to catch it before it hit the ground.

Thankfully, no humans were there to see. He wedged the can between two jars of peanut butter and hoped for the best.

Someone was always at the pack house to make breakfast, but they tried to keep cereal on hand in case the younger kids were too hungry to wait. They could have a bowl of something ridiculously sugary while the nutritious stuff was cooked.

He balanced four boxes against the cart handle, not paying attention to the brands. If the kids were eating it, they'd be hungry enough to inhale whatever it was. It didn't matter as long as there were unreasonable amounts of sugar and calories involved and something to wash it down.

Which reminded him: he should get milk.

Carefully turning, he headed to the dairy section to grab a few gallons, and then he'd have to call it quits. Nothing else was fitting in this cart. As it was, he'd be carrying the milk in his free hand on his way to the checkout.

He'd reached the dairy case when, out of the corner of his eye, he saw Grant Lucas.

Grant made a quick, furtive gesture at him before ducking down an aisle.

That was... not like him.

Frowning, Victor grabbed two gallons and wheeled his cart in the direction the other alpha had disappeared.

He found Grant hidden around a corner, his eyes pressed closed and a hand against a shelf, but the moment

Victor approached, he straightened, his arm falling to his side.

Victor greeted him with a nod. "Alpha Lucas."

"Alpha Mills." Grant nodded back.

Victor still wasn't used to greeting other alphas as equals. Grant had been the leader of his pack for around a decade, since well before Victor had to tag along to his father's meetings with the neighboring alphas.

They stood there, Victor studying him. Grant's ruggedly handsome face was pinched, the lines around his eyes tense. If Victor didn't know better, he'd say Grant seemed tired, but that wasn't a look shifters got often. With their enhanced healing abilities, it was rare for them to get run down to the point they appeared physically exhausted.

"Everything alright?" Victor asked.

"Everything's great." Grant shot him a look he couldn't read. "How's your pack doing?"

It wasn't uncommon for alphas on good terms to inquire after each other's packs, but the instinct to hide any potential weakness was undeniable. Had Grant sensed Victor's wards were failing? Victor hadn't thought it had gotten to that point yet. It was only that one section that had noticeable damage.

Three days remained until the full moon; he could cover until then.

"We're good. Two of our kids just started kindergarten, and they've been whining for a week about having to wake up so early. One of the older kids taught them the word 'nocturnal,' and that's all we've been hearing ever since. How unnatural it is for them to have to go to school when they're 'nocturnal animals.'"

"They always learn that word earlier than they should." Grant's laughter seemed to leave him breathless.

Victor's grin faltered. His father's face flashed through his mind, worn and drawn in the months before Victor had challenged him for control of the pack. Grant looked nothing like his father had, but Victor couldn't shake the image.

"Is everything alright?" he asked again, more insistent. "You're not being—" Victor cut himself off and rephrased the question. Grant didn't smell like magic, but... "You haven't worked with Elijah Lauring lately, have you?"

Grant frowned. "No. Not for six months."

"Another mage?"

"No." Genuine bemusement crossed Grant's face.

Victor held back a sigh of relief. He had to be imagining things.

"Have you seen Alpha MacFarlan recently?"

The topic change was jarring. It was Victor's turn to be unsure where this was going. "No."

Grant searched his face. "Just watch out for your pack. Keep them safe. Make sure they're healthy and protected."

That wasn't the sort of thing Grant normally would have told him.

Without waiting for Victor to respond, Grant nodded to him again and walked away.

Confused, Victor muscled his cart toward the checkout line.

What the hell had that been? Had Grant implied Niall MacFarlan was untrustworthy? Had Niall done something to Grant's pack that made him feel as though he had to warn Victor? That might explain his pinched look and veiled language—stress caused by another alpha moving in on his territory and uncertainty over whose side Victor might choose.

Or did he know what was going on with Victor's wards after all? Was he hinting Niall was behind it?

Fifteen minutes later, after he'd paid for his groceries and packed up his SUV, he still didn't have answers to those questions.

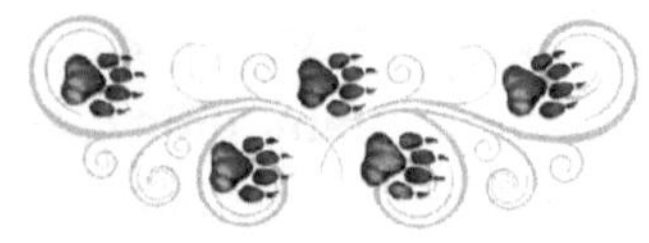

When Victor pulled up to the pack house, Will was lounging in a chair on the porch, his long frame sprawled out, hands behind his head. He stood, stretched, ran fingers through his light brown hair, and strolled down the steps.

Why one of his betas was waiting for him outside, Victor wasn't sure.

"Kade wanted me to check if you'd gotten laid while you were out," Will said by way of greeting.

Well, that answered that question. "I was getting groceries."

"When has Kade let that stop him?"

"Fair point."

"He says you're not allowed back in the house unless you, and these are his words, not mine, have had the restlessness fucked out of you. And since people generally scowl less after a good orgasm, not more, I'm going to assume that didn't happen. In which case, Kade said, again, his words, 'tell him to run around the pack land a few times before we have to deal with his sexually frustrated ass.'"

Whatever Kade thought, being sexually frustrated was *not* one of Victor's problems. "Aren't you supposed to show respect and deference to your alpha?"

"Sorry, you're right, Alpha. We'd like to kindly request

you consider taking an extended stroll around your vast, beautiful territory this evening. It's a lovely night for a run."

Victor growled. If he wanted more than their usual sass, he'd need to command his betas to be respectful, and they knew he wasn't the kind of alpha to abuse his power in that way, to use the control he could exert over them to force submission. Besides, what did he expect when his betas were older than him? He snatched bags out of the back of his SUV with more force than necessary.

Will held up his hands. "His words, not mine. I'm just the messenger."

"How'd you pull the short straw?" Victor asked, handing him multiple bags.

"Kade reminded me I owed him for setting me up with Janell."

"Been a while since he's held that over you. You think he'll ever let it go?"

"Knowing Kade? Never."

"Speaking of your wife, I picked up a bag of those maple bacon chips she's been craving. But if I have to go for a run, maybe I'll see if the kids want them."

Will gave him a once-over. "Huh, would you look at that? I've never seen someone who has so clearly been thoroughly fucked in my life. Dozens of orgasms just written all over your face."

"How is having you on my side worse than when you're on Kade's?"

"It's a talent."

They hauled the bags into the house. The moment they were inside, three of the younger pack members greeted them, drawn by the sound of rustling bags and the promise of food.

The kids swarmed them, anticipation evident in their

inability to stand still, and Victor huffed in amusement at their predictability. He handed them a half dozen bags each. "Everything needs to be unpacked and put away before you open or eat anything." He used his sternest tone, and they nodded, wide-eyed and sincere. He gave that obedience roughly two minutes before the box of dough-nuts he'd bought smashed it to pieces.

Before they dashed into the kitchen, he snagged the chips and tossed them to Will, who mock saluted, then headed to find his wife. She was nearing sixteen weeks pregnant and had just started to show. The baby would be the first since Victor had become alpha, the first in the pack in five years, and damn if it wasn't kicking his instincts into overdrive. New life, a new start, and more reason to keep his pack safe and protected.

Victor stationed himself outside the kitchen doorway, leaning against the wall and waiting for the inevitable.

Two minutes later, right on time, he heard a horrified *"Oliver!"*

The answering "What?" was decidedly doughy.

"We have to put the groceries away before we eat," Cami said. She was the oldest at eleven and did try to be the responsible one.

"It has chocolate frosting *and* sprinkles," Oliver countered with every ounce of his five-year-old certainty.

Victor grinned. Oliver had a point. Who could resist frosting *and* sprinkles?

Emelie gasped. "Do those ones have strawberry filling?" Victor imagined her shooting a glance at the door, torn between the proverbial shoulder angel and devil of Cami and Oliver.

"Yep," Oliver said, mouth still full.

That was enough for Emelie's willpower to give out.

"*Guys.*" The exasperation in Cami's voice was louder than her whisper.

"What are we listening to?" Katrina asked under her breath as she took up position next to him.

"I bought doughnuts."

"Oh, you evil, evil man. Please tell me my son didn't break first."

"I could, but we both know it'd be a lie." Victor then pitched his voice to carry. "I was just heading to the kitchen to get a drink. You want anything?"

What resulted was a chaotic scramble of hissed "I told you so's," frantic bag rustling, slammed cabinet doors, and audible panic.

But when Victor had stopped his shoulders shaking from suppressed laughter and entered the kitchen, the bags were empty.

And half the doughnuts had been eaten.

The kids gave him their best innocent looks. They'd be convincing if it weren't for the chocolate smeared at the corner of Oliver's mouth and the powdered sugar dusting Emelie's lips.

Behind him, Katrina snorted, and when he turned, she was looking into the pantry. To say the kids had put the food away was a world beyond generous. Only a miracle had prevented an avalanche when she'd opened the door.

"Well," she said, grinning, "I guess I've got three volunteers to cook dinner with me."

"Aw, *Mama,*" Oliver groaned, scrunching his freckled face.

Victor snagged a bottle of water from the fridge and nodded at Katrina. "I'll leave you to it."

She winked at him and mouthed thank you.

He was always happy to help.

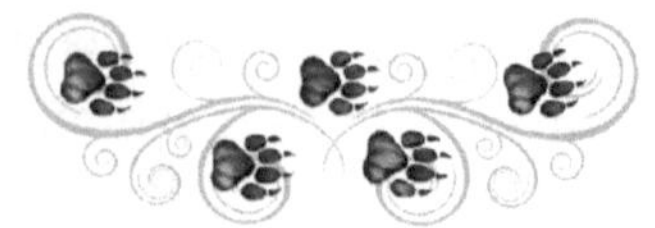

Dinner went by in a blur of passing plates and conversation. The normalcy of it soothed him. Between the food and camaraderie, it was easier to forget about everything outside the pack house. But there was no way he could enjoy himself completely, not when halfway through the meal, he heard Oliver and Emelie whispering to each other.

"My mom says that a mage is coming on the full moon," Emelie said in a conspiratorial tone, leaning her blonde head toward Oliver.

"Mine too."

"Do you think we'll get to see magic?" Emelie sounded excited by the prospect, and Victor found it hard to remember that feeling.

Oliver wrinkled his nose. "If we see it, we'll *smell* it."

"*Oliver.* What did I say?" The admonishment was clear in Katrina's voice, and Oliver shrank in his seat.

"It's not nice to call people smelly," he grumbled.

Katrina ruffled his red hair. In punishment, if his face was anything to go by. "Before you were born, we had a pack mage. We smelled like magic all the time."

Oliver looked stricken at the thought. "*All the time?*"

"Yep. Now finish your vegetables before I decide to add another serving on your plate."

He did as told.

The reminder of what was happening in three days hung there for the rest of the meal, impossible to ignore.

After dinner, Victor stepped out onto the back porch. He descended the stairs into a night crisp with the earliest blush of autumn. Breathing in, he savored the rush of pine needles as they mixed with late-season wildflowers.

He walked to the pond and sat on the stone wall, hands on his knees. He focused on his breath, the rise and fall of his chest, the sound of water flowing out of the pond, bubbling over the stones, streaming out into the forest.

The stars overhead were a brilliant scattering of lights, the moon almost full, calling to him.

Victor turned his gaze to the forest. Elijah's spell lingered there, though it had dimmed somewhat. His magic had been a ghost haunting Victor; there whenever he closed his eyes and sensed the boundary of his territory. The wards had always felt alive, a creature that breathed with him. But now there was that section along the western line that was and wasn't his, that existed in tandem with the rest, that pressed against his wards, wove into them, somehow both foreign and familiar.

There'd been no sign of corruption since Elijah had patched the wards. Victor checked countless times each day. The pack land was healthy and strong, but worry clouded his mind. This was too good to be true. It couldn't be this simple.

His wolf agreed there was something wrong, though it had absolute faith in Elijah being able to fix things, an opinion Victor couldn't cosign.

Maybe he was worried for nothing. The upcoming ritual might have been setting him off, the growing moon agitating his wolf, making him more restless than usual. Or it could be his persistent doubts about his ability to protect his pack.

But the premonition that something was coming wouldn't leave him, and the fear he was powerless to stop it lurked under the surface of his thoughts, no matter how hard he struggled to push it away.

He let out a long, slow exhale and rubbed a hand across his face. Whatever it was, he knew better than to dismiss his instincts when they were this strong. Or, at least, when they were this strong about anything other than mages.

Behind him, he heard soft steps on the path to the pond.

"This broody lone-wolf thing doesn't suit you," Kade said, and Victor scoffed.

"I don't brood."

"Right. You're sitting out here alone, thinking happy thoughts of sunshine and rainbows." Kade took a seat next to him on the wall. "Adorable baby animals and cotton candy."

Victor gave his cousin a flat look. "You don't know me. I might be sneaking cute cat videos on my phone."

Kade snorted. "Not with as shit as reception is out here." He shoved at Victor's shoulder. "And I don't know you? Right. Uh-huh. We're just ignoring the decade-plus you spent trailing after me when you were a pup?"

"Don't say it like you were an adult at the time. You've only got four years on me."

"Five."

"Four and seven months."

"Which rounds to five."

Victor was unable to stop from grinning at the well-worn argument.

"Shit, man. Don't smile. It'll kill the whole brooding thing you've got going on."

Victor shoved him off the wall, happy to use his alpha strength if it meant Kade landed on his ass in the dirt or pond. He didn't; his reflexes were too sharp for that, but it was worth a try.

Kade laughed and retook his seat next to Victor.

A gentle, cooling breeze brushed against their skin and stirred the trees, making leaves rustle and branches sway. Water lapped at the edges of the pond, and the forest echoed with the calls of insects and animals as the moon shone overhead.

"Is everything set?" Victor kept his voice low so as not to disturb the peace that had settled around them.

"Everyone knows where they need to be and what they need to do."

"I want to make sure the territory is guarded. The border will be in flux during the ritual, and if someone is attacking our wards, that'll be their chance to sneak in."

"As you've said before. Repeatedly. It's taken care of. We've got this. The pack can manage one full moon that isn't their usual fun. They'll guard the perimeters while Will, Rick, and I guard the clearing."

"If something happens—"

Kade's sigh was long-suffering. "What's going to happen?"

Victor shrugged. "I have a bad feeling about this."

"Of course you do. You wouldn't be you if you didn't."

They slipped into silence for a few minutes before Kade asked, "What's he like?"

Victor pulled a face. "He's a mage."

"Extremely helpful. It's like I know him already." Kade

leaned back, appearing to study the sky, but Victor felt his gaze on him. "I heard he's easy on the eyes."

Victor grunted.

"I'll take that as a yes."

"Don't even think about it."

Kade's smile was sly. "Think about what?" He wasn't fooling anyone, not with his reputation. He flirted with everything that moved and many things that didn't. "Just saying. It wouldn't hurt if I established a *good relationship* with him. For the pack, of course."

"Thoughts like that are what got this pack in trouble in the first place."

Kade winced, expression sobering. "I don't mean it like that. There are lines I wouldn't cross. One shitty mage, albeit an unbelievably shitty, self-serving one, shouldn't mean we have to stay cut off from magic forever."

"We don't need magic or a pack mage."

Kade snorted. "Every pack needs a mage." Before Victor could argue, he continued. "You're not scared of him, are you?" A hint of taunting crept into his tone.

Victor glowered at him.

"Scared of letting him channel your energy?"

Victor's scowl deepened.

"It's magic," Kade said, serious again. "If you're not a little scared of it, there's something wrong with you. But he won't kill and eat you, Victor. That'd be bad for business."

"I know that."

"Then why? Why are you so determined to keep away from magic?"

"You know why."

"I'm not sure I do. Not really."

Victor didn't have an answer to that. The only sounds

were the gurgling of the creek and the whispering of the forest.

He'd lost count of the times he and Kade had sat like this. Sometimes to talk, sometimes to watch the moon. It'd always been a comfort.

That night, it wasn't.

"Do you remember when you were a kid and used to follow Grandma June around and try to do the spells she did?" Kade asked when the silence grew too heavy.

Another thing Victor didn't need a reminder of. He'd been fascinated by magic as a kid. The way it made his nose tickle like he was about to sneeze, the way the wards shimmered into existence when he touched them, the way it wove through the pack land, an almost tangible thing.

When he was twelve, their grandmother had passed away, and it'd been the first time the pack had been without a mage in over a hundred years.

Victor shook his head. "That was a long time ago. Things have changed."

Kade studied him, then stood. "I'm going to bed. I'll see you in the morning."

He took a few steps away from the pond, stopped, and half turned back. "You're not your father, Victor. You won't make the same mistakes he did."

That was just one more thing Victor had no reply to.

After a moment, Kade walked toward the pack house, though not before throwing one last comment over his shoulder. "Besides, if he's as hot as rumor has it, none of us would blame you for following him around like a pup too."

Victor's jaw clenched. He'd be keeping his interactions with the mage to a minimum. That was best for everyone involved.

He didn't move from his spot by the pond, watching the

moon travel across its surface, swelling ever closer to full, ever closer to the ritual. He let out a breath, trying to calm his wolf, to ease the trepidation that skittered along his skin. It didn't work; his wolf was too agitated, too excited, looking forward to the ritual, and Victor couldn't understand why.

He sat there, conflicted, nerves on edge, until it was time for him to run another patrol.

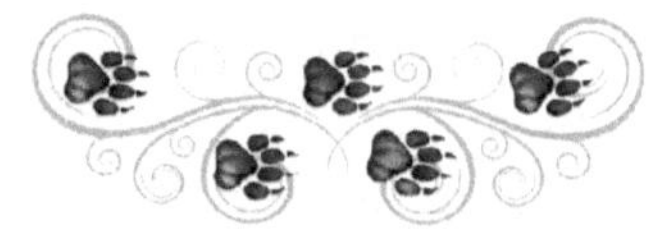

FOUR

It was two hours before sundown when Elijah pulled up to the pack house, and this time, it wasn't empty. A pair of tiny faces were pressed against the glass of a large picture window that overlooked the driveway. Elijah waved at them, and they ducked out of sight, only to pop back up when he looked away. He assumed the kids were being kept inside for the night. The fits that must have sparked had to have been epic.

Thirty-some members of the Mills pack were gathered outside, clustered around Victor. A few cast glances Elijah's way, but most stayed focused on their alpha.

Elijah fought down a frisson of anticipation at the scene. There was something about a full moon that intensified the nature of wolf shifters and made them more animalistic. They were wilder, more impulsive, more powerful. It was in the air, the moonlight that bathed the forest, the primal energy that gripped them. Their wolves were closer to the surface, eclipsing the human parts of themselves. No one could look at them and think they were anything but *other* on a night like this. Not with their eyes flashing, an amber shine taking up most of their irises, and their smiles sharper than a human's could ever be. All the more reason for them to stay on pack lands during full moons, away from people who were unaware of the supernatural.

Shifter packs were bound together by threads of energy that formed an intricate web. It let them feed off each other, share each other's strength. Under the full moon, the force of it reverberated, strongest in the alpha, weakest in the newest members. Victor's pack was thrumming with it, filled to the brim, the blue moon giving them an extra kick.

For a mage, it was heady, all that power at its peak. Elijah's magic leapt at the thought.

He reminded himself of the reasons that energy wasn't as appealing as it seemed; it wasn't worth the strings attached to it. This was work and nothing more. With that firmly in mind, he got out of his car and circled back to the trunk to get his supplies.

"Kade," Victor said, head tilting in Elijah's direction, and the man standing next to him turned and walked toward Elijah as Victor continued to confirm everyone understood their duties for the night. Elijah knew Victor wasn't looking forward to the ritual. Still, nothing in his posture suggested nerves or worry. His voice was commanding and sure, a person who could lead armies.

Out of the corner of his eye, Elijah watched Kade approach. His wavy brown hair fell loose around his face, just this side of shaggy and setting off his scruff and intense stare. He had that obnoxiously attractive shifter energy going on, similar to everyone else in the pack, but amped up by more than the full moon. With that level of power, Elijah's money was on him being Victor's second-in-command.

Even without his appeal currently cranked to eleven, he'd be smoking hot. The type of guy who could blow your mind in the back room of a club, and he knew it too.

Fuckboys, shifter or otherwise, had never appealed to Elijah, but he could appreciate the scenery.

Just once, he wanted to work with a pack that wasn't full of unfairly gorgeous shifters. There were a lot of them in the world; a few had to fall into the homely category.

Elijah shouldered his backpack and picked up the cardboard box he'd packed, propping it on his hip to close the trunk.

"Can I help with that?" Kade asked. His lips quirked in the barest hint of a smirk, well aware Elijah had checked him out.

"Not unless you want to ruin the ritual before it begins."

Kade looked startled. "I'll just show you to the clearing, then?"

"Lead the way."

Kade headed around the house and into the trees. Elijah followed. Hiking through a forest while carrying a heavy box and backpack wouldn't be fun, but he couldn't risk getting his supplies charged with excess shifter energy before he even started, especially the wrong shifter's.

As he passed the pack, Elijah felt eyes on him, but he didn't check to see whose. He didn't have to; the way his magic stirred under that gaze told him everything he needed to know.

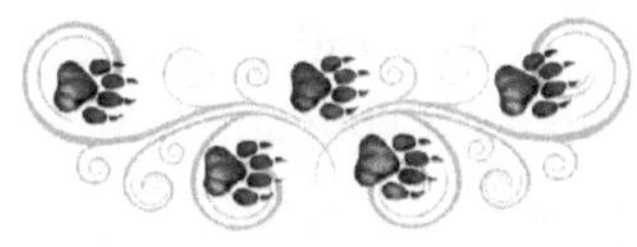

The clearing was large, the earth flat and easy to work with.

"I'll leave you to get yourself prepped for Victor," Kade said. "He'll come for you whenever you want him to."

Elijah raised an eyebrow, but Kade only grinned and left. He couldn't have meant that the way Elijah's brain was trying to take it.

Shaking his head, Elijah cleared his mind, then measured out the dimensions of the clearing with a compass, making sure he was marking the right spots. He had to get this right the first time. There'd be no starting over if he messed it up.

He inscribed a circle with chalk, letting white powder fall from his fingers to decorate the earth. His magic shaped it, guided it to land precisely, symbols and sigils scattering across the ground.

A steady hum resounded through his body, the undercurrent of magic that was always there, but now it was saturating with the energy of the pack. Raw power for Elijah to reach out and take.

It was more than the pack though; it was the clearing itself, every inch steeped with magic. Elijah knew, certain as the stars in the sky, that this was where the mage in Victor's family had performed their rituals. But Victor had said that had been his third great-grandparent, which didn't line up with how recent the magic felt. Another thing for Elijah to be curious about, another thing he'd never get an answer to.

This ritual would be draining, so he hadn't used his magic much over the last few days, and it called to him now, a fire glorious and gleaming, incandescent, tugging at him, demanding he let it consume him. The time for that would come soon.

He didn't look up when he felt someone watching him again, just kept working, kept laying out the circle. When he took a final step back, his magic snapped into place. The lines ignited into a soft white phosphorescence before settling into dormancy, waiting to spark to life once the ritual started.

Wiping the last of the chalk from his hands, he knelt by his box and flipped open the lid. This part didn't require as much concentration, so he allowed himself a glance at Victor.

He was leaning against a tree at the edge of the clearing, his eyes bright and ravenous in the evening light. Even in his human form, he was all wolf at that moment, something predatory lurking in his posture, something impossible to mistake as human.

Elijah picked up a small bag of salt and stood, sprinkling it around the circle as he walked, one extra layer of protection.

By the time he'd made a complete circuit, Kade was standing next to Victor, saying the betas were in position, keeping everyone away from the clearing and ensuring nothing disturbed them. Elijah blocked out their conversation and ran through his mental checklist of preparations.

The ritual that had created Victor's wards had been for bonded pairs and would have been much simpler than what he and Victor would be doing. A mated pair's connection to each other and their pack could be woven into the most indestructible wards possible without the extra trappings Elijah required to do even a rough approximation. He wouldn't have needed this overly complex circle to ground him to the pack land or the symbols he'd use to have full access to Victor's energy.

All a mated pair truly needed was each other. That was something he could never hope to replicate. But if he could weave in the remaining healthy wards, it might be close.

His magic was compatible enough with Victor's energy, and the wards seemed willing to indulge his meddling, likely sensing he was there to help.

He placed various objects in the circle, stones and runes, candles and bowls. He scattered herbs and oils until he was satisfied he'd done everything he could to prepare the clearing. But there was one more thing he needed to do.

Twilight had settled as he approached the tree Victor was leaning against. Kade slipped away, going back to his patrol.

"Everything ready?" Victor's wolf was in control if the hint of a growl in his voice was anything to go by or the way his lips curled to show his teeth—too rapacious to be a smile. He hadn't moved a muscle, yet some primitive part of Elijah's brain coiled, ready to run. The glint in Victor's eyes said he'd like nothing more than a good chase.

No, definitely not human tonight. And whatever hang-ups Victor had about mages, his wolf seemed to disagree.

Elijah didn't speak until he was in front of Victor, less than an arm's length away. His magic tried to ignite in response, but he kept it tamped down. "Everything but you."

Victor cocked an eyebrow at him, and Elijah held up a small jar of mixed herbs, oils, and charcoal.

"You want me shirtless?" If Victor wasn't careful, that'd sound like flirting, even if it was the moon talking, making his wolf reckless.

"*Want* is a rather loaded verb choice."

"*Need?*" Victor pushed away from the tree, crowding into Elijah's space, but Elijah didn't step back.

He snorted. "Let's just say the ritual requires it." He unscrewed the jar's lid, and Victor pulled off his shirt, his gaze not leaving Elijah's.

Elijah tried not to get sidetracked by the tan skin and muscles that were on sudden display.

A tremor ran through him as he dipped his fingers into the mixture and brought them to Victor's chest, starting near his heart, but he steadied himself. The moment he made contact with Victor's skin, a surge of energy scorched through his system, so wild and at the surface with the full moon rising. It was intoxicating enough he could get drunk on that alone.

The decorative patterns and runes he was drawing ensured the shifter's energy flowed smoothly into the ritual. Though with as compatible as Victor's energy and his magic appeared to be, part of him wondered if he'd be able to do it unaided.

The black lines weren't that different from the ones that would unfurl over Victor's chest if Elijah were to tether himself to Victor, to tie them together permanently. Those tattoos would mirror Elijah's own and glow when Elijah channeled his energy. They wouldn't wash away when all this was over like the charcoal would.

"The ritual requires you to shift during it," Elijah warned, more to distract himself from the thoughts of what creating a permanent tether to Victor would entail and to break the silence between them than to inform Victor. He had to have assumed as much.

"So you don't just want me shirtless." Victor kept his voice low, though no one was there to overhear. His eyes dropped to where Elijah was inscribing a symbol on his right pec, then back to his face.

Elijah wasn't sure which was worse: the version of Victor that held him at arm's length and glared with suspicion or this one who leaned forward and inhaled deeply before asking in a teasing voice, "Anything else you want?"

He didn't shiver at that, but it was a close thing.

This was dangerous, and when Victor was more human, he'd regret those words. Elijah did them both a favor by pulling away as much as he could while drawing the patterns over Victor's chest. He donned every cold, calculating guise within himself and looked Victor dead in the eye. "Should I send the bill to the pack again, or will you be paying tonight?"

The moment the human side of Victor crawled to the forefront, his posture changed. Sudden tension laced through how he held himself, and his expression shuttered. "It's still a onetime payment, both in money and energy?"

"Yes."

"And you'll repair the wards to how they were before?"

"I can't repair or replicate the old wards, but I should be able to use them as a base for new ones that are nearly as strong."

"Why can't you repair them?" Victor's stomach clenched as Elijah's fingertips left a twisting line down his side, along his ribs.

"They were made by a bonded mage-alpha pair."

"Isn't that what the ritual is for? To mimic that bond?"

"Yes and no. The connection it establishes will help me access the wards and channel your energy, but the ritual isn't the same." Elijah drew another line over the bumps and ridges of Victor's abs, finding it easier to deal with this less flirty version after all.

"How so?"

Elijah paused and looked up at him. "To put it bluntly? If you want the other version, at minimum, you're going to need to buy me dinner first."

Victor's eyes darted to the lines spiraling over his chest,

ending right above the waist of his pants. He snapped his jaw shut, the faintest red tinting the tips of his ears.

That would not have been the response he'd have gotten if Victor's wolf were in control. Elijah huffed. "I thought so. We'll stick to the basic model for this."

Under Elijah's fingers, Victor was barely breathing. "The connection. Who controls it?"

Elijah frowned, finishing the final lines and stepping back. "I do. But if I channel too much of your energy, pull away, and I'll stop."

Victor nodded, tight and restrained.

"Also," Elijah added, his cheeks heating, but he held Victor's gaze. "Fair warning. The amount of magic this will require can be... euphoric. It's not uncommon for people to react to it the first few times, no matter the type of ritual they're doing. But I don't take more than I need, and I don't take anything not freely given by everyone involved."

Nothing physical was going to happen between them, but there'd be a lot of energy exchanged. He needed to make sure Victor was okay with the way things might go; he couldn't have him panicking mid-ritual because he was getting aroused by magic. Whatever Victor believed mages were capable of, there were lines Elijah wouldn't cross. Not even if they were both drunk on power and Victor's wolf thought it was a good idea, regardless of whether his human side agreed.

Victor's scrutiny was intense. For the life of him, Elijah couldn't tell which part of Victor had more control.

Finally, he nodded again.

Elijah let out a breath. "We'll start as the moon is approaching its zenith," he said, then returned to his supplies, giving both him and Victor time to collect themselves.

He spent the last few minutes before true nightfall getting himself into a focused, relaxed state. He pulled off his jacket and counted his inhales and exhales until they slowed. As he did, currents of power moved through the earth beneath him. Victor stood a few paces away. His energy, the wards, the pack, everything—it hung there, waiting for Elijah.

When his mind calmed, he pressed his hands against the ground, letting its essence rise up to claim him.

With each second that ticked by, the magic within him built, buzzing under his skin, ready for what was to come. It hadn't been this excited in years.

Around them, the forest quieted, even the trees and animals aware something was about to happen.

It was time.

Elijah stood and walked to the circle, while Victor stripped off his jeans before joining him. He could have waited and undressed during the ritual if he'd wanted, but shifters were never shy when it came to nudity.

It took every scrap of his willpower not to check Victor out. It was tempting to let his gaze travel down that muscular body, to watch the graceful way he moved.

As one, they stepped into the circle, and magic washed over them.

The chalk markings kindled to life, silent and steady, illuminating the night. If he'd thought it was hard to resist looking at Victor before, when it was the moonlight and stars on his skin, it was so much more difficult with the lines casting their soft incandescence over the clearing.

Together, they knelt at the center of the circle, their knees close to touching as they faced each other.

Elijah took out his small knife and held it between them, handle toward Victor. "The last thing this needs is blood. It will act as a conduit between us." He gestured to the blank skin he'd left over Victor's heart. "Prick your finger and smear the blood there."

Victor showed his teeth in a sharp, feral imitation of a grin, white and perfect in the dim light. He brought his hand up to his mouth, not breaking eye contact as his canine teeth lengthened and pricked the skin on the pad of his thumb.

Right. No knife necessary. Elijah exhaled. That should not have been hot.

Blood welled up on Victor's thumb, and he dragged it over his skin. The cut had healed by the time he was done.

Resisting the entirely inappropriate urge to ask Victor to bite him too, Elijah used the knife to prick his own thumb. The blood pooled, and he brought it to Victor's chest, following the line he'd drawn.

Their blood mixed, and the world spun, momentarily unmooring him until he regained his bearings.

Goddamn, Victor's energy was potent. Exhilarating, though Elijah hadn't even begun to channel it. He'd need to be careful not to lose himself in the rush.

Everything grew still and distant as he placed his hand against the smooth, firm muscle of Victor's chest, his heart beating beneath Elijah's palm.

He slid into a state somewhere between reality and beyond, where he accessed his magic, where he shaped it and bent the world to his will.

But before he could work on the wards, he had to check the pack and the territory.

Victor's energy pulled him in, and he sank into it, sank into Victor. His perception of the land and the pack spidered outward, bringing them into focus in Elijah's mind. He felt each pack member as they moved through the forest, the bonds between them robust and durable, the land itself alive and healthy, the wards surrounding and protecting them.

The strings that tied the pack together were luminous, and he traced those bonds, following them as they spread out from Victor to the borders of the territory. He ran his awareness through each one until he reached the shifter it led to, examining them to ensure there were no problems. He found none. The three closest to the clearing were the strongest, brilliant threads of energy connecting Victor to his betas. Even knowing nothing of the pack, their bonds alone affirmed Victor was a good leader, that his pack trusted him, that he cared for them and they cared for him in return.

Elijah had worked with multiple packs during his apprenticeship and over the last year; few had bonds this solid. Whatever had caused the wards to fail, it wasn't this. It wasn't the ties between Victor and his pack. But he'd suspected that.

He took one last look at the pack bonds and found, in their midst, a ghost of a thread between himself and Victor, faint and undefined. The temporary connection the ritual had established between them.

Curious, he traced it with his magic. Victor shivered, his energy rippling, and Elijah's magic flared in return, causing the connection to shine in Elijah's mind—thicker, ropelike—before it settled to a faint thread again. Elijah pulled back. There was no need to do more than that, not to something that would be gone as soon as the ritual was over.

Satisfied there was nothing within the pack that was corrupting the wards, Elijah expanded his consciousness outward into the land. Only lush, healthy forest greeted him. At the edges of the territory, the wards breathed as

Victor did, vibrating with his life and energy. They arched up and over them, a dome of protection covering the land.

This was enough for now, enough for him to get started. When he was sure he had the pack land mapped in his mind, when everything was clear, he trailed magical fingers through the river of Victor's energy, letting it wrap around him before grabbing onto it, pulling it toward himself, channeling it. It streamed so easily into him, through him, as he used it to lay a scaffolding of magic above them, the framework he'd be draping with his wards.

More than hearing it, he felt Victor's sharp, shallow inhale and quickened pulse at the rush of energy pouring out of him and into Elijah.

Shifters didn't use their energy this way. It was instinctual for them. They didn't gather and shape it as a mage did with their magic. They didn't control its flow. It was a natural bond between the shifter and the earth, between them and their pack.

It wasn't the heady thrill of magic that Elijah had trained to control, to shape and mold, to leash and tame, to live with it rushing through him like adrenaline, a high most would never experience.

If Elijah opened his eyes, Victor's pupils would be dilated. If he glanced down, he might see proof of the intoxicating magic filling Victor's veins. He remembered that aphrodisiac thrill from the first times he'd opened himself to a large amount of magic and felt it throb inside him. It still affected him. Even now, years and so many spells and rituals later. Especially now, with the unbridled flush of Victor's energy exciting his magic. He rarely got hard while working with magic anymore, but this time, his dick was thickening in his pants.

Had things been different, had they both been comfortable with it, the ritual would diverge from here. Victor wouldn't be shifting in that kind of ritual; they'd connect in another way. Elijah's body responded to the idea, and his magic swelled, twisting through him. Victor's heartbeat roared in his ears, his inhale shaky under Elijah's hand. The magical tattoos on Elijah's arms warmed, coming fully to life even though he'd only begun to use his magic.

Victor rolled his shoulders, a discomforted motion, and Elijah fought to get himself under control, to contain his magic. That wasn't the ritual they were doing. He pushed the idea away. It didn't matter that his cock was showing more interest in magic than it had in years; he couldn't let himself get diverted. He focused on the ritual.

When he reopened his eyes, he was careful to look only at Victor's face.

"Shift," he said, almost inaudible so he wouldn't disturb the stillness of the night, then watched in fascination as Victor shimmered into a wolf.

The smooth muscle beneath his palm changed until his fingers were buried in the fur above Victor's front legs.

He'd seen the shift before, but it never stopped captivating him. There was this strange illusion to it, a sleight of hand, where, if he watched close enough, he'd find the moment man turned to beast. He could never decide if the transformation was beautiful or horrifying, if it looked painful or divine.

Victor was attractive as a man; Elijah couldn't deny that. With his sharp, chiseled features and dark stubble, he was dangerously handsome, exuding a raw magnetism that was impossible to ignore. He was stunning as a wolf too. Large and solid, his fur white and gray, his eyes a piercing amber, and for one odd moment, he reminded Elijah of his cat. A comparison neither would appreciate.

His fingers dug deeper into Victor's fur as he sank into his energy again. It was wilder, more primal when Victor was in this form. Every sound was sharper, every scent more fragrant, every feeling more riveting and raw. The world and all it held gleamed more radiant.

Elijah felt the land and the pack the way Victor did as a wolf. The thrum of magic was a tangible thing, but over it, his ears picked up the whisper of claws on the ground, the sound amplified by the emptiness around them, the size of the clearing. Elijah shivered despite the warmth emanating from Victor.

The constant presence of the wards hovered in the back of his mind, as it did for Victor. Miles away, a deer entered the territory. It was faint, the wards recognizing it wasn't a threat, but it'd been large enough to disturb them, sending a quiver of acknowledgment along their length.

The forest reached out, brushing against him, welcoming him home. It was there, always had been, but now it was closer, more intimate, and the knowledge had Elijah's heart beating faster. It was sweet and slow, honey on his tongue.

Gnarled branches twisted to form a canopy, heated in the day by sunlight, cool shade beneath. Dry leaves scattered along the forest paths, soft under his paws. It smelled of growth, both fresh and old, of earth and trees.

It was all story and memory, freedom and life. Moonlight filtered between leaves; a chill night breeze ruffled his fur. The scent of prey, the thrill of the hunt. Something wintry.

The need to mark and claim.

Elijah sucked in a lungful of air, trying to center himself in that flood so foreign to his own perception.

Magic affected him, but he was used to it. He wasn't

used to this. Even when he'd channeled other shifters' energy, it had never been like this. Never this vivid, never this visceral, never this much. He gasped at the intensity of it, at the way it made his head spin, and Victor whined softly.

But as good as it was to have total access to everything that encompassed Victor, Elijah had work to do.

Pulling back into himself enough that he was no longer lost and overwhelmed, he drew steadily on Victor's energy and the bonds of the pack. They mingled with his magic, and the forest added its essence. He opened himself completely, letting it cascade into him, filling every inch of him until he felt it in his fingertips, in his veins, in his lungs. Magic permeated the air, a rich potency that surged with the life surrounding them.

Elijah let it swirl inside of him, let it rush through him and build, then grasped it to craft the new wards.

But it didn't do what he wanted. Instead, it twisted out of his control and spilled back into Victor, through that thread connecting them until they were sharing the same power, and with it, the same sensations. Victor's pulse thundered; his chest rose and fell. Magic bloomed between them, a mirror image reflected endlessly, Victor's energy feeding it.

It smoldered, hot and electric, like his magic did when it was being channeled, but it was more than that. It doubled in on itself, not forced or controlled, but growing, multiplying, becoming infinitely more with each added reflection, filling him impossibly full.

A shudder ran through him, or maybe through Victor. Through them both.

Elijah had to get himself together, to find equilibrium so he could work.

It took effort, but he balanced himself in those rapids, anchored by his fingers in Victor's fur.

They both let out shaky exhales, and Elijah began to weave, channeling the immense energy inside himself, creating a filigree of magic to wrap around the territory.

For the first time since he'd started doing ward magic, it was instinctual. He'd built wards before, as he'd been taught, all formula and precision, but this was different. This was art. He'd never felt wards like he did now. This alive, this intimate. He'd never been able to manipulate his magic to the point it became something living, something that sprawled out above them and swept over the pack land. Something that breathed with him, with Victor, with the forest. Something that pounded in unison with their hearts.

The drumbeat of energy and magic twining through them formed a rhythm that resonated in his core. With unwavering certainty, he knew he had been meant for this, meant to spin these wards, weaving a new layer into existence, protecting the pack, reinforcing the areas that had eroded, fortifying them.

Elijah stared into the sky, his head tilted back. He lost track of time as sweat formed on his brow and his respiration grew heavy. His tattoos glowed, a pleasant burn on his skin. Magic glittered above them, beautiful, swirling in an imitation of those tattoos. It formed an intricate pattern that danced to the cadence of the blood coursing through their veins.

His magic, Victor's energy, the forest's essence, the pack's life, they fused seamlessly with the old wards, creating new ones, stronger, like nothing he'd ever seen. They painted the deep indigo of the sky, blazing with a silver light brighter than the moon before they faded.

It wasn't until the wards subsided that he drew back into himself, taking in rapid puffs of air, his eyes falling closed as his magic receded. His skin prickled with awareness of the world around him, the soft breeze, the hard ground, the solid strength of Victor before him. The new wards glimmered, dazzling afterimages against his eyelids. All he could do was feel the forest, smell the land, taste the open air. The earth supported him; the moon was as much a part of him as his blood.

Pressing his eyes shut tighter, he forced himself to let go of everything that had filled him.

And then it was done, the intensity of the moment abating.

He was left panting, his heart pounding, his body shaking. Empty and spent but also sated and close to peace, close to contentment.

When he opened his eyes, he saw the wards, an intricate lacework stretching above them. But he blinked, and they were gone, invisible again.

Victor sat in his wolf form, his fur silver in the moonlight, almost ethereal. Elijah's throat tightened, making it difficult to swallow.

At once, the price of the magic he'd used hit him. It was enough to push him forward, and he braced his free hand against the ground while the other remained tangled in Victor's fur, bringing them closer. His arm threatened to give out. It shook under his weight, but his only focus was Victor. How soft his fur was, how heat radiated off him. The wolf's scent was all pine and earth. Elijah's body buzzed in response.

As quickly as he'd shifted into a wolf, Victor was back to his human form, his arms coming up to brace Elijah and keep him from toppling over.

Loopy from the exhaustion, Elijah stared down, the only thought in his mind that his previous efforts to avoid getting an eyeful of Victor's dick had been wasted. From this angle, there was nothing else to look at. This was what he got for doing the right thing. He wasn't sure if it was a reward or punishment, because fuck, he'd be thinking about it again when he had more energy.

It took effort to wrench his gaze up Victor's chest to the black patterns he'd drawn there. His magic had maintained them through Victor's shifts, but it was time to break them and the temporary connection they'd helped facilitate.

With a shaky hand, he dragged his fingers through the carefully drawn lines. Victor's breath hitched as he smeared and smudged them, revealing faint purple beneath.

Elijah squinted, and the color vanished, leaving nothing but tan skin. His vision must have been bleary, the aftermath of all that magic making him see things.

Victor hauled them both to their feet as the magic in the clearing settled. The earth fell into its normal flow, and the light of the chalk lines faded.

Even with Victor's muscular arm around his waist, Elijah swayed, his legs shaking, threatening to give out. Victor wasn't steady on his feet either. They were silent under the moonlight, awash with weariness.

Victor led him to his supplies and helped him sink to his knees, then left to gather his clothes, legs unsteady as he pulled on his pants.

Only when a fatigue-riddled corner of Elijah's mind commented, *Well, that's a shame*, as Victor buttoned his jeans did Elijah notice he was staring.

Looking away, he repacked his things.

The sky was lightening in the east. Now that the electric flame of his magic had left him, the early morning air grazed cold against his skin, and he shrugged into his jacket.

After he'd packed everything in arm's reach, he slumped against a tree, eyes half-closed. He'd move soon. Just a few minutes' rest, then he'd go.

He felt dismantled down to his bones, different in a way he couldn't describe. The weight of it rested on his shoulders, too big to shove away.

Sure, he'd done powerful spells before, but none of them had been like this. He'd never used this much magic before, never been this open during a ritual, never let anyone know how much energy he could channel. Hell, *he* hadn't known.

But more than that, he didn't show the cost of magic. Even after a spell depleted him, he kept his back straight and walked away with his head high, waiting until he was alone, behind his own wards, before he allowed himself to sag and collapse. Because that was the safe thing to do. Because it was never good to broadcast weakness. Particularly in front of wolf shifters on a full moon.

Maintaining that mask was beyond him right now.

Off to the side, Victor was standing in a loose circle with his three betas, exchanging words. They were in a semi-state of dress, likely drawn to the clearing by the wards flashing in the sky, signaling the end of the ritual.

They spoke in hushed voices, but Elijah caught snippets on the breeze. He didn't listen, instead floating in the faint murmur of magic that hung in the air. It hadn't dissipated, not completely, and it never would, if a person knew what to listen for. It'd fade with time, but given how much power had been in that ritual, there'd always be a remnant. Their magic and energy entwined, written in the earth and trees, the stars and sky. Centuries from now, a mage might walk through this clearing and sense those traces, just as Elijah sensed, under everything else, that this was the clearing where Victor's ancestors had first made the pack wards, had first used their bond to create the latticework that spiraled outward from this central point.

As Victor walked toward him, his betas trailing after him, Elijah pulled himself together as best he could. He pushed to his feet and grabbed his things, pretending he'd been adjusting the box on his hip when he swayed.

They stopped in front of him, and Elijah looked at each in turn, but Victor's eyes never left him. Once again, Elijah wasn't sure which side was in control.

Another moment ticked by, or another hour, as they stood there, waiting for someone to speak. Time dragged, but Elijah couldn't wait any longer; he needed to leave before he passed out. "Right. I'm all finished. I'll be going now," he said, his voice hoarse.

If he could get to his car...

But his legs betrayed him as he turned to walk away. He stumbled, barely catching himself and keeping from landing on his ass.

A presence beside him made him glance up to find Victor next to him, watching him, one hand half outstretched, like he wasn't quite sure what to do or how to act. So the human side was still in control after all.

Victor clenched his jaw and reached out, placing a tentative hand on the back of Elijah's neck the way he'd reassure a packmate.

Elijah froze, his next breath catching in his throat, his heart skipping a beat. His magic moved under that touch, coalescing under Victor's palm.

Eyes narrowed, Victor studied him. "You look like hell," he said, voice gruff.

"Thanks." Elijah gave him his best cocky smile, weak and tired as it might be. "So do you."

He didn't. Not really. Elijah wasn't sure that was possible. But Victor looked about as worn-out as he'd seen a shifter get.

Expression somewhere between irritation and contemplation, Victor pulled his hand away and rocked back on his heels. He crossed his arms over his chest. "How are you feeling?"

Elijah resisted the urge to snort. That'd been the most mind-blowing ritual of his life; his best orgasms hadn't gotten him that high or left him this wrung out. Part of him was shocked he hadn't come in his pants like a teenager experimenting with advanced magic.

"I'll be fine," he said instead.

Victor tilted his head in question, but before he could reply, Kade stepped up to Elijah. "Is it going to ruin the ritual if I take that box from you now?"

There was no point in trying to bluff his way out of this. They knew he was dead on his feet. Elijah shook his head, and Kade took the box.

But somehow, the lifting of that weight made his exhaustion hit harder. He swayed again and was startled by the arm Victor wrapped around him. Against his better judgment, Elijah melted into his strength, his warmth.

"You should stay," Victor said, voice so low it had Elijah leaning in to hear him. Then he added, "Just until you've gotten some sleep." As if that needed clarification.

Elijah balked at the idea. Once he fell asleep, he'd be out cold, exposed, defenseless. And while he didn't feel threatened by Victor or his pack, it was always better to play it safe. A few hours of sleep wasn't worth losing control of his magic.

Victor's eyes bore into him, the weight of his gaze lingering for an eternity. Then he pulled Elijah closer still, and for one bewildering moment, it felt like he was nuzzling against Elijah's ear, savoring his scent, but that had to be the fatigue talking again. Or perhaps Victor's wolf had regained control.

"We have rooms you can lock from the inside. No one will disturb you," Victor said, a whisper brushing against his ear, but there was a quiet steel to his tone. "You protected my pack; nothing will happen to you here. I swear it."

Something in Elijah exhaled.

He should argue, should insist that he needed to get home, but he couldn't keep his eyes open anymore, and this didn't set off the alarm bells it should have. Maybe his magic woven into the wards helped put him at ease. That, or he was too drained to care.

"Okay." The word slurred as he allowed himself weakness this one time.

Elijah would have liked to say he got himself to the pack house, but he never would have made it on his own. Victor was taking most of his weight. And while he wasn't entirely stable himself, he refused his betas' offers to take Elijah from him, though one of them did grab Elijah's bag.

Victor pressed against his side. His jacket should have been enough to stop it, but Elijah swore Victor's energy mixed with his magic, a flicker of them combining. He tried to focus on it over his fuzzy mind and the rhythm of their journey through the forest. All he found was the ghost of the ritual. His drowsiness was causing him to imagine things that weren't there.

The betas shadowed them. Elijah didn't check if they were following; he knew they were, though they slipped silently through the trees, stealthy no matter their form. He read a protectiveness in them, a desire to stick close, but that was for Victor's weakened state, not his own.

Once he recovered, he'd be embarrassed that Victor all but carried him up the stairs in the pack house. But he let it be. Let Victor pull him into a bedroom, let himself be lowered into a bed, and gave up the fight to stay conscious the moment his head hit the pillow.

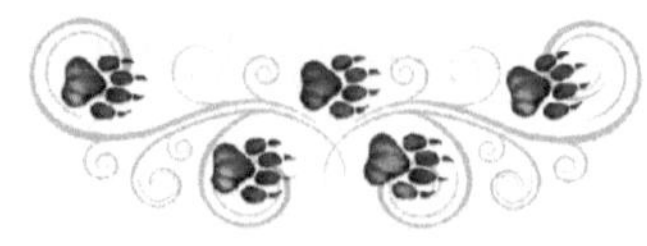

Elijah woke slowly, groggy, limbs pressed into the mattress as if he hadn't moved once while sleeping. He was lying on unfamiliar sheets, in someone else's bed, someone else's house, yet he couldn't remember the last time he'd slept this soundly.

Stretching, he reveled in the bone-deep ache nothing but excessive magic use could cause, leaving him sapped but satisfied. He caught a gust of pine and something else he couldn't name.

He peeled his eyes open and, for a moment, was disorientated. The golden light pouring through the large windows said he'd slept past noon. He'd need another few days to recover fully, but it was enough for now. If anything, he was surprised he hadn't slept into the evening.

With heavy arms, he pushed himself to sitting and considered the bookshelves and dressers that furnished the room, all dark wood and intricately carved. Two chairs sat by the window, their upholstery soft and gray, inviting him to curl up with one of the books crammed on the shelves or gaze out into the forest. On the wall opposite him, a door stood open enough to reveal a connected bathroom.

There were too many belongings for this to be a spare bedroom. Clothes were stuffed in a hamper outside the bathroom, a half-read book sat on the nightstand, personal touches scattered throughout. The room was lived-in. It was someone's space.

Another inhale and recognition clicked. The sheets smelled like Victor; his energy colored the air.

Elijah frowned, not sure what to make of that.

The other side of the bed was undisturbed, which meant Victor had slept somewhere besides his own room. When he'd promised safety, Elijah had believed him, but he hadn't realized Victor would go this far.

His vow of protection implied he knew how vulnerable Elijah had been last night. Another thing that pointed to Victor understanding magic more than he let on. He'd sacrificed his own comfort for Elijah's peace of mind, and Elijah appreciated it.

Besides, this was a *nice* bed. He stretched again, enjoying the caress of sheets on his skin, basking in the shifter energy infused there. He was undoubtedly ruining it for Victor with the scent of magic, but he let himself enjoy it for a few minutes longer, let himself drift in the residual effects of the ritual, the memory of Victor's energy moving through him.

Eyes closed, he ran his hands over the bed, and a tendril of energy stirred, reaching for him. It settled into his body and his bones; it wove itself into him, an echo of the connection from the night before, intoxicating even though it was faint.

He seldom let himself indulge in this state, the one he only fell into after rituals where he connected to shifters. It was such a cliché; he tried not to play into it, to be the mage seduced by shifter energy. But its appeal was too potent to deny. Especially after last night.

Images flashed in his mind of how the ritual could have been different. Him climbing into Victor's lap, sliding down onto his cock, riding Victor and his energy, filled with him in every way possible, using their bodies to strengthen the wards. Them pressed together, the lines he'd so meticulously drawn on Victor's chest smudging onto his own. The wards pulsing with life, stronger and more vibrant than ever, radiating out as they reached completion, their orgasms fueling the ritual and making his magic that much more enduring.

His dick gave a half-hearted twitch, and he laughed. He was too worn-out for anything more than that. Probably a good thing. If he thought his magic was going to ruin Victor's bed for him, it'd pale in comparison to what coming all over his sheets would do.

It also felt creepy to think about fucking Victor while in his room solely because Victor had put Elijah's needs above his own. "Hey, thanks for letting me crash in your bed last night. Don't mind the fact that you'll smell how hard I came in it for as long as you have it."

Not the best way to endear himself to any shifter.

But it didn't stop him from tucking the fantasy away to revisit at a more appropriate time. He'd never done a sex ritual, but he'd always been fascinated by the idea. He didn't know a single mage who wasn't, who hadn't found a book of sex rites when they were an apprentice and purloined it to flip through like a dirty magazine, particularly if it was illustrated. The one Elijah had secreted away for a night of vigorous... study had been illuminating, to say the least. There'd been an entire section dedicated to the spells mages transactionally bonded to wolf shifters could do while knotted, and fuck if that didn't still give him the occasional wet dream five years later. Not that he would admit it to anyone.

It would have been easy to stay in that bed for hours, but he hauled himself to his feet. Which were bare. That was another thing he'd be embarrassed about after he'd recovered. Because he didn't remember getting undressed, but all he had on was his undershirt and boxer-briefs. The rest of his clothes were folded neatly and stacked on a dresser.

The certainty that it had been Victor struck him, and he was more amused than he should be at the idea of Victor stripping him while trying to touch as little of his skin as possible. Well, if it had to be anyone, he felt most comfortable with Victor doing it.

And he was right back to realizing the sad state of his love life when someone's disinterest in him was a virtue.

Instead of dwelling on that, he grabbed his clothes and went into the en suite. The faintest of glows caught his eye in the mirror, a fraction of residual magic leftover in his tattoos, nearly unnoticeable except in the dim bathroom. It was rare for magic to remain in them after a ritual; it'd only happened twice before and never this long. He stared at them, then flicked on the light, drowning out that reminder of how much power he'd used.

He debated taking a quick shower but decided it could wait. Instead, he splashed water on his face, rinsed out his mouth, answered nature's call, then dressed.

The room was remarkably quiet as he stepped back into it. He hadn't noticed it before, but it was impossible not to now. No sound came from outside, though it was unlikely he was the first up. It wasn't until he went to leave that he realized why.

The slightest shimmering of wards flickered as he opened the door. He blinked, then shut it, and they flashed again.

Running his fingers over the frame, he pushed a sliver of magic into the wood until a series of runes lit up, sparkling in the afternoon light. He sensed the familiar magic that had carved them into the frame; it was similar to the magic that had created the pack wards but not quite the same. Again, it felt newer and fresher than something created generations ago.

These wards were smaller, meant for privacy, to sound-proof the room. And, he realized, to keep anyone uninvited out. Victor hadn't just put him in a room that locked from the inside; he'd put him in one only Victor could enter. The safest in the house.

As a distraction from thinking about what that might mean, he studied the wards, impressed.

The mage that had been bonded into Victor's pack generations ago must have been powerful and highly skilled at multiple kinds of ward magic, not just territory wards. Elijah wished he could have met them, to learn from someone who wove such stunning masterpieces.

Reluctantly, he dropped his hand and left the room. The sounds of the pack clattered up to him. He headed that way, assuming he'd find Victor there. His legs were shaky as he descended the stairs, but they grew steadier with each step he took.

Downstairs, he found half the pack but no Victor, sitting at a large table, eating a massive meal.

His stomach growled at the sight of all that food, and the pack members' gazes swung to stare at him. He froze, unsure what to do. But then Kade stood and walked toward him. He leaned in, and Elijah swore he sniffed him before he pulled back to a more socially acceptable distance.

"Elijah," he said with a shit-eating grin. "After the way you went at it last night, I thought you and Victor would want to stay in bed for the rest of the day."

The start of a blush burned his cheeks, but Elijah tried to hold it back. He was a badass mage, goddamnit; he wouldn't get flustered at the hint of an innuendo.

Kade grinned wider.

"Victor wasn't in his room," Elijah said.

"Oh, I know," Kade said, and a few of the adults at the table fought grins of their own.

"Where is he? I should speak to him before I go."

"He's not up yet. Seems like you wore him out last night. But don't worry, he'll be up for you again soon."

Yeah, there was no way Kade wasn't doing this on purpose. The number of shifters trying to hide their smiles increased. The unimpressed look Elijah gave him only got another of those obnoxious grins.

"How about you join us for afternoon breakfast? It's a post-full-moon tradition."

Elijah stared at the piles of food, and his stomach growled a second time.

"Excellent," Kade said, laughing as he slung an arm across Elijah's shoulders, pulling him closer than most shifters would ever want to be with magic. He steered Elijah toward a chair next to the head of the table, then took the seat across from him.

Before Elijah could protest or get a word out, people were handing him multiple dishes at once. Someone passed him a glass of juice. A redheaded woman in her mid-thirties sitting beside him piled his plate high with pancakes, hash browns, fruit, scrambled eggs with veggies, and three kinds of meat, and at that point, it'd be rude to not eat it. There was no good reason to waste food, and he was hungrier than he ever remembered being.

"Thank you," he said and dug in, holding back a moan at the first bite.

Politeness demanded he attempt not to scarf it all down at once, but he couldn't say he succeeded. Every time he cleared a spot, more food snuck onto his plate. The pancakes got replaced by waffles; fried eggs took over for scrambled. Things didn't stop appearing until he slowed.

He was chewing his way through a bagel when a small voice on the other side of the red-haired woman spoke. "You smell funny." The kid leaned around the woman to get a good look at Elijah. His hair was the same shade as hers. "It tickles my nose." He wrinkled said nose to emphasize the point.

"*Oliver*," the woman chided. "We talked about this. That's not how we speak to guests."

Elijah chuckled. "I don't mind. You don't work with shifters as much as I have without developing a thick skin for comments like that."

A brunette preteen sitting across the table a few down sniffed the air. "Actually, you smell kind of nice. Mainly you smell like—" She cut herself off, mouth forming a silent *oh*, her cheeks flushing.

Kade snorted, grinning into his coffee.

Yeah, fine. He smelled like he'd been rolling around in Victor's bed for hours. But that didn't mean he smelled like *they'd* been rolling around *together*. He knew shifters were more than capable of distinguishing between the two.

The kid probably thought he didn't reek because Victor's scent was all over him, and his magic was running on empty. But he was saved from having to reply as the attention of every shifter moved from him to the doorway. A few moments later, Victor entered the room, his hair damp from a shower.

He was subdued as he wended his way down the length of the table, occasionally grasping a shoulder or cupping the back of a neck. He didn't appear exhausted, not exactly, but his movements were slow with lingering lethargy.

The pack members turned with him as he passed, finding comfort under his touch. It was subtle but spoke of a tightly knit pack, reconfirming everything Elijah had sensed in their bonds last night.

Victor took the head seat and glanced sideways at Kade. "Behaving yourself?"

Kade's grin was just as obnoxious when directed at Victor, all wolf that had eaten the canary. "Always," he said, but from Victor's huff, nothing could be further from the truth.

Victor reached for the nearest serving dish, one piled high with bacon, and Elijah's mouth watered. He'd eaten more than he ever had in his life, but suddenly, he was hungry again. Which was ridiculous. His stomach wasn't fitting anything else. If he let it settle, it'd remember he wasn't starving.

An hour later, Elijah was still seated at the table. He should leave, but the easy camaraderie made him want to stay. Conversation flowed around him, kindred bonds filling the room. Victor didn't speak to him—he didn't speak much at all—but he didn't seem opposed to Elijah being there either.

Some shifters shuffled out, only to be replaced by others. Some came and went, bringing dishes to and from the kitchen. He picked at the remaining food on his plate.

Victor ate more than Elijah had, not surprising given how quickly shifters burned through calories and the amount of energy he'd ceded to the wards, but he managed to do it without inhaling the food. If that didn't show self-restraint, nothing did.

When he was finished, he stood. Elijah pushed back his chair and followed. It was well past time for him to leave.

His box and bag were beside the door, and they grabbed them on their way outside.

"Thank you," Victor said as they reached Elijah's car. He was all human again, no longer in the grip of the moon, but he also didn't seem as grudging as he had been the last time he'd gritted out those words. "The wards feel strong, maybe even stronger than before."

Elijah had no response to that. He was unsure what had happened during the ritual. The wards shouldn't have been that receptive to his magic. He shouldn't have been able to repair them the way he had, not to this extent.

"What happens now?" Victor asked.

"It should be a onetime thing," Elijah said. "The wards shouldn't need anything but their connection to you."

"We still don't know what caused them to fail."

"I didn't find any signs of magic or see any issues with your pack bonds or the land. Could it have been how the wards were transferred to you?"

Victor shrugged, his eyes darting away from Elijah. "Possibly." He didn't elaborate.

"Well, whatever happened, it shouldn't happen again. But if there are any problems..."

"I'll call you." The words were forced out. Victor's unwillingness to deal with magic had apparently survived the night.

Elijah opened his trunk to put his things inside. He

closed it, and they stood there for another few moments, neither knowing what to say.

Victor held out his hand, and Elijah eyed it before looking up. There was strain in Victor's expression, but the gesture seemed genuine. Elijah slipped his hand into Victor's. And for a fraction of a second, as they touched, energy glided under his skin, filling him up, an uncanny mimic of what had happened the night before. Elijah pushed away the feeling as he dropped Victor's hand.

He got into his car, his palm tingling. The weight of Victor's gaze followed him as he drove off.

When he passed through the wards, they stroked over him, tugging on him. The sheer amount of his magic in them made them feel more like home than he'd been prepared for. He couldn't sense them the same way Victor could, but they also weren't foreign to him anymore.

The Mills pack seemed like a good, formidable pack. It was a shame Victor distrusted magic. Elijah doubted he'd be seeing them again, outside brief encounters in town. He wouldn't mind doing more work for them, but it was for the best. Given how attracted he was to Victor's energy, it was better if he kept his distance. If he spent too much time with a pack like that, he might be tempted not to leave. And that was something he'd sworn he'd never do. A couple more years, and he'd be out of this damn town.

No way in hell was he ending up a pack mage. No matter what some people might think.

As he drove, he turned the idea over. Maybe staying with a pack forever didn't sound quite as horrifying as it had in the past. If it were the right pack.

But he blamed those thoughts on the ritual; the rational part of his mind must have been temporarily switched off by all that power.

Lady greeted him at the door to his apartment, there to sniff at him with disdain, less than happy about her mage showing up smothered in the pheromones of a wolf pack. Huffing, she got as far from him as his tiny apartment allowed.

He made his way to the bathroom. She had the right idea. Avoiding anything to do with wolf shifters was always the smart choice.

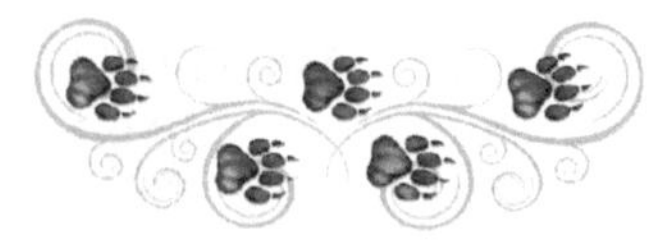

CHAPTER
FIVE

Victor watched Elijah's car disappear from view. Something he didn't bother naming twinged in his chest, but he ignored it and headed into the house. He'd grab another cup of coffee, then check the perimeter to verify everything was as secure as it seemed.

"Well," Kade said, scenting the air as Victor walked into the kitchen, "someone had a good night. And a good morning."

"Shut up." Victor's glare did nothing to quash the mischievous glint in Kade's eyes.

Had he jerked off in the shower? Yes, fine, he had. Was that the norm after a full moon? Also yes. The moon made them ready for action, in more ways than one, and not everyone had a partner to help slake those keyed-up urges. He hadn't been thinking about anyone specific, no matter what Kade's smirk implied.

Kade laughed and leaned against the counter, enjoying this far too much. "So, how was it? It had to have been good if the first thing you did afterwards was drag him to your bed."

"It wasn't like that, and you know it." Victor wouldn't think about how Elijah's magic had throbbed inside him, how it still laced through the wards, curious and alluring.

"Like what?" Kade asked, too devilish to pull off the innocent look he was attempting.

"He couldn't have driven home and wouldn't have stayed otherwise, not if it meant passing out on the full moon in the midst of a bunch of unfamiliar wolf shifters."

"Nothing would happen to him here."

"I know that, you know that, he doesn't. The wards on my room keep everyone else out. It was the place he'd feel safest." There. That passed as a valid excuse. It'd been a selfless act, nothing but sacrifice.

"You care what he thinks now?"

"Of course not. But he was a guest. The least I could do was show him some respect."

"Respect. Sure. Carrying him to bed, undressing him, and tucking him in was *super* respectful. And I had no idea respect caused you to get so growly when anyone else tried to help."

There was no reasoning with Kade. He'd only see what he wanted.

"Can you honestly tell me it didn't feel right?" Kade's gaze was knowing.

Victor scowled but couldn't deny it, not in a way Kade would believe. It *had* felt right; that was the problem. "Whatever you're thinking, stop it. He won't be back."

The noise Kade made was less than convinced.

Victor didn't bother responding. Coffee could wait. It wasn't worth dealing with Kade's assumptions. Assumptions that were wrong. He headed outside.

Late-afternoon light warmed the forest, filtering

through the branches. Victor stayed in his human form, relishing the last vestiges of true summer as he hiked to the perimeter trail.

Kade had no idea what he was talking about. He hadn't seen Victor's wolf respond to Elijah. How reckless and willing it had been. Like it'd learned nothing from their previous encounter with a mage. It would have done anything Elijah wanted, whatever the ritual called for, regardless of Victor's consent or comfort. Elijah's unwillingness to take advantage of that was inconsequential; it didn't make Victor's wolf any less susceptible to magic.

It didn't change how satisfied his wolf had felt seeing Elijah asleep in his bed. Maybe if he'd only been feeling gratitude for what Elijah had done or protectiveness toward someone helpless within his territory, but there'd also been a contentment curling in his chest that was distinctly proprietary at the sight. It had been paired with a certainty that, if his wolf had its way, the next time he undressed Elijah, the mage would be awake and returning the favor.

His gaze had been drawn to Elijah from the moment he'd arrived, the magnetic pull toward him overwhelming, making him unable to look away as Elijah worked. And it'd had nothing to do with wanting to keep an eye on him.

Victor wasn't sure if he'd ever get used to this disconcerting split in his mind. Shifters weren't meant to be two separate beings that shared one body; both sides were supposed to be united. No good could come from dividing himself, compartmentalizing himself. But it was the lesser evil. Trusting his wolf around magic would be infinitely worse.

And Elijah was nothing but magic. It was under his

skin, in his veins. Victor could smell it on him, could hear it crackling in the air around him. It tugged at him every time he saw the mage.

That was dangerous. It led to places he'd never trust himself to go.

He turned down the trail that ringed their territory. To his right, the wards shimmered, vibrant and healthy, not waiting for contact to respond to his presence. They thrummed in his blood. Elijah's magic ran through them, threaded with Victor's energy. It pulsed, vibrating, new but woven seamlessly into the fabric that protected his pack.

The wards shone with power, stronger than they'd felt since he'd taken over. They overflowed with life, with potential.

Elijah had put an insane amount of magic into the ritual. Victor hadn't needed to touch him to sense the fiery power running through him. He'd never felt magic to that extent before. He hadn't known it was possible to experience magic like that, like it was his as much as Elijah's. The way his energy had intertwined with that magic had been undeniable—two parts of the same whole. Destined to be together.

Last night, it'd felt as though Elijah had dedicated himself to this land, to this pack, and that caused more conflicting emotions than Victor could parse.

Elijah's presence differed from what Victor had expected. He'd braced for his magic to be harsh, to rub against him in the unpleasant way non-pack magic often did, but it was smooth and refined, fitting flawlessly into the tapestry of the wards.

Taking a breath, Victor let the wards flow over him, his senses spreading out into the world, into the earth, and back. It was a familiar routine, but it'd been a month since the return came solid and clean.

He continued along the trail, scaling fallen trees and sharp ridges toward the section that had been damaged.

He'd woken in a hazy state that morning. Reality had shifted somehow; the ritual had left him oddly empty, though that had to be a result of the energy drained out of him. Flickers of a dream he couldn't quite recall danced at the edges of his perception; the familiar thrum of post-full-moon arousal coursed through him. He hadn't bothered denying himself, though he'd known he'd get shit for it later.

Finding Elijah eating breakfast with his pack only complicated his feelings.

The night before, as he tried to fall asleep in a room that felt all wrong for reasons he didn't want to examine, part of him had been hoping Elijah would leave before he was up. That way, he could avoid the mage until the full moon had truly passed, until his wolf wasn't so close to the surface. Until he could forget how Elijah's fingers had felt drawing patterns over his chest and look him in the eye without remembering his too-visceral visions of what might have happened if he'd agreed to the other version of the ritual— sliding into Elijah's body, scraping his teeth along his neck, coming inside him.

He wasn't that lucky. When he'd woken, his wolf was entirely too smug with the knowledge that Elijah was still there, in their territory, waiting for them.

He'd been torn between horror and amusement at where his pack had Elijah sit, next to the head of the table, a spot normally reserved for the alpha's mate. They'd argue they were giving Elijah a place of honor, but from the unholy glee in Kade's eyes as Victor entered the room, he doubted it was that guileless.

As he'd passed Elijah's chair to take his own, he caught traces of earth, snow, and magic, mixed with Victor's scent, blending in with his pack's disturbingly well. Kade's scent was on him too, something he was sure had been deliberately done to provoke him.

The energy of so many pack members swirled through the room, filling up the space with their life force, their bonds, and it calmed him, even while he sat beside magic.

Victor had watched Elijah out of the corner of his eye, an easy serenity settling over him. He shouldn't fit, but Victor only needed to see him in that room to know he would. There was no arguing with his wolf on that point.

He shook his head. It didn't matter what his wolf thought. It wasn't happening.

Victor reached the weakened section. Not a hint of damage remained. No one would believe how frail these wards had been. They were just as they used to be, better even.

Relieved, Victor exhaled fully for the first time in weeks. If nothing else, this was worth the inner turmoil he'd gone through about working with magic. His pack was safe. Now things could go back to normal.

And if he spent most of the day wandering through his territory, double-checking everything was as it should be, it was out of an abundance of caution. He wasn't avoiding certain people and their incorrect assumptions.

When it came time to call it a night, he swung by the linen closet and grabbed a set of sheets. Putting Elijah in his bed had been a ridiculous impulse, especially since it meant he'd be changing his sheets afterward. If that would even be enough to get rid of the smell.

But as he stepped into his room, not bothering to turn on the light, he put the sheets on the dresser by the door and walked to his neatly made bed, tugging down the blanket.

The scent rose, infusing the air with magic, wintry earth, sleep, and... arousal? It was faint and covered by magic, but it was there. His fingers ran over the material, and he inhaled. He smoothed the sheets, straightening them with his palm, brushing his hand over them, then stopped when he was hit by the realization that if someone saw him at that moment, it'd look like he was petting his bed.

Really, magic was all over him; there was no point in changing his sheets when it'd be clinging to him either way. He might as well leave them. He'd change them when the scent of the ritual had worn off. Besides, his bed wasn't as repulsive as he'd feared. It mostly smelled like him and pack. He could put up with it for a few nights.

With a bare moment's hesitation, he dropped his clothes where they fell and stretched out on the bed, the soft sheets and that hint of winter caressing his skin.

The wards radiated calming security. After a night crashing in a guest room, his bed was more welcoming than ever. The quiet rush of the wind outside his open window was a lullaby, coaxing him to sleep. Dread about what was happening to his pack no longer haunted him.

He sank into bed, letting the feeling of home envelop him.

All the scenarios he'd conjured during the ritual, all the ways it could have been different, flickered behind his eyelids. Uncensored, unbridled. Unbidden.

Elijah, naked, his skin illuminated by the moon and the lines of the circle. Victor's mouth against his neck, fierce pleasure as his teeth pierced flesh. Elijah's magic under his fingers, under his tongue. The broken gasp of his breath. The intoxicating glide of their bodies, every movement filling them with a keen, dizzying delight.

Those figments of his imagination were burned into his mind. He fisted his hands, making a frustrated noise and staring at the ceiling.

Indulging in this, letting himself get swept up in the delusion, was pointless, even if he could blame it on the near-full moon hanging low in the sky, on his wolf wanting to strengthen their pack by mating with a mage. Any mage.

He closed his eyes and refused to think about it. Refused to believe one additional scent made his bed and his room seem emptier. That an absence was a tangible thing.

He didn't imagine what having a mage permanently in his pack would be like.

Maybe if he were someone else, someone stronger, that level of power wouldn't corrupt him. But he wasn't that person. Whatever his wolf thought, whatever Kade implied, it was better if he stayed away from temptation.

Forcing his mind to stillness, he breathed deep until he fell asleep.

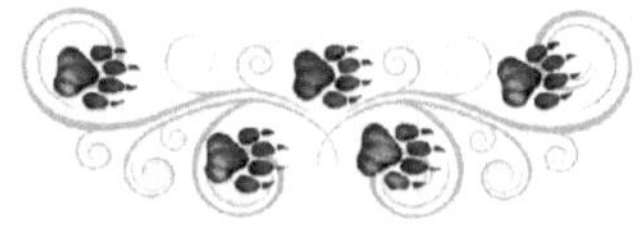

Cool air whispered over Victor's bare skin; the grass below him tickled his back. He had one moment to gaze up into the dazzling night sky, to see the ethereal light of the circle, one moment to realize he was so hard he ached, before a hand wrapped around his cock, grip too loose as it spread lube over him.

He lifted his head and looked down the length of his body to where Elijah straddled his thighs. Moonlight painted him in radiant hues, bathing him in a soft silver that accentuated his sharp cheekbones and brought out the glimmer in his eyes. The magical tattoos decorating his body were visible, already alight in reaction to the energy surrounding them. The swirling scrollwork wound up his arms, showing his strength in the amount of skin it covered.

Victor feasted on the sight of the elegant spirals that twisted around each other in a graceful symphony of curves and loops. They played across all his lithe lines and lean muscles and made Victor itch to trace their sinuous paths.

Elijah's long fingers teased him, gliding his foreskin up and down, but not giving him the pressure he needed.

"Elijah," he ground out, his own fingers digging into the loamy soil, his muscles tensed for what came next.

"Do you remember what you need to do?" Elijah asked, then stole the answer from Victor's lips as he stroked the head of his cock with a feather-light touch.

Victor choked back a moan and nodded. The connection between them was wide open, rushing through him, twining his energy with Elijah's magic and making it diffi-cult to concentrate on anything else. But they'd talked this through, as awkward as that conversation had been. There wasn't a lot he had to do. He just needed to lie there and let Elijah do the work. No matter how much he wanted to take control, he was there for Elijah to use, and he wouldn't be allowed to come before the ritual reached its climax.

"Good," Elijah said, and then his fingers were moving in earnest, stroking and pressing, and Victor couldn't restrain himself.

He thrust up, driving his cock into Elijah's hand,

chasing his release, only to find himself suspended, magic coiled around him, keeping him from toppling over that edge. He nearly whimpered, his body shaking, eyes closed tight. When he opened them, Elijah was looking at him, pupils blown, respiration accelerated, dick hard and leaking, like he felt Victor's orgasm building within himself.

"Ready?" Elijah asked, and all Victor could do was swallow and nod again.

Then Elijah was lining himself up, lowering himself onto Victor's dick. The world froze; it was them and their connection, his energy and Elijah's magic, the circle and the wards.

Part of the ritual or not, Victor brought his hands up to clasp Elijah's hips as he sank onto him.

Elijah rocked against him, fingertips tracing the lines and symbols he'd drawn on Victor, leaving electric trails buzzing as a memento of his touch.

Victor's energy poured out of him and into Elijah as he set a steady rhythm. The sky above them glimmered with magic, the wards weaving themselves into wondrous patterns guided by the arcane words Elijah spoke.

Magic grew and built, but Victor couldn't focus on it, couldn't focus on anything but Elijah bearing down on his cock over and over and over. The sounds they were making, skin slapping against skin, their pants and groans, Elijah's voice faltering as pleasure engulfed him.

His fingers had to be bruising Elijah's hips, but he couldn't bring himself to let go or relax his hold. Belatedly, he noticed his claws were out, pricking pale skin, the faintest hint of blood floating in the air.

Elijah stared at him with eyes that glowed purple, and Victor's flashed in response.

It continued until they were slick with sweat. The stamina Elijah was showing with how relentlessly he was riding him would have been impressive if Victor hadn't been held, hanging on the edge of orgasm for a maddening amount of time, for what felt like hours, like he'd spill at any moment if the magic would let him. Elijah had warned him about it, but that hadn't prepared him for his balls drawn up, impossibly tight, so ready for release but unable to, waiting for the ritual to allow it.

There was a quirk to Elijah's lips that said he was enjoying edging Victor beyond its part in the ritual, that he liked watching him squirm and try to stop himself from begging for permission to come.

But then, finally, *mercifully*, Elijah was taking himself in hand and speaking the last few words of an incantation that Victor didn't comprehend, clenching down as he choked out the final syllables, his come splattering on Victor's chest.

Victor gripped his hips tighter, thrusting up once, burying himself deep, and came with a howl, shaking and shuddering, emptying himself into Elijah, as the wards flared a brilliant white, as they solidified and materialized into being, new and strong and perfect.

The entire world was swallowed by that blinding light before reforming into something equally as new and strong and perfect.

A second, a minute, an hour later, Victor blinked his eyes open. Elijah was braced over him, caught on unsteady forearms, breath rough, puffs of hot air hitting oversensitized skin, his face inches from Victor's.

Victor closed the distance between them, dragging his lips across Elijah's in a drugged, hypnotic dance, liking the shiver it pulled out of him. He stroked the side of Elijah's face with his thumb, cupping his jaw.

His dick softened and slid out of Elijah, his come leaking onto the ground, an offering to the earth, but fuck if he didn't wish he'd been able to knot Elijah, to keep them tied together, keep him filled for as long as possible.

Next time, he'd do exactly that.

They kissed, breathless and unhurried as their bodies cooled, so different from the demanding rhythm the magic had set. It was more intimate than the exacting fuck the ritual required, and Victor didn't want to stop. He wanted to lie there forever, his tongue tangling with Elijah's until they both were ready to go again, and he could explore Elijah's body at his own pace. Something that was for them, not for the magic or the wards or anyone else.

Elijah slipped a hand between them, his fingers skating through his come, using it to trace the lines he'd drawn. A tingling, pulsing warmth bloomed wherever he touched, a pleasant burn that had Victor getting hard again.

"What else do you have to give me?" Elijah asked in a low whisper against Victor's ear.

Victor groaned. His teeth ached with the need to bite, to claim, to show Elijah everything he could give him. But before he could flip them over to do that, Elijah sat up, his eyes a muted purple smolder. He eased himself back onto Victor's dick and pressed one hand firmly over Victor's heart.

"Let's see what you've got."

The lines on Victor's chest ignited, lightning-quick and red-hot, searing before settling into a burn this side of painful.

Victor gasped, his vision locked on Elijah's face. All he

could see was Elijah smirking at him, his expression icy cold, his eyes gleaming purple as energy flooded into him.

Elijah rode him, incessant and demanding, until what little energy Victor had left was ripped out of him, and the world dissolved into blackness.

Victor woke with a start, the pounding of his pulse deafening in his ears. He bolted out of bed and rushed to the mirror over his dresser. His reflection stared back, shaken, chest heaving, as he clawed at the skin over his heart.

Nothing was there.

The lines had washed off. They hadn't left a mark.

But in his mind, they burned.

Even though Elijah didn't seem like he would do that, like he would force a connection on someone and drain them, it hit far too close to home; it brought up too many unpleasant memories.

He rubbed at his chest, trying to clear the thoughts from his mind and make his anxiety dissipate.

As his heart slowed, the panic receded enough for him to notice the residual arousal stirred up by the dream. He was still half-hard, still turned on. He clutched the edge of the dresser, his nails gouging into the wood.

This, *this* was why he couldn't be trusted with magic. In his dream, his energy had been stolen, ripped away from him, drained completely, yet his wolf insisted it was what they wanted. Everything they had was Elijah's to take.

Snarling in frustration, he jumped into the shower, scrubbing away the cold sweat that had gathered on his body. But even standing under freezing water, the heated drumbeat of desire thrummed in his veins.

He groaned and leaned against the wall as the water washed over him.

Fine, he'd give his wolf this. But it was the last time he'd allow weakness regarding magic. He took hold of his dick, calling the earlier parts of the dream to mind as he stroked. Though he told himself, when he came, it was to the slap of flesh against flesh, the tight clench of heat, almost anonymous and impersonal, no different from the rush of magic that had caused him to get turned on during the actual ritual. It wasn't shared breath and the leisurely slide of a tongue against his own that got him off.

He finished his shower quickly and tried not to wonder if that was how it would have gone, if that was something people paid mages for, if Elijah had done that kind of ritual, if he did it often.

His wolf didn't like that idea; the thought of Elijah doing that with anyone else caused a growl to build in his throat. Though it wasn't opposed to those rituals in general. Victor tried to convince himself it was because his wolf wanted to have the best wards possible, whatever they needed to do to get them, not because it wanted Elijah.

Besides, magic was corrupting. Addicting. It left him powerless and out of control. He'd fallen under its sway once before. It'd destroyed his father; it'd almost destroyed his pack.

No matter what he did, where he went, how hard he tried, the pull of magic was too irresistible. He had to stay away from it, from anything to do with the occult. And that meant staying away from Elijah.

He'd be damned if he gave that weak side of himself any more power than he had to.

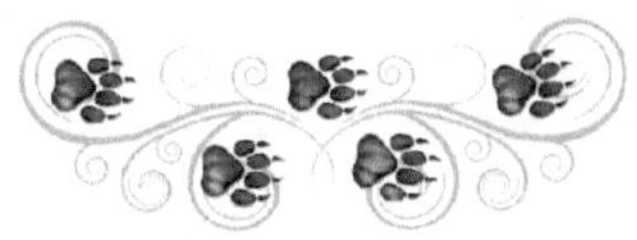

The forest that night held a crisp hint of fall; the wind murmured news of the coming season change through the trees.

Victor stalked along a deer path in his wolf form. He reveled in the sensations that washed over him, the fresh air ruffling his fur, his claws digging into the earth. A rabbit dashed away, scared off by his presence.

After his nightly patrol, he'd gone for a run, letting the burn of his muscles drive him through the forest. Running for the sake of savoring it.

He'd needed this. Needed a good, long run.

In the four days since the ritual, he'd been monitoring the wards, worried the damage might have been too extensive to repair. Even in his best-case scenario, he'd only hoped things would return to normal. But what Elijah had managed was so much more than that. The wards weren't just repaired; they were now diamond-edged steel glittering around his territory.

The ritual magic lingered, humming throughout the land, not interfering with Victor's energy but not withdrawing either. Supporting it, strengthening it.

From time to time, he caught hints of Elijah's scent on his skin and swore he'd change his sheets. But each night, he found a reason not to, even with Kade's smirk growing more shit-eating every passing day.

He'd slept better than he had for weeks, than for the

last year—something surely caused by relief at his wards being fixed and nothing more.

As he turned toward the house, he heard a twig snap behind him. He paused, sniffing the air.

There was a burst of movement, the sound of paws hitting the earth, and then a gray-and-white wolf crashed into him.

He growled, twisting out from under Kade and snapping at him, but Kade danced out of his reach. It would never stop being annoying how Kade managed his cocky grin even in wolf form. The bastard probably practiced it in the mirror to ensure it was that impeccable level of obnoxious.

Victor huffed and waited for the attack. Kade didn't disappoint. He lunged, Victor dodged, and then Kade was pouncing on him again. Victor nipped Kade's ear for his effort.

This was another thing it'd been a while since he'd done. Fighting for the thrill and fun of it.

They'd done this so often as kids, when Kade was bigger and stronger, those four years making a difference. But once they were teens, the playing field had evened out. Now, there was no doubt who had the upper hand.

They rolled around, darting and snapping at each other. Victor wasn't using his full strength, but with Kade, he didn't hold back much.

Kade's growls were like laughter, his joy evident as he dodged Victor's attacks. He took every hit with cheer, then nipped at Victor's tail, more than determined to give as good as he got.

When they were young, they'd chase each other until they were too exhausted to do anything besides flop onto the ground and pant. Tonight was no different. They sparred until they were out of breath, tongues lolling out. Nothing but carefree pups again.

They sprawled out on the leaves, and Victor let himself relax under the watchful eye of the moon before he got up and started to pad his way home. Kade followed behind him, and they shifted near the house, gathering their clothes from where they'd left them next to the porch.

Kade shoved at his shoulder as they climbed the stairs. "Where was your mind? I was stalking you for five minutes, and you didn't notice."

Victor wanted to protest, to claim he'd known Kade was there the whole time, but he'd been oblivious.

"Wait," Kade said, "don't tell me. I can guess."

Victor gave him an unimpressed look. He knew where this was going.

They went through the back door and into the kitchen. Will and Rick were sitting in the little breakfast nook, each with a cup of coffee in hand.

"What have you two been up to?" Rick asked. The silver flecks in his dark hair caught the light as he leaned back from the table.

"I was about to explain to Victor how easy it's been to track him lately," Kade answered.

Both Will and Rick snorted into their coffee, and Victor expanded his disapproving gaze to include them all. It only made them grin wider.

Victor wondered, not for the first time, if he should have chosen betas that were younger than him. Ones who'd regard him with respect and maybe a little awe or fear. But he'd wanted the best shifters for the job—betas who wouldn't hesitate to call him on his bullshit, who'd stand up to him if he endangered the pack.

"He's right," Will said. "The zip of magic in your scent? It's a fucking beacon."

He just hadn't realized that potential for insubordination would spill over into his personal life. He should have known.

And again, he silently vowed to change his sheets. Tomorrow. It was too late to hassle with it tonight.

"Honestly though," Rick said, studying him, "your scents are ridiculously compatible. I was expecting the reek of non-pack magic, but he smelled good with your scent on him."

That did not make Victor happy. Not even remotely.

"That morning after the ritual, he smelled like pack. Spending the night in your bed—" Will cut himself off before Victor could protest. "Yes, yes, I know, I know. It meant nothing, nothing happened. But it also shouldn't have changed his scent to that extent."

"I forget," Kade said, offensively pleased with himself. "Why did you put him in your bed again? Something about respect?"

Victor still had no answer to that, even for himself. It'd felt right, and he hadn't had the energy to fight his instincts over it.

So instead, he changed the subject, not even trying to be subtle about it. "I'm going into town tomorrow. Do any of you need anything?"

"Sage," Rick said, not missing a beat.

"Sage?" Victor asked. "Don't we have a jar in the pantry?"

"No, not for cooking. I mean the bundled type. Used for smudging or whatever."

"That's perfect," Will chimed in. "I was going to ask him to grab me a deck of tarot cards."

Victor groaned and turned to leave the kitchen. "Fuck you guys," he said over his shoulder.

"Not interested," Kade called after him. "But I know a shop where you'll find sage, tarot cards, and someone who might be."

Victor needed new betas. Or, at the very least, a new second-in-command. It'd make his life so much easier.

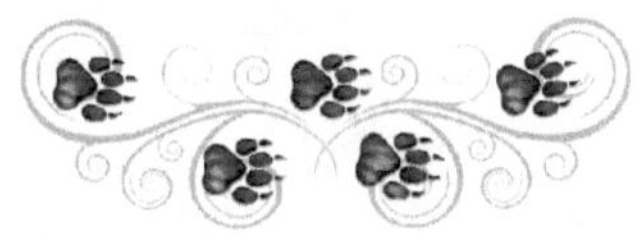

CHAPTER
SIX

Elijah trailed his fingers over the smooth stones, sensing their energy. They were just trinkets, little things people outside the supernatural community adored. A mage wouldn't look at them twice, but the uninitiated who managed to wander into his shop couldn't get enough of the charms. They liked to pretend they were magic. And they were, to a minor extent. He put a spark in each, charging them so they'd give their owner a nudge in whatever direction they needed.

There were a dozen combinations, symbolic animals carved from special kinds of rocks. For safety, for health, for luck. Most magic users considered them worthless—the natural, raw properties of perfectly good stones and crystals rendered useless by Elijah's magic tainting them and how they'd been shaped. Elijah, however, had a soft spot for the knickknacks; they were frivolous but brought people joy. Plus, they had a decent profit margin and didn't take up much space in his shop.

He picked up a malachite frog and held it between his forefinger and thumb, its green swirls catching the light.

The card included with it would explain it was meant to be placed in an entryway to ensure the owner and their family always returned home safely.

The stone warming against his fingertips, he closed his eyes, concentrated, and let his magic flow into it. It didn't need much.

But he'd apparently forgotten to tell his magic that. It surged into the frog. A sharp crack echoed in the silence of his office.

Elijah opened his eyes as the frog split apart. Three pieces fell into his palm, and he blinked at them.

That was not how this was supposed to work.

He grabbed another frog, examining it for weaknesses or damage. The first might have had an internal fracture or defect that had caused charging the charm to go awry. This one looked fine.

With a delicate touch, he threaded his magic through the stone. But as he pulled back, another rush swelled through him and into the malachite, cracking it.

Confused, he stared at the charm. At least it hadn't broken apart, but a deep crack ran through it now. There was no way he'd be able to sell it like this.

Setting it aside with the other frog, he chose a pig carved out of snowflake obsidian, meant to attract wealth. The sleek black-and-white stone felt good in his hand.

Closing his eyes once more, he focused and carefully fed the tiniest hint of magic into it. This time, when the flood of magic came, it rapidly heated the stone, nearly burning him. He dropped the charm with a curse. When it hit the floor, it shattered into pieces.

What the absolute fuck?

Shards of black littered the floor. Nothing like this had

happened with the other charms he'd sold from the same supplier. The problem wasn't with the stones.

He rubbed a hand over his face. It'd been four days since the ritual, and his magic still didn't feel right.

The first few days had found him feeling a combination of drained and oddly full. The small things he'd tried had gone less than spectacularly, so he'd held off, figuring it was better not to push himself. Even if the thought of all that wasted time left him restless, he'd forced himself to take a break. It'd never taken him more than a day or two to recover.

When he'd woken that morning, his magic had seemed closer to normal. Which was perfect—he was itching to get caught up on work.

He must have misjudged things.

Scowling, he found a broom and swept up. As he tossed the pieces into the bin, the bells above the door jingled.

Good, a distraction to get his mind off whatever the hell his magic was doing.

The imposing figure of Niall MacFarlan, alpha of one of the local packs, loomed in the shop. He was in his mid-forties but still in his prime. His hair was graying, making him more distinguished than anything, and the energy he gave off was undeniably alpha. Though, Elijah had to admit, it was far less appealing than Victor's.

Behind Niall was his second. Pierce was nearing thirty and being groomed to take over the pack when it came time for Niall to retire. His energy hovered in that same not beta but not yet alpha range as Kade's, and man, was he gorgeous, all sincere puppy-dog eyes and genuine smiles, offset by the nicest pair of arms Elijah had ever seen. But today, his brow was furrowed, strain written in the lines of his face.

Niall had hired Elijah once before, and as far as shifters went, he was decent enough. He hadn't made any unnecessary comments about the scent of Elijah's magic and had been thankful when Elijah removed a nasty hex on a dagger that had belonged to his grandfather.

"Alpha MacFarlan," Elijah said in greeting, nodding to him, then his second. "Pierce."

Niall glanced around the shop, confirming they were alone before he approached the counter. Pierce followed, also scanning their surroundings. Elijah had the strangest impression both expected an ambush would spring out of nowhere.

"Mage Lauring," Niall said.

"What can I do for you today?"

A car drove by the shop, and Niall paused, watching it go, waiting a long beat until it had driven around the corner at the end of the block.

"I need you to..." he said before glancing around again. He stepped closer to Elijah, lowering his voice. "There's a problem..."

He leaned in even closer and froze, his nostrils flaring. He took a deep breath and scrutinized Elijah's face.

They stood there, and Elijah waited for him to continue as Niall's gaze darted around.

"There's a problem?" Elijah prompted. He glanced toward Pierce, who was frowning, eyes jumping between them.

Niall shook his head. "No."

"You need me to do something for you?"

Niall turned, walking toward the door. "Never mind," he called over his shoulder, gesturing for Pierce to follow. "It's taken care of."

Pierce hesitated for a moment, expression torn. He

looked at his alpha's retreating back, then at Elijah, studying him. He opened his mouth to speak.

"*Pierce*," Niall repeated, voice deeper, demanding. Elijah fought down a shiver at the power laced through his tone. "We're leaving. *Now*."

Pierce straightened and followed Niall out the door without a word.

Elijah watched them go. He didn't know Niall beyond their one business transaction, but he hadn't seemed like the type to use his alpha command to force pack members to obey his orders. Hell, Elijah had only seen an alpha use that voice once, when he was an apprentice, and the shifter it'd been used on had been well out of line.

What had gotten into him?

An idea formed, and Elijah cursed.

"Lady," he called.

She hopped down from the shelf she'd been lying on and strolled over, sitting in front of him on the counter and blinking slowly.

"Do I smell like Victor Mills?"

Her tail flicked hard against the glass as she glared at him with judgment.

"Goddamnit. If I just lost business because that bastard thought it was a good idea to put me in his bed..." This was precisely why he should stay away from shifters.

Lady headbutted his stomach, then rubbed her body against him.

He huffed, scratching behind her ears. "Thanks. But I don't know how much that's going to help."

She rubbed against him a second time, then hopped off the counter and found a new perch where she could observe the shop.

Elijah scowled. He better not lose any more business because of this.

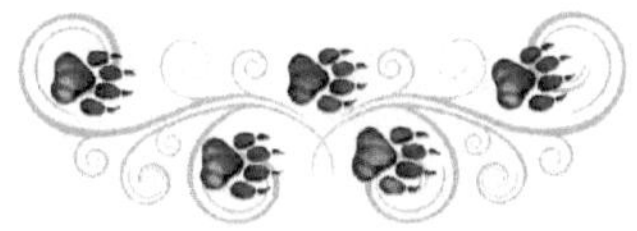

Preparing himself for the shit he was about to get, Elijah stared at his phone before he pulled up the messenger app. He settled onto his bed and opened the group chat with his three best friends. Two he'd met during his apprenticeship, and the other, Liam, had been his ride or die since they were preteens. They'd scattered to different parts of the country now that their primary apprenticeships were over. Liam had headed to the East Coast to establish a grimoire-archiving project through the largest magical library in the country, while Aran and Miles had been accepted to secondary apprenticeships focusing on druid magic and healing, respectively. But they kept in near-daily contact and were usually free this late in the evening.

ELIJAH

You guys there?

It didn't take long for three dots to appear at the bottom of his screen. A moment later, he got a reply.

ARAN

Hey! How's my favorite shop owner doing?

ELIJAH

I'm good, but my magic is acting up.

ARAN

I was talking about Lady. Obviously.

ELIJAH

Lady's fine. Annoyed with me.

ARAN

Ooh, if she's annoyed with you, that can
only mean one of two things.

LIAM

Wait. What's this about your magic?

ELIJAH

TWO things?

ARAN

Ah, priorities.

ELIJAH

She only gets annoyed when I work with
shifters.

ARAN

And?

ELIJAH

And what? That's the only time she's gotten
pissy with me.

MILES

Aran's right. That's not the only time.

Elijah narrowed his eyes. Aran might try to pull one over on him, but Miles wouldn't. What the hell were they talking about?

ARAN

Oh, man. I feel bad for those dudes. Were
those dates that unmemorable?

In the last year, Elijah had been on exactly three dates. Two he'd made the mistake of bringing back to his apartment. Lady had been less than pleased.

ELIJAH

They would have been more memorable if I'd actually gotten sex out of them.

Lady was a cockblocker of the highest degree. He didn't mention the week she'd refused to acknowledge his existence after the date he'd been smart enough to take elsewhere. She might not like shifters, wolf shifters in particular, but non-magical humans were a bridge too far.

The string of amused emojis Aran sent did nothing to help.

MILES

She's protecting your honor.

ARAN

snort "honor"

LIAM

Guys.

Focus.

Elijah's magic.

ELIJAH

I knew there was a reason you were my favorite.

LIAM

Seriously, what's going on?

ELIJAH

It's been erratic the last few days.

LIAM

What set it off?

ELIJAH

I did a full-moon ritual. Reset a local pack's wards.

He didn't normally give specifics about the contract work he did, even to his friends. Privacy had to be respected, but there were limits to that. His magic misbehaving was one.

ARAN

Ward reset? What kind of ritual?

ELIJAH

Not that kind.

ARAN

Is there any other?

Elijah rolled his eyes but typed out a description of the ritual, including how thoroughly it'd wiped him out.

LIAM

Elijah, that was dangerous.

What if they'd tried to bond you while you were unconscious?

ELIJAH

I know, but I wasn't getting home by myself and the alpha gave me his room for the night.

I was as safe as I could be.

Not that he'd known it before passing out, but Liam would worry too much if he knew that.

ARAN

A pack alpha put you in his bed?

ELIJAH

Nothing happened.

ARAN

That's a shame. Is he hot?

ELIJAH

Aren't they all?

LIAM

Would you guys focus?

What's happened since then?

ELIJAH

Two issues.

First, I still smell like him.

MILES

But that was four days ago.

ELIJAH

Lady confirmed it.

LIAM

For the love of fucking god.

Your magic.

What's happening?

The ritual caused your magic to act up?

Elijah groaned.

ELIJAH

It was fine during the ritual, but afterward…

It feels like I have too much power built up and no controlled way to use it or burn it off.

It was like the strings restraining his magic had been cut, letting it run wild.

LIAM

This hasn't happened when you've worked with shifters in the past?

ELIJAH

Nope.

MILES

You said the ritual went well?

ELIJAH

Yeah. I was able to channel more energy than ever before.

ARAN

I'm about to say something, and being who I am, I know you all are going to take it the wrong way. But hear me out.

Elijah braced himself and waited for Aran to send his next message. Three dots appeared, paused, then appeared again. After an eternity, the message popped up on Elijah's screen.

ARAN

I think the ritual stretched you open. Basically, you're used to two fingers but have just taken a good, hard, night-long pounding from a giant alpha shifter dick. It might take longer than usual for your channels to return to normal. And until that happens, even an average-sized dick will slide in easier. And if you do have some of his energy left in your system, it might be trying to keep you ready for more of that thick shifter cock.

All the bracing in the world would not have prepared him for that. Why were these his friends?

ELIJAH

It wasn't that kind of ritual!

ARAN

Metaphorically! Not everything is about sex!

ELIJAH

Says the guy who used an extended anal sex metaphor to describe the current state of my magic.

ARAN

I mean, if the dick fits.

MILES

I didn't think it was possible, but Aran has ruined magic for me.

Whenever I use magic from this moment on, I'm going to get these intrusive images of Elijah being stretched open by some insanely huge, metaphorical shifter dick.

I don't need those images in my head every time I try to cast a spell.

ELIJAH

How do you think I feel?

LIAM

Please tell me he didn't compare remnant energy to a buttplug.

MILES

Pretty sure he did.

ARAN

Do you think shifters have magical knots too?

LIAM

Aran, I swear to god.

I'm taking away your group chat privileges if you keep this up.

ARAN

What? It's a legit question. Their energy could act more like a knot than a buttplug. You know, not just keeping their bonded mage ready for more, but actively stretching them wide and filled with shifter energy.

ELIJAH

Not a legit question. There was no bonding, so there was no knotting, magical or otherwise.

MILES

I think I've been friends with Aran too long because that sounded almost logical?

It's pretty well documented that a mage's access to magic increases after a shifter bonds them.

And that's regardless of whether they're near the shifter at the time.

Maybe it is the shifter's energy forcing their channels open wider than they've ever been before.

There was a pause, and then...

MILES

Oh god, I didn't just write that.

I regret every life decision that has led me to this point.

ARAN

See! Miles agrees!

MILES

Unwillingly.

But the theory only fits (don't even, Aran) if they're bonded.

ELIJAH

THERE WAS NO BONDING.

There was no biting.

There was no knotting.

There never will be.

He isn't interested.

LIAM

HE isn't?

ELIJAH

I'M not interested either. That should go without saying!

ARAN

Right. We know. We've heard it all before. No shifter dick for you. (eye roll)

ELIJAH

I thought you agreed with me on that.

ARAN

On bonding, yes. Not on your absurd disavowal of shifter dick. Though, it's unfortunate you need the former to get the full benefits of the latter.

ELIJAH

Liam? Miles?

LIAM

Definitely no on the bonding.

ELIJAH

And the dick?

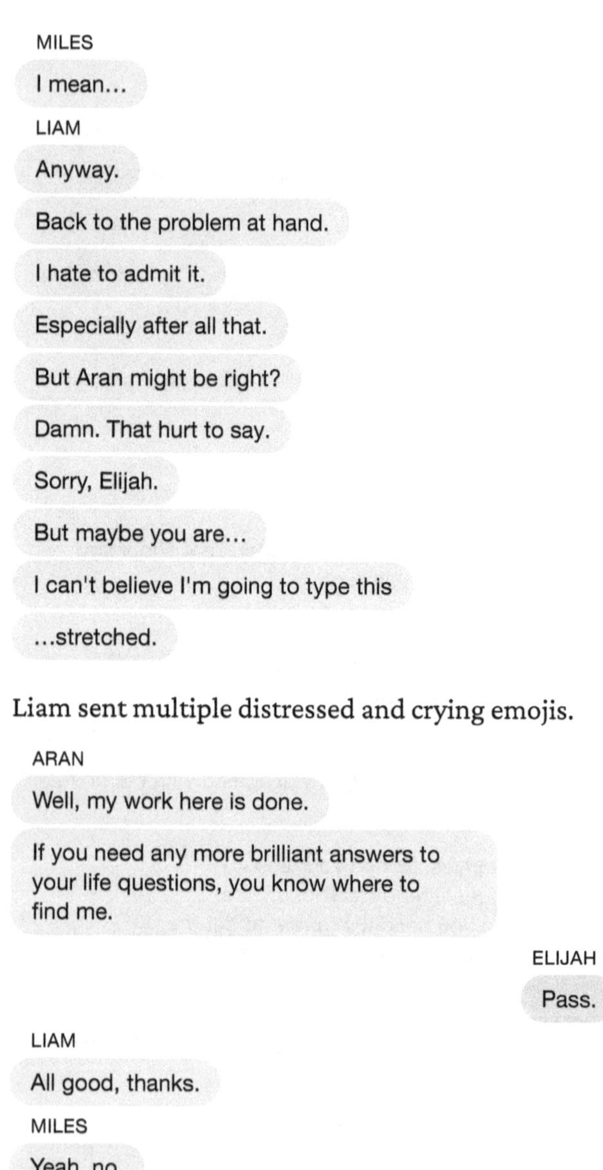

Liam sent multiple distressed and crying emojis.

Give it a few more days and see if things go back to normal.

If they don't, message me and Liam privately, and we'll figure it out.

ARAN

Hey!

ELIJAH

Thanks.

ARAN

Before you go. Even if there was a disappointing lack of sex, he had to shift, right? How did the actual (eggplant emoji) compare to the metaphorical one?

ELIJAH

And that's my cue to leave.

Goodnight, guys.

Elijah exited the app before thoughts of being magically stretched open could change to being physically stretched open.

He really should consider getting new friends.

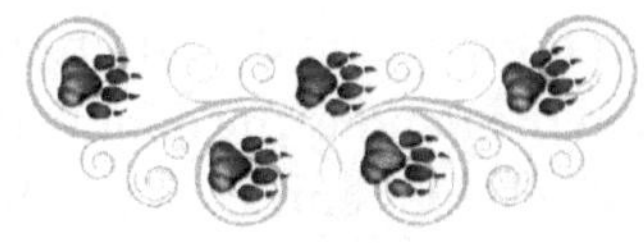

SEVEN

Victor ran fingers through his short hair and glanced at the Ziploc bag in his other hand. Inside were half a dozen leaves in vibrant fall colors, though it was only the first week of September. A few were stained with blotches of brown.

He hoped he was being paranoid, but he needed to check. That was the only reason he was walking up to the magic shop. No ulterior motives at all.

A Closed sign hung in the window, but there were still a few hours before the shop should be shuttered for the night, and when he tested the handle, the door was unlocked.

The bells announced his entrance, and he was hit by the wall of magic that waited inside. But above all, it was the scent of snow-covered earth that greeted him, more notice-able than before, distracting him from the overwhelming amount of magic in the enclosed space. He caught a hint of his own scent in the mix and wondered how it'd lasted over two weeks since his previous visit.

His wolf stirred, but he ignored it. He didn't need any of

its input while he was here. Rubbing his chest absentmindedly, he walked toward the counter.

A small explosion and a string of curses came from the office, and a moment later, a highly irritated Elijah strode out of the room, a trail of smoke and a fluffy white-and-gray cat following him. Elijah didn't seem surprised to see Victor, just miffed.

"The sign says Closed." Elijah's voice was as frosty as his eyes. The professional air he cloaked himself in had been tossed aside, leaving him nothing but annoyed. His cat took up a better vantage point on the glass counter to glower at Victor, tail swishing.

"The door wasn't locked." Victor didn't step closer, didn't inhale deeper, didn't let his gaze travel the length of Elijah's body.

"Most people don't try it when the sign's there."

"I needed to talk to you."

"You couldn't have called?"

"I did. Multiple times. Do you ever answer?" After his third try, he'd given up and gotten into his SUV.

"Not when I'm doing work that requires concentration. That's what voicemail is for."

"Do you answer your voicemail?"

"I would have after I finished."

Victor hadn't been prepared for this. He'd planned to come in, ask about the leaves, and then go back to being done with magic. But now Elijah and his damn cat were glaring at him like he'd done something wrong. This was not how this conversation was supposed to go.

He stepped up to the counter, setting the plastic bag down. "Was this caused by magic?"

Elijah's brow furrowed, irritation diminishing as he

reached for the bag. "Where are these from? I thought it'd be another few weeks before autumn kicked in."

"They're from the damaged section of the wards. One line of trees right at the edge of the border."

Elijah's frown deepened. "When did this start?"

"I noticed it today. We've been patrolling regularly, but that area is off the path."

Elijah examined the leaves in the bag. He set them down and turned, grabbing a few objects from the shelves and piles around him. While his focus was on gathering the supplies, Victor's eyes roamed to his lithe form. The memory of Elijah drawing lines on his chest was still too vivid.

His wolf chose to take a longer detour, imagining what it would feel like to touch Elijah instead.

He forced the thought away.

Elijah opened a massive tome on the counter. It was filled with detailed botanical drawings, and Victor watched, transfixed by his nimble fingers flipping through the pages.

Magic inched along Victor's skin. Everything sharpened in a way that told him his wolf was coming to the surface. He leaned in before he could stop himself, catching the impossible ghost of his scent on Elijah as he breathed in. When Elijah glanced up, a trace of purple kindled in his icy blue eyes, too faint for human vision to detect.

He studied Victor, his expression guarded, and again, Victor wished the oversaturation of magic didn't keep him from discerning the hints of Elijah's emotions in his scent.

"Do you think I did this?" he asked, voice quiet in the minimal space between them.

"No," Victor answered, too quick to know which side of

himself was saying it. Either way, it wasn't a lie, but he reined his wolf in before it could do anything he'd regret.

Elijah hummed, consulting his book once more, but the tension in his body had eased a fraction. "As far as I can tell, there's no magic to this. It looks natural."

"But why in that location? This early?"

Elijah shrugged. "The forest lent a lot of energy to the ritual, and that has to come from somewhere. That area had the weakest wards. If I had to guess, I'd say the forest sacrificed something from those trees to help reinforce the new wards, and whatever normal senescence they should have gone through got accelerated."

"So it's nothing to worry about?"

"I don't think so. Just keep an eye on it." If Elijah was lying, he gave no indication of it.

Victor nodded. "I will."

With the reason he'd come taken care of, Victor went to leave. He made it five steps, then stopped. He did have another errand he could cross off his list while he was here.

Turning back, he asked, "Do you have tarot cards and sage?"

Elijah raised an eyebrow. "Obviously. Why?"

"I need a deck and... a bundle?"

Elijah's expression grew more bemused. "Do you know what you're doing with either of those?"

"I do. I'm fucking with my betas."

The remainder of Elijah's iciness melted, replaced by a mischievous glint in his eyes. "Valid use. Any specific reason?"

"They're assholes."

Elijah's laughter was warm and genuine, and it settled in Victor's chest. "Aren't all good friends?"

Victor couldn't quite repress a smile. "If they ask, I deny them being anything remotely friend-like."

"I heard nothing of the sort." Elijah ducked into his office, then reemerged with a half-burned bundle of sage and a worn deck of cards.

As he put them in a simple paper shopping bag, his cat jumped down and paraded toward Victor, stopping to sniff at him before strolling off. Even by feline standards, the look Victor received had been monumentally unimpressed. He watched the cat disappear between the jumble of shelves.

Another laugh from Elijah drew Victor's attention. "That was downright friendly compared to how she usually reacts to wolf shifters."

Victor huffed. Cats, in general, weren't fans of canine shifters. "In that case, I'm glad I'm not the worst ever. What's her name?"

"Lady."

"Like Lady and the Tramp?"

"If you want to continue to not be the worst, don't let her hear you suggest she was named after a dog. And no, it's a shortened version of her full name."

"Which is?"

"Lady of Dread and Slaughter, Lady of the East, Female Devourer, Mistress of the Oracle," he intoned.

"You named her after the Egyptian cat goddess Bastet?"

"When she decided to adopt me, it was the only name she'd answer to." Elijah's tone was amused and fond. "I'd say it went to her head, but she's always been like that."

"Is it safe to let her run loose in the shop? She could get into something."

"She knows this place better than I do." He slid the bag across the counter to Victor. "On the house. Never let it be said I don't support the cause of fucking with obnoxious friends." He leaned forward, grin positively devilish. "I can do you one better. A little trick that will let you give them a tarot reading they won't forget."

Victor shifted closer. "I'm listening."

"It requires magic," Elijah warned.

Victor hesitated. "And my energy?"

"No," Elijah said. "Here. Give me your left hand. If it's uncomfortable, tell me to stop, and I will."

Victor exhaled, his heart pounding. If it wasn't Elijah taking from him, if it meant a chance to turn the tables on his betas...

He held his hand between them.

Elijah reached over the counter and pressed his palm against Victor's. The moment they touched, Victor had to restrain from shivering at the flutter of magic. The tattoos peeking out from under Elijah's cuff glowed softly, and Victor couldn't tear his gaze away, couldn't deny he desired to undo that cuff, push it back, reveal Elijah's skin and the designs that decorated it.

Magic streamed into his hand. Victor looked up in question and saw purple in Elijah's eyes before he blinked it away.

"That'll last an hour or two max, so you'll have to use it right when you get home. Tell them you're going to see what their future holds. Let them shuffle the deck. You'll know which three cards to pick." The wicked delight in his grin had Victor suppressing another shiver.

The prickle of magic was bizarre but not as unpleasant as Victor would have expected. He stared at his hand, flexing his fingers. It appeared the same as always, but each movement stirred the magic under his skin.

Elijah was watching him with the same expression

Victor had seen before, that near-imperceptible head tilt and one corner of his mouth quirked up like he was trying to figure Victor out.

Victor took the bag, finding himself more confused than when he'd entered the shop, though for entirely different reasons. "Thanks." Not sure what else to say, he nodded to Elijah and left.

Dusk fell as he drove home, his attention divided between the road and the tingle of magic inside him. He touched as little as possible with his left hand, unsure what would happen if he did, and was thankful Elijah hadn't asked for his dominant one.

As soon as he stepped inside, his betas were on him.

"Where have you been?" Kade's eyes gleamed, fiendish as ever. Rick and Will followed behind him. Victor knew he must reek of magic; there was no hiding it.

"Oh, I got those items you guys requested." He pulled out the cards and sage, holding the former out to Will. "Give these a shuffle. Let's see what'll happen if you keep giving me shit."

Will scoffed but shuffled the deck, fanning it out on a nearby table.

Victor hovered his hand over the cards and got a quick zap from one. "Kade," he said and barely maintained his neutral expression as he flipped it over. A dead body lay on the ground, ten swords sticking out of it.

He picked two more that gave him that same jolt—a tower being struck by lightning for Will and Death on a white horse for Rick.

They stared at the cards for a blessedly silent minute before looking up at him in suspicion.

"How did you do that?" Kade asked.

"No clue what you're talking about. Have a good night."

He grinned at them and headed to his room. Those cards meant nothing to him; they could have positive meanings for all he knew, but the surprise and concern on their faces had been worth the forty-minute drive awkwardly holding his hand in the air. He so rarely got them to shut the hell up.

He shook out his hand after he closed his bedroom door. Whatever that had been, besides satisfying, hadn't used up the magic Elijah had transferred into him. It wasn't as strong, but it remained. How long until it wore off?

Victor rubbed his palm on his denim-clad thigh, eyes widening as magic seeped into the skin there, causing a shudder to run through him. That felt... remarkably good.

He swallowed as a thought stampeded into his mind. One that had to violate some ethical or moral code about how loaned magic could be used.

He tried to think of something else, anything else, but his dick was already hardening. The goddamn traitor strained against his jeans, fully on board with his tremendously bad idea.

Ethics be damned; his cock did not care.

Almost without volition, his fingers traced over his thigh. He let out a shaky breath and sat on his bed. Yeah, that felt exactly as pleasurable as it had the first time.

The mental gymnastics going on in his brain were Olympic-level. He was supposed to be avoiding magic. But really, it wasn't magic he should avoid so much as mages. And if there were no mages around, this couldn't hurt, could it? As long as it was just this once.

Knowing he'd be thoroughly horrified after he was done, but also unable to convince himself not to, he popped open the button on his jeans, undid his fly, and pulled himself out.

He groaned as he wrapped his hand around his cock.

This was a horrible idea. The worst in his life.

But that didn't stop him from experimentally tugging on his dick. He rolled back the silky skin to expose his glistening tip. The cool air of the room caressed the sensitive head, a torturous counterpoint to the heat of Elijah's magic.

Using his nondominant hand was awkward, but the hum of magic more than compensated for what he lacked in finesse. Each stroke delivered tingling sparks into his shaft and made them pool in his balls.

It took effort to force himself to stop long enough to grab lube from his nightstand and lie back. But when he had, the now slick slide ratcheted up the sensation.

Eyes screwed shut, toes curling, he twisted on the bed, drawing in graceless, ragged gasps of air. He'd never felt anything like this before. He couldn't have described it even if he'd been able to form coherent words. It overwhelmed him, a whirling euphoria that sucked him in, submerged and enraptured him, left him lost in a world of intoxicating pleasure, where his hips moved on their own, where the stimulation was so intense he was close to crying from it.

He clenched the sheets with his right hand, one desperate lifeline to reality, while he thrust up into his left, not holding back, not trying to make it last, just jerking himself, hard and fast, greedy for the release that was barreling toward him.

His orgasm crashed into him, and he came with enough force a spatter hit his jaw. He worked himself through it, kept stroking until the aftershocks abated and the final traces of magic drained out of him. Then he lay there, panting, wrung out, staring at his ceiling in a daze, his wolf smug and satisfied.

Fuck, he thought. Apparently the only word his brain

was capable of producing as it painstakingly reassembled itself from a thousand shattered pieces.

Was that what sex with Elijah would be like? Would his magic gather inside Victor, driving him higher, making him come that much harder? Or would it be better? How would it feel to have fingers buzzing with that magic stretching him open, pressing into his ass?

As his body cooled, he grimaced. This had been such a bad idea. Not only had he used Elijah's magic for something he doubted the mage would approve of, but he'd probably ruined himself for non-magical orgasms for the rest of his life. And, he realized, looking down at himself, he'd done his best to ruin a shirt in the process. There was more come on it than he wanted to attempt to rinse out. Had he emptied his entire balls?

Note to self, he thought. *Undress before any future magical orgasms.*

Not that there were going to be any. He'd let himself get too comfortable around magic over the last few days if this was the result. He had to be more careful.

Groaning, he hauled himself out of bed, legs unsteady, and made his way to the bathroom to clean up.

CHAPTER

EIGHT

Elijah grimaced at the parchment he'd been working on before Victor had arrived, now nothing but a charred mess. The pile of ash had been well on its way to becoming a binding contract of nonaggression between a pack of wolf shifters and a colony of mountain lion shifters.

Grumbling to himself, he scrubbed his workbench clean, then gathered supplies to start over.

It was a layered spell, more time-consuming than complicated, with only the last stage being particularly difficult. He spread out fresh parchment and mixed finely ground herbs into a new batch of ink.

The first step didn't even require magic, just a steady hand. He wrote the agreed-upon terms in clear, unequivocal language. After that, he added a simple charm that would protect the paper from being destroyed by non-magical means.

As he worked, his magic buzzed, aching to be used. It usually brought him a sense of satisfaction and purpose; it was a welcome companion he always carried with him. But even with Victor gone, his energy remained, chaotic in Elijah's veins. Touching Victor had been a boneheaded move. He'd known it might make things worse but hadn't been able to resist. And now his magic ran as wild as Victor's energy, unpredictable and restless as it twisted through him.

It was an ill omen of how this next part would go.

The contract would be signed without him present, which meant the magic he infused into it needed to capture the oaths sworn, binding the spirit of the spoken words to the document, ratified by signatures of blood.

Elijah closed his eyes and tried to still his thoughts. He pictured the sigils that needed to be inscribed with magic, each with their own meaning, their own covenant to embody—alliance and honor, security and integrity. They swam behind his eyelids. Right there, waiting. All he had to do was transfer them onto the parchment.

He should be able to do this. There was no reason having excess energy in his system should stop him. He settled into his magic, trying to regulate its flow, but it jumped, dancing away, slipping out of his control. He gritted his teeth and tried again.

If he could focus, if he could calm his magic, he could do this.

But it wasn't happening. Every time he tried to manipulate his magic, it slithered out of his grasp, elusive, unwilling to be tamed.

It was so close. Just a little more...

He latched onto it and felt something give in his mind. Magic rushed through him, washing away the sigils he'd been picturing in a surge of raw power.

Frustrated and cursing, Elijah opened his eyes to find the parchment smoldering at the edges.

Well, at least it hadn't exploded. That was progress, he supposed. A sad, pathetic amount of progress.

He shoved back from the workbench and left his office, locking the shop before making his way upstairs. No point attempting to get any more work done tonight.

He flopped onto his bed, not surprised to find notifications from the group chat when he pulled out his phone.

LIAM

Elijah, how's your magic doing?

I see you typing, Aran.

Don't even think about it.

ARAN

Think about what?

MILES

Don't pretend you're all innocent.

We know you too well for that.

Aran had replied with a string of angel emojis.
Elijah snorted. Not likely.
He stared at his screen. Did he want to tell them this?
No, he didn't.
Sighing, he started to type.

ELIJAH

I think it was getting better. It felt more under control yesterday and this morning.

LIAM

I don't like the past tense in those sentences.

ELIJAH

Neither do I.

LIAM

What happened?

ELIJAH

He came into the shop today, and I exploded a binding contract.

The number of shocked emojis they sent was disturbing. Nearly as disturbing as not being able to control his magic.

ELIJAH

And that was before I touched him.

ON THE HAND!

He added that detail quickly before Aran could ask where.

ELIJAH

Now it's as bad as it was a few days ago. Maybe worse.

ARAN

That makes sense. If you keep taking that shifter dick, it's gonna leave you wide open.

ELIJAH

There was no dick-taking, metaphorical or otherwise!

MILES

Okay, Aran's ridiculous metaphors aside, did you channel his energy?

ELIJAH

No. I fed him some of my magic so he could do a trick tarot reading.

But that's it.

ARAN

How did he take it?

LIAM

Aran, don't.

ARAN

I'm being serious. If the wolf was on the receiving end of things, that shouldn't have affected Elijah. My theory only works if Elijah's the one taking that big shifter energy.

MILES

Why does everything you say sound dirty?

But he's right, Elijah. Touching him shouldn't be enough to mess with your magic.

ELIJAH

So. The thing is.

Ever since we first touched?

Literally just touched.

Even before I channeled his energy.

I've been getting bits of it.

Without trying.

All it takes is skin contact.

MILES

That's not normal. It's never that easy to channel energy.

LIAM

Definitely not normal.

And something you should have told us last time.

ELIJAH

I wasn't thinking about it then.

I've been too focused on how weird my magic is being.

LIAM

Anything else you're not telling us?

Elijah winced. If they were going to help him, he had to be honest.

ELIJAH

Uh. The exploding contract?

That might have happened before I'd even seen him?

I was in my office. He'd just entered the shop.

And my magic went haywire. It knew he was there.

Cringing, he waited for the response that would get. The chat stayed quiet for long enough he force stopped the app, then restarted it.

No, it hadn't malfunctioned. They simply weren't responding. The fact that Aran hadn't cracked a joke yet was making Elijah sweat.

Finally, three dots popped up, and Elijah held his breath until a message appeared.

MILES

What do you know about tethering to shifters, Liam?

Have you done any research on that?

ELIJAH

Wait. What?

LIAM

Not much.

I can check the library.

There's a section on magical connections.

It has a lot on both tethers and bonds.

ELIJAH

Guys, no. I didn't tether myself to him.

Pretty sure I'd remember that.

MILES

Not saying you did.

But I've also never heard of mages who could channel shifter energy that easily without a permanent connection.

LIAM

Neither have I.

They were right. Channeling shifter energy should entail at least a little effort. It wasn't supposed to be automatic the moment skin met skin, and his magic had never reacted to any shifter the way it did to Victor.

ARAN

You must have freakishly compatible magical signatures.

ELIJAH

Apparently.

But seriously. There's no connection between us. Bond, tether, or otherwise.

LIAM

Miles has a point, Elijah.

What you're describing…

It sounds an awful lot like you could have a
tether to your shifter.

ELIJAH

He's not my shifter.

And I told you, it wasn't that kind of ritual.

Have you ever heard of someone tethering
themselves to a shifter WITHOUT sex of
some kind involved?

Without intending it? With neither party
wanting it?

LIAM

No.

But there are countless things I haven't
heard of.

Doesn't mean they don't exist.

If it's not a tether, what about a bond?

Weird shit can happen during rituals.

Maybe it was a fluke?

Some kind of accident?

ELIJAH

How would that even work?

I slipped, fell, landed on his knot during the
ritual?

ARAN

> Ooh! I love that one! The mage makes the best face when he lands. You've got to watch it. Hold on, I'll find you the MateHub link.

Elijah's *NO* beat the ones sent by Liam and Miles, but only barely.

ARAN

> Your loss. It's super hot. Richard Knotz is a fucking legend.

Ignoring Aran, Elijah exhaled, slow and measured. He hated to admit it, but they might have a point.

ELIJAH

> Fine. I still don't think it's possible.

> But, Liam, if you find even one case of a mage and a shifter forming either a tether or a bond WITHOUT sex, biting, knotting, or it being deliberately done...

> I'll run interference the next time your mother tries to set you up on a blind date.

LIAM

> Next three times and you're on.

> I'll check the archive.

> There have to be answers there.

> In the meantime...

> Are you going to see him again?

ARAN

> More importantly, are you going to touch him again?

Elijah rolled his eyes.

ELIJAH

Not planning on it.

And he dislikes magic, so I doubt he'll be a regular customer.

LIAM

Okay.

You need to avoid him if you can.

That might help.

And I'll also see if I can find something that will act as a...

I don't know.

A barrier or buffer of sorts?

ARAN

Magical prophylactic.

MILES

I'm pretending I didn't see Aran's last message.

ELIJAH

Good plan.

LIAM

Don't worry, Elijah.

We'll figure this out.

ELIJAH

Thanks.

He groaned and shut the app. If his magic didn't behave soon, it'd make running his shop a whole hell of a lot harder.

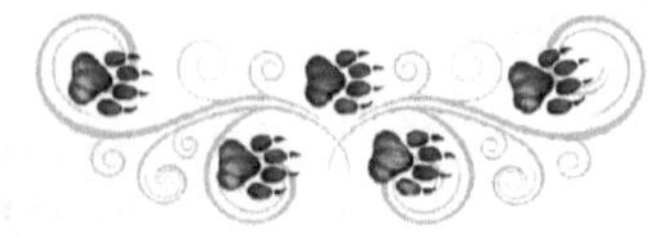

Elijah woke up, groggy and disoriented. The reality of where he was, who he was, crawled back to him.

This was his bed. He was in his apartment. But he had the strangest impression he was somewhere else. He was someone else.

He shook his head, trying to clear it.

It had been a dream. Racing through the forest on four legs instead of two. If that was where his subconscious was going, shifters had been occupying his recent thoughts entirely too much.

His body comfortable and relaxed, he rolled onto his side, and a yawn forced its way out of his mouth. A glance at the clock confirmed it was after nine, and as tempting as it was to become one with his pillow again, he always opened the shop by ten on days he didn't have a house call.

Laziness wasn't a luxury he often indulged in. He had too many responsibilities, too much ground to cover. But since the ritual, his usual, naturally early start had turned into sleeping late. If this kept up, he'd have to set an alarm.

He rolled out of bed, already two hours behind his regular schedule.

The day didn't get better from there.

His magic was volatile enough he didn't want to risk any challenging spells, and there was no message from Liam with stunning insight into what was wrong. Not that he'd expected it to happen overnight, but when Liam got it in mind to research a topic, superfluous things like sleep rarely stopped him.

Liam had been like that since the day they'd met in their final year of elementary school. Constantly carrying around at least one book, always so fixated and focused whenever some new academic puzzle presented itself to him.

After a decade of Elijah's parents telling him the only thing he needed to know about magic was how to suppress it, meeting Liam, feeling magic in another person for the first time, had been a seismic change to Elijah's eleven-year-old self. And for all his parents' insistence he stay away from *that boy*, they'd become closer than brothers, even if they were opposites in so many ways. Elijah's drive and ambition contrasted by Liam's contentment as long as he had books to lose himself in, Elijah's pragmatic streak versus Liam's tendency to worry, Elijah's pale skin an outlier when surrounded by the mixed Creole heritage of Liam, his parents, and his younger siblings in family pictures.

They'd been there for every important moment in each other's lives, including when Liam, Aran, and Miles had helped Elijah move into his shop.

His shop, which was empty for most of the day, a rarity for a Saturday. It was normally his busiest day. Not good for business but probably for the best, considering the state of his magic. If anyone had needed something urgent done, he didn't think he could have obliged.

So instead of helping customers, he spent his time scouring the shop's stock of books. He'd searched his own library the night before, though he'd known he wouldn't find answers there.

But it didn't matter where he looked; he found nothing. No explanation for Victor's energy affecting his magic over a week after the ritual.

He sighed and stretched, working out the kink in his back, then restocked the books he'd been listlessly flipping through. It was almost closing time, and the hours of frustration had left him in need of a drink.

After locking up, he walked the few blocks necessary to hit Main Street, thankful Lost Creek was large enough to justify a bar, multiple even. Not that he'd found many small towns that weren't.

The bar was half-full, a few people already drunk, talking in too-loud voices over the twang of country music. Its decor was dated but in fair condition—with a few worn posters on the walls for bands that had long since broken up, red vinyl stools faded to the color of dried blood, and a pool table and some dartboards that had seen better days. The whole establishment was tidier than Elijah would have expected from a dive bar in the middle of nowhere. Its dozen or so wooden tables were always reasonably clean, the floor freshly mopped, and the rows of bottles lined up neatly, their labels exposed. The air was heavy with alcohol, spiked by sweat, perfume, and the almost forgotten scent of cigarette smoke that would have hung in hazy clouds years ago.

When he got to the counter, the bartender had just finished pouring a drink for another customer.

"The usual?" she asked, turning toward Elijah. She was in her mid-forties, her auburn hair streaked with white and pulled back in a low ponytail. He nodded.

A minute later, she slid the layered Guinness stout and Bass pale ale across the counter, thanking him when he passed her a few bills and told her to keep the change.

As he walked to a table in the corner, the two layers began to mix, dispersing into each other.

He sat and took a long drink, letting the alcohol relax

him. This was exactly what he needed. He leaned back and surveyed the room, his out-of-the-way table giving him the perfect vantage point for people-watching. The patrons were mostly middle-aged, with one group of younger ranch hands playing pool. It was a far cry from the clubs he and his friends had gone to during their apprenticeship, but he'd take what he could get.

His magic stirred, and he glanced at the door, both surprised and not, to see Victor and Kade walk in. Kade's smile was wide, while Victor's expression was the epitome of long-suffering.

Elijah had figured this was a safe place if he wanted to avoid Victor. The music was loud enough it couldn't be pleasant for shifters. Hell, even he'd have liked it turned down a few notches, and his hearing was perfectly human. Add that to the scents and smells, the half-shouted conversations, the way alcohol didn't affect shifters that much, and he'd assumed none of the local shifters were frequent visitors. The handful of evenings he'd killed there over the last year had reinforced that belief; he'd never seen one inside.

Obviously he'd been wrong.

There was a chance they might not notice him, right?

That hope lasted all of three seconds, but then Victor inhaled, and his attention snapped to Elijah. Kade tracked his line of sight, his grin growing wicked. He spoke, his lips moving, the music drowning out his words. Elijah hadn't heard him, but Victor had. He flashed his teeth in a warning that Kade ignored.

Kade said something else, smirking at him. Victor narrowed his eyes, and over the din, Elijah could swear an irritated growl rumbled through the bar, but Kade just turned to stalk toward Elijah's table.

He walked with a swagger that had heads turning. His hair, tousled from the breeze outside, framed features that were strong and sharp, though softened by the warmth in his brown eyes.

One of the ranch hands missed the shot he'd lined up, his focus more on Kade than the pool table, and Kade's full lips curved into a smile that reminded Elijah of the moments when Aran acquired a target for the night.

He was gorgeous, but he wasn't the one that drew Elijah's gaze.

Victor glared after Kade for a beat before he followed.

Where Kade was a study of playboy good looks, Victor was classically handsome, a bit of dark stubble dusting his chiseled jawline. The natural ease in his movements made it look like no matter what he did, it'd be graceful. He carried himself with a quiet confidence and a mesmerizing air of strength. His dark jeans and black T-shirt hugged his muscular frame in a way that had Elijah taking another sip of his drink.

Elijah rose to his feet, his magic humming in anticipation as they got closer. It'd been quieter as he drank, the alcohol dimming its presence, but it flared back to life now.

The smell of stale beer and too much cologne was momentarily covered by pine, summer, and something uniquely shifter. Elijah frowned, confused. He must have been imagining things again because he most certainly did not have the ability to pick out scents like that.

They wove through the last few tables, and Elijah tried not to be distracted by how his magic was demanding he reach out, pull Victor closer, get lost in his intoxicating energy.

Elijah's fingertips prickled, and he rubbed his thumbs against them to dispel the feeling. Victor's eyes flickered downward, and Elijah stopped the motion, his ears suddenly feeling hot.

"Mage Lauring." Kade's voice was a hint suggestive as he held out a hand.

Elijah stared at it. No shifter volunteered to have skin-on-skin contact that would leave them smelling like magic. When Victor had, it'd been to prove something to Elijah. Looking up at Kade with suspicion, Elijah offered his hand, calling his bluff.

Kade's grip was warm and strong, his fingers stroking along the inside of Elijah's wrist before curling around his hand in an almost lewd fashion that could have been dismissed as unintentional if it weren't for the circles his thumb was drawing on Elijah's skin.

He didn't drop Elijah's hand immediately. Instead, he tilted it subtly, trying to turn his palm facedown.

Irritation spiked through Elijah at the attempted show of dominance. He kept his grip firm and held Kade's gaze without wavering. They both knew Kade could force the matter; Elijah was nowhere near as physically strong as a shifter, and he'd rather not use magic in public, even subtle magic, as retaliation. But Kade eased his pressure.

"Can I buy you a drink?" Flirtation still dripped off Kade's words.

"I'm good, thanks." Elijah had over half his drink left and no interest in getting involved in whatever game Kade was playing.

"Suit yourself." Kade dropped his hand and his indecent tone before moving away, though his eyes gleamed as he turned toward Victor.

Victor shot him a look, thunderheads in his glare, and Kade held up his hands in mock surrender.

Elijah really wasn't the only one with obnoxious friends.

As they stared each other down, Elijah realized he hadn't noticed Kade's energy. There'd been no transfer like with Victor. He didn't know if he was relieved by that or not. Was it better if his magic acted up around all shifters or just one?

"Mage Lauring." Victor inclined his head, oddly formal about the greeting.

"Alpha Mills," Elijah replied in kind.

They stood there, Kade watching them. Neither of them made a move to speak. A thread of discomfort wound through Elijah.

"Well," Kade said, standing up straighter. "As fun as this is, we're here to get this one something hard."

Elijah raised an eyebrow at him.

"Liquor," Victor clarified. "Hard liquor."

"Like I said, he's been craving something hard all day. And I'd be a terrible friend if I didn't make sure he got it. I suggested driving to the city, but it seems like Victor has a taste for something more local. So here we are." He grinned wolfishly at Victor before advancing on Elijah.

But this time, Victor took a step forward too, turning his body toward Kade, putting himself in Kade's path so he'd need to push past him to get to Elijah.

Kade leaned around Victor, ignoring a warning growl so low Elijah only registered it from the reverberations in his chest.

"If you decide you do want that drink, or if you'd also like to make sure Victor gets something hard tonight, we'll be at the bar." Kade winked at Elijah, then strolled in that direction.

Victor turned to face Elijah, the movement bringing

them into close proximity. Elijah's left hand tingled, his toes wanted to curl in his shoes, and his breath caught as an image of Victor invaded his mind. For one heartbeat, all he could see was Victor on his bed, dick out, back arching as he came.

His magic swelled, causing the lights in the bar to flicker, and it took him a moment to focus, to bring himself under control.

Victor cleared his throat, and Elijah blinked away the vision. His cheeks burned, and his ears felt hot again.

Great, Elijah, super professional.

"Sorry about him," Victor said, voice rough. "As much as we've tried, we've never quite housebroken him."

Elijah huffed out a laugh. "You did say your betas were obnoxious."

"Him more than the rest."

"We all have one of those."

Victor seemed like he was about to ask, but instead, he stepped out of Elijah's personal space and nodded. "Elijah."

"Victor." Elijah liked the sound of that much more than the traditional greeting.

With that, Victor headed to the bar and slid onto a stool next to Kade, who gave him a disapproving look worthy of Lady.

Elijah watched them, his magic wilder now than it had been this morning, a reminder to stay away from Victor Mills. Even if he fascinated Elijah more than anything else this town had to offer, even if he had the kind of energy a mage could get addicted to, even if he was searingly hot and one of the best alphas Elijah had worked with. None of that mattered. Elijah had plans. Plans that necessitated neutrality, plans that required his magic to behave.

He didn't bother sitting. Instead, he threw back the rest of his drink and made for the door.

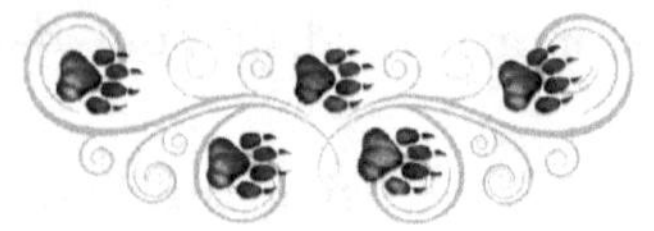

NINE

Night fell with no moon to illuminate the land. Victor walked his patrol on four legs, senses alert. Most of his pack was safe inside. There'd been no issues since the ritual, but tonight required vigilance. They were at their weakest during new moons, and if someone planned to attack, this was the time to do it.

The forest brimmed with life even when bathed in darkness. Small nocturnal animals crept through the undergrowth and moved in the trees above him, little paws scurrying over leaves and branches—there and gone with nothing but a soft rustle. A family of raccoons marauded not far away, their musky odor mingling with the evergreen balm that permeated the air. An owl swooped high through the canopy, the fluid grace of its silent wings almost supernatural under the starry sky. Roots dug deep, pushing through the earth in search of nourishment. A chorus of calls, croaks, and caws echoed around him, so melodious Victor paused to listen.

He felt his land with all his senses. It was part of him, as he was part of it.

He followed the path ringing his territory, enjoying the crisp breeze. The wards beckoned him, luring him closer, but he brushed the temptation away.

A gust of wind drifted by him, carrying a hint of something through the trees.

Victor closed his eyes and inhaled. His senses weren't as sharp tonight, but in this form, they were better than a human's, and the air tasted wrong. A chill shivered along his spine.

It was subtle at first. He might not have noticed it if he hadn't been taking his time, so in tune with his surroundings. But now, it stuck out, one sour note of death in a forest full of sweet life. Something was amiss, and it wasn't the wards.

He rounded a bend and reeled at what he saw.

The area ahead of him was silent—a stark contrast to the murmurs of night at his back. No birds chirped, no insects buzzed. A stretch of land, from the tops of the trees to the dirt beneath, stood preternaturally still. The finality of it sent a shudder coursing through him.

There was no life in sight. The usual animals were missing. What replaced them was so much worse.

The shadows of night couldn't hide the black sickness coating every branch. Leaves dripped with it, weeping a tarry slime that fell in heavy splatters to the forest floor.

He sucked in a breath, nearly choking on the scent of decay. Phantom lice crawled through his fur, and he shook his body to rid himself of the sensation. The ground was sticky under his paws.

What the hell was this?

He stepped back, trying to comprehend what lay before him.

It was more than the leaves; whole trees were dying.

They were withered, branches bare earlier than the onset of fall could explain. Rot saturated the air. Plants died in the forest every day, but never like this. Not years' worth of disease in a night.

He shifted to his human form, the flash of pleasure-pain that came with it sweeping over him, but he ignored it. He stayed crouched, attempting to determine how far down it extended, but all that answered was sickness and decay.

The trees were infected, the plants, the soil. Everything.

Victor stood, the weight of the forest pressing down on him. This land didn't feel like his anymore. He traced his finger over a branch and brought a leaf to his nose but couldn't name the scent that clung to it beyond the fetid reek of death.

This wasn't natural. Not when it was this pervasive, when it'd spread this quickly.

He reached out to the wards, checking for intrusions. But there was nothing. They weren't registering this as a threat, as unbelievable as that seemed.

Something glinted in the undergrowth, a dull gleam in the moonless night, but when he turned his head, it vanished.

Victor changed back into his wolf form and ran, panic building as he found more rotting areas scattered throughout the territory.

They hadn't been there the day before. He or someone else in his pack would have noticed.

He kept heading in the direction the blight seemed to point, and his chest tightened as he realized where he was going.

The spots grew as he neared the western border, the place where the wards had weakened, where Elijah had cast the reinforcement spell. They radiated outward from there, sapping life from the land in ever greater amounts the closer they were to that deathly epicenter. The plants were shriveled, the leaves tinged sickly hues, splotched with oil-slick mold as they drooped on their stems, crude sludge fouling the ground.

Was magic responsible for this? Had Victor risked his pack's safety by inviting a mage onto their land?

Elijah seemed trustworthy; he'd sworn an oath not to harm them. But what did Victor know? Did parchment that glowed for a few seconds guarantee anything? Maybe it was for show, and Elijah hadn't vowed to do shit.

But even with his suspicions toward mages, that didn't ring true. The thought of Elijah betraying his pack caused all of Victor's muscles to clench. Elijah gained nothing from screwing them over.

If he wanted to undermine Victor's pack, why pour so much of his magic into the ritual? There was no way for him to fake that. He could have done a half-assed job—enough to make it look like he'd tried but not enough to help.

And yet no one else with the ability to do this had access to their land. Unless someone managed to sneak through the wards before they were fixed?

Victor headed toward the pack house, mind spinning through a list of potential causes. Was it a symptom of whatever had damaged the wards or a sign of Victor's weakness after all? Was it related to the ritual, or was it something else?

He pushed forward, determined to get home, paws eating up the distance.

When he reached the backstairs, he faltered.

His grandmother had been fond of fairy tales and fables, any story with a moral, anything that taught a lesson. And not the sanitized versions made into family-friendly cartoons.

One had stuck with him for years.

It was a story about a pack of wolves that didn't follow the laws of the land. Driven by jealousy of neighboring packs whose alphas were mated to mages, they craved more power, more territory, more respect. And the best means to get that was by having a mage of their own. So they took one.

Victor hadn't known what that meant as a child, but when he was older, he knew how to fill in the part she never told.

The mage's family sought revenge, sought to ensure the pack didn't abuse anyone else, didn't take more power that wasn't theirs. They cursed the pack.

A blood rot, his grandmother called it. A decay that swept over the pack land, dripping off the trees like blood, destroying and consuming everything in its path and the pack with it. The curse contaminated the territory until it was uninhabitable and damned the shifters to waste away, bleeding from their eyes and noses. It'd been virtually unstoppable.

When he'd learned their oral histories, he'd found out it wasn't just a story, and it hadn't been only one pack. Hundreds of years ago, greedy shifters forcibly bonded mages. There'd been a sadistic tradition to it too—always on a full moon, when the shifter was at the height of their power.

Those atrocities ruined the centuries of alliance between their kinds that his grandmother referred to simply as the time before. Before the abductions, before the hostilities that came after, when the mages retaliated. Packs that allowed it to happen had been obliterated, one by one, every single member from oldest to youngest, until it became the worst sin a shifter could commit, condemning their pack to a death sentence in their quest for power.

Forcing anyone into a bond was abhorrent. But for a mage, it was even worse. The one-sided bond stripped them of control over their magic, leaving them at the mercy of the shifter who'd bonded them against their will. It turned Victor's stomach and left him firmly on the side of vengeance.

Even when a mage fully drained a shifter's energy, taking more than they should, the shifter retained their agency. To establish a permanent connection, mages needed a willing shifter. They weren't able to keep shifters bound to them, restrained and obedient, like a shifter could keep a mage. Their wolves couldn't be leashed by magic.

Or at least, most of their wolves couldn't.

Victor understood why mages were wary around unknown shifters. Why Elijah, alone and exhausted, hadn't wanted to pass out in the middle of his territory on the full moon. A couple hundred years after the practice had been expressly forbidden by all shifter councils, distrust still festered. They'd settled into an uneasy truce that'd given way to the first tentative transactional bonds, but those were weak imitations of the once predominant true bonds that had since become impossibly rare.

He stared into the forest, breath caught in his throat, mouth dry, heart hammering.

That couldn't be it.

They'd done nothing to justify a curse.

He shifted and entered the house, his bare feet causing a couple steps to creak as he climbed the stairs.

Before he dressed, he showered. Whatever had polluted

the forest, just being near it made him feel tainted and dirty. He cranked the water up as hot as it would go, scouring himself until his skin was red and raw and he felt clean again.

A cold, creeping dread filled him as he pulled on jeans and a T-shirt.

It was three in the morning. The magic shop wasn't open, but Victor didn't care. He picked up his phone and dialed, pacing as it rang.

And rang.

And rang.

Finally, the line connected, and Victor inhaled, ready to speak, only to growl as it went to voicemail. He left a message, his tone brisk. "This is Victor Mills. Call me as soon as you get this."

An invisible vice gripped his lungs, squeezing tight, and he rubbed a hand over his chest, trying to ease the tension, but it was useless.

Victor stared out the window at the predawn sky, then forced himself to move. He needed to know if Elijah had put this into motion, and it'd be easier to detect any lies in person.

His wolf was faint but protesting the conclusions he'd jumped to. Elijah wouldn't hurt them, *couldn't* hurt them. Victor had to verify that before he'd believe it.

If Elijah's oath still held, he could test it. It'd piss Elijah off, but Victor would do whatever it took.

He grabbed a plastic bag and ran back to gather a few leaves, using the bag like a glove to avoid touching the filth as he collected them. They smeared sickening tar inside.

Even ignoring the speed limit, the miles stretched out longer than the last time he'd made this journey. The entire drive there, thoughts tumbled through his mind.

He called twice more but got no answer.

Victor parked in front of the shop, snatched the bag off the seat next to him, and got out of his SUV.

A light shone deep inside the shop, and the door was unlocked again.

He opened it and remembered one more lesson from their oral histories.

The only way to stop a blood rot was to kill the mage who'd summoned it.

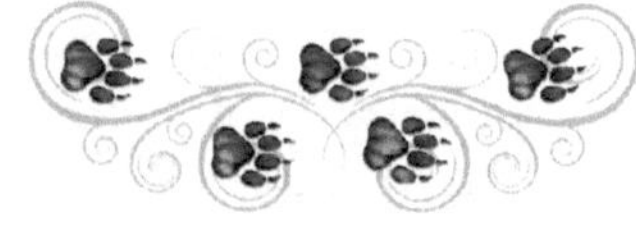

TEN

Elijah sprinkled dried lavender into the cauldron, infusing the flowers with magic. The potion was simmering low; its rich floral scent filled his office. This elixir—meant to aid sleep—was his favorite to brew. It required a delicate touch and the right balance of magic so as not to overpower the properties of the oils and herbs.

He'd been putting it off for days, but as the moon had waned, his magic had stabilized, and there'd been significantly fewer explosions in his shop. Always a good thing.

As much as he hoped that meant he'd recovered from the ritual, the timing couldn't be dismissed as coincidental. He had to wait for the moon to grow full again. Until then, he had work to do.

After messing up as many charms, spells, and potions as he had over the last two weeks, he had a backlog of orders. No good could come from keeping customers waiting half a month for things he normally provided within a day. That was not the reputation he wanted for his shop.

So here he was, getting as many tasks knocked off his

to-do list as he could while his magic was playing nice. He wasn't certain what time it was; he'd lost track hours ago and hadn't bothered checking. Productivity was more important. If he went a night without sleep, so be it. His bed would be there tomorrow night. Or was it tonight? He'd check after this potion was done.

He added juniper to the mix, then stirred it once and let his senses flow into the gently swirling liquid, adjusting the magic that had seeped into it. Three minutes until he scratched one more item off his list.

The door to his shop opened, but he was so close to finishing this, and he was pretty sure it wasn't technically business hours anymore... or yet? Depending on the time. Had he remembered to flip the sign to Closed? He'd been so busy he might not have. But it'd be just another minute. Whoever it was could wait.

He was about to yell he'd be right there, but before he got the words out, his magic churned, flooding into the potion. Not to the extent it would have a week ago, but still overwhelming the ingredients, causing it to hiss in a sickly fashion. Its smell soured. Cursing, he reined his magic in and extinguished the flame beneath the cauldron. He sighed.

Well, that was an hour of his life wasted, and he now knew who was there. Even weakened by the new moon, that energy called to his magic, and it irritated the shit out of him.

He was better than this. He had more control than this.

Grinding his teeth, Elijah stepped into the shop, unsurprised to find Victor standing there, a scowl on his face. He flung a bag of leaves onto the counter. They were splotched with ugly decay.

"What the hell is this?" Victor's tone was accusatory.

Before Elijah had a chance to inspect anything, he continued. "Did you do this?"

Elijah's hackles rose. They'd never be on friendly terms, but he'd thought they'd reached an understanding. Apparently not.

He grabbed the bag off the counter, grimacing at the state of the leaves inside. "Do what exactly? Introduce a leaf fungus to your territory?"

"You know it's not a fungus."

"Really? Please tell me what else I know. If you're so knowledgeable, what is it?"

"It's a blood rot."

Icy rage washed over Elijah. "Are you accusing me of cursing your pack? Of literally trying to kill every single member? Including the ones that aren't complete assholes. Do you think I'd try to murder children?"

Doubt crept into Victor's expression, but he didn't back down. "If not you, who? You're the only mage who's been in my territory all year."

"Have you done something that would warrant a wholesale slaughter?" Each word was bitten out, crisp and vehement.

"Of course not."

"Then why would your mind immediately jump to the worst curse a mage can call the moment you see a few dead leaves?"

"It's not a few dead leaves. There are pockets of this shit littered throughout my territory, places where every plant is infested with it. And they spiral out from the spot you did the reinforcement spell. How could that not be your fault? Not be your doing?"

Despite himself, a spark of curiosity ignited inside

Elijah. It'd been a week since he'd seen Victor, and he hadn't mentioned this then. "When did this start?"

"There were those trees last week. But this? This started tonight."

Elijah's eyes widened, and he frowned at the bag. If that was true, something was seriously wrong. The leaves were covered in decay. This sort of thing didn't happen overnight. Victor's suspicion made more sense, but the accusation still stung. And that pissed him off. "You honestly think I did this?"

"It isn't natural, so it has to be magic."

Elijah tossed the bag down and gestured at it. "There's no magic in that. I don't know what the fuck it is, but it's not a blood rot. I saw one once. You can feel the magic in it; it's unmistakable. Also, red, not black. Hence the name. And even if it were, and we set aside the fact that I have no reason to curse your damn pack, I'm absolutely shit with plant-related magic. I wouldn't have been able to summon it."

He knew someone who could, but he wouldn't bring Aran into this.

Victor looked skeptical. "Prove it."

"Prove that I can't summon a curse to massacre your pack? How? By not doing it? Okay, done. In case you forgot, you made me swear an oath not to harm your pack."

"That oath only lasted until you fixed the wards." Victor grabbed Elijah's shirt and pulled him up against the glass counter between them. He picked up a small ritual dagger from the piles of merchandise and wrapped Elijah's fingers around it before covering Elijah's hand with his own. His was large and warm, and magic sparked under his touch, annoying Elijah further.

He jerked back, but Victor's grip was too strong. "What the fuck are you doing?"

"Prove you can't hurt us."

"I can't. You said it yourself. The oath ended after I reset your wards."

But Victor wasn't listening. He yanked Elijah's hand toward him.

The oath kicked in like a blow to the chest. Elijah wasn't fighting Victor, but his arm went rigid. The closer the dagger came to Victor's skin, the more Elijah's body shook. Violent spasms ran through him, trying to drop the weapon, trying to keep it from cutting flesh.

Spurred on by Victor's energy, Elijah's magic whirled, uncontrolled and chaotic as it strove to avoid what Victor was attempting to make him do. His tattoos glowed hot on his skin, exposed by the sleeves he'd rolled up while working.

His magic strained against Victor, but he bore against it, refusing to budge, and it couldn't do more than that without injuring him in the process.

"Stop it," Elijah gritted out.

How was he still bound by the oath? Had he screwed up the ward ritual after all?

Victor pressed his hand down. Physically, he was so much stronger than Elijah. Under any normal circumstance, there was no way Elijah could have resisted his strength. But no matter how hard Victor pushed, it didn't bridge the gap that would cause the dagger to slice along his skin. The entire time, Victor kept his eyes on Elijah's face, watching his reaction.

Elijah's whole body was locked up, his breath coming in gasps. If this continued, Victor would break his fucking arm.

"The oath won't let me hurt you."

"If you did your job, why weren't you released?"

"It must be the wording. I said until I fixed the problem with your wards. This has to be related."

Victor shoved harder for one second more, then let go. The sudden absence of pressure caused Elijah to stagger. He caught himself against the counter, panting as he leaned, shaking as his magic subsided, glaring up at Victor.

"Did that prove your point? Do you feel better?" This asshole. Why was he so distrustful of mages? He could fuck off and take the mage council with him. Their unwillingness to disclose what had happened with the previous shop owner and Victor's pack had left Elijah unprepared for this shit. "I'm going to say this very clearly so it gets through your thick alpha skull: I don't want to hurt your pack. I *can't* hurt your pack." Elijah didn't add *right now*, though he was tempted.

Victor didn't apologize or acknowledge he'd been mistaken; he just asked, "So what is it?"

Elijah wanted to be done with this, but his oath hadn't been fulfilled. The only way to be released was to fix the problem. And that meant working with this paranoid shithead.

Standing straight, he stared Victor dead in the eye. "Probably whatever caused your wards to deteriorate. It must have gotten inside and is eating away at your land. You never did answer me. Was there an issue with how the wards were transferred to you?"

"How do I stop it?" Victor asked instead.

"I don't know. I've never seen anything like this. It might be a curse, but I have to check it out myself. Maybe there's a magical signature I can detect."

Victor nodded, short and abrupt. "Fine. We go now."

Elijah clenched his jaw. He hated being ordered around, but he wasn't getting any more work finished anytime soon. His magic teemed, infused with Victor's energy. He grinned his coldest customer service smile. "I'll get my things."

Victor's gaze followed him into the office, but at least the jackass didn't follow as well.

Once inside, Elijah sucked in an unsteady lungful of air and rubbed his hand. Victor's iron grip still branded his skin. Even with his magic accelerating his healing, there'd be bruises.

Goddamn shifters. This was precisely why he avoided associating with them. Especially the alphas. They were too volatile.

He threw together a bag with supplies he might need, but he had too many questions. There were too many unknowns, forcing him to guess and go from there. He slung the bag over his shoulder and exited the office.

Lady was sitting on the counter, ears flattened as her tail flicked. She was coiled, ready to pounce. A growl rumbled in her chest, promising piercing claws and a slow, painful death.

Victor stood frozen, expression holding genuine concern.

Elijah stopped to pet her. Her back arched as he scratched along it, and she butted against his hand, then sat, her tail twitching again. So much for her thinking Victor wasn't the worst. Elijah was surprised she hadn't bitten him while he was pulling his little stunt.

Victor darted a glance at him. "Is she going to attack me?"

He smiled at Victor, sharp and vicious. "Well, she didn't swear an oath, did she?"

With one last scratch under her chin, Elijah walked out from behind the counter.

"You're coming with me," Victor said.

Elijah shot him a disbelieving look. "What? You don't trust me to drive to your place by myself? Think I'll disappear on you?"

Victor didn't bother denying it. "You're not leaving my sight until this is over."

Elijah scoffed. "That, I didn't swear to."

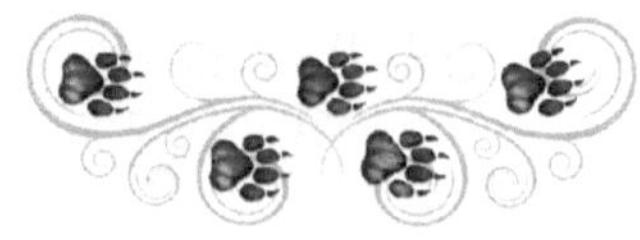

The drive to the Mills pack territory was one of the least pleasant in Elijah's life. Being trapped in a car with someone who suspected he was sabotaging their land and capable of killing five-year-olds wasn't high on the list of activities he considered a good time.

But Elijah wasn't one to sit silently. "What the hell happened between your pack and the previous shop owner?"

Victor's eyes didn't leave the road. His hands gripped the wheel tight enough to turn his knuckles white, tight enough to remind Elijah how easily he could break it. "Didn't they tell you when you took over?"

"I know the council had to remove the previous owner because of something he did to your pack. I'm assuming with or to the former alpha. They stripped him of his position and threatened to strip him of his magic, which means whatever he did was inexcusable. They didn't give me details beyond that. Hell, the only reason I know his name was Darius Caldwell was because I saw it on paperwork in the shop. The council wasn't exactly forthcoming on the matter."

Victor snorted. "The former alpha, my father, thought we needed a pack mage. He said if we'd had one, my mother wouldn't have died. So he decided to *court* that bastard."

Elijah glared out the window. Too many shifters were like that. To them, it didn't matter who the mage was, as long as they had one. They lured in any mage who might have them with their energy and pack resources. It was transactional and nothing more. The shifter and their pack got a mage, the mage got access to shifter energy, both exploited each other, and no one was truly satisfied.

"That doesn't explain why the council disciplined the mage."

"Apparently the council doesn't look fondly on mages who defraud multiple packs. The bastard siphoned off my father's energy. Left him completely drained most nights, so depleted he couldn't move. And then he took our money, because I guess the energy wasn't enough. He had no intention of becoming a pack mage. My father kept trying to justify it, but the longer it went on, the weaker he became. And you know what happens to a pack with a weak alpha."

Elijah winced, able to see where this was going.

"I tried to cover for him, but the pack started to fracture. I sensed it in the wards, in the land, in our bonds. So I challenged him before anyone else could. Then I told that fucking mage to never return, sent my father off to live with relatives, and filed a complaint with the mage council. We weren't the only pack whose alpha fell for his bullshit. He'd done the same thing to others. The council gave us monetary compensation, but that doesn't make up for what he did."

Victor might be an unmitigated ass, but no one deserved that.

There was a strange dynamic to relationships between shifters and mages. Shifter energy was tempting, this beautiful well of power waiting to be used. Shifters knew mages liked it, but they also were repulsed by the scent of magic, happy to keep mages at arm's length, not willing to give up their energy except when required. Or to trade it to enhance their pack's status because the strongest packs were the ones with pack mages. So when shifters did pursue mages, particularly when alphas did, it was almost always with selfish designs.

More than a few shifters had made passes at Elijah. Those willing to ignore what their senses were telling them in order to get a mage for their pack. After everything that had happened between mages and shifters, with all the suspicion between them, it was rare for them to reach a point they sincerely knew and respected each other, let alone wanted a relationship on grounds beyond what was mutually beneficial. But that was preferable to how things had been.

If a mage wanted that kind of arrangement, to each their own. It wasn't for Elijah. Even if being bonded to a shifter wouldn't obliterate his neutrality, and his shop with it, being in a loveless relationship for the sake of power had no appeal.

And although it was frustrating to have shifters pretend they were interested in anything other than the amount of magic he wielded, he could never condone harming a pack. Part of him understood the mentality of wanting to get something out of the shifters who tried to scam mages into relationships. But that didn't make it right, and it wouldn't save the mage from the consequences of unbalanced magic if they took more energy than they needed to the detriment of the shifter.

Elijah let out a breath. "You won't believe me when I say this, but most mages would never do that. Shifter energy isn't worth endangering an entire pack by weakening their alpha."

Victor huffed. "Are you telling me that mages aren't drawn to our energy?"

"You know I can't say that, but there's a difference. No reputable mage would drain someone like that. It's not healthy. It's not sustainable. We only take what we need, whether it's from the earth, a shifter, or ourselves. Everything requires balance. Taking too much destroys that, especially in the rare cases it's taken by force. And the things you do with unbalanced magic become twisted and tarnished. If your magic gets corrupted, you can't do anything good with it. No healing spells, nothing that encourages growth, no cleansing. There's a whole list."

And that explained why the shop had initially made his skin crawl, why he'd needed to cleanse the building before he was comfortable there. He hadn't been imagining it; the place had been tainted.

He couldn't tell if Victor believed him, but the hard set of his mouth had Elijah leaning toward not. His eyes were narrowed as he focused on the road, and the muscles of his shoulders were bunched with tension. Even like this, he was frustratingly handsome, the planes of his face sharp and strong, dark scruff accentuating the line of his jaw. Energy radiated off him, a siren song threatening to entice any mage who came too close.

Elijah shook his head and trained his gaze on the lightening eastern edges of the sky.

None of that mattered. He'd figure out what was causing the problem, fix it, fulfill his oath, and then they could both go their own way and happily not have to deal with each other again.

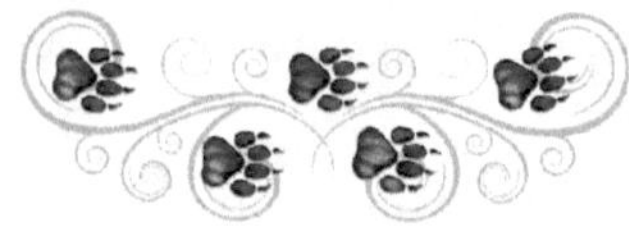

ELEVEN

onflicting emotions warred inside Victor as he led Elijah to one of the diseased areas. His instincts told him Elijah was trustworthy. The mage wouldn't harm his pack; he'd fix this. That same part of himself raged at him for doubting Elijah, for demanding proof of something so obvious. But he knew where those thoughts were coming from, and the main benefit of the new moon was that he could ignore them easier than at any other point in the lunar cycle.

He'd needed to test Elijah to ease the more suspicious side of himself, needed to assess what Elijah was capable of. He might not trust himself around magic, but as long as the oath bound Elijah, Victor's weakness didn't matter. Although conditional, it was the closest he'd get to trusting a mage.

As they moved through the forest, tension rolled off Elijah. The early morning light filtering through the trees was bright enough he had no problem hiking along the trail.

Like every time Victor had seen him, his tailored dress

shirt and slacks fit perfectly, but for once, he wasn't immaculate. The fractionally more disheveled look fascinated Victor. His gaze kept catching on Elijah's unbuttoned collar, rolled-up sleeves, and dark, unstyled hair. And as much as he wished he could, there was no blaming that on his wolf. Elijah's presence would be captivating without the added allure of attraction, but that changed nothing.

The forest's scent curdled as they neared the decay—growth and life defiled by mold and death.

Victor watched Elijah as they entered an area overrun by rot. His eyes widened as he took in the forest and the sickness spreading throughout. Only a few of the largest, oldest trees were withstanding its effects.

The first touch of autumn had colored the foliage a few days before, but this was different. The leaves weren't the reds and yellows of fall; they were splotchy black and sickly brown. They wept and oozed with it. The trees sagged, burdened by some unseen force, and the air felt wrong. Each breath slithered down his throat, stomach-churning and slimy.

Elijah's face showed his shock and horror. He placed a tentative hand against a tree. Victor sensed the forest trying to respond to him, but it was sluggish, not the jubilant way it had reacted to his magic the previous times he'd been there. This was a painful crawl, dragging itself forward, straining to get to Elijah, almost unable to make it.

The tree shuddered, an unnatural wind causing its leaves to rattle. Some fell to the ground, showering them. Victor shook them off, suppressing a shudder of his own at their tainted brush against his skin.

Elijah's brow furrowed as he crouched and cleared away the fallen leaves. Hesitantly, he sank his fingers into the dirt. His lips pressed together; disgust twisted his face.

After a moment, he stood, brushing his hand clean. "I've never come across anything like this. It's not natural."

Victor barely stopped himself from saying no shit. "Is it magic?"

Elijah studied the canopy before answering. "I don't think so. Something is there, but I can't..." He trailed off.

He huffed, then turned toward Victor, determination clear. "May I?" he asked, holding his right hand out. He didn't specify what he wanted, but Victor could guess.

If he needed to, he'd do this. He gave a curt nod but didn't move to meet Elijah. Instead, he stood there, arms crossed over his chest, forcing Elijah to close the distance between them.

The scowl he sent Victor was less than pleased. There was another flicker of hesitation, and then Elijah's hand grazed over the bare skin on Victor's neck, his fingers slipping under the edge of his T-shirt. His thumb rested against the notch of Victor's collarbone in a position that would have been threatening if it didn't feel so much like a caress.

Victor kept his gaze trained on Elijah as his energy jumped under that touch. Even as subdued as it always was this close to a new moon, his wolf pushed forward.

A hint of purple bloomed in Elijah's eyes before they slid shut. His tattoos smoldered to life in a delicate filigree that swooped around his forearms and disappeared under his rolled-up sleeves. They all but taunted Victor to trace their elegant lines, dared him to reveal the path they danced over Elijah's skin.

The energy he channeled from Victor was a mere trickle, but there was more to it than that. There was an echo. Not just his energy but his energy as Elijah perceived it. The buzz of it combining with Elijah's magic, weaving through his body, lighting it ablaze. His chest warmed, and his hands prickled, static electricity on his fingertips. He carefully didn't think about what he'd done with that the last time.

Was this how mages felt using shifter energy? It had been a part of him for his entire life, something he took for granted. But now, experiencing it as Elijah did—that wild, unbridled power coming directly from his wolf—he could understand why someone might crave this, why it might call to them.

Elijah reached through Victor with his magic, tracing the connections that spiraled out from him to every member of the pack, to the land, to the wards. He didn't linger on them; it was a quick confirmation and nothing more.

Even with that exhilarating rush filling him, as soon as he'd checked everything, he pulled back and stepped away. When his eyes opened, Victor wasn't sure if he'd ever seen the purple in them so vivid.

Elijah shook out his hand and pressed his eyelids closed before he looked at Victor again with his usual icy stare, his skin a blank canvas once more as his tattoos faded. "There's nothing in the bonds of your pack that could cause this. No corruption, or at least none that I can find. It all feels like it should, and the wards seem to be fine. It's only these areas."

"What does that mean?"

Elijah grimaced. "I'm not sure. I don't have the kind of magic that lends itself well to living things. Mine is earth-based, best for barriers, wards, and the like. I have a friend who specializes in plant magic though."

Victor's lip curled before Elijah got the suggestion out. The last thing he wanted was another mage on his territory.

Able to read his wordless answer, Elijah narrowed his eyes. "Fine. But I have to consult him."

Despite his misgivings, Victor had no choice but to concede. "Don't tell him who it's for."

"I would never reveal customer information, especially if it might make a pack vulnerable." Elijah tilted his head as if thinking, then scoffed. "This oath probably wouldn't even let me."

That was good enough for Victor. "Do you need to see the other areas?"

"If they're the same as this, there won't be much to learn from them. But I'd like to, just in case."

As they walked, the gentle hum of Elijah's magic swirled inside Victor. It wasn't the surface-level tingle from before; it had settled deeper into him. Whatever energy Elijah had drawn from him, there'd been an exchange. The same thing had happened on the full moon, but he'd convinced himself he'd imagined it. Now that he was clear-headed, he knew he hadn't.

The magic was light in his mind. It shimmered through his energy, mixing in a way he wasn't comfortable with. His younger self would have been thrilled to have magic running through his veins, unusable though it might be. His younger self had been an idiot.

They spent the morning and into the afternoon working through the territory. By the end, Elijah was more rumpled than when they'd begun. There were dark smudges under his eyes, and Victor had to wonder how long it'd been since he'd slept. But he was still far more put together than Victor would have thought possible after hours of hiking through a forest.

From time to time, Elijah paused to touch a tree or the earth. Each time he did, he shook his head, not getting anything more and not finding the underlying cause. He snapped pictures of the rot, zooming in on the leaves. He didn't ask to channel Victor's energy again, but he did try a few spells using supplies he pulled from his bag. Whatever they were supposed to do, from the occasional odd fizzle of magic and the crease between Elijah's brows, they weren't doing it.

He even managed to set a tree on fire, though that only produced a noxious tarry smoke and a string of curses from Elijah filthier than anything Victor had ever heard, including multiple in languages he didn't know. After Elijah put it out, he glared at Victor with such intensity he might have been trying to incinerate him as well, like Victor was the one setting things alight. Elijah didn't try many spells after that.

Once, near the territory line, Elijah detoured toward the wards. He raised a hand to them, and they flashed, glittering with a ripple of magic that ran down their length. Surprise jolted Elijah's body as a tendril formed and snaked around his wrist before fading into the barrier. It was fleeting but undeniably there.

Victor's breath caught in his throat. They didn't do that to anyone but him. They reacted when people passed through them but never greeted the rest of the pack that way.

The fact that his wards liked Elijah should reassure Victor. They were a remarkably good judge of character for something technically inanimate and insentient. But he couldn't stop himself from wondering what Elijah had done to make them act like that.

When they reached the pack house, Elijah leveled a blunt look at him and said, "I have to research this, and I can't do that here."

Victor was reluctant to let him go; he wanted to keep Elijah there. Just until this was solved. But he knew that was irrational. So he drove Elijah to town, the noise of the road filling the silence that stretched between them.

Elijah paid him little attention, choosing instead to focus on his phone, while Victor was less successful in his attempts to ignore the way Elijah's scent tried to curl around him in the close quarters of the vehicle. Somehow it was even more noticeable after he'd dropped him off.

By the time Victor got home, he was restless and agitated after an hour and a half trapped in his SUV. He stripped and shifted, enjoying the pleasant burn that came with the change, a momentary distraction from the thoughts cluttering his mind. Then he headed into the forest.

His wolf knew the exact path Elijah had walked, but Victor took another. There was no point following a trail he'd already taken.

The lack of answers frustrated him, but all he could do was wait for Elijah to return.

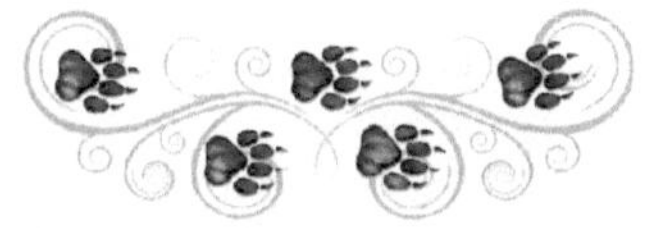

TWELVE

Halfway into town, when the silence became too oppressive, Elijah pulled out his phone and opened the messenger app.

ELIJAH

I need all hands on deck.

The replies were immediate.

LIAM

Is your magic still acting up?

I haven't found anything concrete yet.

ELIJAH

It stabilized over the new moon. And yes, that does play into your theory.

But that can wait. There's a bigger problem.

Victor watched him out of the corner of his eye, trying to see what he was typing, but Elijah blocked him out. He explained the situation and fielded his friends' many questions, though most of his answers were in the vein of *I don't know* and *I'm not sure*. The pictures caused the chat to go quiet for two whole, nerve-racking minutes.

ARAN

I've never seen anything like this before, but
I'll find out what I can.

The decay had brought out the serious side he rarely showed. There were times even Elijah couldn't wrap his head around the difference between this focused, intense version of Aran and the one he'd met in a club years ago—pretty as sin, body graceful and lithe, full-sleeve tattoos on display, streaked with glitter that hadn't been his own.

Aran, for all his bad-boy looks, would give the most avid horticulturist a run for their money with his plant obsession. His experiments with different species strove to unlock the secrets of their powers, to harness their full strength and magical essence. He was quickly ascending the ranks of the world's most skilled mages in botanical-based magic. He could already coax the most obstinate plants into doing his bidding. It was only a matter of time until his abilities were unrivaled.

Elijah couldn't say he enjoyed the no-nonsense Aran; he'd rather have the constant innuendos and inappropriate jokes. When Aran was serious, things were beyond fucked-up, and he was unrelenting until the problem was eliminated.

But all of Elijah's friends were equally relentless.

Liam planned to search the library, while Miles would join Elijah in combing through the digital archives, which weren't as extensive but might have something useful. If information was out there, between the four of them, they'd find it. Elijah had no doubt of that.

Victor dropped him off in front of the shop.

"I'll call you tonight with an update," Elijah said, sticking around long enough to get a terse nod before he got out of the SUV and climbed the stairs to his apartment. It was late afternoon; his shop could stay closed for the day.

Once inside, he spared a moment to gaze longingly at his bed. If he'd known this shitstorm was on the horizon, he wouldn't have worked through the night. But sleep would have to wait. He put some coffee on to brew while he jumped in the shower to scrub off the skin-crawling sensation he'd felt since the moment he saw the rot. Then he grabbed his laptop and got started.

He had no clue what he was searching for, what could cause this, but it wasn't magic. When he'd told Victor magic was about balance, he hadn't been lying, and whatever was affecting Victor's territory was the furthest thing from balanced. No true mage would do that.

He stared at his computer screen until his eyes weren't just dry; they felt like they'd been sandblasted. Lady's contribution to his effort was a steadfast attempt to keep his lap warm. Her low, rumbling purr calmed him.

By the end of the evening, they still didn't have definitive answers, but they had a list of a dozen things for him to try. It was a start, even if none were a guaranteed solution.

Around midnight, he found Victor's number on the shop's phone and dialed it, unsurprised when Victor answered before the second ring.

"Hello." Tension dripped from that one word.

"It's Elijah. I've got some spells to test out. I'll be there first thing tomorrow."

"Do you need us to prepare anything?"

"Not right now. But if that changes, I'll let you know."

"Will you want—" Victor stopped, then rephrased. "Will this require my energy?"

"Everything I'm going to try is pretty basic; no energy needed. If those don't work, maybe."

When Victor spoke again, he was forcing out the words. "How much is this going to cost?"

It was normal to ask, but it set Elijah on edge. "I said I'd fix your wards, and this has to be connected."

Those were the best damn wards he'd ever created. Someone like him, someone not bonded into the pack, shouldn't have been able to repair them to that extent. The problem wasn't the wards but what had caused them to fail. He hadn't noticed it during the ritual, which made this his fault, and he would absolutely figure out what had gone wrong.

"You aren't doing this for free." Victor's voice was tight with suspicion.

Elijah understood where his mistrust was coming from, but the assumption didn't nettle any less. "If I misread the situation and overlooked some underlying problem, you better fucking believe I correct my own mistakes."

When Victor didn't immediately respond, Elijah decided it was time to end the call. "I'll see you in the morning." He hung up and glared at his phone.

He'd fix this, whatever it was, and make damn sure Victor knew that he, at least, was trustworthy before it was over.

Morning came far too early. Elijah staggered out of bed and into the shower, but the water didn't wash away his exhaustion. Neither did the coffee he downed on his way out the door.

Driving to Victor's territory on four hours of sleep was less than advisable, not with the combination of narrow roads and a groggy mind, but Elijah was determined to get this done.

The brush of the wards as he drove through them roused him more than the caffeine had.

When he pulled up to the pack house, Victor was standing on the porch, leaning a hip against the railing. His expression was guarded and composed, but under that facade, worry ran deep.

The bastard looked annoyingly good in his jeans and T-shirt, even though he probably hadn't had any more sleep than Elijah over the last forty-eight hours.

"You've got everything you need?" Victor asked as soon as Elijah was out of the car, slinging his bag over his shoulder.

Elijah pointed to the trunk. "There's more in there, but that's for later."

"What are you going to do?"

Elijah stared out into the forest. From the safety of the house, it was hard to imagine something so wrong beyond those trees, something his magic couldn't explain.

"First up is a more complicated sensing spell. It focuses less on you and your pack, which was what I checked yesterday, and more on the plants."

"To check the extent of the damage?"

"And hopefully what's causing it."

"Then what?"

"I've got a few spells for cleansing and revitalizing that might clear out whatever's fouling up the forest."

This wasn't Elijah's area of expertise, never had been. While he was good with earth, his secondary affinity was fire, and that combination predisposed him to be better at destruction and protection than growth and regeneration. Wards, he could do. Plants, not so much. With his skills in water and earth, Aran should be the one out there. But since he wasn't, he'd given Elijah several enchantments that might help the forest fight off the rot.

The day before, Elijah had tried simple healing spells, but they'd done nothing. Or, more accurately, they'd done nothing when they hadn't backfired. He'd set a goddamn tree on fire like it was a fucking matchstick. He hadn't told his friends, and if the universe was willing, they'd never find out. His pride wasn't likely to survive admitting his best attempt at healing had gone up in literal smoke because his magic kept rampaging through him, craving the tempting well of energy standing so close, but not nearly close enough.

He really needed to get his shit together.

"Are you positive it's a 'what' and not a 'who'?" Victor asked.

"No. But unless I find a magical signature or residue, I have to go off what's there, and what's there doesn't·feel like magic."

"Okay. Do what you have to."

They went around to the back of the house. Elijah stopped at the tree line and took his bag off his shoulder.

Victor turned toward him. "Here?"

Elijah nodded.

"Do you think it extends this far?"

"Hopefully not, but it seems logical to start here."

The preparations were quick, only a circle drawn with salt and a candle inside. He knelt and pressed his palms to the earth, his eyes closing as he gathered his magic, sending up a prayer to any power listening that it'd play nice. This was too important for it not to. It had to behave.

A warm hand came to rest on his neck, and he jumped, startled out of the beginning of his trance. His magic jumped as well, and the hand was jerked away.

Elijah glanced up at Victor. Part of him wanted to check if anyone else was around, but they were alone, and he'd recognize that energy anywhere.

"Sorry," Victor said, then swallowed audibly. "I shouldn't have done that."

Elijah studied him. Were the tips of his ears turning red? "Actually, it might help. If you don't mind."

Victor made a noise of acknowledgment, his jaw clenched, but he was looking at the forest, not Elijah.

Well, Victor initiating voluntary physical contact had been unexpected. Elijah focused on the candle, his breath held as he waited to see if he'd do it again.

The touch was more tentative this time, fingers sliding over his neck, threatening to elicit a shiver, before Victor's palm settled once more. His hand was firm, steadying Elijah, but he concentrated on his magic and tried not to think about that weight against his skin. He couldn't afford that distraction. Not now, not ever.

His energy was a drug, calling to Elijah with every stroke of Victor's thumb along the side of his neck. Elijah shuddered under the caress, not sure when Victor's fingers had started moving but also not wanting him to stop. He didn't pull away, didn't even consider it.

Magic pooled in the pit of his stomach, and he prepared

for the surge he knew was coming. When it swept through him, he used it.

A pulse shot out of him, through the earth, engulfing the nearby trees, rushing through the forest. The candle flickered, green and gold, as magic flooded the land. He poured more of himself into the spell, pushing it as hard as he dared, stretching it across the territory, trusting the strength of Victor's energy to carry it through.

He was uncertain of what to expect. Possibly some backlash or resistance as the magic met whatever was in the forest. But then he sensed it. Something that didn't belong. Something unclean. His spell struck it in a sharp burst that reverberated, strange and uncomfortable, soiled and slick, a blow to the chest that constricted his lungs.

It wasn't so much a presence amongst the flora but a blight. A tentacled disease full of thorny hooks and glistening teeth that pierced the land.

Elijah marked it with his magic, and the wards flared, flashing in the sky, reacting to the rot, finally recognizing it as a threat.

The forest was fighting, but it was losing. He felt the places death was taking over, felt how deep the decay had seeped into the earth. At its worst, deeper than most roots grew.

He shuddered for an entirely different reason, repulsed by the slimy sensation against his magic. Victor's grip on his neck tightened, a lifeline keeping him grounded.

When he had the shape of it in his mind, he opened his eyes and pulled his hands away from the earth. The candle extinguished as the spell ebbed out of existence.

"What is it?" Victor asked.

"No idea..." Elijah trailed off, trying to determine what

would produce that reaction. "It isn't magic, but it's not natural either."

"Supernatural but not magic?"

Elijah shrugged. The movement must have made Victor realize his hand was still on Elijah's neck because he snatched it away, leaving cold skin behind.

"Is it sentient?"

Frowning, Elijah considered it, then shook his head. "It felt more like a disease. A virus, maybe?" He looked up at Victor. "It's spreading, but there doesn't seem to be a consciousness to it."

"Can you get rid of it?"

"I sure as hell am going to try."

Elijah's magic churned, mixing with the energy that had bled into his system.

If he'd had any doubt about what was causing his magic to be erratic, that simple contact had laid it to rest. When Victor was touching him, when he was acting as an anchor, he amplified Elijah's magic. When he wasn't, his energy remained, wild and chaotic, volatile and impossible to control.

Elijah shied away from giving that connection the label his friends might. Because that didn't make sense; it wasn't possible.

But acknowledging there was *something* between them didn't mean he knew what, and he certainly didn't have the mental capacity to deal with that on top of everything else. His priority had to be fixing what was wrong with Victor's territory, and then he'd sort out his magic.

He had spells to try, spells that didn't require shifter energy and wouldn't warrant the graze of fingers on his skin. Elijah was hesitant to spend an entire day finding excuses to justify Victor's hands on him. He quailed to think of the state that would leave his magic. Basic charms would blow up in his face for the rest of his life after that.

Given the unpredictability of his magic around Victor, he didn't love his chances of doing anything with him in close proximity. But if Victor wasn't there, he might get them to work.

He walked to his car and grabbed the box of supplies out of his trunk, resting it on his hip before turning to Victor.

"I'd rather you didn't come with me for this."

Victor's brow furrowed. "Why?"

Elijah let out a sigh. He didn't want to tell Victor the truth—that his energy drew Elijah in and made him unstable. That would not go over well. So he obfuscated, latching onto the first idea that sounded remotely plausible. "If this is feeding off your land, it could be strengthened by your energy. I'd like to try a few things without you there in case that helps." It might be an issue, but that wasn't the real reason.

Victor hesitated, then said, "I'll send one of my betas with you."

"I can do it by myself."

"No one goes into the forest alone until this is taken care of. I've told my pack that, and it applies to you as well."

There was no point in asking if that applied to Victor; Elijah knew the answer.

He wasn't surprised when he discovered who'd be babysitting him. The looming threat of a multi-hour deluge of innuendos seemed a fitting punishment for lying.

Victor shot a warning glare at Kade before they headed out, but it only made the quirk to Kade's lips more impish as he took Elijah's box from him.

Kade kept his comments to himself until they were out of Victor's earshot, but not much longer than that.

"You left so quickly the other night at the bar. If you'd stuck around, I would have gotten you something hard too."

Elijah snorted. "Generous of you."

"It's one of the many services I offer. Beta, forest guide, wingman, whatever you desire."

"Victor doesn't seem like he'd give your services a glowing recommendation."

"There's no pleasing some people. But that doesn't mean I can't please you." He winked at Elijah.

"It's sweet you think you could." Years of friendship with Aran made it easy to counter incessant, meaningless flirting.

"There's only one thing stopping me."

"The fact that I'm completely uninterested?"

"Two things. Two things stopping me."

Elijah huffed out a laugh. "What's the other?"

Kade muttered something about stubborn idiots that Elijah didn't catch. But before he could ask Kade to repeat himself, a pocket of decay opened up before them, freezing them in place.

"I swear it gets worse every time I see it." Kade scanned the trees, his nostrils flaring, suddenly serious.

Elijah grimaced. "Let's see if I can fix that."

With a steadying breath through his mouth, he stepped up to a tree. If he allowed the stench to invade his senses, it'd overwhelm his ability to focus.

He'd seen the rotting wood and felt the sickness down to the roots, but this was so much worse. Healing the tree required connecting to it, and that meant connecting to the decay itself.

But this tree, the forest, would not die. Not if he had any say in the matter.

He placed a hand against the bark, reaching out to the rot within, delving into the ground, trying to get to the root tips far below.

Then he began.

The spell built, twisting into the roots beneath. It sank into that rotting mass, deep into the earth, as Elijah's magic flowed out, a river to the sea.

New life budded and blossomed, subtle at first, then stronger and more vibrant as it spread through the ground, up the tree, into the branches and leaves. It overtook the rot, smothering it, driving it out, using death to feed growth.

After half a dozen false starts and failed attempts, it was working.

Beside him, Kade gasped, but Elijah resisted the urge to visually confirm what he was sensing. Instead, he gathered more magic. He braided it through the tree, twining it around the roots and branches, wrapping it from the bottom to the top until every inch was covered and sweat trickled down his temple.

Then he released his magic and blinked his eyes open, smiling when he saw the results.

The rot was gone, and the branches were dotted with new leaves. Vibrant, green, healthy.

He turned to Kade. "Fucking finally."

Kade's eyebrows were raised in disbelief, and he clapped a few times. "What did you just do?"

Relief ran through Elijah. "Since I suck at healing, that used the destruction of the rot to feed the life of the tree. A friend suggested it."

It'd be impossible to restore them all this way; there were too many of them, and it took too much magic, but he could save a few, then ask Liam to modify the spell for larger areas. He was about to say that when Kade inhaled deeply, a frown marring his expression as he scrutinized the tree.

Elijah's heart dropped into his stomach when he looked. The new leaves were vibrant and green no more. They shriveled and died. Decay sprouted on the bark, and Elijah took a step back, dismayed.

"What the hell?" Kade asked.

"Maybe I didn't put enough magic into it. I thought I'd gotten it all, but there must have been some left. Or it might need pack energy to tie it to the land?" He rubbed his face, then turned toward Kade. "Can I try using yours?"

Kade glanced at him. "I don't mind, but wouldn't you rather have me go get Victor?" His tone was teasing, but the crease of his brow betrayed his concern.

"You should be fine." If it worked, he could try with Victor later.

A hint of nerves showed through Kade's bravado. "What do you need me to do?"

Individual energy signatures within a pack were similar more often than not. They helped mark shifters as members of a certain pack. Given how compatible he and Victor were, Kade's energy should be easy to use.

Elijah reached out, palm up. "Grab my hand. That should be enough."

"And if it isn't?"

The grin Elijah gave him was more than a little wicked; he enjoyed seeing Kade not quite as cocky for once. "Then I get out my knife, and we do it the hard way."

Kade took his hand. "Remind me not to get on your bad side."

Elijah waited for the flow of energy.

But it didn't come.

Kade's energy buzzed against his awareness, amped up by his position in the pack, but it was elusive. It hovered mere inches from Elijah's grasping fingers, on the other side of glass.

Elijah let his magic gather and then wrapped it around Kade. His energy shimmered, but Elijah couldn't connect with it. He felt it, but his magic wasn't interested.

He exhaled and centered himself. The hard way of doing this held no appeal. Kade might heal instantly from a cut, but it'd take longer for Elijah to do the same. Victor's energy had spoiled him. That easy, automatic connection wasn't the norm.

Huffing in frustration, he dropped Kade's hand and took out his knife.

"I thought you were kidding about that," Kade said.

"Sadly, no." Elijah pricked his thumb, then smeared the blood on the inside of Kade's wrist. "On the plus side, you'll get to tell people you've had my bodily fluids all over you."

Kade laughed, relaxing some. "That sounds like a fun way to get my ass kicked. Do I get to cover you in mine?"

"No. But I'm assuming it won't be the first time you'll be covered in your own."

"You know me so well. You sure about being completely uninterested?"

"Positive."

Kade took the knife and copied Elijah's action. Elijah wrapped his hand around Kade's wrist. Their blood prickled hot beneath his palm, but no energy flowed into him.

He felt Kade, felt his presence, his energy, his connections to his pack, the land, his alpha. Not letting himself think it over too much, he reached for that last connection, *through* that connection, and tugged.

Kade sucked in a breath as his energy flowed into Elijah. Scarcely a dribble but enough to use.

Elijah laid his other hand on the trunk, channeling magic and energy into it, redoing the spell. The rot receded, giving way to new life. When he thought he was done, he bore down harder, pouring more into the tree, making damn sure he'd exterminated every speck of decay.

Once he was finished, he dropped his arms to his sides. The forest was quiet except for his labored breathing.

Time stretched out, one second ticking after another, a minute, two... and when Elijah's hopes were at their highest, splotches of mold oozed into existence on the bark.

He cursed and heard Kade do the same.

So much for that idea.

So much for all his ideas.

He was dead tired and depleted; he'd tried everything he'd been prepared to do that day and was exactly where he'd started. Now with more ways to fail.

He groaned.

"Unless you've got more witchery to try, let's get out of here. I could use a drink," Kade said.

"You want something hard?"

Kade chuckled. "If you're offering."

"I'm not."

"Care to rethink that? Asking for a friend."

Some of the tension in Elijah's shoulders bled out at Kade's ridiculousness. Today was a bust; that didn't mean tomorrow had to be. There were a few enchantments he hadn't tried. One might work.

As they picked their way through the forest, Kade kept up a steady stream of conversation. For all his rakishness, he was easy to talk to between the offhanded flirting. Plus, he insisted on carrying Elijah's box, which was downright gentlemanly of him.

"Did Victor tell you what he was like as a kid?"

Elijah scoffed. "You say that like Victor and I actually talk."

"You should."

"Because we have so much in common?"

"You'd be surprised."

"Okay, surprise me."

"Victor loves magic."

Elijah stumbled as a burst of laughter caught him off guard. He glanced at Kade, who didn't bother concealing his amusement. "I said surprise me, not lie to me."

"It's not a lie."

"And the other one's got bells on."

"I'm serious. When he was a kid, he thought it was the coolest thing ever. He was absolutely fascinated by it. Our grandma was a mage. Our pack has a long history of alphas and other members being bonded to mages. True bonds, not transactional arrangements."

That did surprise Elijah. He'd sensed a true bond in the wards but had assumed it was one pair, generations ago. That type of connection was beyond rare. But in this pack, apparently not.

"He used to follow our grandma everywhere," Kade continued. "Always wanted to help her. Preparing herbs, drawing circles, whatever she'd let him do. Anytime another mage visited, he'd ask them a couple hundred questions. I swear he even tried to do spells of his own."

That mental picture contained a level of adorableness Elijah was not prepared to handle. A miniature Victor, scowl firmly in place, attempting magic.

"Grandma always said he'd be the next to bond with a mage, that the line of mages wouldn't end with her. She told me once, after Victor found his, I—" Kade cut himself off, shaking his head. "We've assumed that was true since he was five. She was clear it would be Victor, not his father."

"She had foresight?" It was rare but not unheard of. None of his friends had it.

Kade ducked under a branch that hung low across the path. "A little. More vague premonitions than visions, from what I understood. But I think she was getting hints that something bad would happen to Victor's father if he got involved with a mage."

Elijah grimaced.

"He told you about that, then?"

"I assume there's more to it, but yeah, he told me the basics."

"The pack doesn't even know the specifics."

Elijah cocked an eyebrow at him. From what he gathered, it wasn't easy to keep secrets in a shifter pack.

"Oh, don't get me wrong, they've pieced most of it together. But besides Victor, only Will and Rick were privy to it all. They were his father's betas. I've heard some of it from them, but at the time, I wasn't a beta. I knew what everyone else knew. Something was going on between Victor's father and the mage who owned the shop before you. We felt him weakening, and then we felt Victor become alpha.

"None of us realized how bad it had gotten though. That the mage was keeping Victor's father almost entirely drained, that he was taking pack money. Will and Rick said that when the pack bonds started deteriorating, the three of them decided to remove Victor's father before it got worse. I think Victor was putting a lot of his energy into our bonds, trying to keep them stable so the pack wouldn't notice, but eventually, that wasn't enough. It's not the same when a beta does it."

"Doesn't tradition demand the pack witness any challenge to the alpha? I thought that's how that worked."

"Normally it is. But Victor's father was weak, and Victor was unwilling to fight him in front of the pack. So they took him aside and gave him an ultimatum. Victor won't talk about it, and Will and Rick are tight-lipped on the details, but they must have fought. Even if his father had been at full strength, my money would have been on Victor. As a beta, he was absurdly strong, and fuck, he can fight. His father wouldn't have been a match for him physically, not as drained as he was, but I also don't think he would have given up control without being near death."

Elijah swallowed around the queasy lump in his throat, unable to imagine what it'd been like for Victor to have to beat his own father within an inch of his life in order to save his pack.

"They told us leadership had been transferred to Victor and that his father was going to live with a pack of distant relatives. It was implied that he was still grieving his wife and needed time away from a place that held so many memories. That wasn't a lie. We're pretty sure he became obsessed with getting a new pack mage because of her death. Like if we'd had a mage, they would have saved her."

"What did she die from?" Shifter life spans weren't

particularly different from human ones, but even with that, Victor's mother must have died young.

"Honestly? We never figured it out. We think she might have been poisoned by hunters but have zero proof of that. Alpha Lucas lost his mate around the same time, and that's not something we could write off as coincidental. But given how strong our three packs are and how solid our alliance is, hunters are usually smart enough not to fuck with us. There weren't any more mysterious deaths after those two." He shrugged, uncomfortable. "Anyway, Will took Victor's father to another pack, and Victor took over. He kept Will and Rick as his betas and appointed me as his second."

Elijah let the subject drop, though he wanted to know if there were hunters in the area. He'd have to keep that in mind while figuring out what was happening to Victor's territory. But for the time being, he followed where Kade was steering the conversation. "That's strange, right?"

"Me being a beta and trusted enough to be second-in-command?"

"Also that. But I meant keeping the same betas."

"He did what was best for the pack. Keeping them as betas offered stability. But yeah, typically a new alpha would want betas of their own choosing, ones that will serve them well."

"I.e. be respectful. Which I take it you guys are not."

"We tease because we love."

"And because it's fun."

"That too."

The banter with Kade distracted Elijah from thoughts of what Victor had gone through, how he'd been keeping that bottled up inside himself. "The pack doesn't mind they were lied to about the transfer?"

"From what I can tell? They respect that Victor let his

father save face. Victor did it to protect the pack; nothing's more important than that. The change of ownership at the shop was confirmation enough the mage was involved. They didn't need anyone to spell it out for them."

"I'm surprised at how welcoming you all have been to me after that."

"Like I said, we have a history of mages in our pack. We can distinguish between one corrupt asshole and mages in general. Immoral mages are rare. I know that, the pack knows that, even Victor knows it. You may smell weird, but generally, you're good people."

"Thanks. I think."

"You're not bad though. For a mage. Do you know what you smell like?"

"Magic?"

"Beneath that."

"More magic?"

"Earth and snow."

Elijah wondered if the earth scent was connected to his affinity for earth-based magic, but Kade was already jumping to a new topic.

"How much did you learn about shifters during your apprenticeship?"

Elijah wasn't sure where he was going with this. "Not much. General overviews of pack hierarchies, politics, and traditions. The primary focus was on how to use your energy to amplify magic."

"So you didn't learn how we bond?"

"Can't say that was part of the curriculum. But I suppose there's always MateHub if I get really curious."

Kade snorted. "*Bond*, not fuck."

"Don't they go hand in hand?"

"Sometimes, but those aren't the body parts I'd pick."

It was Elijah's turn to snort. He'd left himself open for that one. "Okay, fine. I'm going to regret asking this, but how do you bond?"

"When two shifters love each other very much—"

"I am perfectly capable of throwing a fireball at your head." As long as he didn't aim to hit, there should be sufficient wiggle room in the oath for that.

"You're no fun, so I'll skip to my main point, which is that we don't have destined mates we recognize the moment we meet. It's not like we see someone and the heavens part, angels sing, and all that. But we do have people we're more compatible with, people who we fit with better than anyone else."

This was not a conversation Elijah ever would have predicted, but he was too curious to interrupt.

"Shifters who are highly compatible have scents that complement each other. There's this way they combine, something about them, that's perfect. Not that either scent is incomplete or lacking without the other. But together, they're better, fuller, almost sublime."

That was lovely. Elijah hadn't known. "So you can smell when two people are compatible?"

Kade nodded. "Sometimes, if a shifter's head is so far up their own ass their nose isn't functioning properly, the people closest to them will notice it before they do."

Elijah shot him a look. "Why are you telling me this?"

"Because after a whole day with me, I figured you'd be eager to give shifters a try." Kade winked at him again.

"You offering?"

Kade thoroughly checked him out, then said, "Nah. You're hot and all but don't smell right for me."

"Small blessings." They walked on in silence before Elijah spoke again. "You're wrong though."

"About you being hot?"

"Obviously I'm hot. But you're wrong about Victor. You said he loves magic. He *loved* magic. After that, there's no way he still does."

"Magic isn't the problem."

"Then what is?"

"Victor." Elijah opened his mouth to protest, but Kade continued. "It's not magic; it's that he doesn't trust himself around magic. He remembers being obsessed with it; he saw what happened when his father became consumed by it. And now he's afraid history is going to repeat itself, that he's weak and will destroy the pack for magic."

"That's bullshit. I've felt your pack bonds. They're strong. You don't get that kind of strength in a pack without a good leader. Without someone powerful and protective." There was no doubt in Elijah's mind that Victor would give his life for his pack. He'd sacrifice everything he had for them.

"Agreed. I just haven't figured out a way to convince Victor of that yet."

They fell into silence again as they neared the house.

"Do you know what Victor smells like?" Kade asked so softly Elijah almost didn't hear him.

"Pine," he said automatically, certain he was correct. "Pine and another scent." A scent he didn't have a name for.

"Pine, yes, and the night on a full moon."

A flash of the forest on a wintry night with the full moon shining flickered through Elijah's mind, but then they came around a curve in the path, and Elijah saw slivers of the house through the trees.

"And do you know what I smell like?" Kade's tone was more boisterous again as he returned to his incorrigible self.

"Frat houses and the back rooms of seedy gay bars?"

Kade clutched at his chest. "You wound me. That second note is nothing but the back rooms at the *finest* gay clubs."

"How could I have made such a foolish mistake? You're all discreet gentlemen's establishments and beer bongs."

"You bet your damn ass that's right."

Elijah smiled despite himself, and the memory of Victor and Kade approaching him in the bar hit him.

"Summer," he said. "I don't know what it is, but somehow, you smell like summer."

Kade tilted his head, an eyebrow raised, but then he grinned. "And that's why we can tragically never be together, no matter how much you yearn for me. Diametrically opposed seasons. I'm way too hot for your wintry ass to handle."

Elijah snorted again. "Thank god for that."

He stepped past the last few trees into the clearing surrounding the house, his mind brimming with everything he'd just learned.

He made his excuses before Kade could invite him in, not ready to face the shifters waiting inside. Particularly not the one watching them through a window. Instead, he escaped to his car and updated his friends.

ELIJAH

Nothing worked. That phoenix spell nearly did, but the rot overtook it.

I'll try the rest tomorrow.

LIAM

How's your magic holding up while working with your shifter?

ELIJAH

He's not my shifter.

And I'm not working with him. I had his second with me today.

ARAN

And how did this new shifter's energy treat you?

ELIJAH

It didn't. I barely got any out of him.

LIAM

What do you mean?

You couldn't connect with him?

ELIJAH

Basically. Something was blocking me.

There was a pause while they processed that. Elijah braced himself for the comments he was about to receive. To his surprise, Miles was the first to respond with a flurry of messages.

MILES

Aran, if you say it's because Elijah already has one metaphorical shifter dick in him

Or some metaphorical shifter knot keeping him stretched open and full, so he can't fit another

Or that Elijah is being metaphorically shifter cockblocked

So help me, I will drive the thirty-fucking-six hours necessary to punch you.

Elijah stared at the screen, eyes wide.

ARAN

Clearly I don't have to say that since you've said it for me.

The string of expletives Miles replied with was truly impressive. It was official. Aran had corrupted their sweetest friend. If they'd been on a video call, Miles would be bright red.

He'd been such a gentle, caring soul when they'd met him. This golden ray of sunshine determined to heal everything wrong with the world. And he still was, but after being friends with them for years, his innocence appeared to have been obliterated. Not that it'd had much chance of surviving Aran.

ELIJAH

Alright, if any of you have any ideas that are not related to metaphorical shifter anatomy, you know where to find me.

But until then, I'm fucking exhausted. I'm heading to the shop to shower off this filth then crash for a few hours.

LIAM

Get some rest. We'll keep researching.

Elijah closed the app and started his car. He needed sleep so he could wake up too early even for him and do this again tomorrow.

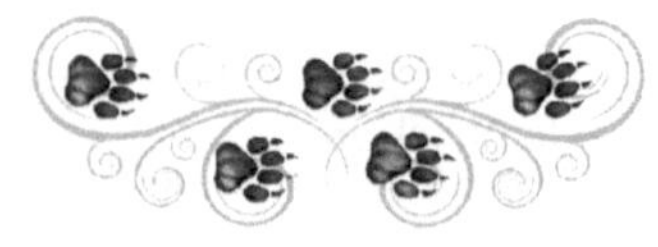

THIRTEEN

Victor paced from the kitchen to the living room and back, trying to shake off his excess energy.

Something was happening in the forest. An hour ago, he'd felt a tug of some kind, a pull under his sternum. It'd come through Kade but had been all Elijah. Kade's energy had flowed through Victor, though he didn't understand how or why.

It'd taken every scrap of his willpower not to hunt them down. For the sole reason of making sure they were fine and nothing more.

Being anxious for them to return was normal; the urge to go out there and find them was understandable. They'd been gone for hours, and he needed to know what was happening. To his land. He wanted information, wanted this over so he could get Elijah away from his pack.

But if Elijah thought Victor's energy might make things worse, he wouldn't interfere. For now. Whatever it took to fix this.

It had nothing to do with Kade and Elijah being alone. Kade was like a brother to him. He trusted him completely.

And if he couldn't go himself, Kade, as his second-in-command, was the most logical replacement.

A relentlessly flirty, obnoxiously charming replacement.

That pull had to have been Elijah using Kade's energy. Had Kade gotten lost in the intense torrent of magic sweeping through him?

It wasn't like Victor's stomach dropped at the thought of Elijah doing that with Kade. That'd be ridiculous. It was just that he knew how Kade got. If he experienced that, it'd add an extra layer to his teasing. There'd be a month of never-ending magic-as-sex innuendos. The pack shouldn't have to endure that, not with everything else they were facing.

When they finally emerged from the trees, Victor was in the kitchen. He'd been getting a glass of water, not staring out the window in the direction they'd departed.

Elijah was side-eyeing Kade as they approached the house. He shook his head, but his expression was amused and more open than any he'd given Victor. It wasn't hard to imagine the things Kade might say to get that reaction.

They stopped far enough away that Victor couldn't make out their conversation, only its faint rhythm. Elijah's smile fell as he glanced into the forest, every line of him tired and shaken, but then his gaze hardened, determination overtaking despair. They exchanged a few more words before Elijah turned to leave. His eyes caught Victor's through the window, and he froze, then gave a brief nod of acknowledgment before walking toward the front of the house.

Kade came in through the back door, bringing with him the scent of magic, decay, and a hint of blood. Victor fixated on the red smeared across the inside of Kade's wrist as he went to the sink to wash it off.

"No luck?" Victor asked, his arms folded across his chest. He tried to keep his tone neutral, tried to pretend he hadn't watched them through the window, but it sounded fake even to his own ears.

"Nothing worked." Kade dried his hands, but the iron tang of blood remained. "He's going to his place to do more research and consult with his friends. They have a few more ideas, but he needs other supplies. He'll be back tomorrow morning."

Victor nodded, the movement short and tight.

Kade scrubbed a hand over his jaw, then grinned, unapologetically wolfish. "You sure you don't want him?"

"Of course I don't." The answer was too rushed and forceful to sound like the truth.

"If that's the case, do you mind if I have a go?"

"Leave him alone, Kade." There was more than a little growl in Victor's voice.

Kade stalked toward him, clasped his shoulder, and leaned in. Snow and earth invaded Victor's senses. "I'll leave him alone if you pull your head out of your ass."

"What's that supposed to mean?"

"You know damn well what it means," Kade said as he left the kitchen.

"When this is over," Victor called after him, "I'm getting new betas."

Kade laughed. "No, you won't."

And the annoying thing was, Kade was right.

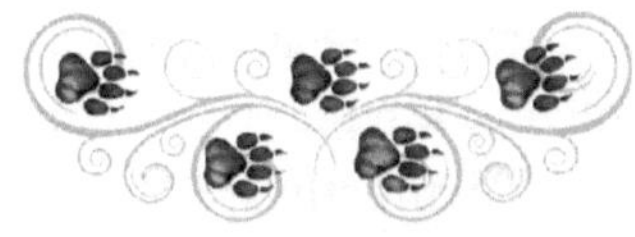

The next day was much the same. Elijah disappeared with Kade for multiple hours while Victor had to restrain himself from going after them. He told himself repeatedly it was for the best that Elijah was keeping him at arm's length. Especially after that bizarre pull came through Kade twice more and his wolf insisted they should be out there instead.

The afternoon was warm for mid-September, and the sun glittered off the small creek that meandered past the house. The three youngest pack children were playing outside, scampering noisily about. They weren't allowed in the forest anymore, not without an adult, but they didn't care as long as they had room to run.

Victor had been perched on the stone wall by the pond, watching them for the last thirty minutes, letting their delighted shrieks remind him there was life in the middle of this decaying forest. They were what needed protecting.

A gust of wind blew by, carrying sharp ozone and the hiss of magic. The scent prickled across his skin, but he couldn't pinpoint its origin beyond that it had come from Elijah somewhere out amongst the trees.

It was midafternoon when they returned. Fatigue was etched onto Elijah's features, and the dark circles under his eyes evidenced a string of sleepless nights. Victor smothered the desire to go to him and do something other than get an update on the rot. Any impulse to comfort Elijah was a natural instinct to reassure and protect someone in distress on his land.

But before Victor did anything ill-advised, Oliver spotted Elijah and hurtled toward him, demanding to know if he could fly. Cami and Emelie weren't far behind, forming a mini-stampede aimed directly at Elijah.

He grinned, some of the exhaustion hanging around him lifting. "Sorry, no flying here."

"If you can't fly, what can you do?" Emelie asked. She and Oliver threw questions at Elijah faster than he could answer.

"Can you stop time?"

"Or make zombies?"

"Or turn people into frogs?"

Elijah laughed, good-natured and genuine. The sound settled in Victor's chest. "You'll be able to turn into wolves in a few years. Surely turning someone into a frog can't be that impressive."

"Then can you make tornadoes?"

"Or summon a tiger?"

"Or freeze things with your mind?"

"Or make them explode with your eyes?"

There was a chagrined cast to Elijah's chuckle over that last one. He looked bewildered by the onslaught of their questions, but his shoulders had lost their taut line, more of his stress falling away.

"Is there anything you *can* do?" Oliver asked, skeptical after so many negative responses.

"How about this?" Elijah crouched and pressed his palm to the earth. A second later, the dirt under Oliver pushed up, creating a platform that lifted him a foot off the ground.

Oliver's face lit up in surprise, and he whooped. He jumped off the pedestal. "Do it again!"

"What about this instead?"

Elijah held out his hand, and a purple flame flashed to life, hovering above it, earning him appreciative *oohs*. Tiny sparks broke free, flitting around the yard, and the kids spun, attempting to watch them all at once.

"You can try to catch them. They won't burn you."

That was the only encouragement necessary for them to chase the magical fireflies.

The corner of Victor's mouth twitched as he watched Elijah run through a couple more spells, little things, not much more than party tricks, but the kids loved every second.

Victor had no defense against this kind of scene.

Kade took a seat beside him, and Victor barely refrained from jumping. He needed to be more vigilant; he hadn't noticed Kade walking over. Though given how Elijah's magic clung to him, Victor should have. The combination of winter and summer wasn't a good one.

When Victor looked at him, Kade tilted his head toward Elijah, a self-satisfied smirk twisting his lips.

Victor scowled but couldn't deny it. Elijah fit into his pack better than he had any right to, but that changed nothing. He was saved from responding by Katrina calling the kids inside to help with dinner.

"But Mama," Oliver yelled, "Elijah's doing magic!"

"Then invite him for dinner and ask him nicely to do more afterwards."

A wild excitement swept through the children, their expressions glinting with anticipation as they turned toward Elijah.

Kade snorted. "Uh-oh. There's no escaping now." He might have been talking about Elijah, but it felt a whole hell of a lot like he meant Victor.

"You're staying for dinner?" Oliver asked.

"Oliver," Cami hissed. "You have to ask *nicely*."

"Fine. You're staying for dinner, right?"

Cami slapped a hand to her face. "Not like that! 'Would you please join us for dinner?'"

He huffed before parroting her. "Would you please join us for dinner?"

Elijah's eyes flicked over, meeting Victor's. Victor assented with a reluctant nod solely to prevent any tantrums it'd cause if he said no.

Elijah turned back to the kids. "I'd love to."

They cheered and ran inside, Oliver shouting at Elijah, "Mama makes the best food ever!"

"Well," Kade said, strolling toward the house, "I better warn Katrina to bring her A game."

Elijah hesitated before wandering over, taking Kade's abandoned seat.

"How'd it go?" Victor guessed the answer and regretted the question when it made the line of Elijah's shoulders tense again.

Elijah grimaced. "It didn't go. Nothing's working."

"Anything I can do?"

Elijah sighed. "Actually, yeah. I have a few spells to try tomorrow that will require you to be there. I'd like to use your energy."

"Kade's won't work?"

"No. I can't—" He cut himself off, then started again. "It has to be yours."

The idea that Kade wasn't enough, that Victor was who Elijah needed, shouldn't graze down his spine and curl in his stomach. It was absurd; he knew that, but the instinct to be the one to protect his pack drove him. "Just tell me if you need anything else."

Elijah nodded, and silence overtook them. Victor couldn't decide if it was awkward or companionable, but he also had no intention of breaking it. So he sat there, the breeze bringing constant hits of Elijah's scent, until Oliver came racing out to announce food would be ready soon and that his mom said they had to wash their hands before they ate, no excuses. That second part had been aimed at Oliver, not them, but they assured him they would.

As Victor entered the house, calm rolled over him. Maybe it was because his mind had been so focused on the decay over the last few days, but he savored being with his pack more than usual. The smell of dinner wafted through the air, the kids were laughing, and a murmur of voices floated from the living room where the adults were sitting. Nothing was amiss in here.

Will passed them, making his way toward the kitchen to help bring food to the table. As he did, his hand came up and squeezed Elijah's shoulder. It was such a familiar move. Humans might mistake it for a friendly greeting, but it was more than that. It was an affirmation of pack, how members greeted each other.

Elijah blinked, his surprise evident. Victor doubted many shifters touched him, let alone in such a welcoming way.

The perfection of it struck Victor then. How easily Elijah could be there more often, more permanently. He wasn't even surprised when the chair on his right was offered to Elijah again after he returned from washing up, his skin scrubbed clean of any trace of decay, making his natural scent that much more noticeable, that much more distracting.

What he didn't expect was the all-out brawl that took place over the seat on Elijah's other side. There was a mad scramble between Oliver and Emelie to get into the chair first. Elijah leaned away from the fray, his expression mildly concerned.

"I guess you aren't the coolest anymore," Kade said as he slid into his regular place on Victor's left.

Victor cleared his throat. When that failed to get their attention, he cleared it louder. Both children froze, heads turning haltingly toward him.

Other than Kade sitting beside him, he'd never bothered much with hierarchy in eating arrangements. But that didn't mean poor manners should be on display when they had a guest.

"Leave that chair for your mother, Oliver."

There was grumbling, but they took the next two available seats, and Katrina sat next to Elijah, grinning. "I promise I won't bombard you with so many questions you aren't able to eat."

"Thanks. But maybe don't try to feed me quite as much as last time?"

"That, I make no promises about."

As they ate, conversation wound its way around the table, everyone going out of their way to include Elijah.

Kade leaned in and said, under his breath, "You're dangerously close to smiling right now. It's pretty disgusting. I can't even look at you."

Victor shoved him, attracting Elijah's notice. He fixed them with a curious stare.

"I was telling Victor he should bring you up to the attic after dinner," Kade announced, more than loud enough for everyone at the table to hear, hushing the room.

Victor gave him a flat glower, which Kade met with unrepentant smugness.

The attention of every pack member was on them now. Amusement poured off the adults while the kids looked around, aware they were missing something.

"The attic?" Elijah asked, understandably confused.

Victor shook his head. "It's nothing."

Halfway down the table, Rick spoke. "You should show him. There might be something useful up there."

The piercing interest in Elijah's eyes became more pronounced.

Victor shrugged, uncomfortable, but Rick wasn't wrong, and his pack's safety trumped Victor's unease over letting Elijah up there.

"Fine. You can show him."

"No. You need to," Rick said with all the deference of Kade at his cockiest.

Victor raised an eyebrow at him. His betas gave him shit, but they never contradicted him this directly, especially not in front of outsiders.

Rick held his gaze, challenge clear. Tension built, thick and heavy between them, Victor against his entire pack.

Elijah shifted in his seat. "It's okay. You don't have to show me."

Victor took the opportunity to break his stare-off with Rick. He wasn't caving; he was replying to Elijah. "There are things you might be able to use."

Perplexed, Elijah waited for someone to explain further, but Victor didn't offer more information, and the pack seemed content to keep it a surprise.

The rest of the meal was spent obsessing over how Elijah would react and whether this was the best decision.

Dinner ended both too slowly and too quickly. Victor found himself leading Elijah upstairs and through the hall, then up another narrow flight tucked into the back of the house.

He sensed the pack tracking them, not physically following, though they wanted to. Their interest was palpable, trailing after Victor and Elijah as they climbed the stairs.

Victor pushed on the attic door. Its hinges creaked, but it swung open smoothly. It'd been months since anyone had been up there.

Inside was dark, but he saw the outlines of the roof's steep slope, low enough in the corners he'd have to duck his head. Thick, wooden beams stretched across the length of it, evenly spaced, and a single bare bulb hung from the ceiling. He walked to it and pulled the string.

The sudden light made Elijah blink, but the moment he realized what Victor was showing him, his curiosity and confusion transformed into astonishment. He was held captivated and spellbound. The rise and fall of his chest was quick and shallow.

"What is this?" His voice was hushed, like if he spoke too loud, he'd disturb the sacred tranquility blanketing the space.

He stepped deeper inside, his movements slow and soft. His eyes were wide and full of wonder as he took in the shelves overflowing with books, crystals, and rows of jars. A grandfather clock ticked solemnly in the corner, and the air was filled with a strange, beautiful electricity and the musty smell of forgotten secrets. He tore his gaze from the clutter of dressers, cabinets, and boxes strewn throughout the attic to look at Victor.

Victor shrugged, uncertain what to make of the jumbled emotions Elijah's presence in that space elicited. It implied things he wasn't ready to admit. "Our pack has had several mages over the years."

Elijah's focus was fully on him now, but it was with intrigue, not surprise. Victor would bet every item in there that Kade had been talking out of turn.

"These were my grandmother's. Hers and all our mages. Stuff that's been handed down through the generations."

"You kept it all?"

"Before she passed, she was pretty insistent on us keeping everything."

Even if she hadn't been, they wouldn't have gotten rid of this much history, glimpses into the past and the life they'd built.

She'd also been insistent that it was for *Victor's* mage, but Elijah didn't need to know that.

"There's so much magic in here," Elijah said. "The wards on this room are stunning to keep it from leaking out."

No one came up there, not with how saturated with magic it was. It might be pack magic, but it was magic all the same.

"I'm honestly surprised that—" Elijah grimaced, not finishing his sentence.

"What?"

"Sorry. It's just that, if that asshole was taking everything from your father..." He trailed off, but Victor filled in the blanks.

"He would have," Victor admitted. "But Rick and Will were a step ahead of him." He wasn't sure how they'd managed it. They hadn't told him beforehand, figuring it'd be easier to ask forgiveness than permission and that Victor would be conflicted about it. They'd loaded it all up and hidden it somewhere off pack territory. Hauled it elsewhere before Victor's father gave it away. He'd never asked where they'd taken it, but his money was on them entrusting it to Grant Lucas. The thought of another alpha in possession of such a large part of their history made Victor squirm. Even as temporary as it had been, even with an alpha as honorable as Grant.

His father had ordered them to return it, but they'd

refused, and with how weakened he'd become, he'd been unable to force them to follow his command. It hadn't reappeared until Victor was firmly cemented as alpha and his father had been exiled.

Victor distracted himself from the softness in Elijah's gaze by gesturing around the room. "So, if there's anything here you think will help with the decay, you can use it."

Elijah turned in a circle, unable to decide where to start.

It was hard not to wonder what the attic looked like through his eyes. It wasn't that dissimilar from the shop, all chaotic mess and a mishmash of magical tools crammed together in a too-small space. To Victor, it smelled of pack, magic, his grandmother, and over a hundred years of history.

Elijah stepped up to a shelf, hesitant as he reached out, his fingers dancing over the spines of the books. He pulled out a tome, his motions subdued and venerating. Those books predated this house, this territory, brought with them when they'd crossed the ocean in hopes of land where they could run free.

"My family doesn't have anything like this," Elijah said, his voice still pitched low. "There were mages in my family for hundreds of years, but everything they had is gone now. My parents wanted no part of it. They don't see the purpose anymore. They think it's better to pretend they belong in the mundane world, that they can't sense the magic around them."

"How did you become a mage then?"

Elijah looked up from the book. "Magic is a part of me. I've felt it since I was a child. I can't *not* feel it, *not* use it. If your parents had pretended to be human, would that make you not a shifter?"

That was impossible. There was no denying the power of the moon over him.

"Luckily, I found Liam, one of my friends. His family had just moved to the town where we lived. The moment we met, I *knew*. Knew he was like me. I recognized the magic in him. His family taught me until I was old enough to do an apprenticeship. My parents hated them, hated that I chose magic over going to a proper university."

"Why?"

Elijah shrugged. "Fewer and fewer people believe in magic. The more technology there is, the less it's needed. Who's going to pay for a telepathy spell when they've got a phone in their pocket? Over half of what healers can do can also be done by modern medicine. Doctors will eventually figure out the rest. Of the jobs that are left for mages, most of them pay shit. Shifter packs are one of the few steady sources of income. They said if I became a mage, I'd end up selling myself to a pack before the year was out. Better magicless than a pack mage, stuck in a backwater town, transactionally bonded to some asshole alpha."

Bonded to an asshole alpha in a backwater town. No, Victor couldn't imagine Elijah being happy with that. "But you have your own shop. They should be proud of you." The workings of the mage council were a mystery to him, but if they trusted Elijah with a shop at his age, that had to be impressive.

"They said I was wasting my money. Once I own a shop in a bigger city, they might care. Liam's family is thrilled though."

At least he had someone to celebrate his successes.

The book engrossed him again, his graceful fingers leafing through the pages before he gently put it back. He ran his hand along the shelf once more before turning away regretfully, and Victor had to stop himself from telling Elijah he could read them, take them, whatever he desired.

Dropping to a crouch in front of a large cedar chest, Elijah flipped its lid open. A tide of magic spilled out, catching Victor's breath as it swept over him. That had been his grandmother's magic. He hadn't felt it that strongly in years. The lump in his throat was hard to swallow around.

Elijah inhaled, steadying himself, his eyes glowing the faintest purple. "I take it this hasn't been opened in a while."

"I guess not." Probably not since she'd passed.

"Thankfully, the ward on it thought I was alright. Not sure what would have happened if it hadn't."

"I would have warned you if I'd known."

"I should have been more careful," Elijah said, but he was distracted, mesmerized by the chest. He leaned over to peer inside, fingers trailing over everything, reverence in his touch.

Victor couldn't help but watch as Elijah went through the contents. There were a handful of pouches, books, and a dozen glass bottles with labels written in a flowing script Victor remembered well.

Elijah pulled out an unlabeled bottle filled with flower petals. Even dried, they were a bright bluish purple. Recognition dawned on his face as he uncorked it and sniffed.

Dread stirred in Victor's gut. He didn't need to get closer to identify it; the soapy fragrance burned his nose from across the attic.

After stoppering the bottle, Elijah placed it back. "Was not expecting to find wolfsbane here. We certainly won't be using that. If you want me to dispose of it, I'll take it off your territory."

That was an offer Victor would have to consider.

The next thing Elijah took out was a battered book, bound in leather, the edges worn and ragged. Victor watched, transfixed, as he unwound the leather ties wrapped around it. He cradled it in his lap as he flipped through it, page by page, savoring it.

Halfway through, he drew a pattern on the dusty floor, and something glimmered outward from that mark, racing along the floorboards and up the walls to the ceiling. Elijah's eyes followed it upward. When it reached the top, he gave an almost noiseless laugh of pure joy and astonishment, then turned toward Victor.

"This has your wards in it. The territory wards, those privacy wards on your room, the ones on this room, on this chest. They're all in here. And so many more. The original spells and rituals, but also notes refining them over generations." His admiration was easy to hear. "I've never seen anything like them, but I think I can do these. Well, most of them." There was heat in his cheeks.

While Elijah lost himself in the pages, Victor lost track of time. If Elijah had been regretful when he'd moved away from the bookshelf, it didn't compare to the way he rebundled the book and returned it to the chest before closing the lid with a nearly inaudible sigh.

But then he was on his feet, going to another shelf, taking in everything, the little trinkets of magic and artifacts of power. Emotions flickered over his face, so different from the deliberately professional shop owner he tried to be. There was unconcealed delight and awe, unguarded amazement and fascination.

Victor leaned against a wall, watching Elijah breathe

life into the attic. The magic surrounding them was changing, shifting, revitalized, new but not foreign.

"I don't know if I can explain it to you," Elijah said. "But the magic in here, in some of these things, it's so old, absolutely incredible. The craft and skill of it, it's gorgeous. A level I can only hope to achieve one day."

None of this truly belonged to Victor, so he pushed aside the pride that praise stirred in him.

Elijah's gaze roamed to the end of the room and back. "I could spend days and not get through all this. At least not as thoroughly as it deserves. That'd take weeks, or months. Or even years. Just that ward book alone..."

The ferocity with which Victor ached to give him that time left a keen longing in his chest he hadn't been prepared for. To let him have this, family and pack, the history it represented.

Elijah wandered to a dresser and peeked inside the top drawer before shutting it, as if resigning himself to not learning what other secrets it held. But his eyes landed on the gilded plateau mirror on top of the dresser. It was dark with age, held up on five scrolled feet. His hands twitched, eager to touch it.

That mirror held more than a few memories from Victor's childhood. He approached Elijah. "Go ahead," he said, voice whisper-quiet.

Elijah rested his fingertips on the beveled edge, and a ripple glided across the glass.

Victor took another step forward.

"What is this?" Elijah asked. "It doesn't feel like it's for scrying."

"It isn't." Victor stopped next to him, placing his own fingers on the edge of the mirror, and Elijah gasped as the gleaming surface rose, showing the pack land in an exact magical hologram.

Victor had loved this as a child, loved the miniature house and all the tiny trees. It'd been over a decade since he'd seen it. There was no real use to it, not like most things in this room, but it was beautiful. It was home.

Elijah leaned in to inspect the scene, their bodies almost pressed together.

Victor's misgivings about showing him the attic were forgotten. There was no question in his mind: Elijah belonged there.

Face flushed, eyes radiant, mischief written in the quirk of his lips, Elijah looked at Victor. "What else have you been hiding?"

Victor's stomach clenched with how much he *wanted*.

"Thank you for letting me see this." Elijah's voice was the softest caress, leaving Victor yearning for more.

He didn't know what to say, so he brushed his fingers against Elijah's shirt, boxing him in against the dresser.

Elijah's breath hitched, but he didn't pull away. This close, it was impossible not to notice how seamlessly he fit there, how enticing he smelled, how under all that magic, his scent sparkled with happiness and increasing arousal.

It shouldn't have been so simple and effortless to lean in, to bury his nose in the crook of Elijah's neck as his hands found Elijah's waist. But it was.

Victor let himself be consumed by the moment. The warmth of Elijah's skin, that tantalizing aroma of rich earth and shimmering snow, intoxicated him with unspoken promises. It curled around him, soothing him with its sweetness, making him want to stay there, breathing Elijah in, until he was full and sated.

Elijah already smelled like pack. How much better

would it be if he were? The idea alone was enough to make Victor's canines ache.

He distracted himself from that line of thought by pulling back so he could take in the contours of Elijah's face, zeroing in on his mouth, his slightly parted lips, then up to the soft purple glow in his irises. As their gazes locked, a jolt coursed through Victor. He wasn't sure what it was—Elijah's magic, his energy, both together—but it was a tangible thing, gusting through the attic, stroking over every inch of him.

Above them, wooden chimes hanging from the rafters shook, the resonant sound out of place in the silence between them.

Elijah exhaled and pressed his eyes shut. When he opened them, they were icy blue, the purple gone. "Is your wolf in control?" The question was whispered and rough-edged.

Victor jerked away, the spell broken, reality hitting him without mercy.

He inhaled sharply, then switched to breathing through his mouth, too overwhelmed by the scents surrounding him. He swallowed hard, his heart leaping into his throat.

"Sorry." He stared over Elijah's shoulder, not sure how to answer his question. "I shouldn't have done that." He'd been saying that too often lately.

"It's fine—"

Victor cut him off before he could continue. "No, it's not." He stood straighter, putting distance between them. His tone was firmer when he said, "It won't happen again."

He didn't let himself think about how the lack of Elijah's heat chilled him, or the way he hungered to press against him, to pick up where they'd left off, to find out if Elijah tasted as good as he smelled.

Elijah straightened his clothes, though they were as immaculate as always, and an awkwardness settled between them that hadn't been there since they'd entered the attic.

Entered hours ago, Victor realized. He resisted the urge to fidget before he spoke. "It's late. You should stay the night."

Elijah glanced up from his cuffs, eyebrows raised, and Victor's ears wanted to burn.

Before Elijah could accuse him of proposing something he wasn't, he clarified. "In a spare bedroom. If you have what you need for tomorrow. It's too late for you to go home, especially if you're planning on getting here early. You shouldn't have to drive an hour and a half between now and dawn."

He hesitated for so long Victor was convinced the answer would be no, but then Elijah nodded. "I have everything."

"I'll show you to a room." Victor led him downstairs. The knowledge that Elijah would be safe under his roof for the night left his feelings in a tangled disarray.

Most of the pack was in bed or gone. Not everyone though. He wasn't surprised to find Kade, his betas, and a few older members in the living room. Their reason for staying up was betrayed by the lull in their conversation as Victor and Elijah reached the bottom of the steps. They might not know what happened in the attic, with its wards and protections, but there was no hiding that something had. They both reeked of lust; no magic was strong enough to cover that scent.

For all their meddling, they stayed silent. Possibly the one and only time his pack had ever had a subtle bone in its collective body.

But after he'd left Elijah in a guest room, that luck didn't hold out.

Kade lounged against the wall outside Victor's room. He opened his mouth to speak.

"Don't," Victor said. "Unless you want your ass kicked, don't say a word."

Kade held up his hands in surrender, but his grin gave him away. "What? I'm here to wish you a good night." There was more innuendo in his words than Victor could deal with.

With a growl, he slammed his door, but not before he heard Kade chuckling. Victor considered shutting him up, but it didn't seem worth the effort. He leaned against the door, fists clenched at his sides, unsure what to do, what to think.

Had his wolf been in control? He hadn't thought so. But then, it wouldn't be the first time it had tried this bullshit. Though it felt so different with Elijah. It felt like something both Victor and his wolf craved.

The ghost of Elijah's body, almost pressing against his, haunted him, as did the scent of him, a memento written on his skin. An additional presence in his house shouldn't change anything, but Victor couldn't dispel the completeness that hung in the air, threatening perfection. He closed his eyes and tried to ignore it.

His father had deluded himself into believing he and that bastard mage were meant to be together. Maybe he was doing the same.

Elijah could be trusted; he wouldn't screw over the pack. But Elijah being trustworthy didn't mean Victor was as well. He could be convincing himself there was something there that wasn't.

There was no point in letting himself indulge in foolish

fantasies. No matter how drawn to Elijah he was, he should keep his distance. It was safer that way.

Besides, Elijah didn't want to be bound to a pack. It'd be better if they forgot what had almost happened. He rubbed at his chest and refused to think about it as he got ready for bed.

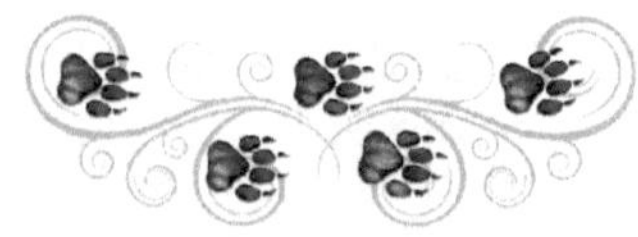

FOURTEEN

Elijah floated, suspended between the real world and wisps of dreams. His physical body was comfortable and serene, safe in the guest room, but his mind was filled with visions of a forest covered in snow. Moonlight gleamed through the trees and bathed him in silver. The wintry air tasted crisp on his tongue. His ears flicked toward the rustling of small nocturnal animals burrowing underground. He ran, racing the wind, dirt beneath his paws.

No, that wasn't right. He didn't have paws.

He surfaced closer to wakefulness but kept his eyes closed. A cool breeze blew through the window and over his exposed skin. He must have kicked the sheets off during the night. Pine-scented air swelled in his lungs, and his body thrummed with contentment, rightness, and energy. Birds chirped in the branches outside.

A low buzz of want pulsed through him. He should ignore it. He might not be in Victor's bed this time, but jerking off in a client's house was never the professional decision.

There was no telling that to his dick though. The urge to get off built as he lay there, half-asleep, his morning semi thickening. He cupped himself through his boxer-briefs, and his cock twitched under the pressure of his palm.

God, it was like he could smell how turned on he was. He pulled himself out and shoved his underwear down. It was a practical move, nothing more. These were the only pair he had with him. A day spent in briefs smeared with precome was a less-than-appealing prospect.

And if his hand found his dick again after that, well, the breeze was chilly. He was just keeping himself warm.

He squeezed once and groaned, shivering as that touch echoed inside him, causing his fingertips to ache and his toes to curl. When had he last woken this wound up? He blamed the night before—Victor so close to him and his own regrettable attack of conscience.

What if he hadn't stopped it, if he hadn't needed confirmation of who was in control? Would Victor have kissed him, crowded him against that dresser as he licked into his mouth? Would he have ended up in Victor's room instead?

As vehemently as he denied it to his friends, he had to admit the appeal to himself at least. Maybe he should let himself indulge once. He didn't care how it went. With the way his entire being responded to Victor, to his energy, whatever they did would be mind-blowing. Even quick handjobs in the attic, Victor stroking him, his teeth grazing Elijah's neck. He could practically feel it.

Fuck it, he thought. It wouldn't take much anyway.

He slung his arm over his eyes, not wanting to face the reality of what he was doing yet. As long as he was in this fuzzy state, it didn't have to mean anything. He only had to think about Victor controlling his pleasure, only had to imagine the fingers wrapped around him were Victor's, not his own. Their bodies aligned, Victor embracing him, breath hot on his ear as he shuttled Elijah's cock through his fist.

His nose pressed against skin and the fucking scent that hadn't left him alone for weeks. It made him want to howl and run, to rut and bite, to claim.

There was no drawing this out. No slow, languid movements, just the need to come, overwhelming and all-consuming. Heat trembled down his spine and pooled in his stomach.

Hand slick with precome, his fingers glided over his shaft as his balls drew up. He was so close. So fucking close.

No matter how tightly he squeezed his eyes shut, silver moonlight and that frustratingly perfect scent invaded his senses.

He bit his lip, stifling a moan, trying to hold on, to make this last a few more seconds.

Ecstasy crashed over him. It exploded behind his eyelids as he flew apart, come spurting onto his chest. His orgasm reverberated, leaving his muscles twitching and shaking, his body alight with it. He worked himself through that rush, picturing Victor's hands driving him to greater heights until it was too much.

Then he collapsed back into the mattress, limbs boneless. Remnants of pleasure shuddered through him. He didn't move, simply breathed, letting himself bask in the afterglow, the heavy heat draped over his bare skin in the snowy-pine breeze, and the luxurious bed beneath him.

Cracking his eyes half open, he squinted at the blurry ceiling above him, higher than it should be.

He blinked against the morning light until the room

sharpened into focus. The ceiling seemed to settle, returning to the height he remembered from the night before. He shifted, no longer weighed down and warm, the bed as firm as it had been when he'd fallen asleep. Not uncomfortable, but also not the kind of mattress that tempted him to sink into it and never get out. When he turned his head to the side, there was no breeze blowing through the window. It was closed. Only a hint of pine remained.

Had he come hard enough to hallucinate he was in Victor's bedroom? No power on earth or in the heavens above would make him admit that.

He winced, trying not to think about what he'd done. What he shouldn't have done.

This was not happening again. Even if it had been one of the better orgasms of his life. Even if he was almost ready to go a second round, like once had barely scratched the itch. He was here to work, not get off to the illicit idea of the pack's alpha on top of him, ravenous and greedy as he—

Nope. Not going there. Again.

With his clean hand, he grabbed his phone to check the time and cursed when he saw it was after six. He'd planned to start earlier than this.

Every muscle loose and relaxed from deep sleep and a good orgasm, he rolled out of bed. He doubted he'd gotten more than five hours, but he was more rested than he'd been in days. His body ached with a delicious soreness, far more post-marathon night of spectacular sex than the expected sleep-starved exhaustion.

He stumbled into the bathroom and took a hot shower, washing away his come and grogginess, then dressed in yesterday's clothing. He wasn't looking forward to wearing the same outfit two days in a row, but he'd deal with it.

Mouthwatering scents wafted through the house as he left the room, but the lack of accompanying noise made him doubt another pack breakfast was waiting for him. Six thirty was too early for that.

As he walked toward the kitchen, a few pack members passed him, dressed for the day and likely heading to jobs in town. Each one gripped his shoulder, wishing him a good morning with smiles more knowing than Elijah was ready to acknowledge. He was unsure how to process those greetings; he'd only ever seen shifters do it to each other, never outsiders. But there was something nice about it, something in him that lolled into the touch.

Lust scorched through him when he stepped into the kitchen and saw Victor with his betas, but he pushed it aside. He didn't want them smelling the desire on him.

But as they turned toward him, he realized it was a lost cause.

The three betas took in deep lungfuls of air, their chests rising. Then they smirked, the comprehension in their eyes almost feral, consummate predators fixating on their prey.

With dawning horror, Elijah belatedly remembered how sharp wolf shifter senses were. Especially alphas and betas. Suddenly, the looks the other pack members had given him made gut-sinking sense.

It didn't matter if they knew what had happened in the attic or that he was fresh from the shower; they were more than capable of discerning things he'd rather not disclose.

That had been a rookie mistake, and he mentally berated himself for it. He'd worked with enough shifters to know he had to be careful about this sort of thing. There was no way he could jerk off in a house full of wolf shifters and expect no one to notice. He hadn't been thinking straight, too caught up in his fantasies to comprehend the consequences of his actions.

He froze in the kitchen doorway, like standing absolutely motionless would shield him from Kade's wicked delight or Rick and Will's less-than-successful attempts to conceal their obvious amusement. Or Victor not quite meeting his eye.

Well, this was going to make working together even more excruciating. Lovely.

"You five grab chairs, and we'll get you fed," Katrina said, causing Elijah to jump. With his vision zeroed in on Victor and his betas, he'd missed her hovering near the stove. Her expression was gentler but no less knowing.

The sudden, intense gratitude he felt over missing breakfast with the pack lessened his dread over the meal he was about to have. He wouldn't have survived another dozen people smelling his morning activities on him; this small group was enough. The embarrassment made his face burn, but it was better than the alternative. Relatively speaking.

They sat at the smaller kitchen table, chairs crowded around it. Elijah wasn't surprised to find himself next to Victor, their legs distractingly close. It was almost intimate; it'd be so easy to press their thighs together if he wanted to.

Which he didn't.

Rick and Will dished up food for them so Katrina could keep cooking for the hoard, as she called them. Being the main pack cook had to be more than a full-time job.

"Elijah," Kade drawled after they'd tucked in, and Elijah braced himself. "How are you this lovely morning?"

"Fine," Elijah replied, failing miserably at stopping color from rising in his cheeks.

"That's great," Kade said. "Mornings can be hard. Particularly after late nights. Isn't that right, Victor?"

Rick snorted into his coffee.

Victor shot Kade a look but didn't answer. The tips of his ears were tinting pink.

Kade ignored whatever had been in that glare and leaned forward, conspiratorial, about to tell Elijah a secret. "Victor's been having quite a few hard mornings lately."

Fucking hell, was he implying what Elijah thought he was implying?

"Kade." The warning was clear in Victor's tone; his ears flushed a progressively darker pink.

"It's understandable, really," Will chimed in. "He's had a lot on his mind these past few weeks."

It was a fairly neutral sentence, but something about it sounded like Will meant more than what was going on with their territory.

Kade nodded solemnly. "That's why we're so glad you're here, Elijah. I can't think of anyone better to help Victor through these hard times."

"Really make sure he grasps the problem," Will added.

"Just get a nice, firm grip on it," Kade said.

"Help him thoroughly work it over."

"Explore and experiment to see what's best."

"Then relentlessly go at it until a resolution is reached."

"One that leaves everyone good and satisfied."

Elijah's gaze darted between Kade and Will before glancing at Rick, who'd been quiet during their banter. He was leisurely peeling a banana. Elijah turned away before he could fit the entire thing into his mouth.

Victor's ears were red now. There was no questioning that, and Elijah's felt his own heat in shared mortification.

He hadn't been kidding about his betas being obnoxious. Elijah would never be able to look him in the eye again.

The rest of breakfast was much the same. Elijah spent it torn between amusement and dying of embarrassment. But at least he wasn't alone.

By unspoken accord, they ate quickly, both more than eager to escape the not-so-subtle scrutiny and even-less-subtle commentary.

Fifteen minutes and far too long later, they were heading toward the worst area of decay, Elijah with his bag of supplies over his shoulder. He was overly conscious of his arms, his breath, his movements. Silence hung around them, as discreet as Kade's earlier remarks.

The sight of Victor's broad back made attraction course through him, but he willed himself to ignore it. He needed to concentrate on the task at hand. And damn if that thought didn't cause a very Aran-like voice in his mind to snark, *I bet you do.*

He couldn't deny it. Whenever he looked at Victor, memories beckoned him. Memories of their not-quite kiss and everything they hadn't done after.

It was disconcerting, and Elijah needed this not to be awkward. So he latched onto the first idea he had and started talking.

"Your betas," he said, picking up Victor's barely audible growl. "They're almost as obnoxious as my three closest friends."

Maybe not the wisest choice of topics, but he needed something to distract him from any tasks Victor might have had in hand that morning. And it was the only thing he could think of, the only thing they had in common.

It seemed to catch Victor off guard. He snorted as he pushed aside a low-hanging branch and held it for Elijah to pass. "No one is more obnoxious than my betas. It's not possible. The universe wouldn't allow it."

"Care to bet on that?"

"Name your terms. You're not winning."

Elijah couldn't stop from chuckling. "You say that now."

"Do your worst. What are your friends like?"

"Well, one of them, Aran, can make anything dirty."

Victor huffed, shaking his head in commiseration. "So you've got your own Kade?"

"If they didn't look completely different, I'd be suspicious that I'd never seen them in the same room. If they were ever to meet..."

"We can't allow that to happen."

"I mean, I should have known. I met him in a club when I foolishly tried to use the bathroom for something other than sex. Aran was in there, not even in a stall, some guy sucking him off."

Victor raised an eyebrow at him, and Elijah continued.

"We recognized the magic in each other. He leered at me and said, 'Hey there. Give me a minute. I'll buy you a drink.' Of course, his hookup wasn't pleased with him hitting on someone else while getting a blowjob. He told Aran to fuck himself, then left him standing there, dick out. Aran looked at me and gestured at it like, 'Any chance you want to help a guy out?'"

The stiff line of Victor's shoulders made Elijah hurry on. Sex probably wasn't the best topic to ease tension after a breakfast full of thinly veiled euphemisms.

"Anyway. There was less than zero chance of that. He sighed, tucked himself away, then offered me his hand like I'd even consider shaking it. Also zero chance. We did grab the drink though, and he has been giving me horny critiques of my life ever since. I'm still not sure Liam has forgiven me for introducing him to our friend group."

Victor chuckled, relaxing some. "Kade's family. We're cousins. Both grew up in this house. He's four years older than me, so there's been no avoiding him."

"I bet you two raised hell when you were kids."

"I will neither confirm nor deny that," Victor said, but his grin told the truth.

It was hard not to wonder what he had been like as a child, before everything had happened with his father, before he'd had the worries of an entire pack resting on him.

"Alright," Victor said. "We'll call our respective Kades a draw. What about your other two?"

"Honestly, the other two aren't that bad. Liam's a worrier. He's the mother of our little group. He's mostly okay, but heaven forbid he starts worrying about you, then you won't have a moment's peace until he's sure you're fine."

"And the third?"

"Miles. He can stay. He's a total sweetheart. I don't know how he puts up with the three of us."

"So Miles wins the most obnoxious friends competition?"

"Hands down. He's got a pervert, a worrier, and me."

"I still might consider trading with him. I've got a pervert, a meddler, and a sadist."

"That does sum up Kade nicely. What about the other two?"

Victor's laughter was pleasant, and it warmed Elijah in the cool morning.

"My turn for honesty. Rick and Will also aren't terrible.

Most of the time. But they've known me my entire life, and Kade's a bad influence."

"I've never heard of betas significantly older than their alpha. Rick has to be in his forties, right?"

"Yeah, Will is in his late thirties. Rick, early forties." Victor shrugged. "They were my father's betas and knew what they were doing, so it seemed senseless to lower their ranks. When they get older, they'll retire, but for now, they're the best shifters for the job."

They walked further before Victor spoke again. "In retrospect, having two guys who have literally seen me grow up isn't the best way to get deference. Hard to go from 'I've changed your diaper' to unquestioning obedience."

Elijah huffed. "No, I can't imagine it would be. What about Kade? Why him?"

"For all his obnoxiousness, he's like a brother. There's no one I trust more. I didn't consider anyone else. All three would do everything in their power to protect the pack, from anything or anyone."

He didn't say from their alpha, from Victor, but the implication was too loud not to hear.

The stench of the decay hit Elijah then, snaking through the forest before splotches appeared on the trees. As they neared the border, full-blown blight surrounded them. Elijah had to cover his nose with his sleeve to keep from gagging. He tried not to touch anything, but his steps skidded on the filthy carpet of rotted leaves.

The area beyond that was so much worse.

The forest was darker, tainted, stripped down to bare trees and death. No longer alive and breathing like it previously had been.

He'd wanted to return to this location to see what they

were facing and if anything had survived. His hope was dying as rapidly as the forest.

But when they got to the epicenter, a few massive trees clung to life. A scattering of leaves clutched their branches, and smaller plants and grass sheltered in their roots as if huddling out of the decay in the protection of their shadows. Everything else was dead, but those giants persisted despite all odds.

Victor looked up at one with a glimmer of hope that stirred some desire inside Elijah to do this, not to prove that he could or to fix his mistake, but for other, less professional reasons.

"They're all cedars," Victor said. "Is there a reason for that?"

"Cedar is used as a symbol of protection. Maybe it's protecting itself and the plants closest to it? I'll ask Aran."

Victor lifted a hand to one as if he couldn't believe it was alive.

The decay had spread in the three days since Elijah had been there. It was still spreading, but as they reached the wards, Elijah stopped, staring at the line of pristine trees ahead of him.

He stepped forward and touched the wards to test his theory. They glittered right at the edge of that line. On their side, it was all disease and death. On the other, life thrived, like Victor's land had before the new moon.

Elijah frowned. "That's neighboring pack territory?"

"Alpha MacFarlan's."

"How far is his territory from yours?"

"A few feet."

"There are healthy trees outside his wards?"

"Yes. So his wards aren't keeping the decay out, mine are keeping it in?"

"Looks like it." Elijah winced and waited for an accusation that didn't come.

Instead, Victor asked, "Can you use that? Use wards to contain it?"

Elijah blinked. He hadn't thought of that, but it was an interesting idea. Definitely worth a try. He was far better at wards than the things he'd been doing. "It'd be a stopgap measure, not a solution. Even if it works, the rot will remain. It just wouldn't spread any further."

"I'll take it. It might give you more time to figure out how to destroy the decay."

Elijah considered how he could do this. He'd used the power of the pack to fix the territory wards, but this was a fraction of the land, a fifth or less. Between that and how easily he could use Victor's energy, it might work.

"Okay," Elijah said, certainty building. "Let's move outside the affected area and see what we can do."

He ran through his mental list of the supplies he'd brought with him as they walked to a healthy part of the forest. They were nothing compared to what he'd used during the full-moon ritual, but the more he mulled it over, the more he realized he didn't need any of that. Half of the ritual was to ensure the mage connected to the shifter and the wards properly and that the flow of energy between them was smooth. That wasn't a problem he had with Victor.

With each step he took, he was more confident. Victor and him, the two of them together, they were enough.

The decay faded. Here, he could almost pretend the forest was fine. He inhaled deeply, savoring the clean air, and found a spot for them to kneel comfortably, facing each other.

"What do you need?" Victor asked.

"I think…" He trailed off and extended a tentative hand, setting it lightly against Victor's collarbone. His heartbeat was strong and steady under Elijah's fingertips, his energy pooling there.

Elijah unfurled the tiniest tendril of magic.

Victor's eyes gleamed in the dim light. He reached out, his palm settling on Elijah's neck, his fingers tangling in the hair at his nape, closing the circuit between them.

Energy flowed into Elijah, feeding his magic, and he immersed himself in that tempting current. His breath came quicker, shallower, as he pulled it into himself. He held it, marveling at how natural it felt, then started to weave the spell.

Through Victor, he sensed the areas of rot scattered throughout the territory, and one at a time, he built wards around them.

Sweat formed on his brow, but this was exhilarating in a way nothing else had ever been. Using magic, channeling energy, it was never like this. Never this easy. Never this exquisite. And the more wards he laid, the more natural it became. Victor's energy inundated him, twining with his magic, flowing out to form perfect, beautiful barriers, walling off the corruption.

He wondered again how it'd feel to tether himself to Victor, to let Victor bond him. To have full access to this whenever and wherever he wanted. How would Victor's tan skin look with the marks of Elijah's magic incandescent on it? If he was able to do this without a permanent connection, what would it be like with one?

And as he had been during the ritual, he was hit by visceral flashes of exactly that—crawling into Victor's lap, sinking down on his cock, connecting with him in every way possible.

His magic surged, responding to his thoughts, tugging harder on Victor's energy, the wards pulsing with strength. Victor let out a shaky exhale. His hand gripped Elijah tighter but nowhere near tight enough. Drunk on the power flooding into him, Elijah pried his heavy eyelids open.

Victor's eyes were closed, his lips parted, his respiration as quick and shallow as Elijah's.

"You okay?" Elijah asked in a breathless whisper. That'd been more than he'd meant to take.

"Yeah," Victor said, voice rough. His eyes half opened, glowing bright yellow. "Keep going."

Elijah soothed his fingers along Victor's neck, watching his lids drift shut as he wet his lips.

So he wasn't alone in feeling this. He shivered and forced himself to focus.

He found all of it. Every area tainted by rot was warded, isolated from the rest of the territory.

When he finished, he held on to that alluring mixture for one more moment, then released it. Most of the energy ebbed out of him, but some remained, its presence increasingly familiar.

Elijah let his hand fall away, and Victor did the same, fingertips skimming along his shoulder, trailing sparks in their wake.

They sat there until their breathing settled and Elijah was willing to risk standing.

Victor stood, offering a hand to Elijah. That easy connection was back as soon as he took it, but he ignored it as best he could.

"It feels like you got it all." Victor's touch lingered before he let go.

"I think I did, but we'll have to wait and see. Until then, I have a few other things to try."

"Lead the way."

Elijah walked into the decay, his wards shimmering against his skin as he passed. His legs were weaker than he'd ever admit, and he tried to surreptitiously adjust himself, though he knew Victor had to be aware of his lust.

Great, Elijah, an absolute credit to your profession, he thought.

"What," Victor started to ask, voice gruff. He cleared his throat, then spoke again. "What now?"

"I tried a spell with Kade to use his energy to burn the sickness out of a tree then help new growth bloom from the ashes."

"I take it the spell didn't work."

"It almost did, but it wasn't strong enough. It didn't get it all. But with you, it might."

Victor's smile spread like a sunrise. Elijah looked away before he did something he'd regret.

Once they entered an area heavy with rot, Elijah stopped in front of a tree. It was hanging on, but it wouldn't be for much longer. He studied it, considering. He had no issue connecting with Victor, but he could ensure things flowed into the spell as smoothly as possible.

The pain was quick as he sliced his knife over his palm, causing blood to well up. He placed his hand against the trunk.

Before Elijah could tell him what to do, Victor stepped up behind him, reaching his hand out to cover Elijah's. A split second before Victor's skin touched his, he saw the blood there. Victor had copied his actions.

That was all the warning he got.

The connection was as instantaneous as always, but the

blood made it more potent. Elijah hadn't thought that was possible. His breath shuddered as everything that was Victor consumed him. His presence behind him, his hand anchoring Elijah's to the tree, his energy ready for Elijah to use, his exhales feathering over Elijah's neck, the instinct to protect his pack, the desire to pull Elijah against him, the breeze that had cooled his feverish skin as he'd lain in bed and jacked off, grip tight, running over his length, as he'd imagined—

Elijah reined in his awareness, attempting to control the connection between them, but not before visions of Victor coming, them almost kissing, and the dazzling scent of snowy earth flickered through his mind.

The blood was a bad idea. A very, very bad idea. But damn, it felt good.

He swallowed, concentrating on the spell and not the hunger that pervaded every inch of space between them. He couldn't lose himself in those images, those fantasies. Focusing on what he needed to do took more willpower than he'd known he possessed.

The blood under his palm heated. This wasn't channeling anymore. It was a simple invitation that Victor's energy rushed to fill.

The magic took hold, delving into the earth, spreading through the roots, twisting around the branches. And then it went further. It flowed through him, through his blood and veins, through the tree, and out into the forest.

There was no comparison between this and working with Kade's energy. One tree had been a struggle, but this, this was effortless, spilling over, extending outward. It saturated the entire warded area, cleansed it, purified it, fortified old life, and established new. The ease of it stole Elijah's breath.

He should have been doing this from the first day instead of shying away from his reaction to Victor. They could have done so much.

The spell came to a crescendo, and Elijah let it fade, though Victor's touch kept their connection alive and radiant, emotions humming between them.

"Did it work?" Victor asked, the words stirring the hair on Elijah's nape. His other hand had found Elijah's waist. They were so close; it'd be so easy to press himself into Victor's chest. He should pull away and break the connection, but that was the last thing he wanted to do.

Elijah held his breath, waiting for the rot to reappear.

A long moment passed, then another and another.

It didn't return.

Joy and elation swooped through him, provocative and powerful, an intoxicating combination, making him giddy.

Victor's fingers slotted through his, squeezing his hand tight. "Did it work?" he asked again.

"I think it did." Elijah heard the relief in his own voice. He turned enough to look at Victor.

When their eyes met, electricity sparked between them. The forest surrounding them froze, even the air seeming to still, held in a trance as surely as Elijah. His pulse thumped with anticipation; the only other movement was the whisper of Victor's breath on his neck.

With his skin golden in the dappled light, Victor looked like a god, solid and strong, so devastatingly handsome the forest itself might bow in worship at his feet.

His dark eyes drank Elijah in, a storm of emotions swirling in their depths, making Elijah want to dive into Victor and stay there forever. He'd never seen Victor's expression so open, so relieved, and it undid Elijah more than anything else.

The gravity of them was undeniable, inextricable. Victor leaned in, a heartbeat away. They stayed like that for an eternity, their breaths mingling, pine and earth permeating the air between them.

Slowly, achingly slowly, yet enough to make his head spin, they closed the last bit of space separating them. Victor brushed his lips against Elijah's gently, carefully. Elijah's eyelids fluttered shut.

It started out chaste, but the way magic was swelling in Elijah's veins felt far from innocent. The awkward angle and twist of his neck were well worth Victor's lips moving against his own with the lightest pressure, a counterpoint to Victor's hand clasping his waist, insistent as he gathered him closer.

The energy under Victor's skin responded to him, and Elijah's magic rose in kind. Its power shook him, a shock wave making him quiver.

When Elijah opened his mouth, inviting Victor in, he was rewarded with a soft sigh, a wordless confession against his lips.

It was impossible not to fit himself against the solid muscle of Victor's body. A heady thrill swept through him. Victor's hips moved in an unhurried, instinctual grind. His hands roamed, sure and exploring, like he had a list of places he'd been wanting to touch and was now knocking them off one by one.

Elijah got lost in the glorious taste of him, the scrape of stubble against his skin, the magic prickling along the entire length of his body. Victor kissed down the side of his neck, then nipped along his jaw before reclaiming his mouth.

Energy swirled around them, stroking over every part of them, every sense. He'd dreamed of this, Victor's lips against his, Victor's hand skating lower to grip him through his pants, Victor's scent enveloping him until he couldn't tell where his ended and Victor's began.

One corner of his mind tried to warn him against this, but Elijah didn't care. He turned in Victor's arms, threading fingers through his hair while pulling him in. The cut across his palm was already fully healed, the effect of so much energy in his system, but that thought was gone when their mouths melted together again.

Victor untucked Elijah's shirt and slipped his hands beneath it and his undershirt, calloused fingers rasping up his back, then down again. He hoisted Elijah up, and Elijah's legs automatically wrapped around his waist. His dick strained against his zipper, caught between them as Victor pinned him against the tree with the relentless rocking of his hips, drawing a groan from Elijah at the friction. The bark was rough through his clothes, but being pressed into it verged on divine.

Victor's fingers made their way under his shirt again, wandering as far up as possible. His hands skimmed Elijah's sides, and a shudder went through him at the caress.

Their connection was still open, magic and energy exchanged with each touch, each kiss. He'd known his magic affected Victor, but feeling it echo inside of himself was like nothing he'd ever experienced.

It was just him and Victor and the connection blazing between them.

So right.

So perfect.

They should have been doing this from the day Elijah moved into town.

He writhed against Victor, working up the willpower to

break away long enough to get him shirtless, to search his bag for oil or something that would work.

But his conscience nagged at him, finally breaking through his stupor with the memory of Victor on the full moon, his wolf in control, reckless and uncaring of what the human side of him wanted.

As difficult as it was to stop, he needed confirmation. He twisted his hand in Victor's hair and pulled, demanding Victor look at him. Their eyes locked, and Elijah saw the flash of Victor's wolf. "Which one of you is in control?"

Victor leaned forward, his mouth hot on Elijah's throat. The graze of his teeth was too sharp to be entirely human, and a muffled sound escaped Elijah as he tilted his head, giving Victor more room.

That wasn't an answer, but Elijah's magic didn't care. It craved more; Victor's energy called to him.

Elijah's hands fisted in Victor's shirt as he warred with himself. He wasn't sure if he was trying to push Victor away or pull him closer. Not that they could be much closer, not with the rhythm of their hips making him gasp and pant, making him forget what he'd asked, making him—

The bark behind Elijah crumbled, the scrape of it gone, replaced by a sickening slide.

Elijah jerked, startled. Victor yanked away from the tree, nostrils flaring. He held Elijah for another moment before lowering him to his feet. Then the reek of dying, rotting plants assaulted Elijah as well.

His head snapped toward the tree. Decay was smeared along the trunk.

With quick fingers, he unbuttoned his shirt and stripped it off, leaving him in his undershirt. He was unsurprised to find the back of his shirt stained with blotches of mold.

He tossed it to the ground and lit it on fire with his magic, watching it go up in noxious smoke. The prickling foulness that seemed to crawl over his skin wasn't as simple to get rid of.

The decay was back. Not as strong as before, but it was back all the same.

He cursed. He'd been so sure it had worked.

Desire was snuffed out, lust doused by frigid water.

"How does this keep happening?" Victor's expression was so haunted it hurt.

"I don't know."

Victor looked at him, dread and worry marring his face. "If we can't fix this, if we can't stop this…"

Resolve formed in Elijah. "We'll figure this out. I swear to you. We *will* fix this. We'll protect your pack. No matter what."

Victor nodded like he believed him—maybe more than Elijah believed in himself—and that was an immense responsibility to bear.

"Whatever it is, I want it eradicated from my land."

"We'll do that," Elijah said, sounding more confident than he felt.

Victor stared silently at the surrounding forest, then walked toward the house. Elijah followed. He had other spells he'd been planning to try—spells that hadn't worked with Kade. But after this failure, there was no point in trying the rest. The result would be the same. They needed something more, something bigger, to take care of it once and for all.

Elijah had messed up. He had a job to do, and it wasn't forgetting himself and making out with Victor. As good as it felt, it got him nowhere. It distracted him. If he couldn't solve this, what did that say about his abilities as a mage?

When they arrived at the house, Elijah saw pack members through the windows. He couldn't deal with more knowing looks and assumptions.

Victor opened his mouth to speak, but Elijah cut him off. He needed distance, and with as charged as his magic was, the more distance, the better.

"I'm going to the shop to do more research and consult my friends."

Victor let him go without a word, his jaw clenched in the same hopeless frustration Elijah felt.

The drive to his place was too long, with too many empty roads that allowed for too much dwelling on what had happened over the last few weeks, about what he wanted and didn't.

Victor and his pack might be this giant, loving family. Obnoxious, but ready to have each other's backs. That didn't matter. Neither did how compatible Victor's energy was with his magic or how easy it was to picture himself at pack dinners. Or in Victor's bed.

None of that aligned with his plans.

He wanted what he always had. To make the shop profitable and then get the hell out of this town. To prove to the council that allowing him to be a shop owner, despite his age, had been the right choice. To show his parents he could be successful at this.

He refused to be the type of mage who'd jump any shifter with attractive energy. He wouldn't end up a pack mage.

Besides, Victor's wolf might be drawn to him physically, and Victor might let himself get swept away in that impulse during a moment of false hope—he might even trust Elijah to save his land—but he wanted a pack mage even less than Elijah wanted to be one.

So he'd fix this goddamn problem, and then they'd go their separate ways as they'd always planned.

When he unlocked his apartment, Lady was there to greet him, complaining loudly about his neglect and the starvation she'd suffered, though there was food in her dish, and they both knew she was perfectly capable of getting herself more. Locked doors rarely contained her; a shut cabinet was merely a nuisance. But why hassle with that? She'd adopted Elijah for a reason.

He had to be covered with Victor's scent, but for once, she didn't shun him. She gave him her trademark unimpressed look after sniffing him—he'd be more concerned if she didn't—but then she curled up in his lap and purred.

CHAPTER
FIFTEEN

Dawn broke as Victor stared out of his bedroom window. He could try to get more sleep, but with as fitful as he had been throughout the night, it seemed unlikely.

Instead, he rolled out of bed and padded downstairs. The house was quiet; it was too early for most pack members to be awake. He slipped outside, stripped off his sweatpants, and shifted. Maybe a run would work off his excess energy before he had to face his pack. He'd check the new wards while he was out there. They'd held for the last two days, but Victor didn't trust his luck enough to believe that'd continue.

Elijah would be spending another day researching. He'd sent Victor a message saying as much after midnight. That caused a whole mess of emotions Victor wasn't ready to sift through. He was also avoiding thoughts of what had almost happened in the attic and what had happened in the forest. With the moon waxing, his wolf made itself more known, and it was doing more than enough thinking about those incidents for both of them. It didn't like Elijah staying away from them, even for forty-eight hours. The constant urge to keep him close, to get him on pack territory, to not let him leave, played like endless TV static in Victor's mind. His wolf was unequivocal about its desires; Victor only scowled as he read Elijah's message because it meant he'd found nothing else to try.

The forest alternated between healthy green dotted with vibrant autumn colors and withered death fouled by putrid decay, Elijah's wards steadfastly separating the two. As Victor approached the epicenter, something unwelcome brushed against his territory wards. His eyes narrowed, and he ran faster, crossing into the rotted section and heading toward that disturbance.

This time, there was a push, an obvious test of the wards' strength. He couldn't tell who was doing it, but there was a distinct trace of alpha shifter in the touch, and he knew whose territory was on the other side of that barrier.

The closer he got to the border, the more certain he was about who he'd find.

The wind changed, bringing a hint of an almost familiar scent. It was Niall MacFarlan's and yet not. Something about it was different, something Victor couldn't identify.

He pushed himself, sprinting flat out, reaching the edge of his territory in time to see Niall stepping away from his wards.

Victor shifted into his human form, controlling his breath so he didn't betray the fact he had run to get there.

"Alpha MacFarlan." He kept his tone as friendly and nonconfrontational as he could make it.

Niall jerked toward him, eyes jumping around the forest before landing on Victor, assessing him.

Victor stood under that gaze and refused to let it make his skin crawl.

"Alpha Mills." Niall took a few steps sideways.

"What are you doing out here?"

"Running a patrol."

It might be the truth, but he was outside his own wards and had crossed the few feet separating their territories. "Is that so?"

"Thought I noticed something odd about your wards," Niall said. "I figured I'd check it out in case there was an issue."

He thought there was a problem with Victor's wards? Why wasn't he commenting on the state of Victor's land? He'd been staring right into the worst of it.

Victor stepped over the border, bringing him closer to Niall. The wards lit up, bright and healthy, a shimmering wave running through them at Victor's touch. Niall's eyes widened a fraction before his expression shuttered again.

"No problem here. Actually, I just had them reinforced. They're the strongest they've ever been."

"So I see." He glanced over Victor's shoulder; Victor didn't look away. "Who did them? That mage in town?"

The question made Victor's blood run cold. Niall shouldn't be allowed anywhere near Elijah, not when he was making Victor's hackles rise. He shrugged. Niall scrutinized him with suspicion.

"Well, have a good day." Niall's smile didn't reach his eyes. He melted into the forest behind him, never showing his back to Victor as he did. When he passed through his wards, something dark swirled through them, so different from the glimmer of energy that should have happened. A chill ran down Victor's spine.

When Victor turned toward his territory, the shock of

what he saw stopped him in his tracks, his chest too tight to breathe.

He should be facing a scene out of a horror movie. Instead, birds flitted through picturesque fall foliage. The idyllic scenery was a punch to his gut. Even the stench was disguised. He would have noticed if he hadn't been so focused on Niall. Was this Elijah's doing, or were his wards doing it on their own? He hadn't known they could, but it was another way they were protecting the pack, keeping outsiders from realizing they were weak.

He changed into his wolf form and checked out the area. Nothing was wrong with the land, but Niall's scent polluted the air, its wrongness unsettling.

That had not been the man he'd known for most of his life, the man he'd met at numerous meetings after he'd become his father's second.

What the hell had that been? Had Niall discovered Victor's failing wards? Was that why he was testing them? Had he weakened them in the first place?

They'd always been on good terms. Victor had a hard time imagining Niall behind this. But that malignant note in his scent made Victor rethink his assumptions.

He returned to the house and pulled on his sweatpants. It was nearly breakfast and easy enough to find Rick and Will.

Ten minutes later, they'd worked out a new patrol schedule, increasing security along that section of the border. They needed to keep an eye out for any signs of meddling from neighboring packs.

With that done, he went to his bedroom, considering whether he should call Elijah. His wolf was certain he should, but that just made Victor more hesitant to do so.

The moment he grabbed the doorknob, he knew Kade

had been inside. Although he could keep his room locked so no one but him was able to enter, he rarely found reason to. What had Kade done this time? Bracing himself, he opened the door.

As soon as he stepped inside, his wolf rumbled its approval. Kade had been there alright, but his scent was overpowered by one that was so much better.

Victor walked to his neatly made bed, dragged toward it, compelled to get closer. He'd left his sheets in disarray when he'd gone for his run.

He paused, then flicked back his comforter.

The pheromones that rose from the sheets had him shuddering in a breath and hardening in his pants.

Elijah.

Arousal.

Sex.

Images of Elijah jerking off in his bed flashed through his mind, overwhelming him.

His brain came online slowly as he clawed control from his more primal side. It took all his willpower not to climb in and roll around in that scent until he was absolutely covered with it.

Goddamn Kade.

That asshole.

He'd taken the sheets from the guest room and put them on Victor's bed.

Plans to get ready forgotten, he ran downstairs, unsurprised to find Kade in the kitchen, self-satisfied and sipping a cup of coffee.

Victor didn't speak or let Kade get a word out. He seized the front of his shirt, growling when he heard Kade chuckle even as he scrambled to put his mug down and follow Victor outside.

"Liked the surprise, I see," he said.

Victor tossed him out the back door. Kade was already stripping, knowing exactly where this was going. Victor shucked off his sweats before he leapt down the stairs two at a time, shifting when he reached the bottom. He had the presence of mind to realize that Will had followed them and was leaning against the railing, watching them.

The grin Kade gave him was wicked and unrepentant. That didn't change as he shifted, or as Victor lunged, sinking his teeth into Kade's shoulder hard enough to show he wasn't playing. Kade swung his head, clipping Victor in the side. Victor charged him again, knocking him to the ground.

Kade sprang up, snapping at Victor's throat. Victor rolled, coming up to bite Kade's leg. He whimpered, and Victor released him, not wanting to cause significant harm. Yet.

But he stayed on the offensive, getting in as many hits as he could, determined to make his point.

Kade should mind his own goddamn business. He was always pushing boundaries, always testing the limits. He needed to leave Victor alone if he knew what was good for him.

Victor had no patience for this. Not with his territory rotting away, not with how he was failing to protect his pack, not with all these conflicted feelings assaulting him, with how restless he felt today. Not with how Elijah's scent and magic had been invading his senses constantly for weeks.

The thought of Elijah and his fucking scent distracted Victor. It was for a mere second, but that was all Kade needed. He attacked, sending Victor sprawling, proving better than anything else why Victor couldn't afford that weakness.

Victor used the momentum to roll into a crouch, but Kade was smirking. It'd been a sloppy mistake; they both knew it.

He didn't bother holding back after that. He went after Kade with his full strength, snarling, snapping, knocking him around, taking every chance to nip at him, bite him, until he pinned him, baring his teeth in one last warning before shifting to human, his point made.

Kade shifted as well, covered in blood and dirt, but his eyes were sparkling with amusement. He didn't speak though, one small miracle.

Victor held out his hand and helped him to his feet. Most of Kade's injuries were minor and already healing. He'd be his obnoxious self again by evening, audacity fully restored. Victor was under no illusions that'd change after one fight.

They walked to the house, gathering their clothes along the way, Kade limping slightly.

Will shook his head as they approached. "I said he'd kick your ass for doing that."

Kade chuckled, then winced. "Worth it. Rick's idea was too good to pass up."

Victor raised an eyebrow at Will.

He held up his hands. "I was not involved. And even if Rick suggested it, he knew better than to do it." He leveled a look at Kade. "He knew not to agitate an already agitated alpha, and definitely not with something like that."

"When have I ever done the smart thing?" Kade grinned at Victor. "Besides, he'll be thanking me for it tonight."

"Enjoy it?" Will said. "Yes. Thank you for it? I wouldn't hold my breath."

Kade huffed. "My hard work is never properly appreciated."

"Whatever you three are trying to do, drop it. It's not going to happen. Nothing has happened. Nothing will happen."

"Your scent says otherwise," Kade said, and Will nodded.

Kicking both of their asses would be too much effort; none of his betas would learn. Instead, Victor growled and headed to his room, where he ignored the bed, took a quick shower, got dressed, and left. With as restless as he was, it'd be better if he wasn't around his pack.

So he got into his SUV and drove into town. To run errands and pick up a few supplies. Not because he was hoping to meet Elijah. That was the furthest thing from his mind.

In the hardware store's parking lot, Victor opened his car door and froze. He inhaled, then swore. He'd recognize that scent anywhere.

Leaving his SUV, he stalked in the direction it was coming from. Two blocks later, he rounded a corner and saw the last person he wanted to see.

His father must have sensed Victor because he spun around to face him. The fabric of his clothes was faded and thin, but it was nothing compared to the man himself. Dark shadows were smudged under his eyes, a sharp contrast to his sallow skin. Gone was the imposing figure of a pack leader—always more alpha than father to Victor

—replaced by shoulders slumped with exhaustion and a premature frailty that had sunk bone-deep. But when he saw Victor, his posture straightened, and his gaze filled with challenge.

He shouldn't be in Lost Creek. He should be with the pack Victor had sent him to.

"What are you doing here?" Victor asked as he closed the remaining distance between them. But as he got closer, he realized the scent wasn't solely his father's. It'd been so long since he'd smelled his father's untainted scent he'd almost forgotten it.

His nostrils flared. There was no way he'd ever forget that bitter, toxic reek. The one of that bastard mage.

He grabbed his father by the arm, wanting to shake sense into him. "Are you still letting that piece of shit use you?"

"He's not using me."

Victor scoffed, but before he could say anything, his father took a deep breath.

"You're one to talk. You're judging me for being with a mage when I can smell that pretty thing from the magic shop all over you?" Victor pulled back, and his father continued, voice harsh and stinging. "I thought so. How long have you been with him? Was that your plan all along? Kick me out and then take the first mage you found?"

"We're not together." But even saying that, he knew how he smelled. He was covered in Elijah's magic. And while he might not smell like they'd bonded or had sex, the way their scents were so mixed on his skin indicated something was going on. It was too much for a simple, professional relationship.

"You're a hypocrite. You've always wanted magic of your own, a mage of your own. Ever since you were a kid.

And you call me weak? Look at you. How much does he take? How often does he use your energy?"

Victor opened his mouth to deny it; his father wasn't listening.

"You said Darius was using me for my energy. You think your mage is any different? That he won't drain you when he can? Make you his pet shifter?"

Again, Victor tried to speak, but this time, his father's head jerked to the side, and he turned to leave.

"Where the hell are you going?"

"I've seen everything I needed to see here."

"Leave and don't return. I might allow you to visit in the future, but for now, stay away. Go back to your new pack until you break ties with that bastard."

His father just laughed. "You may be an alpha now, but you're not my alpha. You can't order me around. And now that I think about it, there's a shop I want to visit. Maybe I'll stay a little longer."

Victor snarled but refrained from attacking. He watched his father disappear around a corner. He didn't have the heart to go after him. But he should warn Elijah.

When he arrived at the magic shop, it was locked with a sign on the door that proclaimed it was closed for the day, call for urgent matters. Victor scowled at it, replaying his father's words.

Was he doing the same thing his father had? He'd already proven he was weak to magic.

Regardless of his feelings, he had to work with Elijah until they fixed his territory. After that, he'd cut ties with the mage, and everything would return to normal.

His restlessness didn't dissipate on the drive home. If anything, it got worse. Another run didn't help either.

He wasn't used to problems like this, problems he

couldn't attack directly. Needing to rely on someone else to fight his battles for him, waiting for Elijah to find a solution —it was maddening. There was nothing he could do, but that knowledge offered little comfort. Even less so when he found rot outside the wards. They seemed to be holding the rot inside, but they apparently hadn't gotten it all because there was one new area away from the rest. It was small—a few plants and trees affected—but it was there.

He wanted to punch things, but that wouldn't help either. Not until he had an enemy he could punch.

Clean sheets in hand, he climbed the stairs to his room, preparing himself for the scent that waited for him inside.

As if reading his mind, his phone buzzed in his pocket the moment he pushed open the door. When he pulled it out, Elijah's name taunted him on the screen. He hesitated before answering it, but only for a heartbeat.

"Elijah," he said. "What's going on?" His gaze landed on his bed. He couldn't sit there while talking to Elijah. He walked over to the chairs by the window and sat, letting the breeze bring in much-needed fresh air.

"Actually, I'm calling to ask you that. Is everything alright? I've had this vague impression that something was off all day and thought I should check."

Victor shifted his weight in the chair, deliberately not breathing through his nose. "Yeah, it's fine."

"Really?" That one word carried Elijah's skepticism loud and clear.

The instinct to cover potential weaknesses was strong, but lying to Elijah would help no one. Victor exhaled. He had to tell him this. "The wards seem to be containing what's inside, but I found a new area of rot outside them."

Elijah cursed. "I thought I got it all. Do you want me to come out there and ward it off?"

The yes came too easily for him to say it aloud, so instead, he said, "Not right now. Let's see if more areas appear. If new areas keep cropping up, your wards won't help. You can't ward off the entire territory."

"That's plan B then."

"Yeah." Victor forced himself to continue. "That's not all though. Niall MacFarlan was testing my wards this morning."

Elijah inhaled sharply. "At the place where they were failing?"

"Yes."

"Fuck," Elijah said. Victor heard the quiet rasp of skin against skin as he rubbed a hand over his face. "Do you think he did something?"

"Our packs have been allied for decades, but there was something off about him. He didn't smell right, and his wards reacted strangely to his touch."

Elijah paused before speaking again. "A few weeks ago, he came by the shop with Pierce. He was different from when we'd worked together. Twitchy. Paranoid."

"What did he want?"

"I'm not sure," Elijah said. There was another hesitation before he continued. "It was right after the full moon. I think he, uh, smelled you on me. He left directly after."

A perverse happiness curled inside Victor, but he smothered it. Elijah wasn't his, and he shouldn't be happy about costing him business. "Sorry," he said, voice gruff.

Elijah made a humming noise that Victor couldn't interpret. "Is he the only suspect so far?"

Victor grimaced. "My father."

"Your father?" The surprise was evident in Elijah's tone.

"I don't know. Maybe not a suspect, but he was in town today. And he smelled like that fucking mage."

"Shit, Victor, that's..." He trailed off like he was unsure what to say, but Victor understood the sentiment.

"Yeah."

"Sorry to ask this, but are they bonded?"

Victor flinched at the idea. "No. There was magic on him, but their scents weren't combined. They were never compatible in the way an actual bonded pair's should be."

"Does that mean they can't bond?"

"They could, but it wouldn't be the same. They aren't a good match."

"So you can smell the difference between shifters and mages that have a transactional bond and ones like your grandparents?"

"Yes," Victor said, remembering the scent of his grandmother's magic, how it'd never been the same after his grandfather had passed. It had still smelled like pack but had never seemed whole again.

He was brought out of the memory when Elijah spoke. "Should I talk to the council?"

"I need to figure this out myself." He'd deal with them if necessary.

"Okay. But if you change your mind..."

"I'll let you know." Victor wasn't sure Elijah believed him; he wasn't even sure he believed himself, but the idea was easier to accept than he would have expected.

Neither spoke for another long moment, somewhere in the undefined space between awkward and companionable. Victor still felt unsettled, but he'd calmed somewhat, and it was too easy to guess why.

"So," Elijah said. "Shitty day, huh?"

Victor let out a huff, not quite a laugh, but close. "Extremely. You?"

"No luck on my end. Just researching while Lady stares at me judgmentally."

"She seems to be excellent at that."

"One of her many talents."

"Ah, she has other hobbies besides glaring at people?"

"General shop guarding, curse detecting, fae capturing, cockblocking."

Victor didn't know where to start with that. No, wait, he did. "Cockblocking?"

Elijah groaned. "Shortly after I moved in, I made the mistake of trying to bring guys here. If you think you've seen her judgmental look, anything she's given you pales in comparison. I swear she saw these guys and sighed in exasperation. If she could roll her eyes, she would have. And I get it. They wouldn't have been my first choice. But have you tried to pick up anyone in this town? I was limited to the few tourists that were passing through."

Victor rubbed his neck, wishing he hadn't asked. "There aren't many options here. Kade goes out of town for the weekend when he wants to get laid." He didn't add he used to go too.

"That does not surprise me." Elijah chuckled. "Lady is the anti-Kade. She does not approve of any form of hooking up. When I brought the one guy home, she wouldn't stop glaring at him. The guy was getting annoyed with her and suggested tossing her out or locking her in the bathroom until he was finished."

"*He* was finished?"

"Yeah. His exact words were 'I can't get off with that thing staring at me.' Needless to say, Lady was not the one tossed out. No one puts Lady in a bathroom. I doubt I was missing out on much, if his kissing skills were any indication. But I also don't think anyone is going to meet her standards of approval."

"She simply has impeccable taste." He liked Elijah's cat more than he'd expected. "She's your... familiar?"

"No, she's a normal cat, as far as I can tell. There's nothing magical about her. And she's eyeing me now as I say this. Don't look at me that way. You're your own special kind of magic." That was clearly not addressed to Victor, but then Elijah spoke to him again. "Familiars aren't that common anymore. Not in the traditional sense. There's not enough balance in those types of connections. We can take energy from any creature, but if everyone involved isn't getting equal benefit, there are consequences. The magic isn't as strong or stable. It's difficult to be truly reciprocal with an animal."

"So shifters replaced familiars?"

"Basically. Even if it's a transactional arrangement, both the mage and shifter should be stronger because of that connection. When it's equal."

He didn't have to say what happened when it wasn't, when the mage was taking and never giving. Victor knew that all too well and didn't want to think about it. But he also didn't want Elijah to stop talking, so he steered the conversation to a safer topic. "If Lady isn't magical, how does she detect curses?"

"I'm still trying to figure that one out." There was a creak and a rustle like Elijah was settling into bed. Another thing he'd rather not contemplate, though for entirely different reasons. But Elijah continued before he could dwell on it. "I'd ordered these crystals that were meant to be placed under your pillow for better sleep. They were these little delicate charms, like glass, and I had them lined up on a shelf. Lady jumped up and started knocking them off one by one, shattering them as they hit the floor. She never does that. I grabbed her, but when I set her down, she jumped up there and knocked more off. So I put her in the apartment, even though I knew she'd hate it and make my life miserable for it, but damn it, those charms weren't cheap."

Lady meowed in protest loud enough for Victor to hear.

"I'm getting there," Elijah said to her, then continued the story. "She shredded my pillow, then somehow got out of the locked apartment on her own. And once she was back in the shop, she broke the rest of the crystals. So I went to clean up and managed to cut myself on a shard, and suddenly, I'm flat on the floor, stuck in this nasty hallucination. We're talking your face melting, bugs crawling under your skin, the world liquefying around you, that sort of thing."

"Were you okay?"

"Eventually. When I came to, Lady was sitting next to me with this expression that screamed, 'Told you so, you idiot.' I examined the pieces, and every single crystal had this malicious little curse embedded inside. Fae magic. I'd completely missed it. They would have given their owners horrible nightmares. So, I won't be buying anything else from that supplier."

"Are you sure she isn't magic?"

"Fairly. But I have my doubts. She's the weirdest cat."

Victor grinned at the understatement. He settled against the chair, muscles letting go of some of their tension. "When did you get her?"

"My first day here, she kept trying to get in as my friends and I moved my stuff in. Then she spent the entire night wailing outside my window. We finally let her in so we could sleep. She used my face as a pillow and then decided to stay. I put up posters but didn't get any calls. Possibly because she was glaring bloody murder in the picture. No idea where she came from."

"She adopted you?"

"Pretty much."

"She's a smart cat."

There was a thud against the phone, and then a rough purr vibrated over the line.

"Would you stop that? Don't scent mark my phone," Elijah said, muffled, followed by an indignant meow.

"Sorry about that," he said into the phone again. "You would not believe the antics she gets up to."

And then he told Victor. Between Elijah's voice and his scent in Victor's room, particularly *that* scent, it was difficult to ignore the low simmer of arousal building in him. But Victor pushed it aside the best he could and let it all wash over him, relaxing him.

"You never told me," Elijah said after a while, "what happened with your betas? Did you do the tarot trick with them?"

Laughter gusted out of Victor at that memory. So he told Elijah, neglecting to mention what he'd done afterward. Then Elijah got him to talk about the ridiculous shenanigans Kade had pulled when they were younger, about his betas, his pack, anything, everything.

He didn't know what had prompted this, why Elijah was telling him these things and listening to Victor's stories in return, but he couldn't say he minded. It was the first time since the new moon his shoulders had relaxed. He wasn't going to acknowledge how warm the sound of Elijah's laughter was or how nice it would be if they were more like this in person.

They talked until the small hours of the night, until

they were both half-asleep, and Victor was floating in a haze of tired contentment. Then they said their goodbyes.

That had been unexpected, but he didn't regret it. It'd given him a few hours to forget all the shit that was happening.

Victor hauled himself out of his chair and looked at his bed. It'd be so, so easy to crawl in. He could blame it on how long his day had been, how late it was.

But he wouldn't let Kade win. His betas were obnoxious enough. They didn't need more ammunition.

He pulled off the sheets and tried not to breathe in too deeply as he did. Though he might have failed on that account. He gathered them up to put them in his clothes basket. Then stopped. It was so far away. Almost halfway across the room. And his dresser was right there. He tossed the sheets on it and made his bed with the clean set, then slipped in with a sigh.

The morning would be busy. He probably wouldn't have time to do his laundry. With everything going on, those sheets might end up sitting on his dresser for days. And until then, they'd be there, balled up, Elijah's scent still very much in the air though not rubbing against his skin. That wouldn't be his fault. No one could say he was doing it on purpose. He'd get to it. Eventually.

And if he slept better than he had in weeks, well, he wasn't to blame for that either.

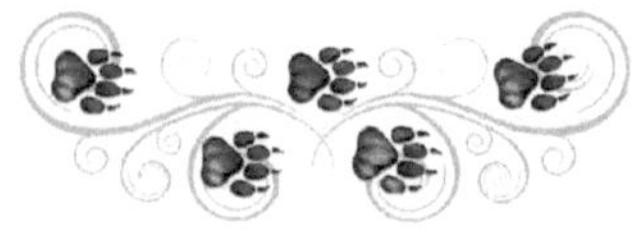

SIXTEEN

Morning sun streamed through Elijah's window, and he rolled over, burying his face in his pillow to block it out. A vibration rumbled from his nightstand, promptly followed by another.

Mind as fuzzy as his dreams, he groped for his phone and squinted at it. The screen read eight thirty. He grimaced; he should have been up and ready by now. After this was over, he'd be realigning his damn sleep schedule.

His phone buzzed again, and he swiped through the notifications—half a dozen of them, all from Aran.

He pulled up the group chat.

> **ARAN**
>
> Elijah, are you there?

More messages had followed less than ten minutes later.

> **ARAN**
>
> You can't seriously be asleep.
>
> I need to talk to you.

And a few more after that.

ARAN

Elijah!

Get your ass up!

Why the hell aren't you awake? It's after 8am. Have you ever slept past 8 in your life?

This could not be good.

ELIJAH

I'm here. What's going on?

Did you figure out why the cedar trees aren't affected?

Instead of a message, Elijah's screen lit up with a call notification. He answered.

"Morning," he said, voice raspy from talking half the night. He'd barely gotten six hours of sleep.

"What were you doing last night?" Aran asked, amused. "No. Never mind. It's you. You weren't doing anything interesting."

Elijah wanted to protest, but it wasn't like he could tell Aran about his conversation with Victor; he knew what that'd earn him.

Aran didn't bother waiting for an answer. "Anyway, it doesn't matter. I found something, but Miles and Liam should hear this too."

Elijah sat up in bed and waited the minute it took for them to join the call.

"Okay," Aran said. "I haven't found anything definitive on the cedars yet, but I did find a report from early last year about a pack in Southern California that was completely destroyed by some kind of rot. I didn't want to mention it until I saw it for myself. Got here this morning."

Elijah held his breath and waited for him to continue.

"It's bad, Elijah. I've never seen anything like it. The whole territory is a dead zone. I attempted to revive a tree, but there was nothing I could do. It's creepy as fuck and has massive wards around it. Prison-grade wards. I was only in there a few minutes, and my skin is still crawling from whatever the fuck is inside. I'm getting a hotel room so I can shower before I drive home, but I'm gonna need to scrub my skin off to feel clean."

"What happened to the pack?" Dread settled in Elijah's stomach, heavy and sick.

"No one's sure. They disappeared but are probably dead. The mage who wrote the report said she'd been helping them for a while. It started as a decay. Her descriptions and pictures match what you're dealing with. She couldn't identify a cause or solution, though there's a whole list of spells she tried. No matter what she did, the disease always returned and never stopped eating away at their land. First it was the plants, then the animals, then the pack itself."

"What do you mean 'the pack itself'?" Elijah already knew he wouldn't like the answer.

"It corrupted the pack bonds, destroyed the pack ties, and then the pack members literally started to rot. She never found their bodies, but she didn't search the entire territory. Which I get—I couldn't stand being in there for more than five minutes. But also, a few members left the pack right before the last stages of the decay kicked in, and she was unable to track them down. It's like the pack vanished."

"How is that even possible?"

"I don't know. But their pack house looks like it's been abandoned for a hundred years, not one. That shit is not structurally sound anymore. You could knock it over with a touch. Not that anyone would voluntarily touch it."

"Nothing worked?" Fear of what that meant for Victor's pack crept over Elijah like a shadow, oppressive and stifling, constricting his lungs.

"I wish I had better news. Maybe the best thing you can do is get them off their land before it affects the pack members. If it's the same shit and they stay there…"

"How can I tell him that his entire pack and territory are going to waste away in front of his eyes?" Elijah asked, despair twisting inside him, wrapping a tight hand around his throat. It'd kill Victor to have to leave his land.

"Sorry, Elijah, I'm out of ideas."

"Actually," Liam said, breaking in. "I might have something."

Elijah jumped. He'd forgotten Liam and Miles were on the line.

"I was planning on messaging you later today once I finished the translation, but I'll share what I've got so far. Hold on. This isn't fully ready."

Elijah heard Liam rummaging around and the rustle of pages turning. It was only a few seconds, but they stretched impossibly long. He tried to steady himself, desperate for any lifeline Liam might be offering.

"Here. It's a full-moon ritual, so you have a week to prepare. And it'll require you to channel quite a bit of energy again. I don't think it'll need as much power as what you described the ward ritual using, but it might mess with your magic."

"That's fine. I'll deal with it afterwards." Until he made

sure Victor's pack was safe, his magic was the least of his concerns.

"Okay, I found a book on crop rituals. This is the most powerful in there."

"The report I read listed multiple spells to destroy crop blights. None worked," Aran said, skepticism in his tone.

Shoulders tense, Elijah let them hash it out.

"That isn't what this is," Liam said. "I think we've been looking at this wrong. We've been focused on destroying the rot, but it seems impossible to eradicate it. So there must be spores or something escaping the spells, right?"

"Spores moving around on the wind would explain why it spreads in patches and keeps coming back. Not seeing how a crop ritual will kill them though."

"This is a four-season ritual."

"I see where you're going with this, but assuming we're dealing with a mold here, odds are a magic-induced winter will deactivate it, not kill it. Once things warm up, it'll start growing again."

"But this isn't just winter. The ritual uses the seasons to purify and reset the land."

"So you think forcing it into a symbolic deep freeze will enable Elijah's magic to thoroughly cleanse all the rot while it's dormant." Aran's doubt was shifting to interest. "And the spring portion will revive the forest."

"That's my theory. The only spell that almost worked operated on a similar principle. This is that but on steroids. Here. I'll send a copy."

Moments later, photos were posted to the group chat, and Elijah opened them. "Uh, Liam. This is in Japanese."

"I said I wasn't finished translating it yet. Actually, Aran, I need your help with a few of the nuances. But I've got the important points outlined in my notes."

"Liam," Aran said, amusement creeping into his voice. Him losing some of his seriousness was a good sign; it eased the pressure on Elijah's lungs. "This is a fertility ritual."

Elijah blinked and hurried to open Liam's notes.

"No, it's not," Liam said. "Well, okay, it is. But not like that. Though, it could be. If Elijah wants it to be. But it's not necessary."

"Uh, no, not would be better," Elijah said. Though... nope, he refused to go there.

"Okay." Wicked delight glittered in Aran's words. "But the 'not' option isn't exactly fluid-free."

"What?" Elijah asked, more of a squeak than an actual word. He skimmed through the notes until he found the relevant part. "Oh. Okay. Well. It says it can be done separately in advance."

He was suddenly glad this wasn't a video call. His cheeks were burning. This was going to be one hell of a conversation to have with Victor.

Aran scoffed. "That's no fun. I mean, come on, Liam, this doesn't even require shifting. You should have at least found one that'll warrant Elijah's shifter stripping down again."

The weight on Elijah's chest lifted as they entered well-worn territory.

"Do you have a better idea?" Liam asked, exasperated.

"I do have that codex of sex magic. I'm sure it's got something Elijah could use to get his shifter naked and finally get some of that thic—"

"Aran," Miles interrupted. "I love you, but I swear to any power listening, if you start talking about the size of anything Elijah's shifter might have, metaphorically or otherwise, or what it might do to Elijah, I'm dosing you with artemisia until you can't use magic for a week."

"You wouldn't." Aran sounded rightfully horrified by the idea.

"If you give me one more mental image of Elijah and his shifter in compromising magical positions, I will. So help me, I will."

"For the hundredth time, can you guys stop calling him my shifter? He's not *my* shifter."

"Riiiight," Aran said. "He's just a random shifter you are so compatible with it only takes a touch for you to use his energy. Nothing strange there."

"You know," Miles said, "out of all of us, I figured you'd be the last to end up with a shifter."

"I'm not ending up with him."

"You say that," Aran said, "but your magic seems to have other ideas."

Elijah exhaled slowly, counting down from ten. He loved his friends. He really did.

"How's your magic?" Liam asked, once again proving why he was Elijah's favorite.

"It still feels wilder than before but more stable now, or I'm getting used to it? I haven't exploded anything in a few days. Knock on wood."

Revealing what helped stabilize it would be making its home at the bottom of his to-do list for the foreseeable future.

"It's stronger?"

"Yeah," Elijah admitted. "Noticeably."

Liam hummed.

"What?"

"You're not going to like it."

"Tell me."

"I've been reading up on bonds and tethers."

Elijah groaned. He took it back. Liam wasn't his favorite. None of them were.

"I said you wouldn't like it, but that doesn't change the facts."

"What facts? We haven't—"

"Yes, yes, I know. You haven't had sex, he hasn't bitten you. But listen, a few of the older books hint at 'how things used to be.' Before the abductions. Before we were constantly suspicious of each other. Finding good sources from that period has been difficult, but I'm convinced there's something there."

"Do you honestly think some sixth-century manuscript holds the key to what's happening with my magic?"

"I was assuming a thirteenth-century grimoire, but yeah."

"Whatever. I told you I'll take care of that later. But I'm not tethered to him. Or bonded."

His friends made various noises of disbelief.

"Is that all? I have a ritual to prepare for."

"Nothing here," Aran said, settling into a semblance of seriousness again. "I'll help Liam finish the translation and get it to you in the next hour or two. But if this definitely-not-a-sex-ritual doesn't fix this, you really should think about getting the pack off that land."

"Noted," Elijah said. They ended the group call.

Elijah sighed before standing and stretching. He was willing to try anything, fertility ritual or otherwise. He couldn't tell Victor there was no hope for his pack. Not yet.

There was another week before the full moon, but at least he could say he had a plan. And if that failed, then and only then would he divulge the information about the other pack. Victor didn't need to know before that; it'd just make him more worried than he already was.

But that didn't keep the story from haunting Elijah.

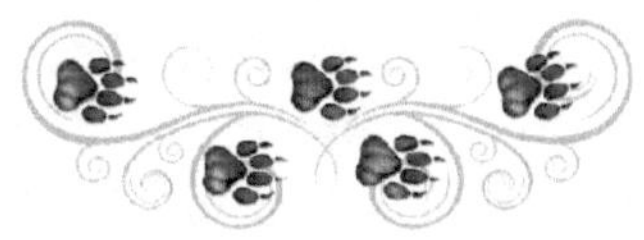

Elijah read through the translation, making a list of everything he had to prepare, all the elements it required. It was fussy and highly symbolic, but he couldn't risk substitutions in case it'd alter the outcome. He'd be spending most of the week spelling candles, carving runes into stones, and brewing potions.

This would work. He'd get it right.

While he gathered his supplies, he rehearsed how to explain the more indecent parts to Victor. There was no delicate way to inform someone they needed to jerk off for him.

Not for *him*.

For the *ritual*.

He had to remember that. It should be brought up tactfully. Preferably not right after he'd spent a good chunk of the afternoon imagining the more hands-on version with increasing amounts of detail until he hadn't been able to do anything but a practice run of the scaled-down version. And as hard as he'd come, it hadn't seemed to ease the need that was clawing at him, driving him to move, to run, to do *something*.

So he did the first thing he could think of. He cleaned up and called Victor.

Victor answered on the third ring, his voice rough,

breath harsh. The sound of it sent heat licking down Elijah's spine, but he did his best to be professional.

He expected the call to be awkward, that their conversation the day before had been a fluke. It wasn't.

It was remarkably easy to talk to Victor over the phone. The walls he'd put up regarding magic didn't activate when they weren't face-to-face, when he couldn't smell Elijah. Even when talking about magic, it was like that distance gave him security.

Elijah explained the ritual. Well, most of it. He didn't quite get through the pre-ritual preparations. There were a lot of them, and he and Victor only talked for the better part of three and a half hours. How could he fit all the details in that amount of time? They had a week to get the necessary pieces, and fluids, in place.

It just meant he had to call Victor to give him more information the following day... and the day after that and the one after that too. It helped distract Elijah. The moon wouldn't wax faster on his account. They had to do this on her timeline, not theirs. That knowledge didn't alleviate his impatience, the itch beneath his skin, the gnawing desire for movement, for action. But his nightly calls with Victor did.

Each night, he updated Victor and checked to see if the decay had spread. His wards were keeping it in check, but new areas kept springing up.

Somehow, their conversations never ended there, neither ready to hang up. And each night, Elijah swore he'd tell Victor the next.

His favorite pastime had quickly become trading horror stories about their friends, Victor matching each of Elijah's ridiculous stories about Aran with one of his own about Kade.

It was impossible not to share a sense of camaraderie with someone who'd suffered the same trauma of going on a road trip, pulling the short straw on roommate assignments, then waking up at some ungodly hour to said roommate fucking the front desk clerk into the mattress of the other bed and not being particularly quiet about it either. Elijah was almost surprised it wasn't the same clerk at the same hotel when they'd realized that.

"They are never allowed to meet," Elijah said, not for the first time, and grinned at Victor's soft huff of laughter.

"Did Aran complain about the wet spot and try to crawl into your bed?"

"He did, but I put up a ward."

"Damn, that would have been handy."

"Is Kade one of those obnoxious bastards who takes up the whole bed?"

"Worse. He's a cuddler."

The thought of Kade spooning a disgruntled Victor made Elijah chuckle.

"Sure. Laugh at my pain. You wouldn't be the first." Victor was grumbling, but his amusement was palpable.

"If it makes you feel any better, my friends do it to me all the time too."

"Given what you've said about them, I wouldn't expect anything less."

"At least the shit they give is out of love. Wish I could say the same for certain other groups of people I have to deal with on a far too regular basis." Elijah couldn't hide the exasperation in his tone.

"This certain group of people wouldn't happen to be made up of a bunch of octogenarians who still haven't fully embraced the Industrial Revolution, would it?"

"Speaking of. I've been curious. How much shit did your council give you for taking over your pack at your age?"

Victor blew out a breath. "They strongly implied I should transfer power to Rick or Will for five or ten more years. Rick and Will then made a few insinuations of their own that if I tried to pawn the pack off on them, they'd retire to cabins in the Northwest Territories where neither I nor the council would find them. How about you? Did the mage council claim you were too young to buy the shop?"

"They were reluctant, to say the least. But I was the only applicant offering them a cash down payment, and it's not like mages were lining up to buy a shop that has never once turned a profit."

"I'm surprised you even wanted a shop way out here."

"I don't." Elijah sighed. "I'm being strategic. What I want is to own a shop in a major city, but the only mages the council ever allows to own those shops are the ones with a proven track record of being able to successfully run a shop. And usually, the only way you do that is by apprenticing in one for a decade or more and then jockeying for ownership with the other apprentices when a shop is ready to change hands. The odds aren't great."

"You can't open your own?"

"I mean, I could. But then someone from the council would give it a visit. You know. 'Lovely shop you've got here. Be a shame if something were to happen to it.' That sort of thing. There's a reason all magic shops are officially sanctioned, and it isn't quality control, regardless of what the council claims."

"So buying a shop in the middle of nowhere increases your odds of climbing the magical ladder?"

"That's what I'm hoping. It was the only shop I had a

chance of buying. It's supposedly cursed to always lose money. And if you can't make a profit, you can't move up to a bigger shop. I have no clue why it isn't profitable though. It's rural, but the nearest shop is four hours away, and there are so many shifter packs and various supernaturals in the area. Even if it isn't especially lucrative, it should be in the black. There's no logical reason it isn't."

Victor made a soft, amused sound. "Ah. That's my pack's fault."

"What? How?" Elijah's mind refused to wrap around that statement.

"We've always had a pack mage, occasionally more than one."

"Right. But they were bonded into your pack. How would that affect the shop?"

"We've *always* had mages. Before the shop existed, before modern transportation made the nearest shop only four hours away, we had mages. Local packs came to us when they needed anything. It was with suspicion initially, but we built up trust over the years to the point that when the shop was established, everyone kept coming to us instead. I think they figured that if our mages hadn't taken over the neighboring packs after decades, we weren't likely to start. And it helped that the bonds were never trans-actional."

Elijah stared at a wall in his apartment but didn't truly see it. He'd never considered that. A transactional bond would indicate a willingness to sacrifice love for power. Mages and shifters who did that were inherently more untrustworthy. But if there was a genuine connection between them...

"Honestly," Victor said, "I'm pretty sure the main

reason there's a shop here at all is because the mage council realized how much business we were doing and wanted a cut."

Elijah snorted. "Well, that didn't turn out so great for them, did it? How is your pack not a massive player in shifter politics after that?"

"We've never cared about that shit. My father was the first with any real ambitions, and look what that got him. After Grandma passed, even before my mother died, he hated not having a pack mage, hated that we'd lost one of our main sources of income. He thought it was ruining our pack's reputation. But everyone before him just wanted a place to run free and be themselves."

That resonated with Elijah more than he would have expected.

And now he knew why the shop had never been profitable in the past, but its current situation still didn't make sense. "How long has it been since you've had a mage?"

"A little over ten years, but even now we get calls from other packs. Sometimes I think my grandmother must have told everyone to keep calling back until—" He cut himself off. "I'll tell the pack to direct any requests your way."

"Thanks. That would be greatly appreciated."

They settled into silence, and Elijah mused over that information, comparing it to what he'd cobbled together from the shoddy financial records he'd found. If there had been an uptick in business around ten years ago, he'd seen no evidence of it. Whether that had been deliberate concealment or gross mismanagement on the part of the previous mage, Elijah wasn't certain. But given the miasma that had festered in the shop before he'd cleansed it, he wouldn't be surprised if, after entering, any shifter had immediately turned tail and driven another four hours.

He'd have to check if the owner of the nearest shop had noticed a spike in new customers instead.

As he considered it, an undefinable pressure built in his mind. The impulse to say something, but he didn't know what. Before he could figure it out, Victor was speaking, hesitant at first but gaining confidence as he went.

"I owe you an apology. I shouldn't have tried to force you to hurt me. It was a complete dick move. You didn't deserve it, and I'm sorry for my actions."

Elijah had not been expecting that, but he heard genuine remorse in Victor's tone.

"You absolutely should not have done that, but I understand where you were coming from. You were trying to protect your pack, and I get that. I'd do the same for my friends." Something in him eased. "But if you ever pull a stunt like that again, I will not be held responsible for what Lady might do in retaliation."

Victor sputtered out a laugh. "The pain and destruction she'd rain down on me would be entirely justified."

"I'm glad we're in agreement."

Elijah took a deep breath. If Victor could apologize for that, then he could say what he needed to. "About the ritual." His cheeks heated, and he was glad they were doing this on the phone.

"What about it?" The tension was clear in Victor's voice as he picked up Elijah's discomfort.

"I didn't explain all of it. Our theory is that destroying the decay isn't enough; the land requires more than that to reset itself. So, it's technically a fertility ritual, and they tend to necessitate... particular things."

"Okay," Victor said haltingly. "Does that mean we... What does that mean? It's sex magic?"

Elijah wasn't able to gauge his reaction. Maybe he

should have told him in person. Though that would have been spectacularly awkward.

"Not exactly. It doesn't require sex in the traditional sense. It's a little more symbolic. But it does involve... an offering of certain bodily fluids. The ritual has four parts, corresponding to the four seasons. Each season is represented by a number of items, including stones carved with runes. And the stones for spring need to be covered with... well, spring needs, um, seed."

"During the ritual?" Victor sounded strangled, so Elijah hurried to clarify.

"We can do it beforehand. Separately. I'll give you one stone, and then that morning, just, uh, do your thing and rub the... offering... into the runes on the stone. And I'll do the same for mine." Elijah swallowed hard enough he was sure Victor heard him.

He didn't bother mentioning that the other options were to do it while setting up the ritual, either individually or helping each other make the offering.

A moment passed while Victor processed that. When he spoke, his voice was gruff. "I can do that."

Shivers of heat ran through Elijah. "Good. Right. Can you have someone pick up the stone tomorrow?"

"I can get it." The gravelly edge to his tone made Elijah's mouth dry. He bit back the urge to say, yes, Victor undoubtedly could. That would not be professional or advisable. In more ways than one.

Over the last week, his magic had settled to something closer to normal as Victor's energy in his system had faded. He assumed the distance from Victor helped that along, and in that case, Elijah should keep away from him for now. He couldn't mess up any of this.

"It'd be better if you sent someone else."

"I'll send one of my betas."

There was no way Elijah heard a hint of hurt in that sentence; he dismissed the idea as ridiculous. "Not Kade."

"Agreed. I'll send Will. Though let's not tell him the details of what he's picking up either?"

"For the sake of both of our sanities, I think that's best."

"Definitely. Is there anything else for me to do?"

"No, that's it. I'm nearly done on my end. All that's left is waiting for the moon."

They spoke for another ten minutes, though Elijah found concentrating on the words difficult. Victor's voice hadn't lost that little extra gruffness, and it threatened to annihilate every ounce of self-control Elijah possessed.

They ended the call, but he already knew they'd find a reason to talk again tomorrow evening. And the remaining two after that.

So Elijah whiled away the hours and tried not to let anxiety consume him, tried not to think about the danger Victor and his pack were facing. About what would happen to them if this didn't work. Until the moon was ready, he had to wait. Wait and have too many dreams about Victor to count. The closer it got to the full moon, the more he woke with ephemeral memories of tantalizing scents, skin sliding against skin, and running through the forest on four legs instead of two.

Once this was finished, his magic and his sleep schedule weren't the only things that needed fixing. He had to get over his attraction to Victor. Or just get laid. He'd been entirely too horny lately. At this rate, his sex drive was going to rival a shifter's. Or Aran's.

But that made it nice and easy when it came time for

the final preparations on the morning of the ritual. His entire body hot and tingling with anticipation, desire curling low and potent in his gut, Elijah grabbed the stone and headed into his bathroom, dick already hardening at the thought of what he was about to do.

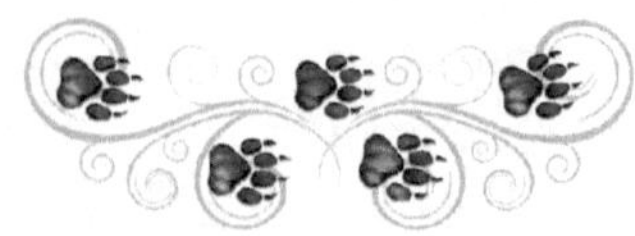

CHAPTER
SEVENTEEN

Victor stared at the smooth, round moonstone. The dim light of the room accentuated its subtle white-and-blue sheen, a piece of the night sky come to rest on his bathroom counter, as alluring as the moon that hung over him, full and waiting for the day to recede before she revealed her true beauty.

He hadn't bothered turning on the light; it wouldn't be necessary for this.

Nervous anticipation built in his stomach, and a heavy awareness settled over every inch of his skin. This would be the weirdest jerk-off session he'd ever had, but his dick was far from opposed to the idea.

He took a deep breath, then another. It didn't help. Warmth coiled around his chest, and his hands wanted to shake, though he didn't let them. He hadn't slept much the night before, too wound up between the looming ritual and the full moon.

His fingers skated over the runes carved on the stone's cool, smooth face. Underneath, Elijah's magic was embedded, finespun and ready for—what had Elijah called it? Victor's offering? He suppressed a shiver.

The things he did for his pack.

Magic sparked against his skin, increasing his excitement. As he palmed himself through his sweats, arousal flooded him. He leaned against the wall opposite the counter.

With the moon less than twelve hours to full, his wolf prowled close to the surface, and it was more than willing to do this, to mark this stone—something it knew their pack needed, something *Elijah* needed. Elijah needing his come woke every primal, untamed instinct inside him.

Victor didn't want to dwell on that, but he didn't have to. His body had decided it was time to do this, his dick tenting his sweats. He pulled himself out and let his pants slide down, the fabric catching on his thighs as he gripped his shaft with his right hand, the moonstone held in his left.

He stroked himself slowly, tugging his foreskin back with each pull before sliding it forward again. His thumb swiped over the head of his cock, through the precome that had beaded there. Every movement sent aching pulses of desire through him.

Elijah hadn't given him details about how to do this. Was there a right way? Did it matter as long as he came on the stone? It must not, or Elijah would have told him. His breath stuttered at the thought of Elijah watching him, telling him precisely what to do.

Had Elijah done this yet? Had he jerked off and come on his own stone?

Victor's vision blurred, and for a moment, the foggy white moonstone was eclipsed by a glossy black.

This wouldn't take long. He'd already leaked more

precome than he knew he could produce. He was on the edge, desperate to come, his entire being consumed by it like he'd been teasing himself for hours.

If he'd been asked what a fertility ritual would require, this wasn't what he would have envisioned. The ward ritual had alternative versions. Did this one as well? Was there a version where they'd be doing this together? He closed his eyes and stroked faster, lost in that fantasy.

What would it have been like to press against Elijah's back as he had in the forest, to have him lean against his chest as Victor jerked him off, scraping his teeth along Elijah's neck right where a mating bite would go? His gums tingled with the impulse to drop his fangs.

Could he have had Elijah's long fingers wrapped around his dick as Elijah sucked at the juncture of his neck, marking him in return? Or both of them thrusting into their joined hands, Elijah's length pressing against his own.

It was impossible not to want that, not to want to continue where they'd left off. To let Elijah's scent and taste drive him higher, relentlessly pushing him toward the brink of his orgasm.

Magic flared in the moonstone, prickling up his left arm. He cupped the stone and pressed it against his cock. His hand tightened, and he let out a low growl as each thrust into his fist dragged his tip over the stone. The zing of Elijah's magic was instant, recognizable, and more welcome than he was willing to admit.

The sensations drove him crazy—the smooth stone against him, his grip strong and slick. It wouldn't take much more to finish, but he tried to draw it out. He wanted the vision of Elijah in his head to be real, to know that, even if he wasn't there with Victor, Elijah had been equally as affected by this. That he'd been thinking about Victor as his hand glided over his shaft, as he held back his orgasm, ravenous for more, shuddering gasps of air amplified in his tiny bathroom, the harsh lights above the desilvering mirror highlighting the flush in his cheeks, the redness of his cock head. His eyes a soft purple glow, his heart racing, mind wild with how this might have been different.

Victor smelled his own arousal, his own precome, but he swore it was mixed with Elijah's. His scent, his lust, how he craved release. Like if he looked, he'd see Elijah's reflection in the mirror, not his own.

"*Fuck*," he muttered, low and rough, as his dick nudged against the stone, against Elijah's magic. He screwed his eyelids shut and gritted his teeth.

His wolf's excitement deepened as his hips jerked and bucked. He groaned and heard Elijah's answering moan cut off as he came, stripes of come landing against the black-and-white stone.

The thought sent a jolt of pleasure through Victor, one he couldn't deny, and he nearly howled, hips thrusting up, cock pulsing, shooting over the stone and the precome smeared there.

He savored his orgasm, the pressure of it. Breathing hard and fast, he stroked himself through the aftershocks. A few more spurts landed on the stone. His hand settled at the base of his dick, and he squeezed, groaning at how gloriously sensitive it was, the hot throb of it.

Panting, he slumped against the wall. Threads of magic wove through him, tugging at him, readying him for the ritual, as undeniable as the moon over him, filling him with her energy.

He glimpsed himself in the mirror, eyes flashing. His jaw ached with how close his canines were to descending, with the need to sink them into something. His wolf was so instinctual under the influence of the moon, so eager for whatever Elijah was willing to give them.

Victor blew out a breath and forced himself to focus. White streaks decorated the stone, and he rubbed his thumb across it, over and over, letting the come soak in, tracing the runes Elijah had carved. As he did, they kindled to a gentle incandescence before fading as he worked in the last of his release, and all that was left was the soft, sticky rasp of his hand in the silence.

An image of Elijah doing the same shot through his mind, his long fingers trailing over the runes on his stone, smearing his come over the white-flecked surface. The thought alone caused Victor's cock to twitch. Even with his shifter stamina, he'd need a few minutes before he could go again, but fuck if that thought wasn't enough to get him there.

When he felt capable of moving, he pushed himself off the wall, still reeling from his orgasm. He turned on the tap and rinsed his right hand while cradling the moonstone in his left, then tugged up his sweats and headed into his room, settling the stone into the box Elijah had sent it in. Victor closed the lid, and a gust of surprised laughter was pulled from him when a light glittered around it, instantly cutting off the telltale scent of what lay inside. That answered the question of how he was going to get it past Kade without him knowing.

He stepped back into the bathroom and blinked. How long had it been this big? He frowned, bemused. Where had that thought come from? He knew how large his bathroom was. He must have come part of his brain out during that orgasm.

Shaking his head, he stripped and started the shower. Not that it'd help with the teasing.

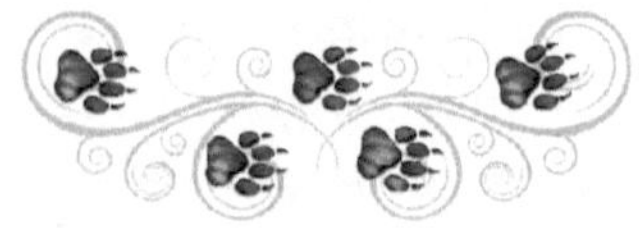

When Victor got downstairs, Kade smirked at him, but for once, he said nothing. Apparently he had enough self-preservation not to push Victor when the moon was full and they were at their most volatile. He'd been less circumspect over the last week. It was like he knew the dreams Victor had been having, which nights he'd had them, and every single time he'd given in to those dreams, because those were the mornings Kade's teasing was relentless.

Victor wanted to blame it on the phone calls. After talking to Elijah for hours, how was he supposed to not dream of him too? To not think about him in less than platonic ways, to not wake up hard and hungry for him. He shouldn't be thinking about Elijah at all, and definitely not like that, not now, but he couldn't bring himself to stop it either, couldn't make himself regret those calls or the dreams that came after.

If anything, he looked forward to both.

And somehow, Kade knew it. The bastard. But he wasn't the only one.

Victor had lost count of the less-than-subtle hints, suggestions, and implications that various pack members had lobbed his way. They'd made it more than clear they supported Victor pursuing a relationship with Elijah, should he want to continue whatever was happening between them.

He didn't, but that didn't stop the comments.

So while Kade kept his mouth shut that morning, Katrina didn't.

"Will Elijah be here for the pre-run dinner?" she asked, cheerfully innocent. It'd be convincing if he hadn't heard similar questions all week.

"Why would he?"

"Because you invited him?"

"That's not a good idea," Victor said, grabbing a slice of toast from the stack she was making.

"You're right. It isn't a good idea," she called after him as he escaped out the door. "It's a great one!"

No, it wasn't. Pre-run dinners were for pack, and his wolf was confused enough about Elijah already. He shouldn't add to that confusion.

He ate the toast and headed into the trees.

Elijah's wards had trapped the rot in most places, but Victor's land felt tainted. He might enjoy their conversations, but they caused progressively more guilt to creep over him. Like he was letting his pack down by allowing himself those self-indulgent moments as his territory lay sick and dying. And more and more, they weren't able to take his mind off things.

But Elijah seemed confident this ritual would work, so Victor had to believe him. That was the only thing he could do. Believe him and hope this would be the last time he walked through his forest with decay polluting everything around him.

It was dusk when Elijah's car pulled up to the house. Victor waited on the porch. His heartbeat sped up, and next to him, Kade snorted. Fuck him. It was simply because he was nervous about this damn ritual, nothing other than that.

But as Elijah got out of his car, Victor couldn't stop his eyes from trailing over his body, admiring how good he looked in his tailored dress shirt and slacks. Relief rushed over him at Elijah being on his territory again.

From his trunk, Elijah grabbed a box, smaller and lighter than the one he'd brought for the previous ritual. As he headed toward them, his fingers ran over the things inside, doing one final check of its contents.

Victor met him halfway.

When Elijah glanced up, there was a hint of color on his cheeks, and Victor's hand curled around the small box he was holding, flashing back to that morning, to the knowledge that, at some point today, Elijah had done the same. And for a handful of drawn-out seconds, they stood in front of his house, both waiting for the other to speak.

Victor's ears burned.

Kade bounded down the stairs behind him. "So, Elijah, all prepared for the ritual?" There was a leer in his tone that was too knowing for Victor's liking.

Elijah's gaze darted to Victor, and Victor shook his head a fraction. No way in hell he'd have told Kade about that.

"Everything's ready," Elijah said.

"That's good. You know, recently, I read a thing that said different woods have different magical properties."

"...they do." Elijah was clearly and rightfully concerned about where this was going.

"Does this ritual require any wood?"

"No."

"Ah, that's a shame. Victor's got a ton of wood I'm sure he'd let you use however you wanted. Some other time." He winked at Elijah, but before Victor could growl or swipe at him, he was heading toward the back of the house, where the pack was waiting. They'd be there at a bonfire until Victor returned after the ritual.

Elijah watched Kade leave before shooting Victor a look. "Seriously. They're never allowed to meet. *Never.*"

Victor gave an amused huff, the tension between them broken.

He inhaled, getting a good hit of Elijah's scent. And for one moment, he was lost in it, lost in that earthy, snowy fragrance and the feeling of home that came with it. It'd been a week since he'd truly scented it, the pile of sheets on his dresser a poor substitute, and it was hard to convince himself he hadn't missed it, hadn't been waiting to get Elijah here so he could have more. Hard to remember the reasons he shouldn't pull Elijah closer and bury his nose in his neck until he was drowning in him. Hard to pretend it was just his wolf craving that.

He managed to turn away and lead Elijah to the clearing, but the moon made him reckless. His wolf demanded he push things, and he couldn't repress the impulse, not completely. "So, do you want my shirt off for this?"

Elijah cocked an eyebrow at him, no doubt remembering the first ritual. "It wouldn't hurt, but it's not required."

Victor wasn't sure if he was disappointed or not.

"Don't let that stop you though," Elijah said, his expression sly.

"That sounded like something Kade would say."

Elijah groaned. "Oh god. Take that back."

When they reached their destination, Elijah set down his box. He knelt at the center of the clearing. Victor stood beside him, unsure what to do until Elijah waved for him to sit across from him.

Elijah rolled up his sleeves and pressed his palms to the ground. "This is one of the greatest benefits of having an affinity to earth." His tattoos lit up, curling across his skin, as he used his magic, pushing it into the soil.

The earth between them moved, four holes opening up, neat and empty, as the dirt piled to one side.

Elijah settled onto his heels and grinned at Victor.

"You must be popular with anyone who likes to build or plant."

"If magic were known, I'd make a killing in construction, gardening, or land excavation." He inched closer to the holes, and Victor did the same on the other side.

Elijah had told him the basics of this. He'd said it was about resetting the land by using the seasonal cycle. What that meant, Victor hadn't been sure, but he was about to find out.

He watched as Elijah took out supplies one by one and laid them in the first hole on his left. A red stone went in, followed by a black one, both with carvings on them. Herbs and flower petals were sprinkled over them before Elijah caught Victor watching him. He tilted his head ever so slightly.

"Carnelian," he explained, pointing to the first stone. "To symbolize the setting sun. And black tourmaline for protection and balance. Sage to drive away evil spirits, acorns for perseverance. Calendula represents transformation and protection, and red spider lilies for the arrival of fall."

Next was a twig with a few brilliant red leaves.

"Maple?" Victor asked.

"Yes, for balance and promise."

"So this does require wood."

"Adding to the list of things Kade never needs to know."

Victor snorted in amusement, and Elijah continued his explanation of the items he put in the second hole, all symbolizing winter, getting more detailed as he recognized Victor's interest. He then hesitated before the third hole.

"I'm guessing it's time for this?" Victor asked, tapping the box beside him.

Elijah wet his lips. "Moonstone," he said, gesturing toward Victor. "For obvious reasons and for growth and abundance."

Then he grabbed a small box, a matched pair to the one he'd given Victor, and opened it. Even before Victor saw the stone, he smelled Elijah's release on it.

"And snowflake obsidian, for balance. And because it felt right." Elijah placed it in the hole. Under the luminous moonlight that spilled over them, the stone was black earth dotted with white snow, streaks of dried come visible on its glassy surface. Victor tried not to pull in a deep lungful of air to get more, but it was impossible. The memory of that morning ran through him like wildfire.

To distract himself, he opened his own box, pulled out the stone, and set it next to Elijah's. Elijah nodded his approval before he went through the rest of the preparations for spring and summer, narrating the whole process.

When he was finished, he pressed his hands flat against the earth again, and the pile of dirt slithered into the holes, almost as if the ground had never been disturbed.

He took out a knife and sliced it across his palm. A thin line of blood appeared, and he let a few drops drip onto each mound of newly packed earth as he held the knife out to Victor. Without asking, Victor copied him, letting his blood spatter to the ground, joining Elijah's.

On top of the refilled holes, Elijah placed thick pillar candles in different colors, their wax carved with intricate symbols Victor couldn't hope to read. Then Elijah pulled out small metal cups, a pair for each season, filling them from four thermoses and placing them next to each candle. Victor caught the scent of spiced cider spiked with whiskey, mulled wine, honeyed milk, and cinnamon tea.

"We'll drink each as the season passes. The milk contains herbs that are technically aphrodisiacs. Whether or not that's the case is questionable, but it will probably make you warm."

Elijah snapped his fingers and ignited the wick of the dark red candle on the first mound. He picked up a cup of spiced cider. "Ready?"

There was a tangle of worry in Victor's gut, gnawing away at him. If this didn't work, he didn't know what they'd do. But he pushed through the doubt and grabbed his cup, surprised to find it warm. He lifted it in acknowledgment to Elijah before drinking its contents, the liquor burning its way to his stomach.

He set the cup beside Elijah's. "Kade will be delighted to learn you gave me something hard while we were out here."

Elijah laughed. "How about we put that on the Never Tell Kade list too?" Still smiling, he held out his left hand, palm up, the cut on it not quite healed. Victor didn't need to be told what to do. He placed his own over Elijah's, grasping tight.

The sharp inhale Elijah took at the contact sounded anything but pained. His eyes shone purple before they drifted shut, and the tattoos on his arms gleamed in the night.

Magic poured off him and cascaded over Victor. A rush of power surged through him, fueling him, twisting and twining with his energy, increasing exponentially before flooding back into Elijah.

Elijah had said this ritual was supposed to require less from them both, but it seemed like more—more magic, more energy. More everything.

Maybe he should close his eyes too, but he was too transfixed by the play of emotion and concentration on Elijah's face. Dark lashes fanned out over his fair skin, accentuating the sharp contours of his cheekbones. His brow was furrowed, and his lips were slightly parted in a way that made Victor want to lean in and do things he shouldn't.

Elijah was doing something with his energy. Victor felt it being woven, bent to Elijah's will. The magic built and grew until there was no way they could contain it between the two of them. Then everything snapped into place, and it rushed out, sweeping through Victor's territory, through the tainted land, into every tree and plant. When it reached his wards, it echoed back.

The forest changed. Trees that had been showing the initial signs of fall burst into vibrant colors. The reds and yellows and oranges of autumn painted the world, then hung there, Victor marveling at the sight.

Elijah squeezed his hand, drawing Victor's attention. His eyes were half-lidded, his breath quick and shallow.

"Next cup," he said in the softest whisper.

When Victor reached for the wine with his free hand, he started. The red candle had melted completely, the barest of flames remaining in the pool of wax.

He drank the wine, and Elijah did the same. They set their cups down, and the flame extinguished in a wisp of smoke before the white candle of winter flickered alight.

Goose bumps pebbled Victor's skin as the clearing took on a chill, and leaves fell like rain. Before the last hit the ground, snow swirled and draped the land in downy blankets of white, softening the bare branches. The area around them stayed clear, but there was no avoiding the cold.

Shivers racked Elijah's body as a deep freeze set in, and all life was held suspended. Even Victor felt it to his bones. He wanted nothing more than to pull Elijah against him, to give him his body heat as well as his energy.

Winter dragged by, their exhales fogging the air. Elijah's magic saturated the land, purging it of decay and corruption, doing things Victor didn't understand, but that resonated deep in his core, like he was being cleansed too, restored, ready to be reborn.

Just when the tremors of Elijah's body hit a point they demanded action, demanded Victor warm him in any way necessary, regardless of what the ritual called for, Elijah reached for the next cup with a trembling hand.

Victor drank from the third cup. The honeyed milk was oddly herbed. Nothing he'd ever choose, but not unpleasant. It slid down his throat, and although the liquid was cool, it warmed him from the inside more than the alcohol had, pooling in his stomach. It didn't go straight to his dick as he expected, but electricity hummed in his veins, making his skin more tender than usual, more sensitive, pulled tight, like the only way to ease that feeling was to touch himself. To run his hands over his thighs, over his chest, see where it'd take him. Or better, to have Elijah do it.

He barely noticed winter thawing around them, the snow melting to glimmering dewdrops as the green candle burned.

Elijah's shivers subsided. His hand gripped tighter, his fingers digging hard into Victor's skin like he needed Victor as an anchor to keep him from being swept away in the riptide of power.

Victor heard Elijah's heart pounding, his ragged gasps.

Arousal wound through Elijah's scent, and although that had to be due to whatever they'd drunk, he wanted it to be because of him, because of his energy. He wanted Elijah to experience this as he did, stretched hot and tight and full of magic.

Even without looking at the forest, he sensed it brimming with new life. It felt like a renewal, smelled like the first buds in spring. It swept through his pack, through their connections, and their surprise and wonder reverberated inside him.

He knew what came next. Without Elijah prompting, he lifted the fourth cup. But instead of drinking it himself, he held it out to Elijah, unable to deny the instinct. His breath caught as Elijah leaned forward, lips parting. Victor tilted the cup and poured the tea into his mouth, watching Elijah's throat work as he swallowed.

Then Elijah held out his cup for Victor to do the same. The heat that had pooled in his gut shot downward, lower. The chance of him not getting hard from this was long gone. He leaned forward, dick thickening in his jeans, eyes locked on Elijah's, opening his mouth for Elijah to fill. Swallowing, he sat on his heels, liking that Elijah's gaze was still on his mouth.

Elijah hovered there, not sitting back, and it took all of Victor's willpower not to lean forward again, to kiss him and see if he tasted like the tea, if his tongue was sweet with cinnamon. If it was better on his lips. He'd wager it was.

But before he could quench that thirst, Elijah jerked out of wherever he'd gone and set his cup on the ground. The final candle lit.

The air was dense and hot with magic, and the freshness of spring gave way to a sultry summer. Elijah's scent surrounded him, filled him, as magic sank into his skin, into his every cell.

Heat settled into his body; it intensified and spread, making him itch to rip off his clothes so he could press himself against Elijah's skin, the only thing that would cool him. His chest heaved, and sweat formed on his brow.

When he thought he wouldn't be able to take it anymore, the magic swelled one final time, filling them so impossibly full as it ran through their veins like moonlight. It threatened to break them, leaving no room for air in their lungs, for thought in their heads, for anything but that exquisite power at its peak. It held them there, suspended, for one endless, heart-stopping moment, and then it rolled out like the tide, like a held breath finally released, leaving them empty and shuddering, every nerve buzzing.

The world fell into place around them. Summer heat faded as the final sparks of magic receded, settling into the land, settling into the trees, the plants, his pack. Everything was now awash with life.

The forest was quiet except for their panting and the racing beats of their hearts.

Elijah didn't drop his hand. His eyes were radiant with magic, and Victor knew his wolf was showing as well.

The flame of the fourth candle guttered out, but the moon hung so bright and low that night he wouldn't have needed his enhanced senses to see.

Elijah's chest rose and fell, his cheeks flushed. Arousal clung to him, its scent murmuring possibilities. Victor longed to close the distance between them and press Elijah into the earth, to bring their bodies together, to find out if touching him, moving with him, coming with him, was as intoxicating as the ritual had been. He was already certain the ritual would never compare.

Elijah blinked, the magic fading from his eyes and tattoos, and hesitantly, he pulled his hand away. His voice was rough when he spoke. "We should check the forest."

As much as Victor wanted other things, Elijah was right. His pack took precedence over his desires.

Elijah put the cups in his box and stood, adjusting himself. There was no hiding that he was still half-hard; Victor was in a similar state. But he supposed that was to be expected with a fertility ritual.

In silence, Victor led him into the forest. Elijah held a flame in his hand, giving himself enough light to walk through the darkness. They headed toward where the worst of the rot had festered, passing through Elijah's wards along the way, and when they arrived, Victor stared in disbelieving wonder.

It wasn't exactly as it had been. The trees held scars from the rot, and a few had been too far gone to be revived, but that was the only evidence it'd left.

In its place was fresh growth, unseasonal this time of year, not yet colored by autumn. With as warm as the night was, it felt like two months earlier, when summer was at its height.

Victor was torn between letting out a relieved sigh and the knowledge that the rot had reappeared before. This was gorgeous, wondrous, a miracle. But would it last?

"It'll be fall again by next week, and nature will take her course from there," Elijah said, voice hushed. His face held a cautious wonder twin to Victor's. He released the fire he was holding, plunging them into night, then lifted his hand. "Can I?"

Victor didn't hesitate. He stepped closer, into Elijah's personal space, and let Elijah's hand slide around his neck, his fingers slipping underneath the collar of his shirt.

Elijah's magic engulfed him again, intimate in a way he'd never imagined possible.

Elijah's awareness spread outward, testing Victor's land, his pack. It was a quick check, but when he finished, he didn't move away. Astonishment cast his features in a euphoric glow. "I can't detect a single trace of it. Hold on. Let me..."

He didn't say what, but Victor sensed it. The wards he'd placed all over the territory fell away before he gazed up at Victor again.

The look in his eyes was something Victor had never seen before, and it filled him with a longing that scorched through his soul. All the sensations from the ritual came roaring back.

He wanted to kiss Elijah, wanted to exchange this all-consuming magic and energy with the brush of their lips, to press their bodies together and let the heat of their desire build between them. The pull toward Elijah was electric, magnetic, divine.

Maybe it was the heady aftermath of the ritual, or he was drunk off relief and gratitude, or his wolf had control. Whatever the reason, he couldn't tear his gaze from Elijah, couldn't even think of letting him go.

Heart hammering, his entire body thrumming with anticipation, he leaned in closer, so close their exhales mingled. His hands settled on Elijah's hips, eyes flickering to his mouth. Elijah's fingers curled tighter against his neck, pulling him in, his grin effervescent and unrestrained.

But then Victor heard a familiar howl, loud and joyous, ringing over the land, quickly joined by a few dozen more. His pack felt it too. They felt the rightness of this. Everything was the way it should be.

Victor understood, but damn if he wasn't about to

strangle Kade, because Elijah had looked away from him, toward the howls. When he turned back, he dropped his hand and stepped away.

The moment was gone, and Victor had to remind himself there was a chance this wasn't over, that it might not be as perfect as it seemed.

"I take it you need to get to your pack." A new ball of fire appeared in Elijah's hand, casting flickering shadows.

He was right; even Victor's wolf couldn't argue with that. Full moons were a time to run, to be with his pack, to revel in their nature under the moonlight.

"What will you do?" Victor asked. They had human members in their pack. Sometimes they joined their mates. There was no reason Elijah couldn't run with them. The thought of it prowled through Victor. If Elijah ran that night, it'd be impossible for Victor not to give chase.

But the invitation caught in his throat as Elijah headed toward the house. "I'll get out of your way."

Victor followed. His wolf whined at the idea of Elijah leaving, and Victor found himself agreeing. He didn't want that; his wolf decidedly didn't. There were so many reasons Elijah shouldn't go, but Victor clung to the safest ones.

"You should stay the night. If you're not taking payment for this, the least I can do is offer you a good breakfast. Especially after all the magic you used. And we should double-check in the morning, to make sure there are no signs of the rot returning."

Elijah hesitated, his footsteps faltering as he glanced over his shoulder. "Same bedroom as before?"

Victor didn't tell Elijah to wait in his room. That wasn't something he had any right to do. Instead, he said, "That one's open."

But it wasn't where Elijah belonged.

Elijah studied him, his expression unreadable, his scent still drenched with lust though clouded with confusion now. It crackled like a fire in the air between them.

Victor had gotten so used to the scent of Elijah's magic it no longer concealed all his emotions. Though that didn't mean he knew how to interpret them beyond knowing Elijah was as conflicted about this as Victor was.

His wolf whispered they should be the one to stoke that fire, to coax out Elijah's secrets.

After an eternity, Elijah nodded. "Then I'll see you at breakfast."

They stopped by the clearing to get Elijah's box, and then Victor showed Elijah back. Though after the last month, Elijah could likely navigate this forest as well as any pack member.

The bonfire behind the house blazed. Enough wood was piled nearby to burn through the night. His pack had waited like he'd ordered, but they were restless, most shifted already and those still in their human forms impatient to. The three exceptions were Will, Lauren, and Alex—all mated to humans. They were always the last to drag themselves away from the fire, torn between the instinct to run with their pack and the desire to stay close to their mates.

Victor had never wanted to stay by the fire on a full moon, but as Janell motioned Elijah over to take an open seat, he had to admit he understood the appeal. Being close to Elijah, scenting the vestiges of the ritual clinging to his skin, seeing the satisfaction on his face as he sat there—it called to him nearly as much as the moon.

Elijah was meant to be there, savoring the night air, the clean breeze coming through the forest, free from the taint of decay. Victor couldn't get over how right he looked.

An idea took root inside him. Maybe he could allow himself to have this, and it wouldn't prove he was weak. It might be okay for him to be close to magic, as long as it was Elijah.

If Elijah let him, if Elijah wanted to stay, wanted to be with him, with his pack.

Victor ached to remain, but he couldn't. Not now. His pack was eager to run, waiting for him, their anticipation coloring the air.

So he stripped off his shirt, and the few members of his pack that hadn't shifted followed. He felt the weight of eyes on him from across the fire and knew without looking who it was. Elijah's gaze devoured Victor as he unbuttoned his jeans and pushed them down.

Victor stayed in human form for longer than he had to. He let Elijah's eyes trace over his body before he gave in to the urge to shift and run, to lead his pack through a forest full of new life and growth. He tried to remember it might not last, tried not to get his hopes up, though it was difficult to hold on to that under the sway of the moon.

The forest blurred by him as he ran. He was high on the thrill, but even that didn't distract him.

For all he relished the pack run, his thoughts were at the house. He had to stop himself from going there, from finding Elijah by the fire or in whatever room he'd chosen, and bringing him to his own bed so he could lose himself in Elijah's scent, in his body. So he could move with Elijah, indulge his whims and pleasures, sate and satisfy him until he never wanted to leave, then ask him to be there, to stay there. Forever. Because he was sure now that Elijah was perfect for his pack. For him. Too perfect to let go.

Fear lingered in one tiny corner of his mind, and doubts hissed he wasn't strong enough, that he didn't deserve it, that all this was too good to be true, that he was being impulsive because it was the full moon and everything was right with his land. He was intoxicated on the moon, on the ritual. He couldn't be trusted like this. But that part of himself held less and less influence.

If he waited until the morning, when he wasn't under the moon's thrall, when the newness of all this life wasn't affecting him as much. After they'd confirmed there were no remnants of the decay, maybe then, before Elijah left, they could see where this thing between them, whatever it was, might go.

The promise of it swelled in his chest, pleasant and warm, like Elijah's magic during the ritual. It kept him company for the rest of his run.

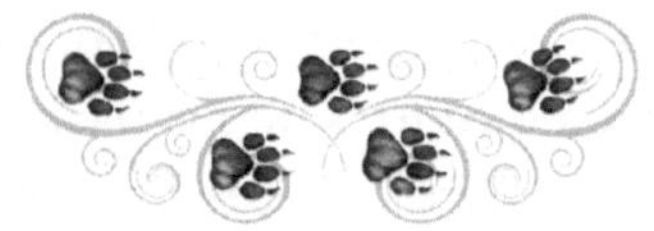

EIGHTEEN

The bonfire crackled, lighting up the night, but its flames were dim compared to the energy blazing through Elijah's body. It ran rampant through his blood, making him as restless as the shifters.

Each time he'd used Victor's energy, it'd gotten easier. From the first spell, it'd been so natural, but he had no words for it now. Their compatibility floored him. That night, when he'd touched Victor, his magic had shifted into something new, something stronger, more powerful. Pure and untamed and everything the forest needed to heal.

No one could blame him for how intoxicating he found it. During the ritual, he'd wanted to crawl into Victor's lap again, to kiss him, to do more. That might be because of the rush of magic, but he'd been attracted to Victor from the moment he'd seen him in the shop. The more he got to know him and saw him with his pack, the more that attraction grew. It didn't help when Victor stood there, naked and glorious, provocative, like he enjoyed Elijah's gaze on his skin as much as Elijah was enjoying the view.

If the world had stopped, Elijah wouldn't have been

able to tear his eyes away, too entranced by Victor bathed in the fire's warm flicker and moon's cool glow. Shadows and light played across his body, over the ridges and planes of his muscles, and Elijah's fingers itched to trace their course. Every line of Victor called to him like a siren song; his gaze held Elijah captive with promises of what could be, if only Elijah would allow it.

But the near-constant amber flare in those dark eyes made Elijah stay in his seat until Victor and his pack disappeared into the trees. Though even that didn't dissipate the whispers of temptation in Elijah's ears.

He knew what Victor's wolf wanted; its desire licked over his skin and sparked along his nerves. What Victor's human side wanted remained more elusive, and the two might not align when morning came.

No matter how reckless Victor's wolf made him on nights like these, at least part of him still distrusted mages. And there was no separating Elijah from his magic.

Even if that had changed, Elijah's plans hadn't. He intended to keep his neutrality and make the shop profitable. He couldn't let his attraction to Victor screw that up.

But if he were brutally honest, the first half of that was already impossible. If a conflict broke out between Victor's pack and another, Elijah wouldn't be able to stay neutral. Not when sitting around this fire with the human members of the pack felt right in ways he wouldn't let himself think about.

Out in the forest, a chorus of howls sounded, and somehow, he recognized Victor's even as they blended together. He stared in the direction of those howls, and when he turned back to the fire, he caught the knowing looks on the faces around him.

Next to him, Will's wife smirked at him, and Elijah

cleared his throat. At least these people couldn't smell him lusting after Victor.

"So," Elijah said, trying to distract himself from the inexplicable need to head into the forest, to run under the moonlight, to track down Victor and let his wolf decide how the rest of their night would go. "How long do you usually stay out here?"

Janell grinned, almost as wolfish as her mate. "All night. Until they return."

Elijah raised an eyebrow. They weren't shifters at the mercy of undeniable instincts to stay out under the moon.

"Oh, believe me, they make it worth the wait." She rubbed the swell of her stomach and winked. "Full-moon baby right here."

His eyebrows rose higher, and she chuckled.

"Honey, if you haven't fucked a wolf shifter on a full moon, you haven't lived." The others nodded before she continued. "They're wild. You'll get fucked within an inch of your life and enjoy every second."

"Or ridden," another added.

"Or both," the third chimed in.

Janell leaned toward him. "Stay up with us, and I'm sure Victor will be more than willing to give you a demonstration when he gets back."

Fucking hell, did every member of this pack want to set them up?

Heat flashed through Elijah at the idea he'd pushed away before. Victor, animalistic and insatiable, his wolf in control. He swallowed and tried to think of something else, anything else, but it lingered, making him too aware of how his clothes rubbed against his skin, how many hours he'd have to wait until dawn.

A heady mix of magic and elation writhed inside him,

too potent for him to sit still. The longer he stayed there, the more restless he became, like he was the one that needed to run to find relief. Tension gathered in his shoulders and neck, a growl building in his throat, an itch under his skin that he couldn't scratch. He tried not to fidget in his chair, but the urge to get up and move overwhelmed him. Holding a conversation was a struggle.

He begged off and told them he was wiped out from the ritual, though their looks said he'd been less than convincing.

Once he was in the guest bedroom, he paced its length, unsure what he wanted, what he needed. Rituals never left him this wired. He should be tired; he wasn't. Not even close.

He'd only used more magic once before, when he'd reset the territory wards. But instead of the post-ritual exhaustion he'd come to expect, he was keyed up, revived as thoroughly as the forest. His body felt tight, too small to contain everything he'd become, his senses too sharp.

Magic buzzed like electricity through his veins; his muscles thrummed with energy. The beat of his heart raced loud in his ears, and the scent in the room was frustratingly not how it should be, lacking in some undefinable way.

He shook his head. Something about this was wrong, but he couldn't concentrate enough to put a name to it or figure out what was happening. And he never would with his mind this scattered and chaotic.

He forced himself into bed. Things would make more sense after he got some rest.

Only years of trance work and meditation allowed him to consciously relax. But even with his training, it took over an hour for him to doze off.

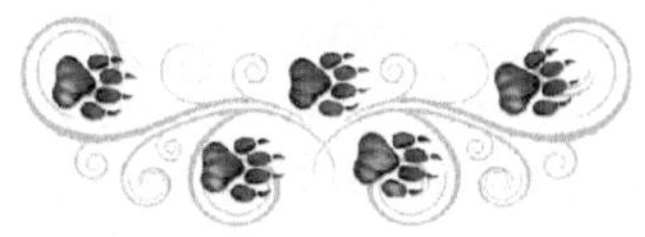

He ran through the trees. His senses were overloaded by the rustle of leaves against his fur, the thud of his paws on the ground. The scents of the forest. His pack running with him. The moon high in the sky, calling to him.

Somewhere in the hazy recesses of his subconscious, Elijah understood he was dreaming.

But not exactly. He'd never had a dream like this. It was too clear, too real.

He reached out with his magic, trying to take control.

Reality snapped into place.

This wasn't a dream, not really.

Elijah might be asleep, but in that moment, he was also Victor.

He ran with him through his territory. The pack bonds sang in his blood.

The lucid part of Elijah cursed. Something must have gone wrong if they were connected like this. The ritual had established a connection, but that should have ended as soon as it was over. He'd been so caught up in Victor's energy, in the sensations flowing between them, he must not have severed it correctly.

It was fine. He'd cut it in the morning. For now, he'd have the strangest dream of his life. There was no harm in that.

Not fighting it, he let himself be sucked into Victor's awareness. Running through the forest was exhilarating. He'd never experience this in his own body. The sheer power in his muscles, the melodies of nature murmuring to him, the perfection of the moon and her sway over him.

Elijah stayed lucid for a little longer, following along with Victor until the rhythm of paws against dirt lulled him into deeper sleep, and the dream faded away.

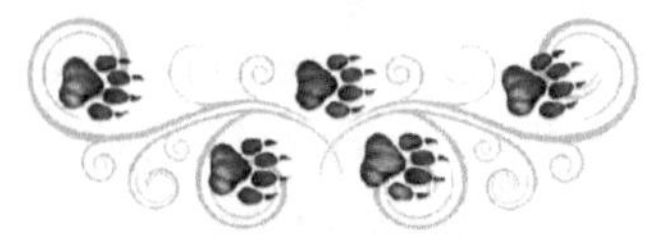

They were running again. Chasing something. Something they were eager to catch.

The scent was so clear. All dark earth and bright snow. Crisp. Easy to follow. Perfect. *Theirs.*

They sprinted toward it with single-minded purpose, shivers of anticipation under their skin, under their fur. They needed it now. Needed to catch it, claim it, possess it. Be possessed by it.

A clearing opened up in front of them, and they saw their target.

The prey they were chasing was Elijah. That scent, so fucking intoxicating, was Elijah.

They read the emotions in his scent. He was being chased through the forest by an enormous wolf, but there was no sour tang of fear. This was fun. He was excited, turned on, ready to be caught.

Their anticipation grew as they slowed. Instead of running down their prey, they stalked him, drawing closer, and he wasn't attempting to get away.

There was something off about this, but they didn't know what. Not that it mattered.

They wanted this, wanted to find a home in that alluring scent, to bring their bodies together and experience the things they'd been fantasizing about for the last month.

They neared Elijah. He smelled so right, so ready; it made their fangs ache.

That thought nagged at them.

Fangs.

No, Elijah didn't have fangs. Because he wasn't a wolf; he wasn't Victor. Clinging to that idea, he used it to keep himself lucid.

Was he running with Victor again? He didn't think so. It didn't feel the same.

Even staring at himself across the clearing, it took effort to grasp the difference.

Before, the forest had been sharp and clear. Now, everything was fuzzy around the edges. Time wasn't moving right. Distance was never consistent. Things flickered and changed.

The two constants were Elijah and the want that coursed through their body—a soul-deep, primal need.

The world tilted, disorientating him. This wasn't Victor in his wolf form as he ran with the pack.

They were dreaming.

Together.

He was in Victor's dream, looking at himself. But *he* was Elijah. That other Elijah wasn't real.

It was so odd to see himself like this, from the outside. Was this how Victor saw him? His pale skin ethereal in the starlight, his eyes sparkling, a hint of magic in their depths.

It shouldn't be possible. It shouldn't be happening.

Elijah tried to focus, tried to figure out how much of this was him, how much was Victor, but their thoughts bled together, entwined, inseparable.

Should he stop this? Did he want to? It should feel

wrong to invade Victor's dreams, but nothing about this felt wrong. Everything was so fucking right, so fucking good. It wasn't hard to sink into the dream, to lose himself in it.

Dream Elijah wasn't evading Victor. He faced them, grinning, backing away as Victor circled him, herding him toward a tree. Because he wanted this as badly as Victor did. As badly as the real Elijah did.

When his back hit the tree, something in them—no, not in *them*, in *Victor*—changed. *Shifted.* And then they were in human form, moonlight caressing their bare skin.

Was that how it felt to shift? That momentary unbecoming, then being reborn, a change so profound it went to a cellular level. Elijah had seen the shift countless times; he'd always been fascinated by it. And now, to feel it...

But that didn't matter either, not when they were closing in on Dream Elijah.

They pinned him against the tree, wove fingers through his hair, and kissed him like they'd been waiting to all night. It was as good as Victor remembered it being, sultry and passionate, everything they craved.

Victor's dick pulsed, rubbing against fabric. It was bizarre to experience these sensations like they were his own, like they came from his body when they didn't.

Breaking away long enough to undress Dream Elijah was a challenge. They wanted to rip off his clothes, but they knew not to do that. They had once, and he hadn't been happy with them. So they unbuttoned his shirt, tugged his pants down, and turned him to face the tree. Then they draped themselves along his back, inhaling his enticing scent, and ground against his ass, the friction of it better than anything else they'd done that night. Running with their pack could never compete with this.

Dream Elijah braced his forearms against the trunk and laughed as Victor dug in his pants, pulling out a packet of lube. "It's good one of us has pockets," he said, and Victor hummed his agreement against his nape, nipping at his skin as they drizzled lube onto their fingers and glided them down the crack of his ass.

They stilled when they met little resistance as they pushed their fingers into his already slick hole.

He huffed out a breath. "Did you really think I'd come out here unprepared? I know how you get on full moons."

Because this wasn't the first time they'd done this. They'd done it so many times before, in this world of infinite full moons where they could run, where they could find each other and come together under endless moonlight.

Victor made sure he was good and prepared, thick fingers working him open, relentlessly seeking out his prostate until Dream Elijah was keening and cursing, demanding Victor fuck him already, and then they were pushing inside. The pleasure sweeping through Victor's body ignited a bone-deep satisfaction like nothing they'd experienced before.

But being inside himself was too strange. Seeing Victor's cock spread him open, feeling it as Victor did, not as himself—it wasn't what he wanted.

Although watching himself get fucked gave him an illicit thrill, it seemed cruel. He was consumed by a shameless desire to feel the sublime burn of Victor sliding into him. Only getting to see it was a maddening tease.

Because, damn, he wanted that. Wanted to be pressed against that tree as Victor fucked him.

The forest flickered. Bark scraped against his forearms, and his breath came in harsh gasps. Victor drilled into him, hips slapping his ass, drowning him in intense, delirious bliss. Just the way he liked it.

Elijah tensed, surprised to find himself on the other side of things. To have Victor driving into him, every hot, thick inch sending him higher. Being fucked instead of doing the fucking. His dick as hard as Victor's had been but leaking in the cool night air, no longer buried in warmth.

Victor paused and fluttered kisses along Elijah's neck, wrapping a hand around his shaft and stroking. "You okay?" he asked, voice concerned. "Need me to go slower? More lube?"

Euphoria coiled through Elijah. His magic shimmered around them, drinking in the energy Victor gave him, his tattoos glittering softly. He couldn't remember the last time he'd felt this alive.

Screw it, he thought. Might as well enjoy the ride. It was never happening in real life.

He bucked his hips and spread his legs as wide as his pants would allow. "I'm good," he said. "Come on. Fuck me."

Victor obeyed. He pounded into him, picking up the rhythm he'd set before.

Elijah clawed at the bark as sharp teeth grazed his neck, biting hard enough Victor was just shy of breaking skin. It stung in the most satisfying way. He tilted his head to the side and met each of Victor's thrusts. His body was ablaze with the need to come.

This was perfection. Nothing would ever be better than this.

The world blurred and tipped.

The rough bark faded to something softer.

Lips brushed against his, sweet and slow, like that kiss

was all they could ever want. Like lovers familiar with every inch of each other's mouths.

Heat clenched around his cock, and Elijah groaned.

Was he Victor again?

That didn't seem right.

He broke the kiss, looking down into Victor's eyes. They were lust blown and dark.

Elijah had enough presence of mind to realize they were in Victor's bedroom, in his bed. His hips rolled, moving in Victor with a sonorous, unhurried momentum that built between them to a smoldering crescendo, a sensual dance that had Victor's fingers digging into his shoulders, holding him tight.

Victor arched beneath him, close to coming, and god, this was beyond unfair. The gorgeous shifter pack alpha was vers and so beautifully responsive? That knowledge would kill him.

Elijah slid a hand over Victor's incredible body, all his taut muscles and the sweat-slick sheen on his chest. He watched, mesmerized, as his fingers skated over skin and lit up the magical tattoos he'd placed there, the intricate patterns spiraling out from Victor's heart. The sight caused fierce possessiveness to curl inside him.

He traced the lines of the tattoos, seeing his magic flicker over Victor's skin, loving the desperate moan it dragged out of him. Pressing forward, he kissed Victor.

His previous thought had been wrong. *This* was perfection.

The world spun again.

His face was buried in his forearms as he braced himself against the tree. They were in the clearing, Victor fucking into him like it was his life's purpose, each thrust stretching him wider as the base of Victor's dick swelled, and this time, it was Elijah letting out a moan, knowing what that meant and so desperate for it.

The lines between himself and Victor blurred further. Ecstasy spiraled in an endless feedback loop. Desire, lust, need, feeding off each other, building like their magic and energy always did.

"Come for me," Victor growled in his ear. "Come on my knot." He gripped Elijah's hips, pounding into him once more. His knot fully expanded, locking them together, as he bit Elijah's neck right over the mark he'd given him months ago.

Elijah couldn't hold back. His come splattered onto the tree, and Victor released inside him, filling him with spurt after spurt. It left him trembling in Victor's arms as he rocked his hips for every last drop. His vision blurred from the intensity of their orgasms.

The night sky above them swirled, spinning them in its dizzying embrace. They stayed like that, suspended in the starlight, as their bodies cooled.

"I knew you were going to do that," Elijah said, voice a breathless laugh, clenching on Victor's cock. "You never can wait until we're back in bed."

Victor nuzzled against his neck, deliberately dragging his stubble over sensitive skin before sucking one last hickey there as Elijah moaned. "Don't worry. I'll knot you again once we are." He sounded far too pleased with himself, and it made Elijah smile.

"Really wasn't worried about that. It's more the chilling for twenty minutes with my dick out in the middle of a forest that has me concerned."

"And yet you're out here every full moon." Victor's hand cupped Elijah's softening length and squeezed, earning him a groan.

"I've never claimed to make the best life choices, and I'm drawing the line once it snows. Not risking frostbite on my balls for you."

Victor trailed kisses along his neck. "Why not? You know I'll keep you warm."

"Why do I put up with you?" There was so much exasperated fondness in his own tone it weighed heavy on his chest, constricting his lungs.

A gentle hand on his jaw turned his head enough for Victor to brush their lips together. Sweet, tender. Loving.

But when he went to deepen the kiss, when Victor's hips started to move again, grinding into him, the dream burst, pushing Elijah out of it and into his body. Waking suddenly to morning light filling the room, he was unsurprised to find he'd come in his underwear.

He groaned and hauled himself out of bed, his legs shakier than he expected as he made his way to the bathroom to clean himself up. He splashed water on his face, then looked at himself in the mirror, his pupils still dilated, his cheeks still flushed.

Then he froze as his eyes settled on his neck, on the dark bruises blooming there, hickeys where Victor had left them in the dream. A shiver ran through him as he remembered Victor's mouth on him.

His shoulder ached, a low throb, and he brought his hand up. As his fingers tentatively prodded it, a spiral of scrollwork lit up, and in his mind, he saw Victor laid out under him, the same magical tattoos decorating his chest.

Elijah's stomach dropped.

His knowledge about permanent tethers would barely fill an index card, but he knew these tattoos; they were part of it and should not be there. Like Victor's marks shouldn't be there either.

He inhaled sharply as it clicked into place. The dreams he'd been having, how he seemed to sense when Victor was at his most agitated, how unstable his magic had been.

This wasn't from screwing up last night. He'd fucked up a month ago, and it had been getting worse with every spell he'd channeled Victor's energy, strengthening some kind of partial tether between them.

No wonder his magic was acting up. The tether hadn't been established properly; it wasn't complete or stable and definitely wasn't balanced.

Pressing his fingers into the marks, he almost groaned as pleasure spiked through him, but he forced himself to focus. He could feel it—the connection leading to Victor. That tiny thread he'd found during the first ritual, but it was infinitely stronger now, reinforced whenever they'd connected, fiber after fiber twining around each other, forging it into a rope that tied them together.

He dropped his hand. God, he'd screwed up massively. Victor was going to be pissed, and rightfully so.

His friends would never let him live this down.

Even with all that, with as fucked-up as this was, he had to admit it had been a hot dream. He'd probably jerk off to the memory of it a pathetic number of times before he got it out of his system, but that just made him more despicable.

He sighed. Beating himself up over it would have to wait.

Shower first, then he'd find Victor and fix this.

He hooked his thumbs in his underwear but paused, worried about what he'd find when he stripped them off. Thankfully the only come in them was his own. Though he swore he felt the ghost of Victor inside of him, his knot stretching him open, leaving him too empty. More a memory than a physical sensation.

Jesus, was that what knotting was like? He'd felt so full, so owned, so connected. He reached behind himself and ran a finger over his entrance, shivering. It wasn't particularly tender. Not quite oversensitized or like he'd been fucked, but also more real than any dream had a right to be, even if the ache it'd left was more spiritual than corporeal.

The laugh that spilled out of him had a half-hysterical edge.

He'd taken a giant metaphorical shifter dick. Or, he supposed, not metaphorical. Metaphysical, maybe? Could cocks be astrally projected?

Aran could *never* know.

Shaking his head, he started the shower. But before he jumped in, he sent a quick message to Liam. And only Liam. He'd deal with the group chat later.

ELIJAH

> Hey, can you maybe send me a summary of your research on tethers?

> And how to sever permanent ones.

> ...asking for a friend.

By the time he'd finished washing up, a dozen notifications flashed on his phone, all from Liam.

LIAM

> Are you okay?

> What the hell happened?

> Elijah?

> Why aren't you answering?

You can't drop something like that on me and disappear.

Elijah!

If you don't reply this instant,

I'm going to tell Aran you tethered yourself to your big-dicked alpha shifter.

Sorry.

I didn't mean that.

But fuck, Elijah.

What the hell?

Answer me!

Okay, fine.

Here are my notes.

BUT ANSWER ME ASAP.

Elijah snorted at the flood of messages. He should have seen that coming.

ELIJAH

Sorry. Had to shower. I'm okay. I promise I'll explain everything tonight.

He ignored the second wave of messages Liam sent, mentally apologizing for making him worry and wait for more detailed answers, but he had to handle this first.

Liam had sent a PDF of everything he had on both tethers and bonds. Ever since middle school, Liam's notes were the best notes. Elijah opened the document and started skimming.

The basics, he knew. Shifters needed to bite someone during sex to bond them. They tended to be serious, once-in-a-lifetime connections. Mages, on the other hand, connected to all manner of things, but a tether, connecting themselves permanently to a specific shifter, required sex, magic, and, most importantly, consent. Transactional bonds and tethers were never as strong as genuine ones. One-sided connections—a shifter biting a mage who couldn't use their magic, or a mage tricking a shifter into a tether without allowing the shifter to bite them in return—were unbalanced and should be avoided at all costs.

Elijah winced. They hadn't had sex, Victor hadn't bitten him, but there was a connection between them. It wasn't full-fledged, but it was there. And it had to be pretty one-sided because there was no way Victor would consent to that. Elijah would never use it to drain his energy against his will, but after everything that had happened to his father, even the possibility of it was the last thing Elijah wanted to put Victor through.

He read on, finding a full page of notes covering how connections were severed. At least it wasn't a shifter bond. Those could only be cut on the new moon, but that gave him cold comfort. Liam had included a note that shifter bonds couldn't be reestablished once severed. There was no similar note on tethers. Elijah didn't think they worked the same way—mages frequently had to reconnect to things—but he wasn't sure if that applied to tethers as well. He didn't bother asking; he didn't need to. This wouldn't be happening again.

The notes explained how to cut a full, permanent tether. It seemed simple enough. But they didn't have that, not truly, and Elijah didn't love the idea of asking to ride Victor's cock so they could establish one for the sole purpose of severing it. He doubted that'd go over well. But maybe all the dream sex they'd been having over the last few weeks would be enough. If he could open it a little further first, he should be able to sever it completely.

This wouldn't be pleasant for either of them, not if the notes were correct about what a real tether felt like. He'd be laid bare and open to Victor, and not in the fun way he had been in their dreams.

After drying off, he got dressed, without the mess that had previously been his underwear, and prepared himself for the conversation he was about to have. If that was even possible.

It'd be the most awkward conversation in his life. The one asking Victor to come on a stone for him had nothing on this.

But this was what he got. He'd fucked up, and now it was time to fix his mistake.

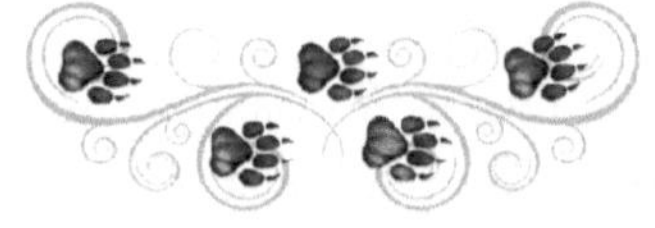

NINETEEN

Victor stretched, more than a little bereft when he realized he was alone in his bedroom, not in the forest with Elijah pressed against him.

His body ached in the glorious way only a full-moon run could leave it, his wolf sated and content, his muscles well used. But there was more to it than that: a sprawling satisfaction had woven through every fiber of his being, something he couldn't attribute to the run. A deep warmth had settled into his bones, and he knew the source with absolute certainty.

He'd had countless dreams about Elijah, but none had been as vivid as this. He swore he still tasted Elijah on his tongue, still felt him clenched hot and tight around his cock. The memory sent pleasure tingling through his body.

They'd been bonded in that dream. He waited for the panic that idea should have caused, but it didn't come. Instead, he basked in unadulterated contentment.

If knotting Elijah was half as good in real life... He squeezed the base of his dick, recalling the morning before, jerking off in the bathroom. Had that been the start of it?

That oversensitive throb. Had he gotten close from the mere thought of getting off with Elijah? Was that even possible? He'd never heard of someone knotting before they were bonded. But then, nothing with Elijah went how he expected, so why would this?

It'd felt so right to be inside Elijah, to have Elijah inside him. Everyone made assumptions about what he liked in bed because of his looks and pack hierarchy, but if Elijah wanted to slow-bone him into the mattress until his need to come was so overwhelming he couldn't remember his own name, well, Victor wouldn't say no to that.

There was no denying it to himself any longer. He wanted that. Wanted it for real. Wanted to experience Elijah's magic moving under his hands as they fucked, to see Elijah gasping and shuddering as he came, to give himself to Elijah and get him in return.

His wolf stirred as the dream replayed in his head, arousal flowing through him. It was right. There was no reason not to let himself have this.

He couldn't believe he was being given a chance at something he hadn't dared to dream about in so long. Ever since he'd first met that bastard mage, after everything that had happened, he'd thought that future had been lost to him.

But now, with Elijah, it didn't seem so impossible.

He stretched again and grimaced as the residue of his dream caused his sheets to cling cool and sticky against his inner thigh. He pushed them aside. That was what he got for sleeping naked. Given the dreams he'd been having lately, he should have known better, but he hadn't been able to pull on clothes after his run, skin too sensitive with his wolf so close to the surface. Now he was going to have to do more laundry as a consequence. He couldn't bring himself to regret it though.

Letting his eyes drift shut, he savored the memory of the dream and absentmindedly rubbed a hand over the warmth pooling around his heart. He'd nearly dozed off again when he heard a hesitant knock on his door.

It'd be so easy to ignore it, to stay in bed and nurse his fantasies, but it wasn't his pack. Most of them would never be up this early, and they knew not to interrupt anyone after a full moon. If it'd been an emergency, Kade or his other betas would have barged in, even if he was asleep. Or otherwise occupied. Though, if he were otherwise occupied with Elijah, he'd have a good reason to use the wards on his room more often.

Which brought him back to the person most likely standing outside his door.

Body humming from the dream, desire making his dick hang heavy—not hard yet, but also not needing much encouragement to get there—he had to admit he wasn't in an ideal state to answer the door, regardless of who was on the other side. But he took a few calming breaths and got out of bed, pulling on a pair of sweats as he made his way to the door, then giving himself and his bed a quick once-over to make sure there were no streaks of come on his stomach or any other incriminating evidence.

When he opened the door, Elijah was waiting, one hand resting on the frame, eyes unfocused, looking at something Victor couldn't see. He was dressed in his usual slacks and button-up shirt, though he'd left the top few buttons undone. His hair was damp from a shower.

"Elijah?"

He jumped, returning from wherever he'd gone. "Sorry. The wards on this room are fascinating. They were listed in that book, but I'd need—" He cut himself off, then looked past Victor into his room. "Can I come in?"

Victor stepped back, opening the door wider. When Elijah walked by him, under the freshly showered scent of body wash and shampoo, Victor smelled sex on him. It was more than someone getting themselves off, but there wasn't the accompanying scent of another person, just wintry earth, more familiar to Victor now than he could have imagined a month ago. That and pack and Victor. To have him here, in this room, smelling like that, was intoxicating.

His gaze flickered down Victor's bare chest before darting around the room, to the rumpled bed, to the sheets on his dresser, to the window, and then to Victor again. He inhaled through his nose, his cheeks coloring, before he forced himself to meet Victor's eyes.

"You should probably shut the door for this."

Victor shut it, one eyebrow raised in question. Elijah didn't want the pack overhearing. That was either very good or very bad.

He visibly steeled himself. "You were right. I fucked up the first ritual."

Victor's brow furrowed. "What do you mean? The wards are fine."

"No, the wards aren't the problem. It's the ritual itself I messed up. The issue is how I ended it. Or, I guess, didn't end it."

Victor's confusion rose. He watched Elijah, reading his nervousness, how uncomfortable he was. Whatever he had to say, he was reluctant to tell Victor.

"If the wards aren't messed up, how did you mess up the ritual?"

Elijah grimaced. "It established a temporary connection that allowed me to use your energy."

Victor knew that much.

"The thing is," Elijah said, avoiding his gaze. "I didn't sever it correctly."

"You think we're still connected?" Elijah nodded, but Victor shook his head. "We aren't. I felt the connection during the rituals and your spells. I can't feel it now."

But even as he said that, his mind spun through the last few weeks. The little flickers of things that hadn't quite lined up.

"It's one-sided, so I don't know how much you'd be able to feel it." Elijah looked chagrined, his cheeks tinting a darker pink. "But I can feel you." He tugged at the collar of his shirt, exposing the juncture of his neck and shoulder.

A line of dark hickeys decorated his pale skin, and Victor had a visceral flashback—his mouth on Elijah's shoulder, biting down as his knot swelled.

Elijah let out a trembling exhale like that rush had coursed through him as strongly as it had through Victor. He looked Victor in the eye. "What did you dream about last night?"

There was no way. He stared at Elijah in disbelief. He'd done that to Elijah in his dream? How?

Victor's stomach dropped. The connection. It'd been open since the last full moon. He'd been under its influence for a month. That morning, his wolf had been so smug and content because of the dream. A dream caused by magic.

Elijah lifted a hand, reaching out for him. Victor recoiled, his eyes widening when Elijah flinched as well.

"I need to check something." His voice was so fucking quiet and tentative it struck Victor harder than any blow.

With effort, he held still. Elijah's touch was uncertain

and light, brushing over Victor's heart, an almost imperceptible buzz of magic on his fingertips. Warmth bloomed across his chest, and when Victor looked down, the faintest glow of purple tattoos marked his skin.

Victor stared at them, his brain all white static and noise. Were he someone else, even just a younger version of himself, he might have been excited to see Elijah's magic written on his skin. But the only thing he saw in that moment was his father, weak and drained, obsessed with the magic that was causing his downfall.

His stomach churned, and panic clawed at his throat. Did this mean Elijah could use his energy whenever he wanted? Could he drain him now, regardless of Victor's consent? Steal from Victor, from his pack, leaving them vulnerable.

Elijah swallowed hard, frantically shaking his head. "I would never take anything you weren't willing to give. This wasn't on purpose. I never would have let it continue this long if I'd realized what was going on."

Victor believed him. He couldn't trust himself, but he read the truth in Elijah's expression, in his scent. Elijah was as horrified by this as he was. Or at least, as he should be. His wolf had no problem with this fucked-up situation. It'd happily let Elijah take whatever he wanted.

Elijah's eyes were wide as he stared at Victor. "I wouldn't do that to anyone. But especially not you."

He really was feeling Victor. That explained how he'd always seemed to call when Victor was at his most restless, how strong the pull toward him had become, how real Victor's dreams had been, especially last night's.

Fuck, that dream.

Victor's eyes fell on Elijah's neck, the marks mostly covered by his collar. "Last night," he said, then scrubbed a hand across his face. "Did I... did you..." Damn it, how did you ask someone if you'd assaulted them in a shared dream?

But Elijah shook his head again, picking up the sick twist in Victor's gut. "No. It was... surprising? But I think I could have stopped it. I just didn't realize how deep the connection was until I saw this." He rubbed at his shoulder, and heat blazed in Victor's chest, making him choke back a groan.

Elijah stopped immediately. He shrugged and straightened his collar. "I can fix this."

"Fix it?" Victor reeled. The idea of fixing it was almost as disconcerting as the connection itself.

"I can cut the tether. I'll sever it properly this time."

To Victor's horror, his wolf growled, pushing to the forefront, demanding control. Victor gritted his teeth and pushed it back, chaining it down with everything he had. "What do we need to do?"

It was best to get this over with, to keep his association with magic as limited as possible. He'd been out of his mind this morning, under the influence of this connection and his wolf. Of course he didn't want to be bonded to a mage, and Elijah didn't want that either.

Whatever he said, the dream must have been uncomfortable for him. The last thing Victor wanted was to make Elijah go through that again because his wolf liked whatever connection they had and was trying to make it more than that, if the marks on his shoulder were anything to go by.

Logically he knew Elijah would never hurt his pack, but Victor couldn't dispel the image of his father's cheeks starting to hollow, how he'd been fading away while convincing himself he wasn't being used.

Elijah gestured to the chairs by the window. "Let's sit."

As they did, Victor's wolf prowled restlessly, straining against the fetters Victor had put on it, raging against what they were about to do.

Elijah scooted his chair closer to Victor's, their knees almost brushing. He held out his hands, and Victor hesitantly took both. Elijah's eyes closed, concentration etched onto his face.

There was a tug inside Victor, a pull that made him want to dive into the connection he hadn't recognized for what it was. Or maybe part of him had, but he'd refused to acknowledge it, had kept pushing it away.

Between himself and Elijah, there was a thread similar to the ones he had to each of his pack members. But it was different, too, forged by magic instead of the moon.

He sensed magic wrapping around it and realized Elijah was there, in his mind, hidden amidst the pack bonds, distant and muted. Victor would never have found him if he hadn't been looking.

Frustration filled Elijah. Whatever he was doing, it wasn't working. There was a crease between his brows. Victor wanted to soothe it away but didn't let himself.

Elijah dropped one of Victor's hands. He leaned forward, and his palm came to rest on Victor's chest. Warmth spiraled out from it, along the lines of the tattoos.

"Can you—" Elijah started to ask, but before he could finish the question, Victor was sliding his hand under the collar of Elijah's shirt, skating it over the marks there.

Without thinking it through, he squeezed, and Elijah gasped, shivery and shallow.

"Yes," he said, barely above a whisper. "Like that."

Victor dug his fingers into his shoulder, and Elijah

moaned, part pain, part pleasure. Almost like it was a real mating bite, always a little extra sensitive to the touch.

"It's," Elijah said, voice breathy. He cleared his throat and pulled himself together. "It's not to you. Not exactly. It's to your wolf." He looked at Victor. "I need you to give your wolf control."

Victor jerked away. "No."

"I don't think I can sever the tether unless you do."

Victor's heart beat wildly.

"I know the difference between what the wolf wants and what you do." Elijah seemed certain about that; Victor wasn't so sure he knew himself.

But he slipped his hand back under Elijah's collar, closed his eyes, and, little by little, let go of the restraint he'd eked out over his wolf, the separation he'd placed between them.

Opening his eyes, he found Elijah studying him. Even without a mirror, he knew the grin that spread on his face was rapacious enough Kade would be proud. He inhaled deeply, reveling in the combination of their scents in his room, though they weren't mixed nearly enough.

Elijah was fucking perfect. His scent, his magic, his everything. No one was better for his pack, for him. He was such an idiot for trying to keep himself from this. Why deny himself? They were inevitable.

He scraped blunt nails over Elijah's shoulder, then dug his fingers in again, massaging the area. Eyelids fluttering shut, Elijah caught his lower lip in his teeth to stop himself from moaning. He'd been holding himself back too. He wanted this just as much.

Victor leaned forward, but Elijah braced his arm to keep him away. His other hand clasped around Victor's wrist, stilling his movement. There was determination in his voice when he spoke.

"Don't."

It was one word, but it was enough to stop Victor cold.

"We have to break this connection. Neither of us wants it."

Neither of them. That cut deep.

Victor relaxed his hand, resting his fingers gently against Elijah's shoulder, and in exchange, Elijah dropped his iron grip on Victor's wrist.

"What if you have to use my energy again?" He attempted to sound neutral, though the idea that breaking a mage tether was the same as breaking a shifter bond, as final and permanent, was making something uncomfortable squirm in his chest.

Elijah shrugged, the motion bumping his shoulder against Victor's hand, causing his eyelids to flutter again. "We fixed your territory. I shouldn't need to."

"What if the rot returns?"

"Breaking this permanent tether shouldn't stop me from connecting to your energy normally. Temporarily." The last word was said to reassure. It didn't.

It also didn't answer Victor's real question. The one he was too afraid to ask. But this had been his plan from the start. Fix the issue with his territory, then never deal with magic again.

Elijah's palm settled against his chest, not pushing him away, just anchored over his heart. The heated shivers along the tattoos increased.

Victor was about to ask what they needed to do next, but then the connection transformed. It flared, bright and sharp, like a lightning strike, and he could sense *everything*.

Elijah, his magic, how strong he was. The dull,

pleasant ache in his shoulder. His mixed emotions—frustration at Victor for his distrust of magic, at himself for this whole situation, and guilt. So much guilt. A whirlwind of it.

Guilt over not realizing he'd messed up sooner, over enjoying Victor's energy so much it'd made him careless, over putting Victor through this after what had happened to his father. And guilt over enjoying the dream they'd shared.

Bark pressed against his forearms, and the hot pleasure of being stretched open overwhelmed him.

Victor's breath hitched, lost in the sensations pouring off Elijah. Hundreds of emotions rushed through him so rapidly he couldn't identify them, but fuck, he wanted to learn them all, every single thought that made Elijah who he was.

And then, as suddenly as that tether had been opened fully, it was severed, a gate slamming shut.

The connection wasn't distant and muted; it was nonexistent.

His wolf whimpered, retreating, leaving Victor with the aftermath of his decisions.

Victor sucked in an unsteady lungful of air, the world around him tilting as he readjusted to the disappearance of whatever they'd had. He hadn't realized it was there until a few minutes ago, but now its absence was stark and obvious.

Elijah was breathing heavily, his eyes wide, concern and shock on his face. When their gazes met, he dropped his hands quickly, and Victor did the same.

"That should do it." His voice sounded as rattled as Victor was. He rubbed his neck, but Victor felt nothing.

Victor concentrated, trying to find the connection, any

leftover trace. It was gone. Not even the slightest thread remained.

He swallowed, unsure what to say.

They sat there, the silence between them thick and uncomfortable.

"Right," Elijah said, drawing in a sharp breath. "I should... I should go?"

Victor nodded numbly. He expected his wolf to protest, but it was quiet, drawn in on itself.

Last night, he'd asked Elijah to stay for breakfast, but he couldn't handle the pack staring at them expectantly, not with this newly carved hollowness under his sternum.

Elijah clenched his jaw and stood. Victor stood as well, the movement drawing them close together. For one moment, the only thought in his mind was how easy it would be to pull Elijah to him, to press him into his bed, sink his teeth into his neck, and replace what they'd just lost with something infinitely better.

But then Elijah stepped away, looking everywhere but Victor, mumbling about getting to his shop to open up, though it was too early for that.

Elijah walked toward the door but stopped before he reached it and turned back to Victor. His pinched expression smashed any hope that might have been foolish enough to spring up.

"We should check the forest before I go."

Spending hours with Elijah walking through the forest right now, after that, was beyond Victor. "I'll check it myself," he said gruffly. Too gruffly. The words made Elijah wince.

"Okay. Just... keep me updated? Let me know if anything's wrong, anything at all?"

A whole hell of a lot was wrong. But that wasn't what Elijah was asking.

"I will. At least until the next full moon. We should know by then if it worked."

In the morning light, he could almost pretend Elijah looked regretful. But then he left the room, and Victor didn't stop him, unsure what exactly had happened except that the thump of the door closing sounded far too much like the end.

He shook himself out of his daze.

This was ridiculous. That ghost of a connection must have been responsible for all his recent conflicted feelings. It had to be why he'd been dreaming about Elijah, why his scent was so damn appealing. He hadn't been thinking straight for a month.

He scowled at his bed and the pile of sheets.

That was the only reason.

Clenching his jaw, he stripped the bed and tossed both sets of sheets into his basket, then brought it to the laundry room. There was no point in delaying this any longer.

He'd been acting ridiculously for the last week, the last month. He didn't want Elijah's scent in his room, and he certainly didn't need it there.

His wolf stirred, whining softly as Victor shoved the sheets into the washing machine, but he ignored it. It kept getting him into these damn situations.

Any attachment the wolf had developed was gone now. Their territory was fine; their pack was protected. They didn't need Elijah anymore. And after it realized that, it would move on.

Kade caught him on his way out of the room and grinned. "Little early to be doing laundry, isn't it?" He was smirking at Victor, but as he stepped closer, that smirk was replaced by a frown. He leaned in and inhaled. "What happened? Your scent is—"

"My scent is the same as it always has been." He didn't need Kade to finish his sentence. He knew his scent was different. The lingering spark of magic had faded. The one that hadn't been on his skin but had wormed its way underneath.

He went to walk away, but Kade stopped him with a hand on his shoulder, his eyes searching Victor's face. "I heard Elijah's car leave."

Victor kept his expression neutral. "Why would he stay? The ritual worked. His business here is finished."

Kade's frown deepened, but he said nothing else as Victor passed.

This had been the plan all along. They'd fixed the problem; Victor never had to work with magic again.

Only it was harder to convince himself of that than it should have been. The hollow emptiness in his chest stubbornly refused to go away, leaving him cold without that constant warmth spreading out from his heart, right where Elijah's marks had been.

But that connection wasn't something he wanted. No matter what Kade thought. No matter the worried frowns his pack sent his way during breakfast when they thought he wasn't looking, especially the times when he forgot himself and rubbed at his chest.

All this would pass, things would return to normal, and Victor would move on.

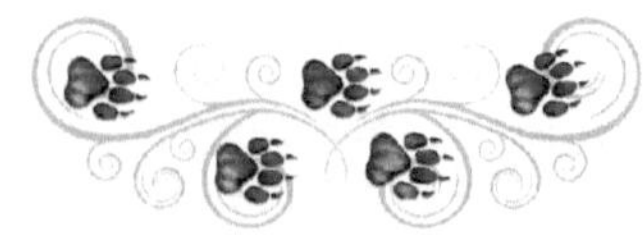

TWENTY

The next two days went by in a fog. Elijah was too busy to think about Victor or his pack or the fading bruises on his neck, which was a relief. He was focused on his long to-do list.

Having full control of his magic and not spending all his waking hours researching meant being able to make a dent in his orders. He had a sizeable backlog to clear but had done enough in the last two days to ease his mind. With a bit of luck, he'd be caught up by the end of the week.

The only reason he hadn't forgotten the matter entirely was the damn group chat. He might have moved on, but his friends hadn't.

He'd ripped the bandage off and told them everything. Minus a few of the more intimate details. He'd be taking Victor's giant metaphysical shifter dick to the grave.

But even without that detail, the teasing had been swift, fierce, and relentless.

ARAN

So my theory of his energy keeping you stretched open and ready was correct!

LIAM

I'm going to regret engaging with this, but…

I think it was the opposite?

It was Elijah's magic keeping them both

Nope.

Stopping there.

ARAN

Either way. Are your channels nice and tight again, Elijah?

ELIJAH

I hate you all.

MILES

Please don't judge me based on Aran's inability to think of anything besides sex.

But seriously, you were so against ending up with a shifter, and then you went and did it subconsciously.

Elijah groaned.

ELIJAH

No. That's not what happened.

It was just a mistake. I made a mistake.

I do that sometimes. We all do that.

ARAN

Sure. A "mistake."

LIAM

You never said.

How did you realize you were connected?

ELIJAH

I told you. The second ritual deepened the connection enough it was obvious.

LIAM

Right.

But all my research points to connections becoming more apparent when heightened emotions are involved.

Anger, fear, sadness, joy, lust.

The stronger the emotion, the more the connection does its thing.

Theoretically because those are the times the connection is most needed.

So there must have been a trigger.

What made you notice it?

He was right. Elijah had spent a good portion of the day after he'd severed the connection reading through the material Liam had sent, then doing as much of his own research as he could. He'd known that question was coming.

ELIJAH

We were both pretty damn elated after the ritual worked.

And it was the full moon. I think his wolf being so close to the surface amplified things.

ARAN

Not to change the subject from one I can easily make jokes about to something serious, but... are you 100% sure it worked? I still have my doubts.

ELIJAH

Cautiously optimistic. I've never felt so much new life before.

LIAM

Told you it'd work.

ARAN

Okay... But tell your shifter to keep an eye out.

ELIJAH

He is. We should know by the next full moon.

ARAN

Besides, checking up on his territory is a good way to see if you can get some non-metaphorical shifter dick. On "accident."

ELIJAH

Leaving now.

Definitely hate you all.

MILES

Hey!

ELIJAH

Except Miles. Miles can stay.

Miles sent a heart emoji, and Elijah closed the app.

It absolutely had been an accident. He hadn't wanted it and certainly hadn't done it on purpose. He wasn't missing the tether to Victor or that connection to his pack. That split second when he'd opened the tether wider didn't haunt him with all the jumbled, disorienting emotions that had poured into him from Victor. It hadn't left him wanting to lose himself completely in that flood, to learn everything he could about Victor through that connection. To leave himself vulnerable and exposed so Victor could do the same to him.

That would be ridiculous. Why would he ever want something like that?

They were a lovely, warm, welcoming pack, and he'd enjoyed spending time with them. But that changed nothing. He had no desire to be a pack mage. That life held no appeal.

Besides, now that the ritual had worked, he wouldn't be seeing Victor again. Because as much as they'd been starting to get along, Victor still distrusted magic. And there was no future for them if Victor couldn't trust such a fundamental part of Elijah.

Not that Elijah had been thinking about any kind of future they might have had.

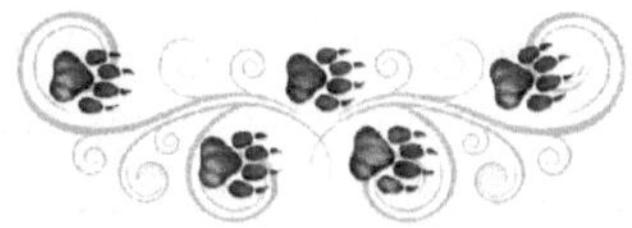

The problem with Elijah's magic working properly was that he'd done everything he needed to do. He'd gotten caught up on his backlog, dusted the hell out of the shop, and finished scanning the latest crate of books Liam had shipped him to archive.

He'd even reached the point he was considering reorganizing the storage rooms. There were two he hadn't managed to fully organize since he took over. It might be time to tackle that.

It didn't help that his sleep schedule had returned to normal. He woke bright and early every morning with no odd half dream, half memory of running through the forest on four legs. And the other dreams he'd had occasionally since then, well, those were his own damn fault. He couldn't blame them on some unintended connection.

Things were perfectly ordinary.

And he had nothing to do.

He sat in his office, stared at the ceiling, and held back a sigh. Lady was curled up in his lap, unconcerned about the sheer boredom he was facing.

This was insane. He shouldn't feel regretful that his magic was behaving. No mage in their right mind would ever think that. He wasn't hoping it'd act up. It'd been frustrating to ruin spell after spell, to not be able to do the simplest charms without them blowing up in his face, sometimes in a spectacularly literal manner.

But now, he could do whatever he wanted with no issue. His magic felt familiar, the same as always. It was no longer unruly and untamed.

He groaned and scratched under Lady's chin. Maybe the rot had infected his brain. There was clearly something wrong with him if he missed his magic being unpredictable.

Lady perked up, listening intently before jumping down and strolling into the shop. Elijah watched her go. He must be boring her too.

The shop door jingled open, and Elijah stood. At least a new customer would distract him, even if it was only fifteen minutes before closing time.

When he stepped out of the office, he blinked in surprise, almost convinced his eyes were playing tricks on him. His heart stuttered a little extra beat.

Victor was there. He was as unfairly attractive as always, in his worn jeans and a tight shirt, a paper shopping bag in one hand. No concern or worry clouded his expression, but why else would he be there?

"Is something wrong?"

"No, I wanted to update you." Victor glanced around and swallowed. "Things are good. There's no sign of the rot."

"That's wonderful news." Elijah waited for him to continue, but Victor stood there like he was expecting something, though Elijah was unsure what.

Lady jumped off the counter and stalked toward Victor. He eyed her warily but held his ground as she approached.

Her tail flicked with annoyance, like it always did around wolf shifters. She sniffed his leg as a look somewhere between concern and horror crossed Victor's face. Elijah bit his lip to hold back a laugh.

After a thorough sniff, Lady took a step forward and rubbed her head against Victor, followed by her entire body. Then she sauntered away and jumped onto a shelf, tail swishing as she vigorously cleaned herself.

Victor stared at her, confusion written on his face.

Elijah chuckled. "I guess that's about as much approval as you'll ever get from her. She marked you as her property and all."

Victor nodded to her. "Thanks," he said, but it sounded more like a question.

Lady ignored him. She sat, haughtily monitoring the shop, her gaze as judgmental as ever.

Indecision and hesitation flickered in Victor's eyes when he looked back at Elijah, like even he didn't know why he was there.

Elijah waited a beat before he asked, "Is there something I can help you with?"

That seemed to jolt Victor into action. "No, I was in town to run some errands and thought I'd stop by to tell you everything's good, and we shouldn't need your services anymore."

"That's great. I'm happy to hear it."

Only he wasn't, not completely. The first part wasn't a lie. It was great they'd fixed Victor's territory. He could return to being the alpha Elijah knew he could be, and it wasn't like Elijah wanted them to need him. But it wouldn't be the worst if the pack hired him for a minor spell from time to time.

"Well, if anything comes up, you know where to find me."

"Will do." Victor hesitated for another moment.

The clocks on the walls ticked, each second obnoxiously loud.

"Also," Victor said, stepping closer and setting his bag on the counter. "This is for you. As a thank you."

Elijah opened his mouth to say that wasn't necessary, but Victor shook his head.

"Have a good day." He winced, likely realizing the time, then turned to leave.

Elijah had the annoying urge to call after him, but he had no idea what he'd say besides thank you. So he said that under his breath, knowing Victor would hear it, and let him go.

Things were better this way. Victor wouldn't want him on his land, and Elijah needed to remember that being successful meant staying neutral. Spending too much time with Victor Mills would be one hell of a way to guarantee he no longer retained his neutrality.

Curiosity getting the best of him, he pulled the bag toward him and reached in to find a book, thick and heavy, wrapped in soft cloth. He unwrapped it, and his breath caught when he saw what was inside.

It was the book from the chest in Victor's attic, the one with the ward spells and rituals.

A tremor ran through his hands as he traced over the cover, not quite believing the book was there, that Victor would give him something this extraordinary. Did he realize what it was worth? Books like this were priceless. They sold for insane amounts at auction, but those numbers didn't come close to touching their true value.

It was too much. Nothing Elijah had done warranted this. Especially not after he'd fucked up the first ritual.

But then, given everything he'd learned about Victor, it shouldn't have been a surprise he'd noticed how, out of all the things in that attic, this was the one Elijah had regretted leaving the most.

Elijah looked over at Lady, sitting on her shelf, glaring as if he'd offended her. She was right. He shouldn't read anything into this. If he were being honest, he should return it, but he couldn't bring himself to do that either.

So he walked to the door, locked it, and flipped the sign to Closed. Then he carefully rebundled the book, carried it upstairs to his apartment, and set it on his table before unwrapping it again.

He sat and stared at it for the longest time, fingers lingering on the cover before he began to peruse it, slower than he had in the attic, examining every page and the marginalia made by a dozen hands.

So much of the Mills pack's history was written in that book, each mage adding their own notes and spells. Most lines of mages had specialties, one area they excelled at more than others, passed down from generation to generation. For the mages in Victor's family, this had to be it.

The flowing scripts and blots of fountain pens were slowly replaced by crisper letters and the regular lines of modern writing implements. Rituals and spells, from big to small, every way Elijah could think to use wards and many he never would have. There were privacy wards, territory wards, a little charm he'd remembered from his first read-through that had inspired the wards he'd put on the boxes for the stones. Some were more ward-adjacent than true wards themselves, protection and preservation spells, even a few meant to break wards. All refined over hundreds of years, little annotations on improvements and variations scattered throughout the pages. The notes on the territory ward ritual made his cheeks heat. That particular ritual might not be something he'd ever be able to do, but most of the rest were. Blank pages in the back waited for more spells, and his fingers itched to add his own.

He didn't, but that urge remained.

Blinking, he realized how late it had gotten. It was past midnight.

His stomach growled, reminding him he should have eaten dinner hours ago. He sighed and shut the book, rewrapping it but leaving it out. He'd be looking through it tomorrow. And probably every day after that.

Most of the supplies he'd need for those spells were in his shop, and now that his backlog was taken care of, maybe he could spend some time working on his own projects.

He placed his hand on the wrapped book one last time, then stood.

There might be things about being in a pack that weren't so bad after all.

He just didn't have to admit that to anyone but himself.

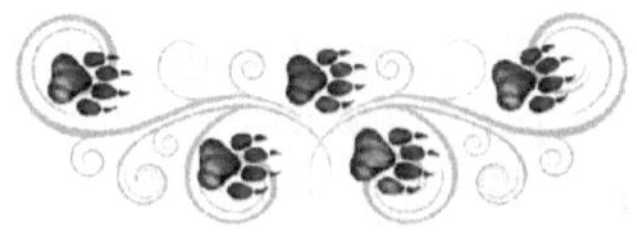

Elijah saw them before they saw him. The benefits of being downwind, he supposed. Victor and Kade were walking together, each pushing a massive cart of groceries out of the store. There was something almost unnatural about them doing such an ordinary activity. It highlighted how different they were from the average human, how they were a little too wild to fit seamlessly into the everyday world.

For a few quickened heartbeats, he considered turning his nonexistent tail and running, but he wasn't that much of a coward. Then Victor spotted him, his next step faltering a fraction, and Kade noticed. He scanned the parking lot in the direction of Victor's gaze. When his eyes landed on Elijah, he grinned, wide and wicked.

There was nothing to it. They'd seen him. He had to say hello. It was only polite.

He tried to walk over casually, but his limbs had transformed into ungainly things, like he'd forgotten how his arms were supposed to move with each stride.

It'd be okay. Neither Victor nor Kade knew about the confusing thoughts that crept into Elijah's head whenever he looked through the book of wards. Which he'd done every evening for the last week, using it to fill the empty hours that were no longer consumed by calls with Victor. Not that he missed those. Something he'd done for a handful of days wasn't a habit.

He didn't need to know how the pack was doing. At least not beyond a professional check-in. Why would he care how Oliver was faring in kindergarten or if Will and Janell had finally settled on a name? None of that was his business. He'd never wanted to be part of a pack before, and he didn't feel a surprisingly intense longing to be in one now. Victor didn't stir anything deep in his chest. That would be absurd and counterproductive to his plans.

It was fine.

Everything was fine.

"Hey," Elijah said.

"Hey," Victor said.

They stood there, waiting for the other to speak. Kade was practically beaming with unholy delight as he watched them, but he stayed blessedly silent.

"Thank you so much for the—" Elijah started to say, but Victor's eyes widened and darted toward Kade. Okay then. "For the update. On your territory. Glad it's doing well." Yeah, that didn't sound lame at all.

Victor looked relieved, but from Kade's palpable amusement, Elijah hadn't been smooth enough to cover whatever that had been. Victor must not want Kade to know he'd given Elijah the book, but why? Was it the teasing he'd get, or was it more than that?

"The forest is still doing well."

"That's good." He should say something else, but his mind was frustratingly blank. They stared at each other, Kade's expression getting more entertained with each passing second, but Elijah forced himself to shake it off. "Well, I need to..." He pointed toward the store entrance.

Victor jerked. "Right. Of course. Have fun." He winced, then marched away.

Kade shot Victor's back an exasperated look. "He'll see you later," he said to Elijah before following.

Elijah walked into the store. As he stepped inside, he

glanced over his shoulder to find Victor watching him, not paying attention to how he stacked bags in his SUV. When their eyes met, they both turned away.

He'd been an idiot to think he'd never see Victor again. Life was not going to be easy if he didn't get over this inadvisable crush he'd developed. Just because a hot guy gave him a book didn't mean he had to act like an awkward teenager. He'd get over it. This town was too small not to.

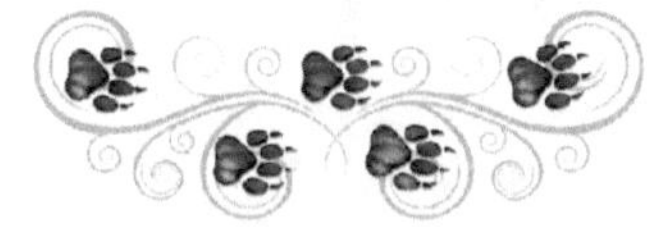

TWENTY-ONE

"Just ask him out," Kade said as they walked through the forest. The night was quiet and dark, the moon a sliver in the sky, two days past new.

"Ask who out?"

"Like you don't know who I'm talking about." It wasn't the first time he'd said something similar and wouldn't be the last.

Victor surveyed the surrounding land, hoping Kade would drop it, but when he looked back, the smirk on Kade's lips said no way in hell.

"Seriously, what's the worst that could happen?"

"Other than me becoming fixated on magic and running my pack into the ground?"

"I thought we were past that. He's trustworthy. Most of them are. He wouldn't jeopardize you or the pack, and you know it."

"It's not him I'm worried about."

"Then give yourself a little more credit. You wouldn't do anything to hurt the pack either."

Victor shrugged. "What's it to you?"

"Yeah." The corner of Kade's mouth quirked up. "What's it to me that my alpha is in a relationship with someone he likes? Hmm. That's a difficult one. It's not like our pack gets stronger as you get stronger or that being in a stable, content relationship would be good for you. And it's definitely not because we've been friends for decades. What kind of horrible person would want to see their friend happy?"

"So it's not about him being a mage?"

Kade groaned. "You're being deliberately obtuse. You like him. For some wholly incomprehensible reason, he seems to like you as well. He's a good guy. I think he'd make you happy. He'd fit well into the pack. The fact that he's a pretty badass mage is a nice bonus, but if a human made you happy, I'd be fine with that too. Besides, he's fucking hot. I fully understand you wanting to—" Victor shoved him into a tree before he could finish that sentence.

He didn't need any help thinking of things he wanted to do to Elijah, and his wolf was less than pleased with Kade talking about him in that way.

"Even if I did like him, and I'm not saying I do, it's been barely a year since I took over. Now's not the time to introduce new members. It's too soon to risk changing pack dynamics."

"Don't tell Will and Janell that."

"Not their baby. An outsider."

"Do you really think of him as an outsider?" Before Victor could respond, Kade continued. "Okay, fine. In that case, how about you and me take a trip to the city for old times' sake? We'll get you laid, because clearly you need it, and then we can build pack bonds or whatever bullshit you're on about."

The idea was not remotely appealing. "I can't leave the pack alone. Not after everything that's happened recently."

Kade scoffed. "The other betas would manage fine without us for a night. Don't get me wrong. They'd thoroughly enjoy your walk of shame in the morning, but they'd understand if you needed a night off."

"I don't need a night off."

"You do need to get laid though."

Victor pushed against his shoulder again. "You're projecting. How long has it been?"

"A fraction of what it's been for you."

Victor couldn't deny it. It had been a while. Between what had happened the last time he'd gone with Kade to find a hookup, his father's descent into madness, taking over the pack, bringing his complaints to the mage council, and then his wards failing, his thoughts hadn't been on hooking up for the better part of two years. That might be why he found Elijah so attractive, even with the connection between them severed.

Maybe getting laid would help. But he'd deal with that later.

They rounded a bend, and Victor froze, his body tensing. Kade stopped beside him, looking at him with concern.

Victor breathed deeply, hoping he was imagining things.

He wasn't.

It was faint but there. A hint of unnatural rot. His pulse skyrocketed.

No. This could not be happening again. They'd fixed it. The forest was fine.

The odor led him to a large cottonwood. Its leaves were bright with autumn colors, not sick and molded. But as he got closer, the stench grew. He circled the tree, examining it. It appeared healthy, except for the smell it was giving off.

He touched the bark, and the outer layer crumbled under his fingers, revealing a streak of sickening decay. Kade inhaled sharply.

Even though he wanted to recoil from the tree, Victor brushed his hand against more healthy-looking bark, and an entire section cascaded to the ground, showering the earth in dusty debris. What lay underneath was stomach-churning, an oily tar that seeped from inside the tree. Without the layer of bark, its stench polluted the air—a fresh kill left too long in the sun. The reek of it crawled over his skin, making him feel unclean and contaminated.

Victor took another step down the path to the next tree and did the same, revealing the sickness beneath that thin veneer of health.

He stumbled backward. Why was this happening? It had to be his fault. Why else would his land be affected by this, with everything dying and decaying? Why couldn't he protect his pack?

His territory was turning into a hellscape, and that had to be because of him. He reeled, but then Kade was behind him, a firm hand on his shoulder, bringing him out of the spiraling chaos consuming his thoughts.

"Whatever you're thinking," he said, his grip steadying, "stop it. Nothing you could have done would have caused this." He paused, then attempted to take on a joking tone that didn't work. "At least you have a reason to contact Elijah again."

They hurried home, checking trees along the way. Most were fine. For now.

It wasn't until they were almost there that they found

another area of decay, one that hadn't been affected by the rot before. It'd never gotten this close to the pack house.

But it was different somehow.

Like before, there was no life. Not a single insect buzzing, no birds in the trees, no animals scurrying in the undergrowth. But it was deeper than that. The forest had never felt this empty, this desolate.

It was Kade, himself, and stillness.

"Where are..." Kade said, trailing off like he was unwilling to break the eerie silence.

Victor moved slowly, his senses on alert. Kade followed behind him as they neared a clearing that had been created by a large tree falling a few years before.

Every hair on Victor's body stood on end, and he had to force himself forward.

When he entered the clearing, his stomach roiled. Nothing lived there either, but that didn't mean there were no animals.

The ground was littered with dozens, their bodies in various states of decay. Rodents, birds, rabbits, a badger, even a small deer. No animal was spared. There were insects too, but instead of feasting off the flesh of the dead, they lay motionless.

Victor took shallow breaths through his mouth, unable to handle the reek of decomposing bodies.

They hadn't been there long. He and Kade had walked a few yards past this clearing on their way out. Even if something were capable of killing these animals in that short period, how were their corpses this decayed?

If they'd been there for more than a day, someone would have noticed. His pack traversed this forest too frequently not to have discovered it. It wasn't in a deep, unreachable area. If the wind shifted right, the smell would have drifted to the house itself.

He swallowed thickly and backed away from the slaughter field the clearing had become. But before he took two steps, he heard movement, something lurching through the trees.

A thing on four legs appeared on the other side of the clearing. Victor's mind refused to accept the creature was a coyote. As decomposed as it was, it had been dead for days but hadn't realized yet. It dragged itself onto the mass of corpses, collapsed, and didn't move again.

Victor met Kade's eyes and saw his own horror reflected.

Whatever this was, it was so much more than a few trees.

With the new moon past, he'd started to believe it was over, that everything was alright.

But he'd been wrong. And the reality of it surpassed his darkest nightmares.

As he drove into town, he called the magic shop. It went to voicemail. He tried Elijah's personal number but got no answer there either. It was late; Elijah was probably asleep. That didn't matter. He needed Elijah, and he needed him now.

When he got to the shop, it was locked, but he found the narrow staircase that led up the back of the building, climbed it, and knocked on Elijah's door.

The seconds stretched out interminably as he waited.

Finally, a half-asleep Elijah answered. A warm gust of his scent spilled out of the apartment, and even though Victor knew he shouldn't, he filled his lungs with it, some part of him feeling better from that alone, wanting to pull Elijah close and bury his nose in his neck, to take comfort there.

Emotions flickered across Elijah's face—a brief flash of surprise followed by confusion then concern as he took Victor in.

"What's wrong?" His voice was sleep-rough.

"I need help." Victor heard his own desperation, the raw emotion in his plea, his weakness laid bare before Elijah. "It's not just the plants. Everything's dying."

His words took a moment to register, but when they did, Elijah's eyes widened, and the color drained from his face. "What do you mean by *everything*?"

Victor ran his hands through his short hair. "Some of the plants, they're... they're worse than they were. But now, there are animals too. There's a clearing full of them. They look like they died weeks ago but couldn't have been there more than a few hours. It's like the trees and animals have been decaying from the inside."

Elijah pulled his door open further, letting Victor step into his apartment. It was crowded, but more than anything, Victor was overwhelmed by how saturated it was with Elijah's scent.

His gaze flickered to Elijah's bed at the far end of the room before taking in his appearance. He was dressed in worn sweats, and for all its inappropriateness, seeing him so casual, not completely buttoned up, left Victor wanting to run his hands over the soft material of Elijah's T-shirt, then sneak them underneath. But he forced himself to focus.

Elijah hurried around the room, gathering supplies, then tossing them into a pile on his table.

"When did it start?" he asked as he shoved things into a bag.

"We found it tonight."

Elijah paused and opened his mouth, about to say something, but then he shook his head and continued packing.

When he finished, he turned and pulled off his shirt, exposing the long, pale lines of his back. He tossed the shirt on his bed before grabbing clothes and slipping into the bathroom to change. Victor didn't know if he was grateful for that or not.

Elijah was out a few minutes later, pulling on a jacket and picking up the bag. "Can you drive?"

Victor nodded, and they rushed down the stairs.

The entire drive, Elijah was sending messages on his phone. Victor wanted to ask if he'd figured something out, but from the way he was cursing under his breath, it was nothing good.

He had to believe Elijah would fix this. If he couldn't, Victor didn't know what he'd do.

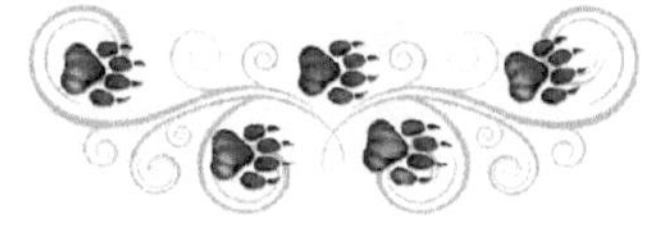

TWENTY-TWO

Elijah held back a gag as he stared at the death in front of him. How Victor was handling it with his heightened senses, he had no idea.

The light in his hand cast eerie shadows over the corpses strewn before him. The stillness was unsettling, like the leaves themselves were holding their breath.

But more than the silence and the death and the stench was how off the forest felt to his magic. Tentatively, he pressed his palm against the nearest tree but had to yank it away in revulsion. The tree looked alive, but decay was hollowing it out, rotting it from the inside. A shiver of dread raced up Elijah's spine. The pack Aran had told him about loomed in his mind.

He turned to Victor and, for once, didn't see the strong, confident leader. Victor was terrified.

Elijah started to speak, but even the air was corrupted, and he choked on it.

Victor gestured toward the house. Once they were far enough away, Elijah took in gasping lungfuls of clean air.

"What the fuck is causing this? A curse? A magical disease?" Victor's fists were balled, like he wanted to punch something but had nothing physical to fight.

An idea struck Elijah. He'd been assuming it was just that. Some type of disease, a fungus spreading through the land. This ran deeper than that. It wasn't mindlessly spreading. It'd started on the wards, eating away at them, then moved to the plants when those wards had been fortified. When they'd purified the plants and trees, it'd adapted again and found somewhere else to infest, and now it was attacking the animals as well, in a way that kept it hidden.

The mage trying to help the other pack had also assumed it was something that spread. Everything she'd tried, like everything Elijah had tried, had been based on that assumption. Spells to fight a crop blight, a mold, a virus, a curse.

But what if it was more than that? What if it didn't spread, it moved?

He'd discarded that possibility because neither he nor Victor had sensed that kind of presence, but maybe they should have been looking for something a little less substantial.

"Do you have a map of your territory?"

"Yes, inside."

Dawn hadn't yet broken, and the pack house lay quiet. Kade and Rick sat at the small table in the kitchen, each with a cup of coffee. They stood, but Victor motioned them to stay. He showed Elijah into an office and pulled out a map.

Elijah dug into his bag until he found his vial of ash. He set down the map and a candle, snapping his fingers to light the latter and dumping ash onto the former.

He concentrated, letting his awareness flow into the map. Without thinking, he held out his hand, and Victor slipped his own into Elijah's. The moment their skin pressed together, the boundaries of Victor's territory burned bright in Elijah's mind. He felt the wards arched over them, Victor beside him, the pack asleep in their beds, and the forest. It wasn't the vibrant, living thing from before, but sickly and dying, struggling to survive.

The connection between them wasn't the same. It was still easier than any he'd experienced before Victor, but it wasn't as overwhelming or all-consuming. It didn't make his magic surge and swell.

He ran magic through the pile of ash, charging it, willing it to mark the things and places he needed marked.

Victor inhaled sharply, and Elijah opened his eyes, then drew in a breath of his own. Even with his working theory, he'd expected the ash to pool where the decay was strongest, and it had, but that wasn't what shocked him.

A long streak of ash oozed over the map, curling like smoke, passing between the splotches of decay. As they watched, it neared the wards, then changed direction, heading back into Victor's land. Elijah stared in horror as it coalesced, an ashy cesspool forming, twisting, gathering. When it moved on, it left behind a smear of darkness, first nothing more than a smudge, but then it grew, spiraling outward—a foul aftermath of its journey, a mold on the land, spores of rot that took root before consuming everything around them.

"What is that?" Victor asked.

"No idea. Can you sense anything?"

Victor's gaze became distant as he focused on his land, but then he grimaced. "No. All I can sense is the forest dying."

"Okay," Elijah said, shaky but pulling himself together. "We can work with this. At least we know it's a thing that moves now. It's leaving the pockets of decay wherever it gathers, and the rot spreads out from there. But those aren't what we need to focus on. Nothing I've done so far has been aimed at whatever that is. We were healing the damage, not addressing the cause. When I put up the wards, they were to contain the rot, not trap the source. If we want this to end, we need to stop that. Whatever it is."

Victor's brow furrowed. "But how? And what is it?"

Elijah didn't have answers to those questions. What could escape both his and Victor's detection? It wasn't magic; he was certain of that, and Victor would sense any hostile creature in his territory.

"This is my fault," Victor said, a half-feral growl punctuating his words.

"Unless you, I don't even know, stole something from the fae? Are they even capable of this? It doesn't matter. There's no way you caused this."

"No. It's my fault. Everything in my life has turned to shit ever since—" He cut himself off.

"Ever since what?"

Victor laughed, bitter and humorless. "You know the previous shop owner?"

"The asshole who took advantage of your pack and deserves to be stripped of his magic? Yeah, I'm familiar."

"My father wasn't the first one he approached."

Elijah's eyebrows shot up. "What?"

"Kade and I had gone to a club in the city. He'd already left with a guy he'd picked up. I was finishing my drink when that bastard came up to me and offered to buy me another. I knew he was a mage immediately. His scent was... I don't know. It seemed off, but I thought it was because I hadn't been around magic for a while. And I was always so stupidly curious about it. So he bought me a drink, and we talked."

Victor rubbed a hand over his face, and Elijah waited. There had to be more to it than that. Finally, Victor spoke again.

"The longer we talked, the more into that bastard my wolf was getting. He was older but decent-looking. He smelled off somehow, but my wolf didn't care. It had never steered me wrong, so I went with it.

"He kept saying all this shit. How he could feel my energy and tell how strong I was, but together, we'd be so much stronger. Saying I'd be stronger for my pack, and we'd both enjoy the process. Asking if I had any experience with sex magic while his hand worked its way up my thigh. I was buzzed, and my wolf was so fucking into it. So I let him keep talking, even though I knew what he was offering was transactional, not true. But I'd been told my entire damn life I'd end up bonded to a mage, and here this bastard was, a minute away from jerking me off in a dark corner of a club. So I considered it."

"But clearly you didn't bond him."

Victor's expression contorted. "We headed to his hotel. By that point, my wolf had total control. I can't explain how strange it was. I'd never felt like that before, like my wolf and I were two separate beings that wanted two completely different things. It would have let that bastard do whatever he wanted, even if that meant bonding him right then and there. But fuck, touching him made my skin crawl. There was something in his scent. Not just his magic, something below that. Something foul."

That didn't sound like anything Elijah had ever heard of

happening to a shifter. "Was he using magic on you? On your wolf?"

Victor shook his head. "I would have noticed active magic. There wasn't any. It was my wolf being weak. Obsessed with magic. With the idea of having a mage."

Before Elijah could protest, Victor continued, his fists clenched tight. "It took every ounce of willpower I had, but I clawed back control from my wolf. I stopped whatever the hell was happening and got out of there. Then a few months later, I caught a hint of that bastard's scent on my father. When I mentioned it, he said he'd gone to the magic shop to pick up some herbs. I hadn't realized the mage in the club was the mage from the shop. I'd never had to deal with him. I should have spoken up then, but I didn't."

"He targeted your father because you rejected him?" Elijah hadn't thought he could hate the asshole more, but he'd been wrong. Anger raged inside him.

"I've got no fucking idea what that bastard was think-ing. But ever since then, everything has gone to hell."

"Whatever he was thinking, none of it is your fault."

"He might not have gone after my father if I hadn't turned him down."

"So what? It'd be better if you were the one having your energy constantly drained?"

"No. Fuck. Maybe? All I know is my grandmother was insistent that I needed to be the next to end up with a mage, not my father. Maybe it would have been different if it had been me, not him. Maybe the pack never would have been in danger. If we hadn't been weakened, this thing might not have attacked us. It wouldn't have gotten into the wards. Maybe that's what was supposed to happen. Maybe that was the best way I could serve my pack."

Elijah stared at him in disbelief. "By sacrificing yourself?"

Victor shrugged.

"You fucking—" Elijah cut off with a growl. "So because some asshole mage didn't like taking no for an answer, you think you deserve to suffer? Because he was greedy and untrustworthy, that reflects on you? His actions are your responsibility?"

"I should have stopped him. Found some way to keep him away from my father. I saw the warning signs but did nothing. If I'd done something, none of this would have happened. I failed my pack."

Elijah cursed. "You haven't told anyone this, have you?"

Victor shrugged again, looking away.

"You should have. Because if you'd told Kade, he would have kicked your ass." Victor flinched, but Elijah continued. "Kicked your ass for thinking you did anything wrong." He stepped closer and jabbed a finger into Victor's chest. "Listen to me very carefully. No one deserves what happened to you, your father, or your pack. Nothing you did or didn't do would justify that asshole's actions. And I might not know your grandmother outside the notes she wrote in the ward book, but she damn well wouldn't have been okay with sacrificing you for the good of the pack or whatever martyr bullshit you've got going on. Understood?"

Victor's eyes were wide, like he was stunned by the vehemence in Elijah's voice. He swallowed and nodded.

Elijah let out a huff. "Good. Now let's go see if we can track down this fucking thing and figure out what the hell it is so we can find a way to defeat it."

Still taken aback, Victor nodded again.

Elijah turned on his heels and headed toward the

kitchen with the map in hand. They were going to need reinforcements.

And once they'd defeated this thing, the next item on his to-do list was finding an asshole mage and kicking his ass.

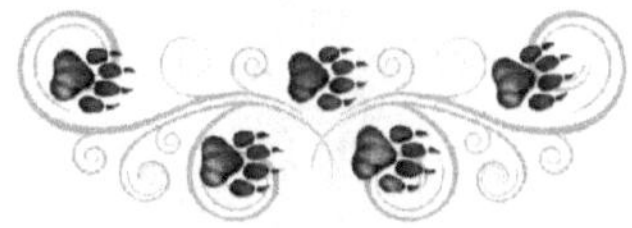

TWENTY-THREE

Victor stuck close to Elijah as they moved through the forest, the sun just high enough to guide their way. Kade and Rick followed behind, but not before Kade had given Victor a look that said he'd overheard at least part of his and Elijah's conversation and they would be talking about it later.

Elijah was right; he should have told Kade. Telling Elijah had eased some of the guilt he'd grown so accustomed to burying. Kade probably would kick his ass, but Victor would handle that when it happened.

As they traveled through the trees, they watched the map, using it to guide them closer to the ashy smear, adjusting their course as the thing moved. Victor marveled at how the ash stayed affixed, constantly flowing over the paper, not falling off.

Along the way, they passed multiple decomposing areas. None had been there the day before, but now they were gaping sores in the landscape.

Victor would have preferred to be in wolf form for tracking, but if anything happened, he'd need to communicate with Elijah.

They quickly realized that whenever they neared the thing, it twisted and oozed away, evading them before they could see what they were facing. When they picked up speed, so did it.

Victor looked at his betas. He tilted his head to one side, then the other. They nodded, breaking off, one in either direction. They'd hunted together enough to not need words for this.

The territory's southwest corner wasn't far, and this thing seemed to shy away from Elijah's wards. They might be able to box it in there.

Victor and Elijah continued straight ahead as Kade circled to the right, Rick mirroring him on the left.

On Elijah's map, the ash switched directions, moving away from the territory border toward where Kade had gone.

Then it froze, gathering briefly before retreating like it'd been cut off, leaving a speck of decay behind.

Victor pressed forward, Elijah at his side, closing in on the place the ash had pooled at the edge of his territory. A presence strained against his wards, and a flash of light rolled through them as they activated, bright enough to be seen even in the morning light.

This fucking thing better not destroy his wards again.

But in Victor's mind, they remained steadfast. The wards weren't allowing it to pass, and they didn't give any indication of weakening.

Victor's hair stood on end as they approached. His skin crawled, feeling suddenly dirty.

The trees weren't showing any sign of decay, but that meant nothing. Ahead, a dark shadow slunk, a suffocating smoke causing an unnatural twilight to creep across the forest floor.

Victor sucked in a breath, nearly choking as the air entered his lungs, heavy and sour. Tainted.

They passed a few more trees. The wards shimmered with white light as they prevented the thing from escaping.

Victor tried to place himself between it and Elijah, but Elijah pushed him aside and stood next to him.

He'd never seen anything like it. The shadow lurked, murky black but with a sheen—filth on polluted water, the rainbow-metallic slick of gasoline floating on a puddle. The wards on the other side were a muted glow through that sickening haze. It swirled disconcertingly, and Victor's eyes refused to focus on it. The constant movement disoriented him, made him unsure which way was up, his stomach churning.

"What the hell is that?"

"It must be some kind of spirit." Elijah held out a hand. A flame kindled over his palm, and then he threw it.

When it hit, there was a sizzle. The fire flared in greens and blues and purples, quick and searing, before it died, fizzling out, leaving behind the scent of sulfur, smoke, and char.

Elijah tried again to much the same effect.

Victor stepped forward, but Elijah placed a hand on his arm. "Don't touch it. I'm not sure what it will do to you."

"If it's dangerous, wouldn't it attack?"

"It might not be strong enough. But it seems to be gaining strength, attacking more complex life forms as it grows. Once it gets more powerful..." He inhaled shakily, then coughed before crouching.

He dug his fingers into the soil, and something shivered through it.

Dirt rose like a grasping hand, but the haze oozed out of the fist that tried to close around it, reducing it to a muddy sludge.

Elijah removed his hand, and the earth settled. He stood, brushing off the dirt. "I wonder if I can trap—"

But before he finished that sentence, the shadow began to coalesce, becoming thicker, denser, all oil slick and toxic waste, equal parts deadly black and consuming corruption, dark and malevolent.

Muscles tense, breath held, Victor prepared to fight, though he had no idea what he was facing.

A midnight tendril slithered its way up a trunk, laboriously hauling itself into the branches. The leaves became tinged with decay, withering as the tree decomposed before their eyes.

The spirit rose higher, into the treetops, spreading out, weighing down limbs, causing the trees to sag under its weight, and Victor reeled in horror.

With a sudden burst, it flowed through the branches, leaving oily trails behind it and showering them in a cascade of leaves, vivid autumn colors marred with decay. It sped off, over their heads, and out into the forest.

Beside him, Elijah cursed.

"Can you ward it?" Victor asked.

"Not while it's moving. To make wards strong enough to hold it, I'd need time, and it's not going to sit still just because we ask nicely."

Victor stared after it, dread twisting his gut. "How the hell are we supposed to fight that? At least if it had a physical body, we could attack it."

Elijah grimaced. "Fuck if I know."

That wasn't the answer Victor wanted. "You've never heard of anything like this?"

Elijah hesitated, then glanced away. Victor didn't need to ask; Elijah was hiding something. He was about to call him on it when leaves rustled off to the side. They both turned and saw Kade coming toward them.

He looked as frustrated and unsettled as Victor felt. "Well, that didn't work."

A moment later, Rick joined them. "What next?" he asked, then dissolved into a coughing fit.

Victor growled. "Let's get back to the house." As much as he wanted this finished, there was nothing they could do until they knew what that thing was and how to destroy it.

But that was going to take time and patience Victor wasn't sure he had.

Victor climbed the stairs, following Elijah up to his apartment and inside. He was getting too used to this, this shared burden, this reliance on someone else, and he didn't know what to think about that. But somehow, being near Elijah made him believe they'd fix this.

Once again, Victor was overwhelmed by the sheer amount of Elijah's scent in that enclosed space, but he pushed down the mixed feelings it caused. There was no time for that.

Elijah said he had research to do. Victor didn't think he'd be much help, but he couldn't sit around and do nothing, so he grabbed one of the tomes Elijah shoved at him.

"Start there. Try to find anything related to spirits or corruption. Anything that seems relevant. Liam will check out the stacks at the main library while Aran, Miles, and I search the digital archive."

Hours dragged by, but they found nothing that fit.

Victor's leg bounced as he flipped through book after book, growing increasingly restless.

Elijah's cat jumped onto his lap, and he jerked in surprise. Even Elijah stopped what he was doing to stare.

Lady blinked at him a few times, then curled up, purring.

"That's her way of telling you to stop fidgeting," Elijah said, a hint of amusement in his voice. "Also, you don't get to move now until she does."

"Fair enough. You're going to have to bring me more books though, so I don't disturb whatever miracle is happening here."

Elijah slid him another pile.

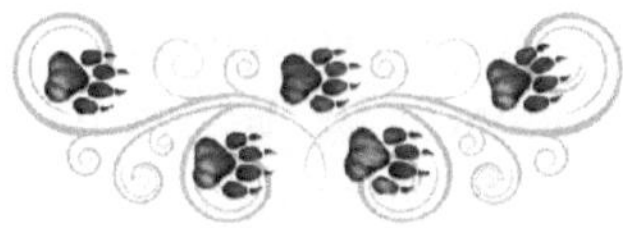

Victor sighed and put his head in his hands. His temples throbbed, and a dull ache had settled in his neck. Outside, the last shadows of dusk stained the horizon. He couldn't remember how many books he'd flipped through. Unease built, taking root inside him.

There was an itch between his shoulder blades, like eyes watching him. He tried to concentrate on the book in front of him, but his thoughts kept returning to that sensation, that gnawing worry.

Stretching out his senses, he followed the threads to his pack, to his land, and immediately was overcome by a wave of nausea. The bonds were there, but they felt corrupted and tenuous.

He stood abruptly, glad Lady had long since abandoned his lap.

Elijah looked at him. "What's going on?"

"There's something wrong with the pack bonds."

Elijah's eyes widened. "Your pack bonds?"

"They're corrupting, like they're being affected by the rot too." Victor had to force the words out.

He held out his hand, and Elijah's fingers immediately wrapped around his wrist. The familiar hum of his magic spread through Victor and into the bonds. Elijah's gasp told Victor he wasn't imagining it; Elijah sensed it too. Horror dawned on his face.

"You know what this is," Victor said. It wasn't a question.

Elijah withdrew his hand, taking his magic with him, and Victor was almost sad to feel it go.

"I don't know what it is." He wasn't lying, but it also wasn't the whole truth. "Aran told me about another pack. He said the pack and their land decayed. A mage tried to help, but nothing she did worked."

"What happened to the pack?"

Elijah shook his head.

Anger simmered through Victor's veins. "You knew about this and didn't tell me?"

"Would it have helped if I had? We aren't sure what this thing is or how to stop it. It couldn't be stopped before. Would you have wanted to hear that?"

"Yes. I would have sent everyone away. Maybe that would have stopped it from hurting them, from doing whatever it's doing to our bonds."

Elijah grimaced. "Leaving didn't help the other pack."

That hit like a punch to the gut, staggering Victor.

"I'd been hoping the ritual fixed it, that it was just the plants that were affected, but now that it's affecting animals and the pack, clearly I was wrong. I'm sorry I didn't tell you."

Victor's phone buzzed before he could respond. He unlocked it and opened the notification.

KADE

You need to get back here NOW. The kids are sick. Oliver just threw up something black.

Victor felt like he might throw up as well. He typed out a quick "On my way," shoved his phone in his pocket, and headed toward the door. Elijah hurried after him, grabbing his bag as he went.

Inside the SUV, Elijah's fingers found his wrist again, wrapping around it. Victor's breath caught.

"Can you drive while I do this?" Elijah asked. Victor nodded. Nothing would stop him from getting home.

As they careened down the dark highway, Elijah's magic flowed into him, along the bonds, through the threads. He couldn't tell what Elijah was doing, but it was similar to his wards, each member getting their own layer of protection, one by one.

He smelled Elijah's sweat as he pushed magic into whatever spell he was weaving. There was a pull on Victor's energy, but he wasn't using much. A tremor ran through his fingers, and he exhaled slowly, withdrawing his hand.

Victor traced his awareness along the threads. They were still damaged but more insulated and protected than before. "Was that a ward?"

Out of the corner of his eye, he saw Elijah shrug. "Something like that. Protection spell. It was in that book you gave me. First time doing it. Not sure how much it will help." His voice was strained.

"Thank you."

Elijah made a noise of acknowledgment, his hands shaking as he pulled out his phone, tapping a message out as fast as his fingers would allow.

"Are you going to be okay?"

"I'll be fine. Just need a few minutes to recover."

"You should have used more of my energy. It wouldn't have affected my driving."

"I used as much as I could." He sounded winded, and Victor's head jerked over to look at him, but he was focused on his phone.

He spent the rest of the drive in a furious conversation via his messenger app. Multiple bubbles popped up, but Victor couldn't read them.

Elijah paused and glanced at him. "Can I use some of the things in your attic?"

"Whatever you need."

Elijah went back to sending messages.

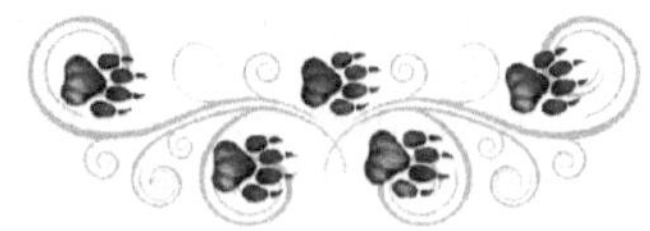

TWENTY-FOUR

Elijah exchanged a flurry of messages with his friends. The building panic in his chest caused his fingers to fly across the screen at a rate he hadn't known he was capable of, but so far, they'd only come up with a handful of ideas, none of which were likely to work.

The problem was they didn't know what they were dealing with. It was some kind of spirit, that was obvious, but it was unlike anything they'd ever heard of. The books they'd combed through had proved to be more frustrating than helpful, the discarded volumes piling up along with his anxiety. They didn't have much to go off and couldn't wait until they had more.

But he had to do something. He wouldn't sit by as Victor's pack was decimated. His heart thundered as he tried to think of a plan and force down the horror rising in his throat, constricting his chest with each breath. He didn't need whatever connection had been between them to feel the panic and fear coming off Victor in waves.

Victor gripped the steering wheel so tightly his knuckles were nearly white, and Elijah's heart ached at the haunted look in his expression. His magic wanted to flare in response, to soothe and calm, though he had no idea what comfort he could offer, not against this.

MILES

I still say your best bet is trapping it. We can destroy it later.

ELIJAH

I'm willing to try, but how?

LIAM

Do you think your wards can contain it?

ELIJAH

Maybe? The territory wards definitely are.

My smaller wards contained the rot it caused.

But I can't ward something that's moving that fast.

LIAM

Can you herd it into a circle?

Use the circle as a temporary restraint.

Then build a ward around the circle.

Elijah scrubbed a hand over his face.

ELIJAH

But then what? Leave a section of the forest warded off?

If it's in the forest, even warded, it's still connected to the land, which means it's connected to the pack.

Will that be enough to stop it from affecting them?

MILES

Can you trap it in something? A box of some kind?

ARAN

You said the cedar trees didn't seem to be affected by the rot. Do you have a cedar box? Or can you put cedar inside whatever you use?

ELIJAH

Guys, this thing is big and keeps growing the more the rot spreads.

It won't fit in a box.

LIAM

If it's feeding on the land and animals,

and that's what makes it larger,

disconnecting it from its energy source should,

theoretically,

shrink it.

ARAN

Also, maybe don't think of it as physical. Do spirits even have mass? Enough that it matters? I mean, look at the fae. They can be tiny balls of light or take on full, solid human forms, yet they're equally evil little bastards either way.

MILES

And once it's warded, without an energy source, it should lose power, making it easier to destroy.

Miles was entirely too optimistic, but that made him who he was.

ELIJAH

Okay, so we lure it into the circle somehow, and then I ward it inside a box.

But how the hell am I supposed to get it in one?

Before his friends could reply, an idea popped into his head.

ELIJAH

Wait. Aran, you're right. I have to stop thinking about it like it's physical.

What if I bind it?

ARAN

Ooh. Like putting a binding contract inside the box?

LIAM

That's gonna take a lot of energy.

ELIJAH

I'll figure it out. I'm going to need a modified binding spell though. Something for a spirit of corruption.

LIAM

Already on it.

Normal binding contracts used sigils for things like honor and integrity to bind the spirit of an oath. Those sigils wouldn't capture the decay; each spirit had to be named. But if anyone could find one for this, it was Liam.

This wasn't a permanent solution, but like Miles had said, destroying it could come later. One problem at a time.

"I need a box," Elijah said to Victor. "Preferably made of cedar."

Victor glanced at him, then back at the road. "What about a chest? There are a few in the attic; at least one is cedar."

"That could work." It was bigger than Elijah had been thinking, but that might be ideal.

Victor shifted in his seat and pulled his phone from his pocket, unlocking it before handing it over. "I have a group chat with my betas. Let them know what you need. And tell them to keep the pack inside. No one goes into the forest."

Elijah opened the messenger app, glad to see the group chat was toward the top.

VICTOR

This is Elijah. Grab the cedar chest in the attic, empty its contents, and bring it to the clearing we used for the rituals.

KADE

What's going on?

VICTOR

We'll explain when we get there. All three of you meet us at the clearing.

Bring the chest and any salt and candles you can find. If you've got any tea tree oil or sage, bring that too.

And Victor says no one is allowed in the forest.

KADE

They won't like that.

VICTOR

He says it's an order. It's not safe.

KADE

So I guess that's where we're going.

VICTOR

Yep. We'll meet you there.

Elijah rummaged through his bag, thankful most of the supplies he needed were fairly standard. And if he was lucky, the earth would remember his circle from the first ritual, which would save time.

He stared out the windshield as the road blurred by them at a speed he wouldn't have been comfortable with if anyone else were driving. Blackness seemed to have swallowed everything around them.

Victor's phone chimed with a new message.

RICK

I found candles.

They don't match or anything.

VICTOR

As long as they'll burn, that's fine.

We're using them for magic, not decorating the clearing.

Rick sent a thumbs-up, and then the phone was silent. Elijah's foot tapped a nervous rhythm against the floorboards until his own phone lit up with a picture from Liam. It was a row of five sigils, the center one as twisted as the spirit it named.

LIAM

Here you go.

The outer four are the basic binding sigils.

The center symbolizes corruption and decay.

ELIJAH

THANK YOU! I'll keep you updated.

LIAM

BE CAREFUL!

MILES

Good luck!

ARAN

Go kick some ass.

Elijah closed the app. He'd do just that.

They reached Victor's territory in record time. As they passed through the wards, the soothing warmth of coming home enveloped Elijah, and he let that feeling seep into his bones, filling him with a steely purpose. He would save this pack.

They were both out of the SUV the moment Victor stopped. It was an hour after midnight, the moon a sliver high in the sky.

Kade and half the pack were waiting on the porch. A chill ran down Elijah's spine at the sight of them. They looked grim, faces drawn and pale.

"Everyone but Kade, inside now," Victor barked out. When no one immediately obeyed, he added, "I will command you if I have to." There was an edge to his tone, a hint of alpha power, though not enough to force compliance, not yet.

The pack didn't look happy, but they filed inside.

"What the hell are you doing, Victor?" Kade asked.

Victor's response was drowned out by the pounding of Elijah's feet against the ground as he rushed ahead.

The territory was at its worst, the pockets of corruption far too frequent and ever closer together. In the flickering of his ball of light, he saw nothing but death and rot. The oppressive scent of decay surrounded him as he ran, his feet slipping on the oily sludge that had dripped off the trees. The forest wasn't going to last much longer if they didn't do something fast.

Victor was right to keep his pack inside the house, but that wouldn't buy them more than another day or two, max.

When he arrived in the clearing, breath harsh and shuddering from the run, he found an old chest at the center with the half-burnt bundle of sage he'd given Victor weeks ago and a small vial of oil beside it. He recognized the chest as the one that had contained the book of wards.

Will and Rick were waiting with a large bag of salt and a box, respectively.

Elijah didn't waste time. "Will, sprinkle the salt along the outside of the circle. Leave an opening big enough for us to get through. Rick, you have the candles?"

Rick lifted the box he was holding.

"How many do you have?"

"Fifteen?"

Elijah tossed him a candle and the compass from his bag. "Put one on each compass point and three between the main directions."

They got to work as Victor and Kade entered the clearing. Elijah only caught bits of their conversation, snippets of Kade asking Victor if this was a good idea. If he knew what he was doing. If they should trust Elijah after all the times he'd failed.

"I'm all ears if you have a better idea," Victor said, his tone terse.

Elijah ignored them and dug his fingers into the earth, asking it to recreate his circle. The energy in the soil greeted him, and a soft white glow lit up the ground. It wasn't perfect after a month and a half had weathered it, but it was close enough. It'd have to do.

Then he turned to the chest, opening the lid and inhaling the scent of cedar. He needed to put a ward on it, something strong, like the territory wards. Something the spirit wouldn't be able to escape.

After all his evenings with the ward book, he knew just the thing.

When he caught Victor's eye, he didn't have to say a word; Victor knew.

Kade watched Victor walk away from him. He said something under his breath that made Victor's gait falter and Will's head jerk up. Whatever he'd said, it'd been too quiet for Elijah to hear.

Victor shook his head and stepped up to Elijah's side. "Blood helps?"

Elijah blinked at him, surprised, but nodded.

Without hesitation, Victor bit his left thumb and smeared blood across his right palm. Elijah tilted his head down, and Victor's hand slid along his skin, settling over the back of his neck.

Like always, Victor's energy flowed easily into him, weaker without the tether but helped by the blood.

It had to be enough.

He marked the wood with the oil, scattered sage in the chest, then wove a new ward around it, using its previous one as a base.

When he finished, he examined the ward. It was the best he'd ever crafted, with two exceptions.

He moved on to the binding contract. They weren't meant for something like this. Using it to capture a literal spirit might be a stretch, but it was the best idea they had, just another thing he'd have to make work.

The last time he'd tried one of these with Victor's energy in his system, it hadn't gone well for him. But now his magic was stable, and he was using that energy in a more controlled manner. It wasn't difficult to embed the sigils into the wooden bottom of the chest. He took out a knife, pricking his finger and letting a drop of blood fall onto each sigil, hoping it would give them a boost. Victor reached over him and did the same with his free hand.

The real issue would be putting enough power into them to capture the spirit. One more thing he'd figure out when he came to it.

He stood, shaky from the magic he'd used but satisfied with the result. Victor's hand fell away from his neck and settled on the small of his back, steadying him.

Rick and Will had also finished their preparations, and they came over as Elijah pulled the map out of his bag.

The spirit itself was even larger than before. Its corruption had spread over significantly more area. It wouldn't be long before the entire territory was covered. One line of ash stretched from the clearing to the house, along the pack bonds. The sight of it made Elijah's chest tighten.

"We need to herd the spirit in here," he said. "Once it's in the circle, we complete the salt ring. That should keep it from escaping temporarily while I try to trap it."

Victor took over from there. They devised a plan to encircle the spirit, then the five of them headed out, following the swirling darkness on Elijah's map. They'd split up once they got closer to the spirit and were ready to drive it toward the circle.

As they made their way through the forest, the rot became even more apparent. The bark on the trees was torn asunder, leaving the oozing filth exposed. From the depths of the forest came the sound of fire. Not the pleasant crackle of a bonfire on the full moon but the raging howls of a forest fire as trees were cracked apart and consumed, thousands of voices shrieking in pain and death. A polluted wind whipped at them, clogging Elijah's throat, and the stench of decay skittered over his skin.

They waded through the rot, toward the spirit, but this time, it wasn't running from them. If anything, it was getting closer, spreading wider on the map.

It took Elijah a moment to realize what it was doing. It was coming straight at them.

They'd been planning to surround it.

It was surrounding *them*.

"Shit," he said, then coughed. It thought it was powerful enough now to take them on. All of them. "Stop! We have to go back."

Victor opened his mouth to protest; Elijah cut him off. "No. It will follow us. I don't want it to catch us out here."

They ran, the forest closing in, as claustrophobic and choking as the air. Elijah tried to avoid touching the rot, but that was impossible. Tar-covered branches reached for him, leaves smeared with mold rained down on them, and the sludge piled on the ground grabbed at his shoes.

Victor's betas pulled ahead, sprinting toward the clearing.

Elijah stumbled, and Victor was there, wrapping an arm around his waist, all but carrying him over a fallen tree.

Unable to take full inhales without coughing, his breath came in labored pants, and his skin felt like it'd never be clean again.

When he could, Elijah glanced at the map. The ashy shadow stalked them, creeping closer.

Behind them, the forest groaned, and heavy, squelching

thuds sounded at regular intervals, getting closer, closer, closer.

Something was chasing them; it wasn't just a disembodied spirit anymore. It rattled the ground and crashed into trees.

A screech tore through the night, sending a shiver of icy dread through Elijah. Another shriek joined the first.

He broke into the clearing, his heart pounding, Victor right beside him, steadying him again. As one, they turned, looking the way they came. Seconds later, the shadow followed.

But it wasn't alone.

There were creatures with it—two twisted things made of rot that loomed in the circle's dim light. Their grotesque forms resembled those of men, but they were massive and hulking, their limbs dripping with decay.

"Close the circle before those get inside," Elijah yelled. Will grabbed the salt, but the creatures crashed through the protective barrier.

"What the fuck are those?" Victor asked.

"Golems," Elijah said, stuffing the map in his pocket. "The spirit's controlling them."

"I did want something I could fight." Victor's tone was grim, but determination hardened his gaze.

They faced the nightmare creatures. Overhead, the shadowy spirit swirled, an oil slick in the darkened sky.

Elijah swallowed his fear and prepared to fight.

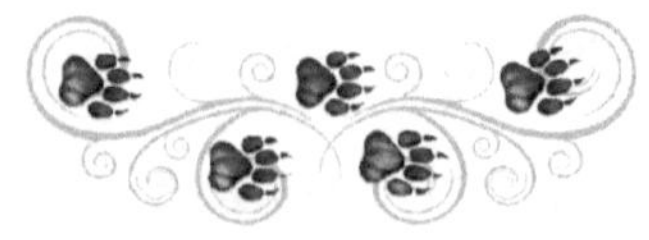

TWENTY-FIVE

Victor pushed Elijah behind him. "Do what you have to. We'll protect you."

He wanted to do more than that, wanted to order his betas to carry Elijah out of there and put him somewhere safe, but Elijah would not appreciate that instinct. As it was, he hesitated before nodding and running toward the chest.

Victor and his betas formed a line between Elijah and the two monstrous creatures. Four on two. He hoped those odds were enough. While they weren't at their weakest, the new moon was barely past, and he wasn't sure even a full moon would help.

His betas knew what to do; he didn't need to give them instructions. Rick and Will would take the creature on the left while he and Kade would handle the one on the right.

Will circled to the side so he and Rick could attack from different directions, and Victor prepared to do the same with Kade.

This would not be a pleasant fight.

The spirit above them swirled, corrupting the air,

making it hard to breathe. Already the grass under his feet was withering. It was just a matter of time before it turned to sludge.

Victor edged to his left; Kade didn't move. Instead, he stood frozen, his breath rattling.

"Kade?" Victor had never seen nerves get the better of him.

But Kade shook himself once and stepped to the right, getting into position.

Victor exhaled. This was it. He crouched low, readying himself to spring forward.

A solid body slammed into him from his right.

Unprepared for the hit, Victor grunted and stumbled. He scarcely had time to register Kade had attacked him before he was doing it again, lunging at Victor.

"What the—" He cut off when he saw Kade's eyes. They were glassy and distant, an unnatural sheen in them. But where his gaze was unfocused, his movements were sharp and precise as he stalked toward Victor.

This wasn't Kade. The spirit must have gotten to him.

Out of the corner of his eye, Victor saw Rick had shifted into his wolf form while Will was partially shifted. He couldn't tell if they were winning, if they were making any progress as they fought the golem.

With Kade distracting Victor, the other creature had started toward Elijah. Victor went to cut it off, but Kade came after him.

He could handle Kade, but the golem and Kade together... That wasn't happening. He had to take Kade out fast, then attack the creature. Elijah would have to protect himself until then.

He wouldn't hurt Kade. Not if he didn't have to. He

needed to knock him out until they could free him from the spirit possessing him.

Mind made up, he threw himself at Kade, trying to slam him to the ground and pin him.

Kade was ready for him. As they fell, he twisted to get Victor underneath him.

They grappled, and Victor struggled for control. Kade's nails lengthened, his teeth elongated, and his body contorted, shifting partially, claws digging into Victor's flesh. The scent of Victor's blood floated in the air. It seemed to spur Kade on.

This wasn't Kade's usual fighting style. There was a viciousness to it that he'd never shown, and his strength and speed were enhanced.

They'd sparred with each other for decades. Victor had gained the upper hand when he was in his late teens; Kade was stronger now.

Over the rushing in his ears, Victor heard Elijah curse, and he risked a glance his way.

The golem had closed in on him, but Elijah had erected a ward. The creature's greasy, muddy arms squished against the barrier.

Victor knocked Kade off him and rolled away, pushing to his feet. He'd been reckless in his attempt to get Kade pinned when he didn't know what his abilities were now. He should have assessed the situation first.

They circled each other, and Victor's eyes darted to the other two fights. Rick and Will had severed the golem's right arm, but the limb was crawling toward Will, and the monster seemed to be growing a new one.

That did not bode well. If these things were capable of regeneration, they'd need to kill the spirit to defeat them. Or, more accurately, *Elijah* would need to. Victor was under no impression he could fight the spiraling sickness that hung above them.

He looked toward Elijah again, and Kade took it as an invitation to attack, charging him, causing Victor to take a few slippery steps to keep his guard up. Victor might not want to hurt him; Kade wasn't returning the courtesy.

Victor blocked Kade's blow and tried to get in one of his own, but Kade moved faster than he ever had before. His next swipe slashed across Victor's stomach, gouging into flesh, cutting him open. Searing pain ripped through Victor, and he gritted his teeth before grabbing Kade's arm, using it to twist him away and get him into a hold.

Kade broke free, flipping around to come at Victor again. The punch Victor landed was answered by a blow to his side, agony stealing his breath. Blood oozed from his stomach, staining his shirt and jeans. His body was trying to heal, but the damage was extensive, and his every movement tore apart the little progress it made.

It'd been a long time since he'd had a fight like this, with someone at his level or above. He had to be smart and figure out how to stop Kade, but his attention was fractured.

Rick and Will weren't having any more luck with the golem they were facing. Rick was in his human form again, and they shouted back and forth, trying to come up with a plan.

"Kade," Victor said, putting all his alpha power and authority into his voice. "*Fight it.* Whatever's possessing you, fight it."

Kade's lips curled as he snarled, showing off pointed teeth. There was black at the corners of his mouth, and it was spreading, spidering outward, crawling over his face.

He surged forward. Victor tried to dodge, only to feel

the razor-sharp bite of claws raking over his wound, deepening the cuts.

The pain staggered him, and Kade pressed his advantage, punching him in the gut. Victor doubled over, stars exploding behind his eyes. Kade kicked his legs out from under him, pinning him on his bloodied stomach.

Victor strained against him but couldn't push him off. This thing possessing him had made him so much stronger. Kade shoved him down, and all Victor could smell was the rot coming off him. He twisted his head and took in the clearing as Kade tore into his back.

Rick cradled his right arm; it looked dislocated. Will limped, seconds away from falling over. But still, they were fighting.

Elijah's ward wavered as the creature pressed against it. Kade wrenched Victor's arm until it felt like it would break, but Victor couldn't tear his eyes away from the black cracks forming throughout Elijah's barrier. The creature was almost through.

He was able to create stronger wards than that; Victor knew he could. His pack territory wards hadn't given in the slightest.

Inside the ward, sweat beaded on Elijah's brow. He'd given up on his spell. The chest sat abandoned. Instead, his shaking hands were pressed against his ward, holding it together.

Victor gasped, half in pain from Kade's claws severing a tendon in his arm and half in realization.

Elijah's ward wasn't as strong because it was missing something.

With his free hand, Victor smeared his fingers through the blood pooled under him.

He inhaled, choking on the air, but forced himself to shout, "Elijah!"

Elijah's eyes widened when he saw Victor pinned down. He glanced at the golem, then back at Victor, and Victor read what he was about to do in the flex of his fingers. He shook his head and reached his free arm out in front of him, sinking his blood-covered fingers into the earth, the way he'd seen Elijah do half a dozen times or more.

Understanding dawned on Elijah's face, and he nodded. He clenched his jaw and removed one hand from the ward, which shuddered and groaned as the golem pushed it to its breaking point. Elijah grasped blindly behind him until he found his knife. He sliced his fingers across the blade, then dug them into the ground.

The connection was instantaneous as the earth bridged the gap between them. Victor's energy was tugged out of him, flowing into Elijah, but when it reached him, something opened between them, and Victor gasped again. Elijah's magic flooded into him, echoing in that endless mirror loop, feeding in on itself, becoming infinitely more. Warmth bloomed in his chest, and he welcomed it.

Elijah's eyes glowed bright purple as he stared at Victor, wonder reflected on his face.

The ward around him flared, flinging the creature away.

Victor wanted to cheer, but Kade's claws dug into his neck. With this extra power inside him, Victor thought he'd be able to knock him off now but wasn't sure if he could withdraw his fingers from the earth.

As if answering that question, Elijah lifted his hand. The connection stayed wide open, their magic and energy tangled together, thrumming through them.

The ground rumbled beneath Elijah's feet, and the tattoos on his arms lit up the night.

Then the ward protecting him vanished.

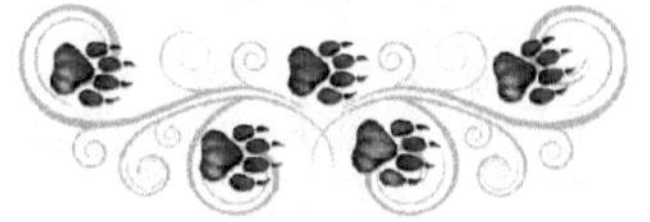

TWENTY-SIX

Victor's energy flooded into him, fueling his magic, alive and wild, more powerful than ever before. Whatever ghost of a connection they'd had, whatever he'd experienced during the full-moon rituals, this eclipsed it all.

He welcomed it, opened for it, let it in.

With it came everything that was Victor. His body, ripped and bloodied. His territory, rotting and failing. His pack, sick and dying. Elijah felt his pain, sorrow, and despair. It made him ache to ease those gut-wrenching emotions.

And through Victor, he sensed Kade, though the bond between them was fouled by the spirit festering inside him, controlling him, using his connections to the pack to spread outward, into the other members.

They had to end this now, or no one would survive.

Elijah released his ward and pressed his palm against the ground as the golem barreled toward him.

The earth groaned as it rose, snaring the creature's feet. It struggled, but soil surrounded it, crawling up its legs and body, dragging it down, and burying it up to the neck with a crushing force that sliced off its head.

The head rolled to a stop and was quickly swallowed by more earth.

Elijah's gaze snapped to where Rick and Will battled the other creature. He didn't hesitate to do the same with the second golem. Victor's betas fell to their knees in relief.

With that threat taken care of, Kade and the spirit remained.

Elijah spun his magic inside himself, gathering fire into his hand, and turned to see Kade's claws scoring across Victor's neck. Victor pushed up, knocking Kade off, and stumbled a few steps, standing to fight. Blood stained his entire front. Elijah's heart clenched at the sight. A desperate, primal need coursed through him, so intense it nearly consumed him. It might have come from Victor or himself or both. It didn't matter; the instinct was the same. Protect the pack, the land, each other.

Kade ignored Victor. Instead, he charged Elijah, coming straight at him.

His face was half-shifted, not the graceful beauty of wolves running through the forest, but a violent, ugly change that was ripping him apart. The bloodlust contorting his features was unmistakable as he lunged forward, sharp teeth bared, a howl of rage in his throat.

Elijah hefted the fireball. It wouldn't kill Kade but should be enough to bring him down. He went to throw it.

Pain lanced through his arm, and the fire extinguished. He hissed and staggered.

Shit, he thought, dodging as Kade rushed him, barely managing to get away. But Kade swung around and came at him again.

The fucking oath was still binding him. He'd never fixed the problem.

Elijah dropped to the ground, his hands hitting the earth, asking it to snare Kade as it had the golems. The earth rumbled, trying to respond to him, but once again, pain shot through him as his magic backfired.

He threw up a ward, and it snapped into place seconds before Kade crashed into it, swiping at it with his claws. Elijah winced, but it held.

Black lines skittered across the barrier as Kade battered it. He snarled when he realized there was no chance of breaking through.

Elijah let out a shaky exhale, coughing on the dirty air. He needed to capture Kade, but he couldn't do anything that might hurt him, and his options were limited while holding this ward—it took too much of his concentration to maintain.

As Elijah considered his next move, Kade seemed to give up on him. His unfocused stare returned to Victor.

Rick lurched forward, but he was too weak to fight. Kade threw him aside and advanced on where Victor stood, swaying, a grim determination on his face.

Elijah dissolved his ward, only to have Kade turn and grab him, a hand finding his neck, his claws piercing Elijah's skin as he hauled him closer. Rot had blackened half of his face.

"Elijah!" Victor cried. He staggered, holding his stomach.

"I can't hurt him," Elijah choked out. Kade's grip tightened around his throat.

Victor's eyes widened with comprehension. "I release you from your oath!"

Something loosened in Elijah. He slammed his palm

into Kade's chest, using the strength of his magic to knock him away. As Kade was forced back, his claws dragged over Elijah's skin, leaving jagged, stinging gashes that seared into his flesh.

Elijah crouched, one hand coming up to rub at his throat. It came away slick with blood.

He pressed his palms against the earth and wove his magic through the soil. It followed his command this time, snaking up Kade's legs, trapping him in place, though he thrashed and struggled to get free.

Elijah wrenched himself up, then hesitated, seeing Victor on his knees. But he had to trust Victor was strong enough to heal from his injuries. Even if he wasn't, Elijah knew what he'd want done.

He threw himself toward the chest, digging his fingers into the ground. He sensed the corruption, the death, the rot.

The magic in his body was overwhelming, thrumming through him, bolstered by Victor's energy. Even the forest lent him its remaining strength to rid itself of the evil that had infected it. Beyond that, the territory wards were radiant and healthy, the only thing unaffected by the rot. It all twined together in a beautiful torrent of power that flowed through him.

Elijah took that power and molded it as his awareness stretched throughout Victor's land.

And then he activated the sigils at the bottom of the chest.

They flared to life, glowing brighter and brighter. A wind picked up, whipping around them, pulling at Elijah's clothes and hair as power surged through him. He gritted his teeth and pushed more magic and energy into the sigils, amplifying them.

The wind became a vortex, swirling over the chest; the sigils shone, blinding in the darkness of a night moments from the first rays of dawn. They pulled the spirit down from the sky, hauling it into the chest, binding it to the bottom.

The rot strained against the binding, clinging to the land, to the pack and their bonds, to the animals and plants, to Kade's mind. But Elijah kept pouring more power into it, and the sigils kept dragging the decay closer, inch by slow, painful inch.

As the spirit's grip loosened on the land, it shrank. Its polluted sheen filled the sky as it coalesced over the clearing, then was trapped in an ever-denser mass inside the chest. It pooled there, sickening, deadly, unlike anything he'd ever seen.

He kept feeding the sigils power until he found no trace of rot left in the bonds and the land outside the circle. Then, very carefully, he directed that pull toward the threads that had woven through Kade. He coaxed them out until the rot receded from his face, and Kade collapsed into the earth encasing him, gasping for air.

The whipping wind died, and Elijah slammed the lid shut, folding the wards he'd prepared around the chest like a second skin, keeping the spirit captured inside.

When he finished, he sagged, panting, drenched with sweat, his eyelids sliding closed. The wounds on his neck itched as they healed.

He checked the pack once more, one by one, to make sure their bonds were whole and clean. Then he let go of the scant remains of his magic, expecting Victor's energy to leave him as well.

But it didn't.

The connection between him and Victor hadn't

dimmed in the slightest. He felt *everything*. The burn of Victor's stomach knitting itself together, his bone-deep relief, his awe at what Elijah had done, and a myriad of other emotions Elijah couldn't begin to put names to, but that left him trembling, his entire body alight with warmth and joy.

Overwhelmed by the magnitude of it all, Elijah dragged a hand through his hair, taking time to breathe and regroup before he looked at Victor. When he did, Victor's eyes flashed golden.

The spirit was trapped. They still needed to destroy it, but Victor's pack was safe. Elijah had finally done what he'd been hired to do.

But now he and Victor were connected in a way that never should have been possible. A tether, thick and rope-like, stretched between them. It shouldn't exist; he knew that much. He just wasn't sure what that meant or what happened next.

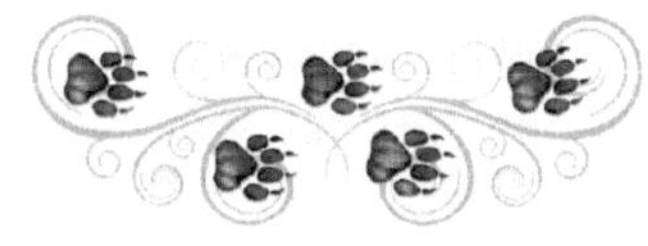

TWENTY-SEVEN

The world slowed and stopped. Victor's every breath, every heartbeat, was filled with Elijah, bursting with his scent, his being, the connection between them. While he reeled with the possibilities, his eyes were transfixed by the sight of Elijah—the rapid rise and fall of his chest, the sweaty, tumbled mess of his hair, the blood dripping down his neck as the cuts from Kade's claws healed. Even like that, he was gorgeous, a vision in dawn's soft light.

There was a solid presence in Victor's mind, a part of him, yet not. It was that intense rush of emotion and sensation he'd experienced for one moment before Elijah had severed their previous connection. But this remained, not snatched away before Victor could truly comprehend its enormity.

Exhaustion from using that amount of magic ached deep in Elijah's bones; relief and joy ran through him. And everything was colored by the same confused wonder that had wrapped Victor in its arms as the world revealed itself to him in a new, extraordinary way, his dreams spilling into reality.

He tried to stand, but his legs weren't cooperating with him. He inhaled sharply as pain stabbed through his stomach. Now that he wasn't trying to fight, it was healing faster than his shifter abilities accounted for, no doubt thanks to Elijah, but it'd still take a few days before he was fully healed.

Elijah didn't trust his own legs either, if Victor was reading his frustrated longing correctly.

Was this what it was like to be bonded to someone? To be so open to them, to know them completely in exchange. The idea sent a thrill through Victor that had Elijah's breath catching, a quiet smile forming on his lips even in the aftermath of what they'd been through.

He felt Elijah's need to touch him, to be close to him; the same need echoed in his own veins.

Fuck his wounds. He had to get to Elijah.

His fingers clawed into the ground as he dragged himself forward, gasping from the pain. He managed a few inches before the delicate new skin on his stomach ripped open, halting his progress. His vision swam, and his arms threatened to give out.

Panic spiked through his mind, and he looked up to find Elijah's startled eyes on him.

Elijah lurched to his feet despite how drained he was, the determination in his expression clear. He wobbled on unsteady legs. His movements were pure momentum, and he stumbled after a few steps, but it was enough to get him to Victor. He collapsed mere inches away, and Victor closed the final distance between them, gathering him in his arms, ignoring the fresh gush of blood the motion caused. It didn't matter; Elijah was there.

Victor grasped onto him, Elijah's touch a desperately needed comfort. The contact made sparks dance between them, like electricity tingling over their skin. Warmth flared inside Victor, and he relaxed into it, into Elijah.

Everything disappeared around them as they sat there, trembling from the ebb of adrenaline out of their systems, leaning together for support, relishing each other's presence.

Underneath the metallic tang of blood and the clinging stench of decay, Elijah's scent pervaded the air, and it caused contentment to roll through Victor. He'd happily stay there forever, taking in lungfuls of that scent. Even through the haze of pain, all he could focus on was Elijah and this new awareness of him.

After two years of guilt and second-guessing himself, Victor had no regrets about the path he'd chosen. This was where he was meant to be.

Their connection left Victor alight with peace and wonder. Elijah's emotions swept through him—his relief, his awe, his elation—as strong as Victor's own.

It was overwhelming, but Victor wanted to know everything about Elijah. Wanted to learn his body and his mind. Wanted to protect him as Elijah had protected his pack.

This was everything he'd ever hoped for, but he had to make sure Elijah wanted it too.

He pulled back enough to meet Elijah's gaze and found himself as lost in his eyes as he was in his emotions.

"This... This tether? It's like a mating bond, isn't it?" Victor asked, stunned. He'd known his grandparents had shared something special, but he'd always assumed the bond caused it. This was better than anything he'd heard bonded pairs describe.

Elijah searched Victor's face before answering. "A

magical version of it. But it shouldn't have been able to form like that."

Victor rubbed his thumb against the inside of Elijah's wrist. "How does it usually work?"

Through the connection, he caught a flash of arousal before Elijah tamped it down. "Sex. Not sex magic, not temporary so I can access your energy. It's supposed to be done at the same time. You bond me; I tether myself to you."

If they were going to get through this conversation, Victor needed to distract himself from the thought of bonding Elijah. "Does that mean we just had some sort of bizarre threesome with the earth?"

Elijah let out a soft huff. "I hope not. I think it acted as a conduit. Really, this shouldn't have happened without a physical connection."

"Do you mind it did?"

Elijah hesitated, his side of their connection a kaleidoscope of emotions that Victor struggled to untangle. "We couldn't have trapped that spirit without it." He paused again, gathering himself before he continued. "When we were connected before, my magic was acting up, but after I severed the connection, it went back to normal. Except somehow, it wasn't *normal* anymore. It was missing something."

Victor knew exactly what he meant. "I've been walking around for the past sixteen days like I've got a hole in my chest."

Elijah's eyes widened at the sincerity in Victor's voice.

"So," Victor said cautiously. "Do we need to sever it?" The idea alone made dread squirm in his gut and his wolf whine.

Elijah's laugh was nervous and shaky. "I mean, we

could try? But I'm honestly not sure it'd work. There shouldn't be a connection between us, and yet it's the strongest thing I've ever felt."

"Do you want to try?"

Elijah glanced away from him, not making eye contact as he said, "I've never wanted to be a pack mage. I wanted to retain my neutrality, make my shop profitable, and prove I could make it on my own."

Victor waited, breath held, inundated by the emotions swirling through Elijah.

He finally looked at Victor again, his expression open and vulnerable; his icy blue eyes glittered like frost in the early morning light. "But I don't think I've been neutral since I met your pack. Being here, with you, feels right in a way I never thought possible. Now all I want is to stay, even if it means those other things won't happen."

Relief rushed through Victor. He gave in to his urges, tangling his fingers into the hair at the nape of Elijah's neck, loving the way it made his eyelids flutter. "I wasn't lying when I said we used to be the pack everyone called when they needed a mage. There's no reason that can't be you."

Elijah seemed to be picturing that, but then his resolve firmed, and he studied Victor. "What about you? Do you want this? All of you. Not just your wolf."

Victor didn't have to think about it; his answer was immediate. "I want this. All of me does. I don't know if I'll ever trust my wolf around magic, but I trust you."

"But right now, while I'm tethered to you, I have unlimited access to your energy. Until we bond, it's one-sided. I have complete control. I could use it to drain you."

Victor shook his head. He wasn't in danger of becoming his

father, not with Elijah, not even close. "You wouldn't. I can feel how much you hate the idea. Also, you said 'until we bond.'" He trailed his fingers down Elijah's throat, careful of the cuts, and then over the juncture of his neck, where the marks from their dream had been. "That sounded like a when, not an if."

"It's a when." Elijah leaned toward him with a slow, deliberate purpose that left Victor dazed and breathless, as if the very air was charged with the potential of what they were destined to become. The electric inevitability of their future crackled between them.

Elijah tilted his head as their lips found each other. The taste of him was just as intoxicating as Victor remembered, their mouths fit together just as perfectly. The spark of pleasure he got from Elijah fed into his own. There was no comparing this to anything else Victor had ever experienced.

He groaned and pressed forward to deepen the kiss, only to groan for a different reason when his stomach objected to the movement.

Elijah pushed him away gently. "Let's maybe wait until you're a little more healed?"

Victor couldn't protest. He wished he could, but with how abused his body was, how much blood he'd lost, how exhaustion was taking over his entire being, he wasn't capable of a fraction of what he'd imagined doing to Elijah. Not yet.

"Okay, but for the record, you using my energy to kick ass? It was the hottest thing I've ever seen. And as soon as we're both recovered..." He pulled Elijah in once more and let his kiss promise all the dirty things he'd do to him, enjoying the lust in Elijah's gaze when they broke apart.

To his right, he heard a groan, and reality came crashing

down around them. Victor forced himself to look away from Elijah and take in the clearing.

His betas were in rough shape. Rick struggled to sit, while Will remained on the ground, panting. Kade was slumped in his earthen trap, passed out but healing now that the rot had been removed. From what Victor could tell, none of them had sustained life-threatening injuries.

He checked on his pack members, following their threads one by one until he'd reassured himself they were fine. Even Oliver's thread—the newest and weakest—was full of life.

Well, second newest. But the thread that tied him to Elijah was far from weak. He traced over it. That touch made Elijah shiver, and he found himself shivering in return when Elijah copied the gesture.

Victor sensed members of his pack approaching, and for once, he was glad they were disobeying his order to stay away. The five of them weren't getting their asses home without help.

Elijah squeezed his hand. "I'm going to release Kade before they get here."

Victor wasn't thrilled with even that much space between them, but he let him go. Elijah managed the dozen steps to Kade, then collapsed with little grace. He pressed his hands to the earth, and the dirt encasing Kade gradually lowered him to the ground. Then he placed a palm on Kade's forehead, and what little magic he had to spare flowed into Kade, infusing him with healing energy. Even with that, it'd be a while before Kade was entirely healed.

A few minutes later, Katrina led a dozen pack members into the clearing.

"How's Oliver?" Victor croaked out as she hauled him up.

"Good as new. No one would ever guess he took ten years off my life tonight. The only way I got him to stay in his room was by promising I'd personally go check on Elijah."

"Elijah, huh?"

"Yeah, sorry. You were an afterthought. You may have some serious competition for Elijah's attention."

"I can't fault his priorities." His eyes jumped to where Elijah swayed on his feet, directing various pack members to grab Kade and the chest. Victor knew he was smiling like an idiot, but he couldn't bring himself to stop.

Katrina beamed at him. "Hey, would you look at that? Whatever happened out here must have finally knocked your head from your ass. It's nice to see your face again."

He scowled at her, but there was no heat behind it, and she grinned wider.

"Everyone else good?"

"All good. Though, seriously. We felt what Elijah did with the pack bonds. If you think you can send him away without a mutiny, you're sorely mistaken."

"He's here for as long as he wants to be."

Elijah turned their way, and while Victor wasn't sure if he'd heard that, the increasing warmth in his chest pointed to yes.

The trek to the house was painful in more ways than one. Victor's stomach was less than happy, his wound threatening to tear open again with every step.

"You do realize this would be easier if you let us carry you." Katrina huffed in exasperation. She was already taking more of his weight than Victor's pride could handle.

"Hey now, let him be the badass, stoic alpha to impress his mage," Lauren said from his other side. "We aren't helping him walk. We're huddling under the protection of his strong, manly arms."

Katrina snorted.

"I'm getting a new pack once I can walk."

"No, you won't," Katrina and Lauren said in unison.

They were annoyingly right. He was rather attached to this one.

But that didn't mean it wasn't driving him insane that he had to allow the pack to help Elijah. His eyes kept being drawn to him, making sure they were treating him well and being careful as they helped him along the path. Though Elijah was in much better condition than Victor, nearly walking on his own.

The forest was still damaged. The rot might be gone, but it'd left scars. Some trees and plants would never recover. And there was something comforting about that. It hadn't been magically restored; it needed time to heal.

Janell was waiting for them on the back porch, and she helped Will inside while other pack members brought Rick and Kade to their rooms. Kade was unconscious but growing stronger, and Katrina promised she'd stay with him until he was awake.

Then they were hauling Victor upstairs. Before he could check to see what they were doing with Elijah, amusement bubbled up in his mind. He glanced over his shoulder, knowing he'd find Elijah there.

His pack hadn't bothered asking if he should be taken to a guest room. They'd made the executive decision to bring him to Victor's.

Victor glimpsed his ragged appearance in the bathroom mirror as Katrina propped him against the counter. His stomach was knitting itself together, but his shirt was in tatters, and there'd be no saving these jeans.

"You going to be able to take care of yourself?" she asked.

He opened his mouth to say of course, but she raised an eyebrow. "I'll manage," he grumbled.

She shot him a skeptical look but stepped away as Elijah was deposited next to him. His clothes were dirty, there was blood on his neck, and his body sagged with weariness, but he was significantly more put together than Victor.

Elijah waved them off. "I'll manage too. And I'll make sure this one doesn't pass out on the bathroom floor."

It was clear they believed Elijah more than him.

"See that you do," Katrina said before leaving them alone.

"They're extremely subtle." Fondness sparkled in Elijah's tone.

Victor snorted. Subtle was one thing his pack would never be.

A comfortable silence settled between them. Elijah was still there, in the back of his mind, though he wasn't as noticeable as he had been.

Victor reached out and glided his fingers across Elijah's hand. His presence sprang forward, snapping into focus, and his emotions flooded into Victor again—his fatigue, his joy, and something else. Something gentle and tender, a comforting murmur, a deep contentment that could never be properly put into words, but that spread out and filled Victor with the thrum of its perfection.

Elijah melted into him as if he'd been waiting for his touch. The intensity of it all bordered on surreal, and Victor let it envelop him.

They stayed there as minutes drifted by, their sides

pressed together, their temples touching, simply breathing, letting everything that had happened sink in.

Victor's eyelids drooped, threatening to close. If he shut them for a minute or two, he'd be fine.

Elijah straightened, pulling out of his embrace. His sudden absence left Victor chilled, and it roused him enough to follow Elijah's words. "No, none of that until you're in your bed. I promised your pack I wouldn't let you pass out in here."

"Our," Victor said in a low, sleepy rumble.

"What?"

"You said *your*. They aren't just my pack. It's not just my bed. Not anymore."

Elijah blinked at him, then a slow, warm smile spread across his face. "Our pack?"

Victor nodded.

"Our bed?" When Elijah leaned in, there was nothing but the feeling of home and happiness in his kiss.

But it was over too soon as he pulled away and appraised Victor's haggard state. "You look like hell." Amusement tickled Victor's mind, and he remembered saying the same thing to Elijah after the first full-moon ritual.

"Thanks." Victor gave him a cocky grin of his own, as spent as Elijah's had been that night. "Can't say the same to you." He looked fucking amazing—blood, filth, and all.

Elijah shook his head and helped him peel out of the blood-crusted tatters of his shirt, his fingers tracing over the tender skin on Victor's stomach. He brushed another kiss against Victor's lips.

"I'm so glad shifters have ridiculous healing abilities."

Victor huffed. "Me too."

"Maybe don't put them to the test in the future?"

"I'll do my best."

Elijah's fingers glided over Victor's left pec, his touch lighting up the scrollwork tattoos that spiraled out from his heart and over his chest, so much brighter than before. A pleasant burn shimmered along the lines, and Victor's breath caught at how right they looked on his skin.

Elijah stripped Victor's bloodied jeans off him, his gaze trailing over his body, lingering on his dick. It gave the tiniest twitch, doing its best to get hard, but it wasn't happening. Not with all the healing he had to do. No matter how much desire was in Elijah's heated stare.

He left Victor naked, resting against the edge of the counter, giving him the perfect view to enjoy the show as Elijah undressed, his movements languid and sluggish.

Victor's eyes devoured every inch of pale skin he exposed. Faint traces of purple glimmered in his tattoos, even under the harsh bathroom light. They seemed to be unfurling as he watched, inching their way over Elijah's shoulders and across his chest, and with a heady satisfaction, he realized that was his doing. His energy infusing with Elijah's magic, making his already formidable strength that much stronger. How much of Elijah's skin would his tattoos cover when they were bonded? Victor's canines ached with the need to find out.

The first chance he had, he'd map that body with his fingers until he had it memorized, trace his tongue along those tattoos, imprint everything that was Elijah in his mind.

They helped each other into the shower, savoring the press of their bodies, even if nothing more could happen. Leaning against the wall, they rinsed off the muck from the fight.

They traded a few more exhausted kisses, but even as

he stood under the hot stream of the shower, holding Elijah, sleep beckoned Victor, and Elijah wasn't doing much better.

Reluctantly, he shut off the water. They dried each other, then stumbled to their bed, falling into it together.

Victor pulled Elijah to him and buried his nose in the crook of his neck.

"God," he mumbled against Elijah's skin. "You have no idea how your scent in this bed was tormenting me. How all I've wanted for the last two weeks was for it to smell like you again."

Elijah relaxed into his embrace. "I think we can manage that."

Victor inhaled deeply and was asleep before he could think of a reply.

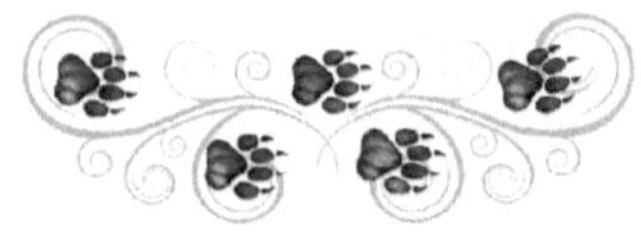

Victor woke to late-afternoon light streaming into his bedroom window. He was draped along Elijah's back, wrapped around his body. The energy between them was potent and familiar.

He closed his eyes, lost in Elijah's scent, so damn sweet and good. Victor couldn't get enough of the way it spread through him. But it wasn't just Elijah's scent anymore; it had started to blend with his own in the most perfect way —all dark earth and deep forest draped in downy snow and the moon's ethereal glow, everything that was home distilled into one sublime scent—and it'd only get better when they completed the bond.

Before last night, he hadn't truly understood how

strong Elijah was. The sheer power at his disposal was incredible. It'd pulsed like a living thing, surging through the air and vibrating in his bones. And now it was around them, blanketing them, filling them both, as perfect as his scent.

As perfect as everything about him. His sharp wit, his magnetic personality, how he interacted with Victor's pack, how similar to Victor he was in so many ways—stubborn and determined, fiercely loyal to those he loved.

Victor shifted his weight on the bed, testing how his stomach was doing, and found it almost healed. Even for him, that was fast. He was tired and sore but wasn't that far from normal. He propped himself up enough he could get a good look at Elijah, relieved when he saw the wounds on his neck were nothing but delicate, silvery lines etching their way across his throat. Those, too, would fade with time.

Relaxing back into his bed, Victor pulled Elijah against him again. He basked in the press of their bodies, but his mind was flush with an endless list of fantasies that were no longer out of his reach—touching every part of Elijah, tasting every inch of his skin, hearing his moans when Victor was inside him.

His well-past-morning wood nestled against Elijah's ass. It perked up even more when Elijah pushed back, half-asleep but practically purring in contentment as he woke.

"Damn shifters," he grumbled. There was fondness in his tone. "I'm not sure I'll be able to keep up if this is what you're like twelve hours after having your guts almost ripped out."

Victor snorted and let his hands explore Elijah's body, running over his chest and abs while he breathed him in. "How are you doing?"

Elijah stretched. "Surprisingly good. Really fucking hungry, but I normally would have slept at least another four or five hours after using even half that amount of magic."

Victor's hands skirted lower, following the line of hair below Elijah's navel further down, pleased to find he wasn't the only one more recovered. He skated his fingers along Elijah's shaft, barely skimming over it, and Elijah groaned.

"Oh god. Are you a tease? I may have to reconsider staying tethered to you if you're a tease."

Victor nipped him on the shoulder and gripped his cock. "I have no intention of teasing you. Edging you until the only word you remember is my name, on the other hand..."

Elijah turned in his arms. His eyes traced down Victor's body, catching on his dick. Victor preened under the attention and gave himself a few slow strokes, rolling his foreskin over the head before retracting it again, just to watch Elijah's gaze darken.

He wet his lips, but then zeroed in on the fresh scars running across Victor's stomach. "Are you healed enough to be doing this?"

"All good." The scars needed a few more days to fade, but no way in hell was he waiting for that. With one fluid motion, he flipped Elijah onto his back and covered him with his body. "Ready to go."

When he kissed Elijah, the steady presence of the tether flared wide open, and he was swept away in a simmering want that was only half his own. He pulled back to look at Elijah. "How does this work?"

Elijah raised an eyebrow at him. "Please tell me I don't have to explain sex to you."

Victor pinched his side. "The tether, you ass."

Elijah shrugged. "I think it's different for every pair. Touching obviously increases the connection. As do strong emotions. We'll probably always be able to find each other, no matter where we are. But this," he said, curling his fingers around the nape of Victor's neck and pulling him in for another kiss, rolling his hips up against Victor's, making them both shudder. "This is when it's the strongest."

"What happens if I..." Victor fixated on the juncture of Elijah's neck. He trailed a finger over the curve.

"Pretty sure it just gets more intense, makes us even stronger." Elijah let out an unsteady breath. His eyes were dark with lust, the icy blue a thin ring around the edges. "That's why the most powerful mages were always the ones with true bonds to shifters."

Desire raced down Victor's spine. It'd been a lifetime of waiting for this. He leaned closer and dragged blunt teeth along Elijah's neck.

Elijah shivered, his fingers digging into Victor's biceps, and Victor couldn't help but grind against him. His body ached for more, for everything. Thoughts of claiming Elijah overpowered him. He could make Elijah his. He could bite him, and they'd be bonded forever.

Victor scraped his teeth over Elijah's skin again, earning him a soft curse before Elijah was tugging on his hair, pulling him back.

"Not saying no, and I realize we're already halfway there, but I'm pretty sure we did this out of order. Shouldn't you buy me dinner first?" he teased, tone light, but under it, there was a frisson of nerves at the idea of Victor biting him.

As much as he'd like to claim him then and there, he could wait until Elijah was as sure as he was. "You want dates before I make an honest mage out of you?"

"Preferably ones that don't involve hunting evil spirits on your territory."

"I can manage that."

Being with Victor, staying there, meant rearranging every plan Elijah had made for his life. The least Victor could do was give him time to adjust to that. He'd date the hell out of Elijah until he was ready.

"I suppose that means we have to wait for other things too." Victor attempted to move toward his side of the bed, but Elijah clung to him.

"Oh, hell no. I was promised mind-blowing edging."

"You said you didn't want me to tease you."

"I was half-asleep. You can't hold me to that."

"Well, if you insist..." Victor reached toward his night-stand and grimaced when the movement caused his insides to twist unpleasantly. He ground his teeth and opened the drawer, rummaging for his lube, but Elijah was scooting out from underneath him.

"Where are you going?" Victor asked, wrapping him in his arms.

Elijah chuckled, though he didn't try to escape, instead letting Victor hold him close. "You're not healed yet."

"Believe me. I'm healed enough for this." Victor rocked against Elijah, trying to kiss him, though Elijah kept turning his head away.

"You can try to be as badass as you want, but I can literally feel you're still in pain," Elijah said, though he was smiling.

"I'll be in pain if you leave me hanging."

Elijah huffed and grabbed the lube. "Fine. Relationships are about compromise, right? On your back. And no moving."

Victor wasn't going to argue with a command like that.

Elijah straddled him and uncapped the bottle. Victor held out his hand, but Elijah hesitated.

"Do you think me having fingers in your ass is going to cause my stomach to rip open?"

"Possibly. I've been told it's a pretty amazing ass." But he drizzled lube on Victor's fingers and scooted up to give him more access.

Victor circled his fingers over Elijah's entrance, causing his eyelids to flutter shut. He was so gorgeous, all his lithe lines and smooth muscles, beautiful and perfect, and Victor's to do with as he pleased. And he did intend to please. He intended to touch, to taste, to claim Elijah in all the ways he'd promised himself he would never do.

"I dreamed about this so many times," Victor said, pressing the tip of his middle finger inside Elijah. "Not just that once."

Elijah's eyes opened, half-lidded as he looked at Victor. "From the morning after the first ritual." It wasn't a question; he knew.

"That morning was vague and fuzzy, but the night after that... You mentioned sex rituals, and I couldn't stop thinking about it." He thrust his finger slowly into Elijah. "What it'd have been like if we'd done that instead. If you'd laid me out in that circle and used my body to strengthen the wards."

A purple glow spiraled through Elijah's tattoos, matching the glimmer that ignited in his irises, and Victor's eyes flashed in response. He slipped another finger into Elijah, somehow feeling both sides of it, the hot clench and the perfect stretch.

"I've never done that," Elijah said, his hand wrapped loosely around his own length as he pushed down on Victor's fingers. "I've never met someone I was willing to do it with. But fuck, that night, you naked in front of me. I wanted to crawl into your lap and ride you until we both saw stars."

Victor nearly whined as that mental image shot through him—Elijah on top of him, coming with him, the heat of Elijah's release coating his stomach. He wanted to experience that with Elijah, to explore sex magic together.

His cock throbbed, eager to get in Elijah, but he didn't speed up, instead savoring the burn of desire. He pressed a third finger into him, working them in and out, adjusting his angle until he was hitting the right spot and Elijah was making soft, breathy noises every time he pushed inside.

Elijah clutched his forearms for support, his head tilting back as he rode Victor's hand like he'd wanted to ride his dick during the ritual.

"Those fucking dreams," Victor continued, "I can't tell you how often I've jerked off to them. They were so real. I could feel your body, how hot and tight you were, the way I hung there, on the edge, at your mercy until you let me come." What had happened after that in his first dream no longer terrified him.

Elijah's gaze was smoldering a steady purple now. Magic buzzed in the air. "We could still do that. That book has the original territory ward ritual in it. We could add layers of our own." His voice was rough and lust-drenched.

"Seems irresponsible of us if we didn't."

Elijah tugged on Victor's wrist, and reluctantly, Victor withdrew his fingers, watching as Elijah snapped open the cap on the lube again and poured some in his hand, slicking Victor's cock, before lining himself up and taking Victor in, as unhurried as Victor had been, their eyes locked.

Victor's lungs refused to work until he was fully seated. They stayed that way for a few heartbeats, awash in their own pleasure and the reflection of the other's, the sensation of being fucked and fucking at the same time. They breathed in sync, getting used to the intensity of it, so close even though they'd scarcely started.

Elijah rocked on his dick, that little movement overwhelming. Magic and energy sparked between them, a swirling current that made Victor shake.

If this was what it was like, it'd be a while before they were anywhere close to edging. Victor couldn't imagine he'd ever last long enough.

"I didn't realize it then, but I think I felt you that morning." Elijah pulled almost all the way off, then slid down, his pace maddeningly slow. "When I woke up, it was with glimpses of some elusive dream. I wanted to stay in your bed. Maybe jack myself off and come all over your sheets."

Victor gripped Elijah's hips hard enough he had to be leaving bruises.

Elijah grinned, tracing Victor's new tattoos. "If I'd known, I would have done it, but I figured you wouldn't be happy to find your bed covered in not only the scent of my magic but also my come."

The idea alone made his head spin as Elijah kept up the leisurely motion of his hips.

"Those dreams of yours, god, I've lost track of the times I've gotten off to them too. Is that what you want? To hunt me down on full-moon nights and fuck me in the forest? Knot me where anyone might see? Will you let me fuck you into this bed, deep and slow?"

Victor didn't know how much longer he could take this. "Whatever you'll let me have."

"Everything." Elijah fell forward, bracing himself with his forearms on either side of Victor's head, bringing their mouths together in a languid kiss as he continued to roll down onto Victor's cock. And for all he'd been told not to move, Victor couldn't stop himself from thrusting up into him, their words faltering as their speed picked up.

But the thought of knotting Elijah wouldn't leave him.

He resisted the urge to flip them over, to press Elijah down, sink his teeth into him, stretch him wide, tie them together.

It wasn't the time for that. They'd get to it. He could wait until Elijah was damn sure he wanted everything Victor was offering him.

His wolf thought he was being ridiculous. Elijah was theirs; they were Elijah's. Bitten or not. If they couldn't claim him, the least they could do was knot him. Those were supposed to go together, but his wolf was more than willing to make an exception for Elijah. They should fill him full, stay tied together as long as possible, show him exactly how good they could make this for him. He'd never want to leave after that.

Victor tried to remind himself that sort of thing required informed consent, not the impulses of a moment as heated as this, but his dick had other ideas. The base of it was hypersensitive as Elijah sank down on him over and over, as they continued to trade kisses that caused pleasure to blaze through his mind.

He worked a hand between them, trying to distract himself as the instinct to knot Elijah built. Maybe if he got Elijah off now, he could come before that happened.

Clenching his jaw, he stroked Elijah's cock. With his other hand, he kept his iron hold on Elijah's hips, slamming into him harder, driving soft grunts out of him. But every thrust made it worse, made the hot pulse of his knot harder to ignore.

Elijah pushed himself up and sat back, looking at

Victor. "You okay?" he panted out. "You feel... fuck. I don't know. Not like you're in pain, but you aren't as into this anymore."

That wasn't the issue at all. He was *too* into this.

Elijah lifted halfway and started sinking down again, like he couldn't help himself, but Victor grasped his hips to hold him still.

"You need to get off," he gritted out. His knot was so ready to expand.

"I was working on that," Elijah joked, then realized what Victor meant. "Oh shit, you mean off you." But when he tried to do that, Victor gripped him tighter, not letting him pull off. He blinked, confused. "I'm getting mixed signals here."

"If you keep riding me like that, I'm going to knot you."

"Oh." Elijah cocked his head like he was listening to something. "So that's how that feels." He snaked a hand down to squeeze the base of Victor's dick, and they both groaned.

"Not helping," Victor said, but thankfully, Elijah didn't take his hand away.

"Don't you need to be bonded first?"

Victor shook his head. "Just need you."

Elijah studied him, then stared him in the eye as his hips pushed against Victor's hands with purpose.

Victor was strong enough physically to stop him but not mentally. Not even close. He let Elijah slip out of his hold until he'd taken him to the hilt. His knot started to swell, making them both shudder.

"You have five seconds to get off me if you don't want this."

Elijah leaned forward. "If you're going to do it, you should do it properly." He tilted his head, offering his neck. There wasn't a trace of hesitation in their connection.

Victor's self-control shattered.

His hips snapped up, each thrust stretching Elijah more.

Elijah's orgasm built in him as if it were his own. It drove him on, guiding him to what Elijah needed, what caused his body to burn with euphoria, how canting his hips at the right angle made ecstasy ripple through him.

He was relentless, driving into Elijah until he was whimpering into the kiss they shared, unable to do anything but experience the pleasure Victor was wringing out of him.

"Do it. Bite me," Elijah gasped, his hands twisting in the sheets as he fucked himself on Victor's cock, too far gone for any thoughts other than the rhythm of their bodies. "Bond me."

Victor growled out something that might have been a yes, but he was so close to coming he couldn't find words. He peeled one hand away from Elijah's hips, weaving fingers in his hair as his knot caught against Elijah's rim.

The desire to bite, the instinct to claim, consumed Victor. His teeth lengthened, and he scraped them along Elijah's neck, biting down, breaking the skin.

The moment he did, the tether wasn't the only connection between them. A mating bond shimmered into existence beside it, braided around it, and fused with it, making everything clearer, sharper, brighter.

Elijah's movements became more erratic, more desperate. "*Harder*," he breathed, half plea, half demand.

Unable to resist that order either, Victor sank his teeth into Elijah as he slammed into him once more, his knot expanding until it tied them together.

Elijah went rigid, strung taut over Victor, arched and

moaning as he came, spilling between them, his body clamping around Victor's knot.

Victor nearly howled, unable to ignore the shudders of Elijah's pleasure coursing through them. His need to come took over, and he grunted as he pushed in deep.

"Yes, that's it," Elijah panted. "Come for me."

After Elijah's orgasm exploding through his mind, it was impossible not to follow. His own climax caused his vision to go white as it tore through him like a thunderclap, radiating out from his heart, through his bones, through every cell. Echoes of it reverberated back to him, filtered through Elijah.

Elijah collapsed, falling onto Victor. Aftershocks made them tremble.

They lay there, breathless and shaking, Elijah's weight grounding him.

Victor's teeth retracted, and he licked over the mark, soothing it as Elijah melted further into his arms.

Elijah tried to shift to the side, belatedly realizing he should be keeping pressure off Victor's stomach. But that only tugged at Victor's knot, and they let out choked-off cries.

"So much for taking it easy on your injuries. Good job with the not moving," Elijah murmured into Victor's shoulder.

Victor rumbled with happiness. "Worth it."

They floated in the blissful aftermath, the world realigning itself as the bond settled between them.

Victor nuzzled into Elijah's neck, reveling in the scent of them, mixed even more with their bond. Elijah smelled like his, as he now smelled like Elijah's. The exquisite perfection of it filled him with each breath. "What happened to waiting?"

"I decided to take a rain check on those dates," Elijah said, voice wrecked. He was joking, avoiding the question, but their bond glittered with affection.

He inhaled deeply, his body boneless as his fingers traced the magical tattoos on Victor's chest. Emotions tumbled through him, and Victor let him sort them out.

Finally, he spoke, just loud enough to hear, vulnerable in a way Victor realized he rarely let himself be. "Pretty much my entire life, I've tried to find a way to make my parents accept me as a mage, some compromise that would allow me to do magic but that they'd be proud of. That they'd consider respectable, even if they never wanted me to be a mage. It was always about what would make them happy, not what makes me happy." He paused, swallowing thickly before continuing. "But you. You make me happy. You and your pack feel like you were meant to be my home, my family. I can't imagine being anywhere else in the world but here, with you. With your pack. *Our* pack."

Victor brushed their lips together, sweet and tender, resplendent with all the warm emotions in the connections between them. No hesitation or regret, only contentment, satisfaction, and love.

"In that case," Victor said as they broke the kiss, "my turn." He offered his neck to Elijah.

Elijah propped himself up to look at him in question, making them groan as Victor's knot tugged at his rim again.

Victor met his gaze. "I know it doesn't mean anything to mages, but I want that mark along with your tattoos. I want everyone to see I'm yours."

Elijah's voice was quiet and serious when he replied. "If it's important to you, it will always mean something to me."

"Then bite me, mark me."

Elijah's eyes sparkled with desire, then drifted shut as he leaned in for a kiss. He sighed, letting his weight rest against Victor.

Victor tilted his head again, and Elijah nipped at the underside of his jaw, taking a detour to suck at a spot under his ear, then down to the crook of his neck. Victor resisted squirming as Elijah sucked harder on the skin there, dragging his tongue over the sensitive flesh.

"Here?" he asked, though he knew damn well where Victor needed him. His mouth hovered above Victor's skin, his exhales gusting over his collarbone.

"I thought I got to be the tease in this relationship."

Elijah chuckled, and it vibrated against Victor's skin. Victor's cock, buried deep in Elijah, throbbed at the sound. "Can't rush this. How often does a mage get the opportunity to bite an alpha wolf shifter?"

Victor's entire body quivered as Elijah's teeth grazed his skin. "You can mark me any time, any place." He relished Elijah's satisfaction at those words.

Elijah nuzzled into his neck, covering Victor's throat with soft kisses. "I'll remember that."

Victor lost himself in their bond as they lay entwined, as magic pulsed between them like a heartbeat, as lust left them aching, already begging for more.

He was unable to think of anything but Elijah's mouth leaving his neck to feather kisses along his jaw. His hips moved on their own, bucking up into Elijah. "If you don't bite me now, I'll explode, and I don't want to come again until you're marking me."

Elijah laughed breathlessly. "Already? Fucking shifters. How am I ever going to keep up with you?" Affection gleamed through their bond, a light, airy thing that defied all laws of gravity.

Victor moaned as Elijah's mouth found his neck again, his lips caressing right where the bite would go.

"*Please.*" He'd beg for this if he had to. Closing his eyes, he held his breath in anticipation.

A few unbearably long moments later, teeth sank into his skin, and Victor soared, a howl caught in his throat, sharp pain turning into the sweetest ecstasy he'd ever known.

He thrust up once more, coming inside Elijah a second time as pleasure washed over him, and Elijah's dick jerked between them, managing a few more spurts of its own before Elijah released him and kissed along the mark. The sensations he got from Elijah's orgasm weren't as overwhelming, but his cock still twitched in sympathy.

Victor made a contented noise, sated and satisfied, eyelids shutting as he settled into the pillows until his knot deflated enough for him to slide out of Elijah, both of them wincing at the loss.

Elijah hummed against his skin. "I came from your second orgasm alone. I wasn't even hard. Didn't know that was possible. Will it always be like this?"

Victor ran his hands over Elijah's sides, pulling a shiver out of them both. When he spoke, his voice was as wrecked as Elijah's. "The first few months are supposed to be the most intense. The bond will demand we stay close, that we reaffirm it. There's a reason newly bonded couples spend most of their time in bed. We'll get better at controlling it, but yeah, I think it'll stay like this."

"A few months in this bed?" Elijah stretched against Victor's body. "I could live with that."

Victor smiled, tightening his arms around Elijah. "So could I."

Elijah grinned back at him. "Especially since I apparently get some shifter-like stamina as part of the deal."

"Another benefit of the bond."

"We should have done this months ago. From the day I moved into town."

"I guess we'll have to make up for lost time." Victor kissed the curve of Elijah's lips.

Elijah skimmed a finger down Victor's neck, over his mark. "For the record, this is so much better than your dreams."

"In my defense, my mind never would have been able to come up with this. When we touch..." He didn't have words for it.

Elijah nodded, understanding what he hadn't said. "Same."

Victor pulled him closer.

As their bodies cooled, everything fell into place around them, so perfect and beautiful. Something Victor hadn't known he was missing.

He exhaled, content and complete.

This was all he'd ever wanted. He'd just needed to let himself have it.

TWENTY-EIGHT

In the late evening, the need for food won out over their desire to stay in bed, learning and enjoying each other's bodies. They showered but had to reek of sex. Not that anyone in the pack was under any misconceptions about what they'd been doing in Victor's room.

Elijah slipped into a pair of Victor's sweatpants and one of his shirts for the trip downstairs. Both were a size too big, but given the way Victor's eyes darkened as he watched him pull them on, Elijah couldn't say he minded. Descending the stairs was an experience Elijah's legs weren't entirely on board with, but it was another thing Victor seemed to enjoy.

Before they'd made it to the bottom, Oliver was there, wiggling with excitement, for all the world looking like a puppy wagging his tail so hard his whole body was vibrating.

"Elijah!" he yelled up the stairs. "Did Mama tell you? I threw up black stuff! It was super gross! Then you were in my head! And you built a wall like *whoooosh*!" The sound effect was accompanied by the most dramatic lifting gesture Elijah had ever seen.

"And *then*—" Oliver paused as Elijah reached the bottom step. His little nose wrinkled. "You smell like Alpha. *A lot.*"

Elijah didn't need enhanced senses to hear the laughter that statement drew from multiple areas of the house.

Victor gripped Elijah's neck right over his bite mark, causing his knees to nearly buckle.

Goddamnit, he couldn't just do that in public. In front of children, no less.

He brushed a kiss against Elijah's cheek and under his breath said, "I have to check on Kade."

Elijah turned his attention back to Oliver.

"Mama said you'd teach me magic!"

From the living room, Katrina yelled, "I said nothing of the sort. I told you if you asked him nicely, he might show you more magic."

Oliver huffed. "Fine. You're gonna teach me magic, right?"

Katrina appeared in the hallway, shaking her head. "At least use the magic word."

"But, *Mama*, I don't know the magic word. Elijah hasn't taught me yet!"

Katrina slapped a hand against her face. "Ladies and gentlemen, my son. Who has a whole pile of crayons to clean up before he gets ready for bed."

"Now?" Oliver asked, looking disgruntled.

"Now."

"But I haven't seen Elijah in *forever.*"

"I have a feeling you'll be seeing Elijah every day from here on out." She winked at Elijah. "He's pack now."

Oliver looked up at him with wide eyes. "Really?"

"Really."

"Awesome!" He hugged Elijah's leg, then dashed off.

Katrina left at a more sedate pace, squeezing his non-bitten shoulder as she passed.

Elijah blinked as he realized every time a pack member had greeted him before, it'd always been his left shoulder, while Victor had bitten him on his right. Hopefully that meant no one would be accidentally touching his insanely sensitive bite mark.

As if summoned by the thought, Victor came up behind him and tugged down his collar enough to trail kisses over his shoulder.

"We're never making it to the kitchen if you keep doing that." Elijah groaned, not completely sold on that being a bad thing. But if he didn't eat something with actual nutritional value soon, he'd pass out, so he tried to pull himself together. "How's Kade?"

Victor sighed. "Asleep. I didn't want to wake him. But Rick said he woke briefly around four, groggy but aware of his surroundings. He thinks it'll take another day before the major internal damage is fully healed and possibly a few more until everything is working normally." He tugged Elijah toward the kitchen. "Come on. Let's get you food."

Victor directed him toward the breakfast nook, then started rummaging through the pantry.

Elijah had barely sat down before Janell was sliding in across from him, blatantly ignoring Victor's warning glare.

"So, I guess you'll be staying up with us next full moon."

Heat rushed through Elijah at the thought of Victor on a full moon. Sex with him was already intense; how would it be after a few more weeks when they knew everything the other liked and Victor was at his full strength? Elijah couldn't hold back the shiver that image caused.

Victor gave up on the pantry, instead drawn toward Elijah, needing to touch him. The desire echoing through their bond was enough to make Elijah's eyes glaze over.

Janell leaned forward like she was about to share a secret, though Victor was standing right there. "One non-shifter to another, you thinking about sex too much is going to drive him fucking wild. Especially in the next few months, while the bond is fresh. So if you ever want to make him utterly crazy, go somewhere nearby he can't easily get to. Then think your filthiest thoughts about him. On loop. When he finally gets his hands on you, it'll be worth it. But FYI, locked doors aren't enough."

Victor growled, dragging Elijah half out of his chair and pressing against him.

"I don't think he needs any encouragement in that department," Elijah managed to get out.

"Something for the future then." She walked away, laughing.

"I'd bust down the fucking door," Victor said.

"Figured as much," Elijah replied.

"But what's this about waiting with the humans? I thought we'd run together. Recreate that dream."

"Hell no. It'll be the end of October. There might be snow."

"I said I'd keep you warm."

"...ask me in April."

Victor seemed far too pleased by that idea if the smugness radiating through their connections was anything to go by.

"What's happening in April?" Will asked from the doorway, but from the amusement in his voice, he'd heard exactly what.

Elijah's cheeks heated. Having an entire pack aware of

an uncomfortable amount of his sex life was going to take some getting used to.

Victor stole one more kiss, then went back to the pantry.

"Newlyweds," Will said, rolling his eyes and chuckling.

Elijah wasn't listening, too distracted by Victor's ass as he leaned over to get something on the bottom shelf. And then did it again.

He swallowed hard. They needed to eat, and they needed to eat *now*. He had dessert waiting for him.

Elijah had thought he'd been prepared for the sly looks and teasing they'd get, but he had been wrong. Very, very wrong.

He also hadn't expected Victor to cook for him. Victor wasn't bad at it either, though he'd likely be better if he didn't keep coming over to touch Elijah. Still, the food was only mildly burnt.

As Victor was cooking and they were eating, a steady stream of pack members found reasons to stop by the kitchen, one by one, claiming they were there for a snack or a drink, though they were fooling no one. The sheer amount of teasing they received would be impressive if it'd been directed at anyone else. The only saving grace was that it was well after dinnertime, and some of the pack had already headed to bed or left for the night.

By the time they'd finished eating, Victor had grown restless. He was getting increasingly handsy, pressing his palm against Elijah's mark, making pleasure spike through him.

It didn't take much for Will to convince Victor they had everything under control. "Don't stay down here on our account. You know, if you have something better to do."

Victor didn't throw Elijah over his shoulder and carry

him upstairs, but it was a close thing. As soon as the door was closed behind them, Victor had him pressed against it, all over him like it'd been weeks since the last time they'd been alone, not an hour.

Not that Elijah was complaining.

"Sorry the pack is full of assholes," he grumbled against Elijah's neck.

Elijah laughed. "I'm sure it could have been worse. Somehow."

"That was them holding back."

"You're kidding."

"Newly mated alphas can be possessive bastards. We tend to get a little twitchy when too many people are around our mates. Particularly in the first few days. Even with pack members."

"I guess I should be grateful they didn't come at us as a grou— Oh, *shit*." Elijah yanked away from Victor and dove for the bathroom. His friends were going to kill him.

By some miracle, his phone had survived the battle and was clinging to the last of its battery life.

He had over one hundred notifications, all from the group chat. He opened the app and scrolled through the messages, though Victor did his best to distract him by plastering himself against Elijah's back, his hands roaming under his shirt. The bulk of it was Liam becoming progressively more worried.

LIAM

Elijah!

It's been 12 hours!

Why haven't you updated us?

You better be alive!

Oh, god.

What if he isn't?

ARAN

It's Elijah. Elijah doesn't lose. He's probably too busy celebrating his inevitable triumph with all the shifter dick he can get his hands on.

MILES

"It's Elijah," he says.

Then immediately says Elijah is doing something Elijah wouldn't do.

ARAN

Nothing like a near-death experience to realign your priorities.

And by priorities, obviously I mean realizing he needs to get his fill of that non-metaphorical dick. Literally. Just positively filled with it.

Well, he wasn't wrong. About any of it.

"Ah," Victor said, reading over his shoulder as he slid a hand into Elijah's sweatpants. "The one that's not allowed to meet Kade. Tell him you're only celebrating with one shifter dick."

"Mmm, yours is more than filling enough."

Victor growled his approval, a sound that went straight to Elijah's cock. He ghosted his stubbled jaw over Elijah's bite mark before mouthing at it while Elijah attempted to keep reading, though it was becoming difficult to focus on the words.

LIAM

What if something happened to him?

ARAN

Then he died like he lived. With a sad lack
of shifter dick.

But seriously, we give him another hour,
then we head out.

MILES

I've got a bag ready just in case.

LIAM

There's a flight I can catch first thing in the
morning.

ARAN

And if he is alive, we should consider
heading out there anyway. To remedy that.
Not updating us for 12 hours is some high-
level bullshit.

Elijah checked the time. It was thirty minutes before their deadline.

He sent a quick message, letting them know he was indeed alive and very sorry, but he'd passed out shortly after capturing the spirit. That was why he hadn't updated them. And his poor battery was on two percent, so he'd have to give them more details later.

None of that was a lie. And if he neglected to tell them about his newly bonded status, he didn't think he was to blame for that either. Victor had been sucking at his mark as he'd typed. He'd tell them. Eventually. But at the moment, he was too busy being hauled back to bed.

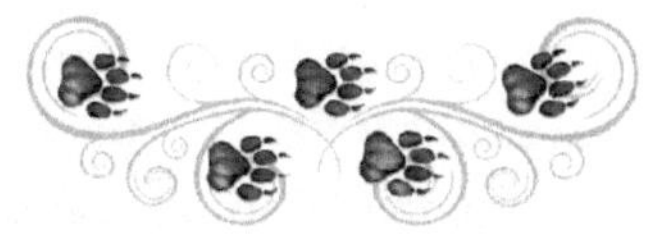

Falling asleep in Victor's arms was as wonderful as waking up in them. But as much as Elijah wanted to stay wrapped in their little cocoon, he had things, and a cat, to take care of. He had no doubt Lady would track him down if he were gone much longer. Whether to kill him for abandoning her or "rescue" him from the evil wolf shifters was a toss-up.

And then he had to figure out what to do about his shop. Maybe he should get an apprentice. As long as they didn't end up bonded into a pack, they could act as a neutral party in situations Elijah couldn't. He loved the idea of all the pearl-clutching he'd cause by telling the mage council he was ready to take on an apprentice well before he was thirty, and oh, by the way, he was bonded to a local alpha.

But first, he had to get ready.

Which was how he found himself in the shower, having one last round before he had to leave. He could spend countless minutes under the warm stream of water, kissing Victor, pressed against him, but all too soon, they were finished, exchanging playful touches as they dried off.

In the mirror, he glimpsed the mark on his neck, new and red, and he couldn't help the grin it caused. He ran a finger over it, shivering at how tender it was. His touch caused the tattoos around the bite to light up; intricate scrollwork now twisted up the right side of his neck and down over his chest, covering more skin than he'd ever thought possible.

Victor wrapped an arm around him as he placed a soft kiss on the mark before going to grab clothes.

Elijah was still unsure what had happened during the battle, how they'd connected. It was so far beyond anything he'd heard of. Sure, he and Victor were ridiculously compatible, but it had to be more than that. It had to be them wanting it, welcoming it. But whatever it was, however it'd happened, it felt right. This was where he was meant to be.

He picked up his pants and shirt from where he'd left them on the bathroom floor. They were cleaner than Victor's had been, but that was a low bar. He'd be wearing more of Victor's clothing to go to his apartment. He emptied the pockets so he could toss the pants. The only thing of note was the crumpled map he'd stuffed in there during the fight, and they wouldn't be needing it now. He unfolded it to give it one last look.

His breath caught in his throat.

This couldn't be right. There had to be a mistake.

On the map, dozens of ashy smudges prowled Victor's territory. They were a fraction of the size of the one they'd captured, smaller than when they'd first seen it, but they were there. The smallest ones were nothing but the faintest specks of ash moving from place to place.

Elijah stared in horror. Had he missed part of the spirit when he trapped it in the chest?

But no, he was sure he'd gotten it all. These weren't that.

"You okay?" Victor's voice was concerned as he came into the bathroom, picking up Elijah's distress, but Elijah couldn't tear his eyes away from the map. He was unable to bring himself to say the words.

Victor put an arm around his waist and looked at the map. When he registered what was happening, his body tensed. "What the hell is that?"

"No idea."

As the initial shock wore off, he realized each smudge was moving in a unique way. Where the rot had oozed over the map, these were different. Some roamed chaotically, with no discernible pattern to their movements. Others spiraled or skittered, curved or waved. Some moved haltingly; others darted rapidly. A few left trails of *something* behind them, though there was no telling what.

"There's more rot?" The turmoil of Victor's emotions was evident on his face and in their bond.

Elijah shook his head. "I think they're all different."

"Can we trap them?"

"How are we supposed to track and trap all these?" Elijah asked.

Victor hesitated before he spoke. "Would your friends be willing to help?"

"Are you okay with that?"

"If you trust them, I trust them too."

Elijah squeezed his hand. "I'll ask them. Unless they have something important they're working on, they should be here by the weekend. Until then, let's see if we can trap a few of these ourselves."

Victor's face was grim. His arm around Elijah tightened, and worry churned in his mind.

"We'll fix this," Elijah said.

Victor nodded with determination.

They might not know what had caused this, *who* had caused this, but they'd figure it out together.

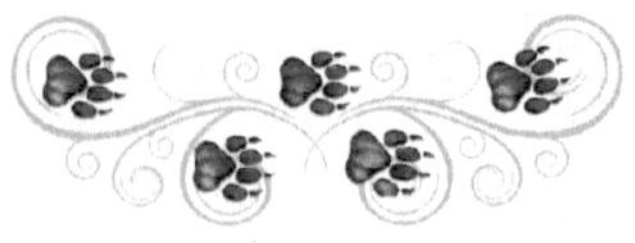

Elijah waited until he was in his apartment to contact his friends. But only after he'd dealt with Lady being less than impressed with his absence. Though, from the way she'd curled up in his lap, not even giving him an offended sniff, she was surprisingly not put off by how much he must smell like Victor.

He plugged in his phone, opened the group chat, and started typing.

ELIJAH

I need you guys here ASAP.

Like I said, we were able to trap the spirit causing the rot.

But there are a lot more, and I'm not going to be able to do this by myself.

LIAM

Shit. Elijah.

I'll be there.

Will send you my flight info after I've booked it.

Can you pick me up at the nearest airport?

ELIJAH

Absolutely.

ARAN

I'll drive up. Give me two days.

MILES

Same here. Should be there by Saturday evening.

And that was why he loved his friends. No questions asked, just there when he needed them.

ELIJAH

Also. In hopes that this will keep the in-person teasing to a minimum…

He sent them a selfie, the collar of Victor's shirt pulled aside to reveal the bite mark.

There was silence for a good minute, long enough for Elijah to stare at the screen and sweat, and then the chat exploded.

LIAM

ELIJAH.

DID YOU GET BONDED TO THAT ALPHA SHIFTER?

MILES

Congratulations!

ARAN

Holy shit. Look at Mr. Never Gonna Get Bonded to a Shifter. How's that definitely not metaphorical shifter dick treating you?

LIAM

DID HE ASK BEFORE HE BIT YOU?

ARAN

Details! Details! DETAILS!

ELIJAH

Shouldn't you be packing?

ARAN

I can multitask.

MILES

Me too. I also want details.

But not the same ones Aran wants.

ELIJAH

Fine.

Yes, Liam, he asked. And I bit him in return.

And I'm tethered to him. Properly this time.

> It's pretty fucking amazing. The connection, the sex, him. Everything is amazing.

> Minus these fucking spirits.

ARAN

> Which we will help you get rid of. So you can spend more time with that amazing, not-at-all-metaphorical dick.

LIAM

> But how's your magic?

Elijah gave a small start. He hadn't thought to check. While he hadn't used it since the fight, it felt normal.

Gaze zeroing in on a candle across the room, he snapped his fingers. A fireball burst over it, but it lit the wick and only caused minor scorch marks on his wall.

Well, fuck. He should have expected that.

When he closed his eyes, Victor's energy waited for him, a pool of strength there for the taking, refilled by his magic.

ELIJAH

> It doesn't feel unstable, but I seem to be significantly stronger.

LIAM

> That's good it's no longer unstable.

> You'll have to get used to the new level of power available to you.

MILES

> And since we're all waiting for it...

> (insert Aran's inappropriate comment about metaphorical dicks stretching things open here)

ARAN

Hey! I had my hands full! The metaphorical
shifter dick was coming!

MILES

...

Can someone else please make a "that's
what he said" joke before I have to?

ELIJAH

Aran.

There's no question now. You have
corrupted Miles.

This is an unforgivable offense.

ARAN

Nah. He's always been like that. He's just
better at hiding it than me. It's always the
sweet, quiet ones you have to watch
out for.

Anyway, I'm packed. Taking off in ten. Will
keep you updated on the way.

ELIJAH

THANK YOU. All of you.

I owe you massively.

If you need anything, just name it.

ARAN

Any other hot shifters lying around?

ELIJAH

Plenty. But you're on your own with
that one.

ARAN

Probably for the best. I doubt your newly
bonded would want you to join me.

Aran sent a string of kissy face emojis, and Elijah grinned at his phone before closing the app.

When his friends got there, everything would be alright. There was nothing they couldn't fix.

And maybe he'd get lucky and convince one of them they should stay on at the shop when this was over.

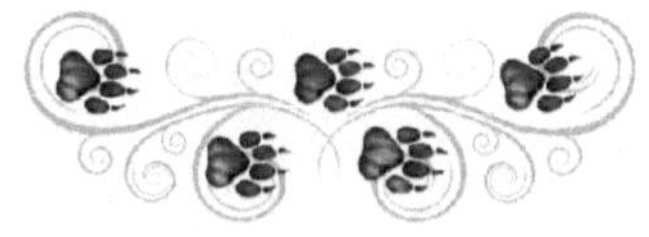

TWENTY-NINE

Victor sat by the pond and stared at the number and name showing on his screen. It was the last person he wanted to hear from, but he answered it.

"Can I help you, Father?"

"Actually," his father said, a cockiness to his voice that grated on Victor's nerves. "There's something I can help you with."

"Not interested."

"You will be. Meet me at the coffee shop the day after tomorrow."

"No. I told you already. You're not welcome here right now."

His father chuckled, low and tinged with insanity, barely sounding like the man he knew. "You'll change your mind. And when you do, you've got my number."

The line disconnected, and Victor glared at his phone. What the fuck had that been about?

Before he could think it through, a new notification popped up.

It was three in the afternoon. Of course he wasn't asleep. Grant must have hit Send too soon, but no more messages came.

When ten minutes had passed with no reply, he dialed Grant. It rang and rang, but no one answered.

Out of the corner of his eye, he saw Kade approaching him, his steps hesitant, so he hung up. He'd call Grant later if he hadn't heard from him by evening.

Kade leaned against the rock wall next to him, arms crossed over his chest, not quite meeting Victor's gaze. It was a relief to see him out of his room, but he was pale and drawn from all the healing his body had done.

Even with the sun past its zenith, the heat of the day stayed with them, unseasonably warm for mid-October. Sweat trickled down Victor's neck.

"How are you feeling?"

"Like I need to apologize." Kade's face was pinched in a grimace instead of his usual easy grin.

Victor shook his head. "You were possessed. Not your fault."

"I should have fought it harder. I was conscious the entire time. It's just, I couldn't control what I was doing. But I should have stopped myself from attacking you and Elijah."

"Neither of us blames you for that. It wasn't you."

He didn't look convinced, and Victor wondered how

many times they'd have this conversation before Kade no longer beat himself up over it.

"How did it happen?" Victor didn't want to push while it was still raw for Kade, but they needed to know. With so many spirits in the forest, they had to ensure it didn't happen again.

"It was when we were tracking it and I was off by myself. It came straight toward me. I thought it was going to attack me. It was all around me, like being in water. Filthy, polluted water. I couldn't breathe. Then it was gone. I felt dirty, like I needed a shower, but that's how I always felt when I was near the rot. Other than that, I thought I was fine. And I..."

He scrubbed at his face.

"There was so much else going on. I didn't want you to worry about me too. But fuck, I wish I'd told you. Elijah might have been able to do something. Or you could have locked me up until we were sure I wouldn't hurt anyone."

Victor clasped his shoulder. "Maybe it would have been different if you'd told us, but everything turned out alright. I'm just glad you're better. And we've got a couple dozen more of these things to fight, so you'll get a shot at revenge."

After a beat, Victor asked, "How's the healing coming?"

Kade shrugged. "Decently enough, but my sense of smell is fucked-up, and lunch tasted like shit. Don't tell Katrina. Totally not her fault."

Sometimes it took a little extra time for their senses to recalibrate after they were damaged. The structures themselves healed, but the brain had to remember the proper settings.

"If you need to sit out these next few rounds until you're at full strength, that's understandable."

"No, I'm good. Whatever you need."

"In that case, Elijah sent a message. One of his friends is flying in tomorrow. Would you mind picking him up?"

Kade gave him a smile that didn't reach his eyes. "If he's even half as hot as Elijah, do you really have to ask if I'll try to pick him up?"

He was trying to be the same carefree flirt he always was. It didn't quite land.

Victor didn't comment on it. Instead, he said, "If you hit on Elijah's friends, I'm pretty sure Elijah will have something to say about it. It's your funeral."

Kade rubbed his neck. "Right. Well. I just wanted to say I'm sorry."

He backed away, and even in his human form, Victor swore his tail was between his legs. But then he stopped and looked Victor in the eye.

"About what I said in the clearing. I didn't mean it."

"I know you didn't. That wasn't you talking."

"It still needs to be said. You're nothing like your father. And I'm happy you finally got your mage." His tone was genuine and heartfelt.

"Thank you."

Kade nodded before heading toward the house. He was halfway there when Elijah appeared around the corner. Kade flinched but didn't avoid him.

Elijah waved off his apologies as quickly as Victor had, insisting he was fine and the cuts on his neck were healed. He then took Kade's hand and checked him with his magic before Kade went inside.

Victor was staring at the door that Kade had shut behind him when Elijah sat beside him. He tugged Elijah closer, loving the feeling of them pressed together, the way it sparked life into their bond. His scent was instantly calming.

"Is he going to be alright?" Elijah asked.

"I think he needs more time to recover. He's not completely healed yet."

Elijah frowned. "There's no trace of the decay left in him, but when Miles gets here, he can check him over. This side of death, there's nothing he can't heal."

They sat quietly for a moment, enjoying the peace of the early evening.

"Don't tell him," Elijah said, "but I might miss the constant flirting and innuendos. That was the first conversation we've had that didn't involve some kind of dick-related double entendre."

Victor raised an eyebrow at him.

"You know what I mean. He isn't himself."

"As long as it's only flirting." He kissed Elijah, a quick press of their lips, but it soothed the restless part of himself. Elijah had been gone too long, even if it'd been less than eight hours. The desire to have his mate on his territory had been eating away at him, but everything was better now.

Elijah leaned his forehead against Victor's. "Are *you* okay?"

"More so than I've been in years." He squeezed Elijah against him. "Just tired of this."

Elijah wrapped his arms around Victor. "Whatever it is, we'll defeat it. I picked up a bunch of cedar at the hardware store to make boxes and get them ready. I want at least a dozen made before everyone gets here."

Victor was amazed at how the idea of four mages on his land didn't bother him. With Elijah at his side, there was nothing he couldn't face.

He pulled Elijah in for another kiss, this one slow,

sweet, and perfect. He couldn't believe he'd been afraid of this, that he'd tried to deny himself this. Their bond thrummed between them, and Victor closed his eyes, truly at peace with himself for the first time in a long, long while.

They had evil spirits and an unknown enemy to deal with, but whatever it was, they'd fight it together. And they would win.

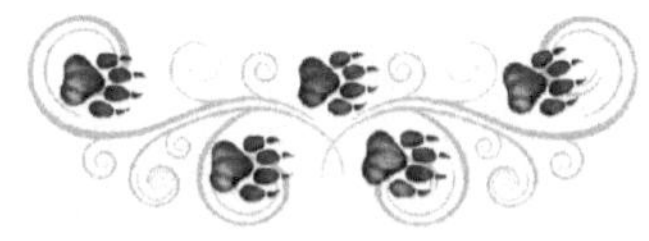

End of Accidental Bonds (Elemental Bonds Book One)

Thank you for reading!

If you'd like bonus scenes of Elijah moving in with the help of his friends (and Lady!), then moving out with a few distractions from Victor, please join my newsletter. You'll be the first to hear about my upcoming releases and get an occasional free story.

IMPULSIVE CONNECTIONS

The story continues in *Impulsive Connections (Elemental Bonds Book Two)*.

After a run-in with a malicious spirit leaves Kade Mills reluctantly bonded to a bookish mage, he struggles to resist the heady pull of their unwanted connection. But he soon discovers that bond could be the key to saving everything he holds dear... and it might not be as unwelcome as he thought.

Available now on Amazon and in Kindle Unlimited.

MATEHUB: LEGEND

Elijah's *NO* beat the ones sent by Liam and Miles, but only barely.

Just because Elijah, Liam, and Miles are missing out, doesn't mean you have to.

Meet Aran's (and Kade's) favorite MateHub star, Richard Knotz, in *MateHub: Legend*.

The contract was simple: three months, seven scenes, zero feelings. Following it was not.

In the world of supernatural adult entertainment, Richard Knotz is a legend, and knotting scenes are his brand. No human could ever threaten to tear his empire to the ground, no matter how tempting that human smells.

Available now on Amazon and in Kindle Unlimited.

ACKNOWLEDGMENTS

Accidental Bonds is my debut novel, and it's been an exhilarating ride. I've learned so much while writing and publishing it, though I know I'm only at the start of my author journey. As someone who has wanted to be a published author since early elementary school, being able to hold a physical copy of a book I've written is a literal dream come true... and more than a little addictive. I want an entire bookshelf of these things. RIP my social life as I try to find a way to write fifty books a year.

I want to thank both of my beta readers for their excellent feedback on this novel. They were amazing to work with, and this book would not be the same without them.

Amy was the first person to read this back when it was in much rougher shape, and her feedback made it infinitely better while also frequently making me laugh. If I ever end up writing a MateHub novel, you can blame/thank Amy for encouraging me to feed that particular plot bunny.

Next, Megan's suggestions on the ending truly helped make it more impactful. She was even willing to read pages of me babbling about where this series is going and assure me the overarching plot actually does make sense outside of the chaos that is my brain.

I'd also like to express my gratitude to Sandra for catching the pesky typos that managed to ninja their way through the roughly five hundred times I reread this thing.

And to you, dear reader, I want to offer my sincere

thanks for giving a debut author a chance. I hope you enjoyed reading this book as much as I enjoyed writing it.

Currently, I'm working on Elemental Bonds Book 2 and will get it out as soon as I possibly can. I'd be honored if you wanted to stick around and see Elijah's friends and Kade find their HEAs too.

If you feel inclined and could spare a moment to leave a review of *Accidental Bonds* on the platform where you made your purchase, or on a review site such as Goodreads or BookBub, I'd be immensely grateful. Reviews help indie authors gain visibility and reach more readers. Your support means the world to me, and I appreciate every review, no matter how long or short.

Please feel free to reach out to me on any of the social media sites listed on my About the Author page. I'd love to hear from you.

Once again, thank you for joining me on this leg of my journey. I am looking forward to sharing more stories and connecting with you through the pages of my books in the future.

Until then, may your TBR list be filled with nothing but your favorite tropes and all the captivating stories your heart desires! Happy reading!

About the Author

Marie Reynard is an American in Japan, teaching English by day and writing M/M paranormal romance by night. Her steamy, snarky stories will take you from first kiss to forever with a few Fs in between—including found family, flirty banter, fake dating, and a fair amount of fu...n. Check out her website for more information on her books, and join her mailing list to get a free story or two and be the first to know about upcoming releases!

Website - https://www.mariereynard.com/
Newsletter - https://subscribepage.io/nuxe5R
Facebook Group - https://facebook.com/groups/
mariereynardsden/

facebook.com/authormariereynard

tiktok.com/@marie_reynard

x.com/marie_reynard

instagram.com/marie_reynard

amazon.com/author/mariereynard

goodreads.com/mariereynard

bookbub.com/profile/marie-reynard